THE TEMERAIRE SERIES BY NAOMI NOVIK

His Majesty's Dragon

Throne of Jade

Black Powder War

Empire of Ivory

Victory of Eagles

Tongues of Serpents

Crucible of Gold

Crucible of Gold

Crucible of Gold

Naomi Novik

BALLANTINE BOOKS · NEW YORK

To Betsy Mitchell, editor extraordinaire,
who gave Temeraire his wings

Published in the United States by Del Rey, an imprint of The Random House Publishing Group, a division of Random House, Inc., New York.

DEL REY is a registered trademark and the Del Rey colophon is a trademark of Random House, Inc.

Library of Congress Cataloging-in-Publication Data

Novik, Naomi.
Crucible of gold / Naomi Novik.
p. cm.
ISBN 978-0-345-52286-3 (hardback)—ISBN 978-0-345-52288-7 (ebook)
1. Napoleonic Wars, 1800–1815—Fiction. 2. Great Britain. Royal Navy—Officers—Fiction. 3. Ship captains—Fiction.
4. Dragons—Fiction. I. Title.
PS3614.O93C78 2012
813'.6—dc23   2011046994

Printed in the United States of America on acid-free paper

www.delreybooks.com

2 4 6 8 9 7 5 3 1

First Edition

ACKNOWLEDGMENTS

Heaps of thanks to beta-readers Georgina Paterson, Vanessa Len, Rachel Barenblat, and N. K. Jemisin (if you haven't read her novel *The Hundred Thousand Kingdoms* do yourself a favor and run to snatch it up), who gave me wonderful feedback and helped me improve this novel in myriad ways.

Thanks also to my terrific agent, Cynthia Manson, not least because she brought me and Temeraire together with my fantastic editor, Betsy Mitchell, to whose passion and encouragement I owe not only a million and one improvements but the vast sprawl of this saga of Laurence and Temeraire's ongoing adventures, which I had only dimly glimpsed when I first jumped on board the deck of the *Reliant* as it captured a dragon egg.

All my love and thanks and gratitude to Charles, always my first and best and most exacting reader, and also to our new daughter, Evidence, who did her very best to interfere with every stage of this book.

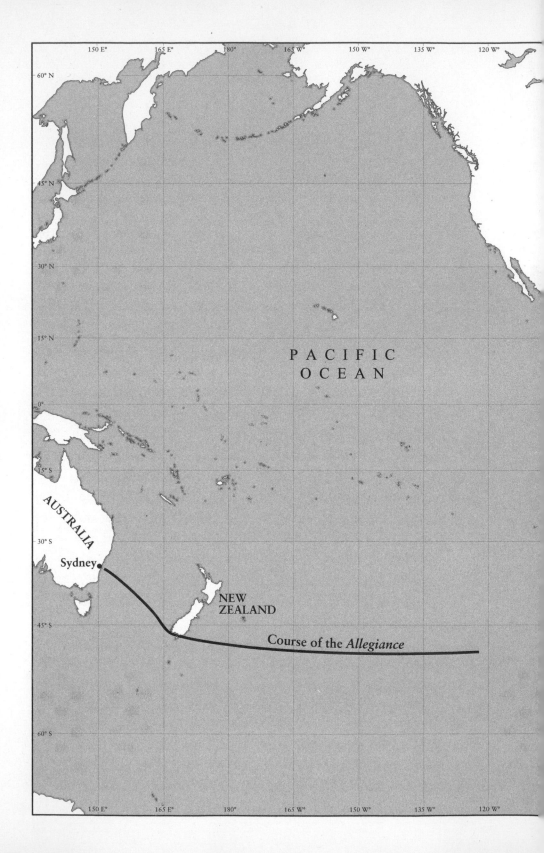

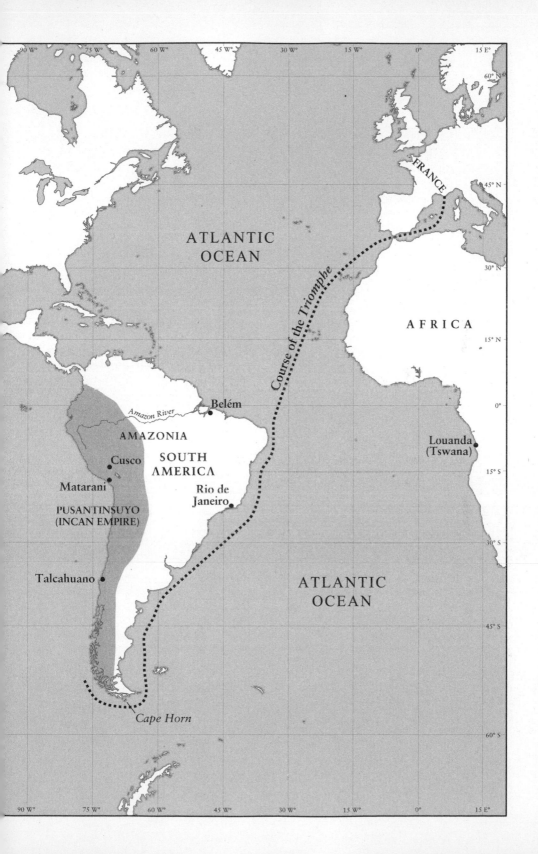

Crucible of Gold

Prologue

❦

ARTHUR HAMMOND PRIDED HIMSELF on a certain degree of insensibility in the cause of duty—an indifference to physical discomfort and even to social awkwardness—a squelching of the natural repugnances, when these should interfere with the progress of a diplomatic mission. Other men, blessed with a greater share of the graces, could afford delicacy; he acknowledged himself a blunter instrument, and if he must be so, he must be the ideal blunt instrument—must be seen to be as heedless of himself as of others, the only possible justification—to be thought of, if grudgingly, "Oh, Hammond—intolerable, but he *will* see the job through."

So he had cultivated where native tendency led, and seized without compunction or politesse whatever opportunity offered itself, with the consequence that he could while not yet thirty years of age call himself ambassador plenipotentiary to China: a post which he himself had contrived to establish.

And which in turn had led him to his present miserable state, which put to bitter test his determined self-neglect: frost grimed over the surface of the woolen blankets which he had wrapped even over his head, and the hideous swoop-and-lift of the great pale blue wings as the dragon dived to eat, at intervals too far apart to grow used to and yet too near to recover fully from one to the other. Hunger warred with nausea at every moment; there was meat and rice in his satchel, but he scarcely managed to worm his hand out of the coverings to feed himself once a day, and half his provisions were taken off by the wind in any case. He subsisted mostly on the strong rice wine in his flask, in rationed swallows, and passed from one day to another in a daze of blurred vision—his glasses were carefully tucked inside his coat—and illness.

His figurative insensibility had become, by the end of three weeks, nearly a literal one: he did not notice for a long time when the descent at last began, and when the courier folded her wings and put her head around and said, "We have had a very pleasant flight," Hammond was unable to remove himself from the harness for half-an-hour together, hands shaking and clumsy.

Shen Li politely did not remark on his difficulties, but bent her head to the water-hole and drank very deeply for a long stretch; then she raised her head and shook off the water from her muzzle. "I do not see the most honorable Lung Tien Xiang," she observed, while Hammond continued to struggle with the clasps, "but you see the pavilion which he has commanded to be built, there on the mountain—"

Hammond did not see, until he had managed to wrest out his glasses and wipe the lenses, and peering saw the pavilion standing on a cliffside at the far end of the valley where Shen Li had landed. It was an ambitious edifice: something neighbor to the Parthenon in size by the columns of yellow stone which paced out its perimeter, as yet without a roof and circled round by makeshift huts.

"Yes, I do; but are we not very far away?" Hammond said—or meant to say; a dry croak was all that emerged, and he gave up the attempt to converse, in favor of getting off the harness. At the moment he felt he would gladly have walked all the remaining distance in bare feet, over thorns, before going aloft again.

He let himself down from Shen Li's back in the indecorously slow manner used in China only by small children and the infirm, moving one hand or foot at a time. When he had reached the ground he sank down upon a broad smooth stone near the waterside.

"Perhaps I will go and hunt before we continue to the pavilion, if you would care to compose yourself a little," Shen Li said, a hint he could not manage to be ashamed to require. She shook out the immense wings and went aloft in a scattering of leaves and pebbles. Left behind, Hammond sat and gazed at the surface, churned-dark, and imagined drinking: the reality should have to wait another half-an-hour, he thought, before he might dare trust his legs to carry him across the two yards separating him from the water.

He gradually became aware, as the sun penetrated the intense chill which had settled into him, that the day was immensely hot. In Peking it was presently winter: as though he had been aloft for months instead of three weeks, or transported by some fairy-tale mechanism into another season. He began weakly to disentangle himself from one blanket and then another, more urgently as sweat gathered and rolled down his back, until at last he gave up all dignity and put his head and arms down and wriggled out of the rest. Abandoning his cocoon and dignity both, he simply crawled over the rock to the water and put his face into its cool relief.

He lifted it out dripping and rolled over onto his back, gasping, for once wholly aware of his body and grateful beyond measure for warmth and sated thirst, and then a pair of clawed, scaled limbs lunged flashing out from the bushes, seized upon the pile of bundling, and dragged it out of sight: he had only a glimpse of a saw-toothed maw and glittering black eyes, and then all vanished.

Hammond stared, and then leapt to his feet: his legs wavered and shook, and he fled in a shambling stumbling run, shuddering away from every branch and leaf which trembled in the wind. Horror gave him strength, and the hissed disappointment behind him: the mistake had been discovered. But he was unequal to the task; he felt a peculiar stirring beneath his feet, and he halted: a head was peering out from the bushes ahead, hungry and malicious, and there was no shelter anywhere to be seen; he was alone.

Evidently though it preferred to hunt from ambush, the creature was not unwilling to confront solitary prey; it crept one leg and then another out of the shrub-growth and came towards him at a slow deliberate pace: forelegs with long, many-jointed talons, scaled in dark shades of brown and green, with heavy sloping shoulders. Hammond turned to flee and halted: there was another half-emerged from a hole up the slope a little way, watching, jaw hung open in a gruesomely eager smile, and another two heads just peering out.

His breath was loud in his ears, labored, even while terror held him for a moment immobile; then he was running, hopelessly, and crying out, "Shen Li! Shen Li!" in hiccoughed bursts as he scrambled up the one narrow rocky slope barren of growth, with the sleek bodies flowing almost leisurely in pursuit.

He heard a coughing note which might have been a noise of amusement going around the creatures, behind him, and then he fell over the far side and tumbling came to rest at the feet of another man: a ragged backwoods hunter, bearded and dusty, in loose shirt and trousers and a broad-brimmed hat with, oh the blessings of Heaven, a rifle in his hand—but he was only one man, and already the five scaly heads were looking over the ridge down at the both of them.

The hunter did not pause; he raised the rifle and fired, but over the creatures' heads, and then lowering the gun said, "That is enough: be off, the lot of you, or we will clear your nest out to the bare rock."

The creatures hissed, and then as quickly, they vanished: a terrible immense shadow had fallen over them, the ground trembling. Hammond only just swallowed a shriek of dismay: teeth upon teeth gleaming around an endless red mouth, and an inhuman voice saying, "Oh! We ought to, anyway; how dare the bunyips, when they know very well I will not have them hunting men here."

"Temeraire," said Hammond, gulping, "that is Temeraire; it is all right," a reassurance to himself which he did not entirely believe; every nerve quivered with desire to flee.

"Hammond?" the huntsman said.

Hammond stared up at him even while taking the hand which had been offered him: a broad and callused grip, and skin tanned dark beneath the shaggy yellow beard; blue eyes; and Hammond said slowly, "Captain Laurence? Is that you?"

I

Chapter 1

"I AM AFRAID HIS ATTENTION is much given to material things," Shen Li observed in a mild way, while Temeraire strove in the distance lifting up the great carved-out slab of stone which should form the central part of the floor of the pavilion: a curious opinion to hear from a dragon, who were nearly all of them inclined to extreme attachment to material things; but perhaps her long stretches in the air, over the barren distances of the Australian deserts and the southern Pacific, had inclined the great-winged Chinese courier to adopt a philosophy more suited to her lot.

"It is of course an admirable work," she added, "but such attachments inevitably must lead to suffering."

Laurence answered her with only a small part of his attention: Temeraire had managed to get the slab aloft, and Laurence now waved the team of men forward to raise the skids which should guide it into its final resting place; but even this immediate work did not hold his thoughts. Those were bent upon the low hut some ten yards distant, under a stand of trees and the coolest place in their ragged encampment, where Hammond lay recovering: and with him all the world, come back to knock at Laurence's threshold when he had thought it done with.

The slab swayed uncertainly in mid-air, then steadied as it reached the long wooden braces; Temeraire sighed out his breath and lowered slowly away, and the stone scraped bark and shreds of wood down onto the workers as the slab eased gently down and settled in, the men backing away with their staves as it slid.

"Well, and a miracle it is no-one was crushed, or lost a hand," Mr. O'Dea said with something of an air of disappointment, as he paid off the men with their tots of rum and a few coins of silver; he had made a great many predictions of disaster over Temeraire's obstinate determination to have the single enormous slab of beautifully marbled stone preserved at the heart of his pavilion.

"It would have been quite criminal to cut it up smaller," Temeraire said, "and spoil the pattern; not that I do not admire mosaics very much, particularly if they are made of gems, but this is quite out of the common way, even though *some* might say it is just ordinary rock."

He had finished inspecting all the supports, sniffing at the fresh mortar anxiously, and now sank down with some relief beside Laurence and Shen Li for a drink of water from the flowing stream. "Do you not agree?"

"It is very handsome," Shen Li said, "although I can see no evil in admiring it in the valley where it was formed."

"I do not mean to be rude, Laurence," Temeraire said quietly aside, when she had turned her attention elsewhere, "but Shen Li can be rather dampening to one's spirits; although I must be grateful to her for being so obliging as to come and bring us letters and visitors: how kind of Mr. Hammond to travel so long a way to see us."

"Yes," Laurence said soberly, as he undid the wrappings on the mail: a large and heavy scroll wrapped on rollers of jade, for Temeraire from his mother, Qian, which accompanied a book of poetry; and a thick sealed packet which Laurence turned over several times and at last had to remove the outer layer of covering to find it addressed to Gong Su with no more direction than his name.

"Thank you, Captain," Gong Su said, and taking it went into his own small lean-to; shortly Laurence could see him performing the Chinese ritual of obeisance to it, and supposed it must be a communication from his father.

There was also, more incongruously, a heavily crossed note for a Mr. Richard Shipley: "Can this be for you, Mr. Shipley?" Laurence asked, doubtfully, wondering how a former convict should have come by a correspondent in China.

"Aye, sir," the young man said, taking it, "my brother's in the *Willow-Tree* as runs the Canton route, and much obliged to you."

Shen Li had brought also a small mailbag to be passed along to Sydney, but these were all the letters directed to the members of their own small company of laborers. Laurence closed up the bag: O'Dea would take it to Port Jackson tomorrow, and perhaps Hammond would go along with it. His business might well be there, with Captain Rankin, who after all was the senior officer of the Corps in this country.

Laurence could not persuade himself to believe it, however. While the cows roasted on spits, for the dragons' dinner, he walked out over the newly laid floor of the pavilion to its edge and looked down upon the broad valley, already sprouting with the first seed crops, and the browsing herd of sheep and cattle lowing soft to one another in the late afternoon. The war was only a distant storm passing on the other side of the mountains, a faint, far-away noise; here there was peace, and honest labor, without the clinging stink of murder and treachery which seemed to have by slow octopoid measures attached itself to his life. Laurence had found himself content to forget the world, and to be forgotten by it.

"Thank you, I *will*," he heard Hammond saying, and turned: Hammond had at last emerged from the hut and was by the fireside accepting a glass of rum from Mr. O'Dea and sinking into an offered camp-chair. Laurence rubbed a hand over his jaw, over the hard prickle of the beard, grown familiar. No: Hammond had not come from Peking to bring a few letters and some conversation.

"Pray allow me to renew my gratitude," Hammond said, struggling back to his feet, when Laurence had joined him. "I have slept all the day!—and I am astonished to see you so far advanced." He nodded towards the pavilion.

"Yes, indeed," Temeraire said, swinging his head around at the compliment, "everything is coming along splendidly, and we have thought up several small improvements to the ordinary design. You must walk through it; when you are feeling more the thing, of course: you cannot have had a comfortable journey."

"No," Hammond said, very decidedly, "—but I ought not be complaining; Laurence, will you think of it, three weeks!—this time three Sundays ago I was taking tea in Peking; it is scarcely to be believed. Although I am not certain I have survived the experience; yes, thank you, I *will* take another."

Hammond was not a bulky man, and not given much to drink; three tots of strong unwatered rum worked upon his caution, or perhaps he would not have spoken so readily when Laurence said, "Sir, while your company must always be welcome, I must confess myself at a loss to answer for your presence here; you cannot have made such a journey for some trivial purpose."

"Oh!" Hammond said, and looking round in vain for a table at last set down his glass upon the ground, and straightened up beaming, "but I must tell you at once: I am here to restore you to the list, Captain; you are reinstated, and—" Laurence was staring, while Hammond turned to rummaging in the inner pockets of his coat. "I even have them here, with me," and brought out the two narrow gold bars which marked a captain of the Aerial Corps.

Laurence held himself very still a moment, against the involuntary betraying jerk of movement which nearly escaped: if the bars had not been lying across Hammond's palm Laurence would have imagined it a sort of wretched joke, a twist of the mind inspired by exhaustion and liquor, but so much premeditation made it true: true, and no less absurd for that. He was a traitor. If he had done anything of note in the invasion of Britain to merit a lessening of the natural penalty for his crime, he had already been granted the clemency of transportation instead of hanging for services rendered, and since had done nothing which should merit the favorable attention of Whitehall: had indeed refused the orders of a Navy officer point-blank.

"Oh! Oh, Mr. Hammond, how could you not say so at once? But I must not reproach you, when you have brought such splendid news," Temeraire was saying, head bent low and turned so that one enormous eye could survey the bars. "Laurence, you must have your green coat, at once; Mr. Shipley! Mr. Shipley, pray fetch Laurence's chest here—"

"No," Laurence said, "—no, I thank you. Sir," he said to Hammond, with more courtesy than he could feel under the circumstances, "I am very sensible of the kindness you mean to do me by coming all this way with the news, but I must decline."

He had said it: the only possible answer he could make, and bitter to give. The bars still hung upon Hammond's palm before him: small and unadorned to represent as they did the lifting of a blot upon his name and his family, whose shame he had with so much effort learned not to think of, as he could do nothing to repair it.

Hammond stared, his hand still outstretched, and Temeraire said, "But Laurence, surely you cannot mean it," looking at the gold bars.

"There can be only one purpose for ordering my reinstatement in such a manner, in our present circumstances," Laurence said flatly, "and that is to charge me with oversetting the rebellion here in Sydney: no. I am sorry, sir, but I will not be the Government's butcher again. I have no great sympathy for Mr. MacArthur and his grab for independence, but he has not acted without cause or without sense, and I will not slaughter British soldiers to march him to a scaffold."

"Oh—but—" Hammond said, stuttering, "no; no, Captain—I mean, of course, Mr. Laurence; I ought not presume, but—sir, you have mistaken me. I do have business with Governor MacArthur;

of course this notion of independence is all nonsense and cannot be allowed to stand, but that is not—while certainly your assistance would be convenient if—"

He paused, collecting himself, while Laurence steeled himself against the hope which demanded its long-abandoned place, and which he ought to have known better than to indulge: if Hammond had brought a mission which any honorable officer of the Corps might be asked to undertake, such an officer would have been asked. But Hammond had drawn himself up more formally: whatever he might now offer would certainly be cloaked in more tempting accents, and all the more difficult to resist.

"First," Hammond said, "allow me to say I entirely understand your sentiments, sir; I beg your pardon for not expressing myself in a more sensible mode. I will also add for your ears that in many quarters, Mr. MacArthur's *other* actions have been seen in nothing less than a prudential light. I hope you can imagine that cooler minds have regarded the prospect of outright war with China, which Captain Willoughby's—out of courtesy, I will not say folly— which Captain Willoughby's intentions would have induced, as sheer madness, and not in any accord with the spirit of his orders."

Laurence only nodded, austerely; he had expressed much the same sentiments in his report on the matter to Jane Roland, which if it had not been officially taken notice of had certainly been seen: Hammond did not have to study far to know his feelings on that subject.

"Insofar as Mr. MacArthur has shown better judgment in rebelling than in acceding to so disastrous a course, he may well be pardoned for the extremity to which he has gone," Hammond went on, "provided he should acknowledge his mistake and recant. You of course, having direct knowledge of the gentleman, can better say if he can be swayed by reason, but I assuredly have not come with the *intention* to work upon him by violence, or merely to treat him as a felon."

"I am very sure Mr. MacArthur will be sensible," Temeraire put in anxiously: his wings were pinned back flat and the expressive ruff also. Laurence knew Temeraire valued his lost captaincy all the more for blaming himself for its loss and that of the better part of Laurence's fortune. Though Laurence was unable to value either so high as the honor which he had sacrificed, Temeraire had proven unable to accept his assurances on that score: perhaps for the greater chance which the former had, of ever being recovered.

But however Laurence thought of MacArthur—a second-rate Napoleon, whose talents were not more outsize than his ambitions—he could do him this much credit, or perhaps calumny: if Hammond indeed bore such an offer, Laurence thought it would indeed be accepted. Certainly MacArthur had proclaimed often enough that he had not rebelled on his own account, or for selfish reasons, but only to protect the colony. If that were not entirely the truth, at least MacArthur had deliberately kept open a line of defense less likely to lead him to the gallows; and if he were not inclined to be as sensible as Temeraire hoped, his wife, a wiser woman, likely would be on his behalf.

"Then for what purpose do you require me a captain, instead of a farmer?" Laurence said.

"Nothing at all to do with the rebellion," Hammond said, and then qualified himself, "at least, perhaps—I do not wish to be accused of deceiving you, sir; it may have been considered as an adjunct to the main thrust of our deliberations, that your reinstatement should perhaps give my discussions with Mr. MacArthur a certain—a degree of—let us say, potency—"

"Yes," Laurence said, dryly.

Hammond cleared his throat. "But that is not at all our central purpose: any dragon, any first-rate, might be deployed here for such an action, should it prove necessary, and certainly if you have any objection I would consider myself empowered to—that is, you should not have to undertake the mission yourself; after all there is nothing very urgent in correcting the situation, so long as Mr. MacArthur continues to accept the convict ships, as he has. No: it is the situation in Brazilia; perhaps you have heard something of it?"

Laurence paused; he had heard only the most wild hearsay, borne by an American sea-captain. "That Napoleon had shipped some number of the Tswana dragons there, to attack the colony; to Rio, I understand, if it is not only rumor." They heard only a little news in their isolate valley, and he had not pursued more than what came of its own accord.

"No—no, not rumor," Hammond said. "Bonaparte has conveyed, at last report, more than a dozen beasts of the most fearsome description, who have wholly laid waste Rio; and there is every expectation of his shipping still more as soon as his transports should return to Africa for them."

Laurence began to understand, now, what might have brought Hammond here, and his anxious look. "Yet I was only a prisoner among them, sir," Laurence said slowly, remembering that sudden and dreadful captivity: borne over a thousand miles into the heart of a continent and separated from Temeraire without warning and, at the time, no understanding of the purpose behind his abduction.

"That is more familiarity than nearly any other person can claim," Hammond said, "and in particular with their language— their customs—"

He stammered over it, and Laurence listened with skepticism: what he had learned over the course of those months of captivity, most of it spent in a prison-cave, he had conveyed in his reports, and he found it difficult to believe that his small experience of the Tswana should have rendered him an acceptable ambassador in the eyes of their Lordships.

To this Hammond said, "I believe—that is to say, I have heard— that his Grace of Wellington thought it not inadvisable—"

"If Wellington maintains any sentiments towards myself or

Temeraire past the liveliest impatience, I should be astonished to hear it," Laurence said.

"Well," Hammond said, "rather, as I understand it—a certain suggestion—"

Hammond tried for a little longer to dress it up: but when at last he came out with a description which Laurence could swallow, it seemed Wellington had expressed the opinion that if anyone might be hoped to have success at talking sense into a band of uncontrollable dragons, it should be the two of them; as long as someone was sent along to be sure they did not in the process give away three-quarters of the colony.

"I am sure we *should* be splendid ambassadors," Temeraire put in, peering down at Laurence hopefully, "however uncomplimentary Wellington may have been about it. Not that I was not quite angry with the Tswana at the time, for after all they had no right to take *you*, but one must make allowances for their people being taken for slaves, and I am sure the Tswana can be reasonable. Indeed, I do not see why we might not satisfy them at once, by returning those who were stolen."

"Ah," Hammond said awkwardly, "yes, well—of course, the interests of our allies must be considered—the difficulty of tracing particular individuals—and naturally the position of the Government vis-à-vis the, the property rights of—"

"Oh! Property rights! That is perfectly absurd to say," Temeraire said. "If I should take a cow to eat, even if no-one was watching it, you should call it stealing; and if I should give it away to Kulingile for some opals, you would not say that *he* had any property rights, I am sure, particularly if he knew perfectly well that it was not my own cow at the time."

Hammond began to take on again the harried look familiar from several occasions of their first mission together, to China, and Laurence was unable to resist, with a certain dour amusement, some speculation whether Hammond would not quickly regret having allowed time to soften his impressions of those past difficulties—and to add a roseate glow to the final triumph—and having volunteered himself as the man intended to keep a leash upon them in this proposed endeavor.

For his own part, Laurence was entirely sure that the number of slaves who would be returned in such a programme as Temeraire proposed would not satisfy the Tswana. Even if the Portuguese were willing to hand over their slaves honestly, they could not raise up the dead devoured by the cruel labor of their mines and plantations, and by the hopelessness of their captivity. Nor could he conceive of making himself in any way the agent of slave-owners, which Hammond had ought to have known, if not from acquaintance with Laurence himself, then from the reputation of his father: Lord Allendale had long been a passionate advocate for abolition.

"But nothing of the sort is conceived, I assure you," Hammond protested. "Indeed, I will go so far as to say that the Portuguese are quite prepared—under the circumstances, a certain readiness to compromise—" He halted, before making any outright promises, and added, "but in any case, you should not at all be *their* agent, but ours."

"And our interest in the matter?" Laurence said.

"The establishment of peace," Hammond said, "which surely you cannot dispute to be desirable."

"Peace is not unpleasant, or nearly so boring as one might expect," Temeraire said, with a faintly wistful note that gave him the lie, "but I do not see why you should be particularly interested in peace in Brazil; if you thought it so splendid you might make peace with Napoleon, in Europe, first: not that I at all wish to promote such a thing," he added hastily, "at least, not while Lien is lording it over in France: I hope we shall never be at peace with *her*."

"Ah," Hammond said, fumbling, and then stopped, visibly irresolute before saying, "Sir, if I may rely upon your discretion—the utmost secrecy—"

"I am sure you may," Temeraire said with interest, pricking

forward his ruff as he leaned in; Hammond looked still more uncertain, as a large dragon's notion of confidential whispering might
be heard a good ten yards away.

"So far as it is in our power, you may," Laurence said, "and for
what we cannot control, you may rely, sir, on your news being of
only scant interest locally, and unlikely of being carried on in any
manner which should render it worth relying upon, to any hostile
agent."

That, at least, was very true: there was commerce to and from
Port Jackson, but there was not a man laboring in the valley who
might reasonably expect to leave this country again; where poverty
and perpetual inebriation did not bar them, the law would, and
they were as trapped here as Laurence had thought himself and
Temeraire to be. Britain was another world; the war a distant
fairy-story; none of them would care, if they overheard.

"Then I will be so bold as to reveal to you," Hammond said,
"Napoleon has overreached, with the failure of his invasion, and
now the jaws of a trap are laid open for him at last: we will shortly
be landing our own troops in Portugal. We mean to bleed him from
the south, while the Russians and the Prussians come at him from
the east; and Wellington is confident of our eventual victory."

Audacious in its very extremity: Laurence could only imagine
the slog of this proposed war, their troops clawing one inch at a
time slowly up the Peninsula through Portugal, through Spain,
through the Pyrenees at last to France. Napoleon had indeed suffered dreadful losses in Britain, and left behind an army of prisoners in making his own escape, but whether those losses had been
sufficient to leave him vulnerable to final defeat in a grinding cam-
paign, Laurence was not nearly so certain.

"But there can be no hope of victory at all, without a foothold
established," he said.

"Yes," Hammond said. "We must have Portugal. And if the
Prince Regent should have to flee Brazil and return, with Napoleon
already occupying Spain—"

"You doubt their continued willingness to permit our passage," Laurence said.

Hammond nodded. "We must have Portugal," he repeated.

Temeraire had scarcely understood at first what Hammond was about; it did not seem reasonable to him that anything so momentous should be attended with so little ceremony or notice, but he recalled that just so had it happened to begin with that Laurence had lost his rank. Temeraire had known nothing of it, until one afternoon someone was calling him *Mr. Laurence,* and the golden bars had gone; and now here they appeared again as swiftly, a lovely gleam in Hammond's palm.

Laurence was silent, when Hammond had finished expounding on the mission; Temeraire looked at him anxiously. "It does not seem to me there is anything very unpleasant in what Hammond is asking," he ventured. He could not—naturally he did not wish Laurence to accept his commission back, if it only meant being ordered to do something dreadful, which they should have to refuse, and then have the same unpleasantness of being called traitors all over again; but it was very hard to have such a chance extended and then snatched away.

"You must be tired, sir, after your journey," Laurence said to Hammond. "If you would care to refresh yourself, my hut is at your disposal, and there is clean water to hand here above the falls; Mr. Shipley will, I hope, be so good as to show you the way," beckoning to that fellow.

"Oh—oh, certainly," Hammond said, and went away, though he looked over his shoulder more than once, despite the rough ground, as if to read Laurence's thoughts off his face.

"Of course you shall not do anything you would dislike, Laurence," Temeraire said, when Hammond had gone away, and left them in privacy, "only, it does not seem to me there is anything to object to in going to Brazil, and you should have your title back, and your rank."

"That, my dear, can be nothing more than a polite fiction," Laurence said. "I cannot pretend that I am in any real sense an officer of any corps when I am determined never again to submit to orders which my own judgment should find immoral."

A fiction which brought with it bars of gold, and changed entirely the mode in which persons addressed you, seemed to Temeraire real enough for anyone's taste. "And after all, it is not as though they *must* give you dreadful orders: perhaps they will have learned their lesson, and think better of it, from now on," he said hopefully. He did not have any great reliance on the wisdom of the Government, but anyone might be expected to learn, after so many proofs, that he and Laurence were not to be cowed into doing anything which was not just.

"I am sure they will not rely upon either of us to any extent further than they must," Laurence said.

He was silent again: standing, with his hands clasped behind his back, and looking out over the great expanse of the valley; even in his rough clothes his shoulders were as straight as though they still bore the golden epaulets in which Temeraire had first seen him, and only a little imagination was required to restore to him his uniform, his green coat and the leather harness, and the golden bars. Laurence paused and after a moment longer asked, "Do you *wish* to go, then?"

It only then occurred to Temeraire that of course, the mission would require leaving their valley. He turned and looked at the pavilion, and the herd of cattle milling below among the grass; the prospect of tree-furred gorges stretched out before them, carved through the yellow and ochre rock of the mountains. He curled his tail in, the tip wanting to switch uneasily through the air; it seemed as though they had only just come and begun the work.

Perhaps it was not so exciting as battles—Temeraire could not argue that—but there was something splendid even in seeing plants grow, when one had helped to sow the fields, and the pavilion half-finished seemed already lonely and abandoned when he thought of going away.

"I suppose—we have been happy here?" Temeraire said, half-questioning. "And I would not like to leave things undone, but—" He looked at Laurence. "Would you rather stay?"

Temeraire drowsed off a few hours later; the handful of small fires near the campsite died away to embers yellow as cream, and the great swath of southern stars came out overhead. From the far side of the valley Laurence heard faintly a song, rising and falling, too distantly for words: the Wiradjuri in their summer camp along the river.

Tomorrow was Tuesday: he should ordinarily have gone down to meet with them and exchange goods, and present for their approval Temeraire's next intended step in the pavilion's construction, the acquisition of timber from a stand of large old trees to the north, for the wall-paneling and to build out the rooms which Laurence himself should occupy, and any of their human guests.

O'Dea would go to Sydney with the mail, and return in a week's time perhaps with some new book. In the meantime, there was the rest of the floor to be laid down, and two of the men had already been set to working upon the shingles for the eventual roof. In a few days the cattle would be moved to fresh pasture; in the evenings Laurence would puzzle out the new volume of Chinese poetry under Temeraire's guidance: the ordinary daily course of their new life.

Or instead they might be aloft for Port Jackson and Brazil: a couple of pebbles briefly cast up and allowed to rest on the shore, carried away again into the ocean by the retreating tide.

Laurence knew his decision already made; perhaps had been made even before Hammond had spoken. He wished he could be certain his choice was not driven by pride, by the lingering grip of shame: he had done his best to make his peace with his own treason, since it had been a necessary evil, but he could not deny Hammond had laid out a potent bribe. Easy enough to hope, to plan, that they should do more good than evil in the grander orbits of the world, if they should re-enter that sphere; easier still for those hopes to prove false.

Easier than that, to allow those fears to imprison them more securely even than the miles of ocean. Laurence laid a hand on the warm scaled hide of Temeraire's foreleg. If nothing else, Temeraire was not made to lie idle, in a peaceful valley at the far ends of the earth.

Temeraire slitted open one blue eye and made an interrogative noise, not quite awake.

"No; go back to sleep, all is well," Laurence said, and when the heavy lid had slid closed again, he stood up; and went down to the river to shave.

Chapter 2

"**I** CANNOT SAY MUCH FOR A PAVILION without a roof," Iskierka said, with quite unbearable superiority, "and anyway you cannot bring it along, so even if it were finished, it would not be of any use. I do not think anyone can disagree I have used my time better."

Temeraire *could* disagree, very vehemently, but when Iskierka had chivvied a few of her crew—newly brought on in Madras—into bringing up the sea-chests from below, and throwing open the lids to let the sunlight in upon the heaped golden vessels, and even one small casket of beautifully cut gemstones, he found his arguments did ring a little hollow. It seemed the *Allegiance* had in her lumbering way still managed to get into flying distance of not one but *three* lawful prizes, on the way to Madras, and another one on the way back, when Hammond's urgent need of a transport to carry Temeraire to Rio had necessitated her abrupt about-face and return.

"It does not seem very fair," Temeraire said to Laurence, "when one considers how much sea-journeying we have done, without even one French merchantman coming anywhere in reach; and I do not find that Riley expects we should meet others on the way to Brazil, either."

"No, but we may meet a whaler or two, if you like," Laurence said absently. Temeraire was not mollified; whales were perfectly tolerable creatures, very good eating when not excessively large, but no-one could compare them to cartloads of gems and gold; and as for ambergris, he did not care for the scent.

Laurence was presently interviewing the aviators at the covert to form their new crew—a small and undistinguished group to choose from, even though swelled by other men whom Granby had brought back from Madras, the coverts there having been half-emptied of dragons by the plague. But it seemed Iskierka had already taken her pick of the available men for her own crew. Temeraire and Laurence were only to have the leavings, even though, Temeraire thought, they had the greater seniority and also the greater need, as one could not conveniently get very many men on Iskierka's back to begin with thanks to her endlessly steaming spikes.

Temeraire could only console himself that at least he now had Fellowes back as his very own ground-crew master, and Emily Roland was once more officially Laurence's ensign; but apart from this he had been stripped almost entirely. At least Gong Su had remained with them all along, so Temeraire had *one* properly loyal crew member—but Dorset for no very good reason had decided not to rejoin them. There had been some suggestion that it was his duty to stay with the covert, which had no other surgeon; but why Dorset might not come along, and Iskierka's new surgeon remain behind instead, Temeraire did not understand at all.

"Sir," Lieutenant Blincoln said, standing rather awkwardly outside the clearing where Laurence was sitting with his writing-table, "sir, I hoped I might have a word."

Laurence looked up from his notes, and Blincoln began to stumble over an apology—very sorry if he should ever have failed in proper respect; hoped he had done his duty as best he could, always; begged leave to recommend himself to Captain Laurence's attention—

"Mr. Blincoln," Laurence said, interrupting him, "I have no complaint to make of your manner towards me under the previous circumstances; if any apology on that score is merited, you may consider it accepted if you wish. I should by far be more inclined to hire a man who had abused me to my face, for a just conviction, than one who has to my own certain knowledge and further credible report behaved in an outrageous and underhanded fashion towards a young officer, friendless and without that defense which he ought have had from your superiors, and knowingly and with selfish intent interfered with the rearing of a beast not his own."

Laurence meant Demane: evidently the aviators in Sydney had continued their attempts to sway Kulingile away from him, and it was no surprise to Temeraire that Rankin should have done nothing to prevent it. Although, Temeraire did not think it should have been anything so very dreadful if one of the other aviators had succeeded. After all, Demane should have been very welcome back in his own crew, and been much better off, if his dragon had proven so very faithless. Not, of course, that Temeraire wished for any such thing to happen; only, if it *had*—well, it had not; he sighed, peering over at the sadly abbreviated list of officers that Laurence had jotted down.

Blincoln meanwhile would have protested, but Laurence cut him short. "No," he said, "I have no interest in hearing whatever explanations you can dredge up, and that your casting of lures was condoned by your senior officer and imitated by many of your fellows as little excuses you as it does credit to any of them. It was wrong in you, and you knew it so; I must ask you and any other man who has acted in similar fashion to expect nothing from me but the strongest possible censure."

Blincoln hastily retreated; and Laurence put down his pen. "I find I am more given to haste, these days; I have grown too used to a more select company," he said to Temeraire ruefully.

"It was certainly no more than he deserved," Temeraire said, "for imagining we should take him for my crew; *I* certainly have not forgotten how rude he was to you."

"I can make allowances for any man who might object to treason," Laurence said, with far more tolerance than Temeraire thought merited, since they had not properly been traitors after all, and now even the Government had admitted it. "But not of this selfish and underhanded leech-work; and now I think on it, we cannot leave Kulingile and Demane here under Rankin's command. I must speak with Hammond: between us and Granby, I think we have enough authority to make off with a heavyweight, particularly as he has never been formally issued orders since the hatching. Otherwise those men will never let them alone; and if they should think my reinstatement means my ill-report of them will have more credence, they will only grow all the more vicious, for having less to lose by it."

"Of course Demane should come with us," Temeraire said, brightening, "and if Kulingile chooses, I do not see any objection. He might come *instead* of Iskierka?" he suggested hopefully. Unfortunately, it seemed that Hammond quite insisted on her accompanying them: more of this unreasonable favoritism towards fire-breathers.

But at least Kulingile's coming meant that Temeraire should not be parted from Demane and from Sipho—whom Temeraire was also not prepared to cede from his own crew, even though as Demane's brother his proper posting might be contested. "But I have an egg-mate back in China, and it is not as though we are always together; so it does not *necessarily* follow," Temeraire said to himself, arguing it out.

"Mr. O'Dea will come with us, also, I think," Laurence said. "He has grown steady, these last few months; and at least that will mean one decent hand in the log-book; and Mr. Shipley. Yes, Roland?"

Emily Roland had come into the clearing, and said in a low tone, "Sir, I beg your pardon; they won't let him come up, but I thought—I was sure you would wish—"

Temeraire looked down the hill, where the all but unnecessary gate to the covert was manned rather to occupy the aviators than to prevent any incursions from the town: a man in ordinary clothing was being barred. "Why," Temeraire said with pleasure, after squinting to be sure, although the shock of reddish brown hair was immediately familiar, "I think that is Lieutenant Ferris; whyever should they not let him come up?"

Laurence looked very pale, and said quietly, "Roland, if you please, run and tell those men to stand aside, and that Mr. Ferris is my guest."

She nodded and dashed away, and shortly Ferris came into the clearing: quite altered, Temeraire found on closer inspection. He had grown heavier-set, especially in the shoulders, and perhaps he had been sunburnt so often that the color had finally stuck, for he was florid in the cheeks, and seemed older than he must be. Temeraire was delighted nevertheless: Ferris had perhaps not been so good a first lieutenant as Granby, but he had been very young at the time, and in any case he should certainly be an improvement over any of the officers here, and of Iskierka's crew, also.

Poor Ferris looked very ill, Laurence thought as he stood to meet him: untimely aged beyond his twenty and three, and, Laurence was sorry to see, the marks of strong drink beginning to be visible in his face.

"I am very happy to see you again, Mr. Ferris," Temeraire was saying, inclining his head, "however you have come here; are you lately arrived?"

Ferris a little stumblingly said he had come on a recent colony ship—he had heard—and there trailed off; Laurence said, "Temeraire, if you will excuse us; Mr. Ferris, perhaps you will walk with me a moment."

Ferris came with him to the small tent which Laurence was using for shelter: set apart from the other aviators, to avoid grating too often against Rankin; Laurence was doubly grateful for the privacy now. He waved Ferris to one of the small camp-chairs, and sitting said quietly, "I am also very glad indeed to see you again, and to have the opportunity to make my apologies, if you can indeed have the grace to accept them: I know of no man I have wronged more deeply."

Ferris darkened a little in the cheeks, and took Laurence's offered hand with a low and half-muttered word, not intelligible.

Laurence paused, but Ferris did not speak further, his eyes still downcast. Laurence hardly knew how to proceed—to offer amends at once impossible and insulting. He had thought to protect Ferris, and his other officers, by concealing from them his treason and Temeraire's; but the court-martial had struck wherever a target might be found, and for the sin of ignorance, Ferris had been dismissed from the service. A promising career blighted, a family heritage disgraced, and the only thing Laurence could not reproach himself for was that by some small grace they had not hanged him.

"We looked for word of you," Laurence said finally, "but—I could not presume to write your family—"

"No, of course," Ferris said, low. "I know you were in prison, when—" and they were silent once again.

"I can hardly offer you any recompense which should be adequate," Laurence said at last: as futile as the offer might be, still it must be made. "But whatever remedy should be in my power to make you—if you have come here intending to establish an estate, I would—" Laurence swallowed his distaste. "I can presume on some acquaintance with the governor, MacArthur; if you should—"

"No, sir, I don't, that—I heard you had gone, and Temeraire, to start the breeding grounds here," Ferris said. "I thought, if you were not an officer yourself, anymore, then perhaps you might— that I might be of use, if I came. And in any case—" He stopped, and indeed did not need to go on to make abundantly clear the other motives which should have made such a flimsy hope sufficient to induce him to take ship around the world, for a tiny and ill-run prison colony: the worst sort of disgrace and mortification, and the life of an outcast. "But I hear you are restored to the list, sir."

Laurence scarcely repressed a flinch: *he,* the actual traitor, had been reinstated, and guiltless Ferris had not. And that very injustice now barred Laurence from giving him a real place: as a captain of the Aerial Corps, he could appoint only aviators to Temeraire's crew. He might contrive to offer Ferris some unofficial position, as a hanger-on of sorts; but such a situation could only be deeply painful, putting Ferris in daily company with aviators less gifted and likely to offer him the same disdain which Laurence with more justice had met.

He made the offer nevertheless. "If you should care for such employment as should offer itself," he said, the details of necessity remaining vague, "and would not object to the journey, I would be glad of your—" There he stopped, and finished awkwardly with, "—company," as the best of inadequate choices.

"I would be glad of—of the opportunity," Ferris said, also awkward; that he perceived all the same disadvantages as did Laurence was plain, and equally plain that he was resigned to them. Laurence could not help but recognize he had no other alternative that was preferable: a miserable situation in which to offer a man work, knowing him unable to refuse.

"I will send word to the *Allegiance;* if you will be so good as to transfer your things there," Laurence said. "We leave at the earliest opportunity."

"I am very sorry not to be able to oblige you, Captain," Hammond said, "but of course, you understand that only Royal dispensation can make any remedy—I would be happy to write a letter, in this regard—"

Laurence had written before now, more than once, and knew that Jane would have gladly seen Ferris reinstated as well if she could; he was not in the least sanguine. "Sir," he said, "I beg you will forgive me; I have made no demands, nor have I any for myself or for Temeraire, but I must make this my price, as little as I like to have one. You must see there is no just cause why I should have my rank restored, and Mr. Ferris not."

"He does not have a dragon," Hammond said, brutally. "No," he added, "I do understand your sentiments, Captain, and without exceeding myself I will venture so far as to say, the successful accomplishment of our mission should certainly have a material and beneficial effect on his suit; particularly if the young man in question—I understand he will be accompanying us?—should manage to be of service during the expedition."

With such scant assurances, insufficient even to mention to Ferris, Laurence was forced to content himself; and he regretted the lack even more when he had completed his interviews: the crew he had managed to assemble was not one such as to inspire great confidence. He had taken on Lieutenant Forthing, who had shown himself a competent officer if not a brilliant one, during their crossing of the continent; and for midshipmen three of the younger men: Cavendish, Bellew, and Avery. These were distinguished from the others mainly for their having had less time in their careers to demonstrate a lack of initiative or skill, so he could have some small hope of uncovering some previously hidden talent.

The farewell dinner, given by Mrs. MacArthur, was an event of considerable magnificence despite the limitations of the colony; her husband *had* been reasonable, or at least sufficiently so to persuade Hammond to endorse the occasion. "You know, Ambassador, I don't care if I shall call myself First Minister or Governor or Grand High Master of Kangaroos, in the least," MacArthur had said to him, and repeated at nearly every opportunity, with small variations, wherever witnesses would listen to him, "so long as it is understood we must be allowed to know our business better than anyone else, and let to settle it ourselves, instead of this sitting fire waiting eight months for word from Westminster, or worse, having some Navy officer with more will than mother-wit come blundering in to set us at logger-heads with our nearer neighbors, and they only looking for good trading partners, as we would anyhow care to be."

The distinction between this position and real independence seemed to Laurence a vague semantical thing, but at least for the moment Hammond professed himself satisfied to indeed call MacArthur *Governor,* and to see the British colors on the flagpole above the Government House, and to attend his dinner there.

The table was lopsided, almost inevitably, but Mrs. MacArthur had managed to find enough women to intersperse between any men of the rank of lieutenant or higher, so at least the upper half of her table preserved the appearance of even numbers. There was still very little in the way of society in the colony, and Laurence found himself seated beside the particularly beautiful wife of a captain in the New South Wales Corps, one of MacArthur's subordinates, whom a very little conversation sufficed to discover had come over on a convict ship, for pickpocketing.

Mrs. Gerald could not be called respectable except in the article of her marriage, which she did not scruple to avow, over her third glass, "the best joke, because Timothy would always go on as he was hanging out for a rich woman, when he should go back to England; and nothing more tiresome for a girl to hear. So I wrote out a long letter to myself, and put on it the name of an old beau of mine back home, saying as how he was coming out and meant to have me, *with* a ring if you please, and I left it about where Timothy should see it: meaning only to keep him from going on as though I was beneath thinking of for anybody. But he went into a rage, and stormed about so, that I lost my temper quite and said he might marry me himself, or else go about his business; and so here I am! And I swear he is none the worse by it, for I am sure no rich woman would know the first thing about how to get on in a country like this."

She was, despite lacking any shade of sensibility, an amiable dinner companion, more so than the wretched creature on Laurence's other side, whom he would have been astonished to find a day above fifteen years of age, evidently released from the schoolroom just in time for the event. Despite a better share of the virtues of birth and education than Mrs. Gerald, Miss Hershelm was stricken with so much shyness that all Laurence's efforts could barely win a syllable from her lips; she did not raise her eyes from her plate even once.

He could not think the occasion ideal for such a child, particularly when the younger men lower down the table began to show signs of forgetting their company, and growing boisterous. Laurence saw Mrs. MacArthur glance down the table, and a quick word to her butler followed; an assemblage of cheeses and sweets came to the table accompanying the pudding, in a rather incoherent combination. Laurence rather suspected another two courses had been intended and forgone, though no-one could have complained of the menu so far: fresh-caught roughy in a sauce of lemons and oranges, with fresh peas; an exceedingly handsome crown roast of lamb ornamented with preserved cherries; new potatoes in their skins presented alongside veal chops dressed with brown butter; a whole tunny baked in salt crust, occupying half the table.

But when the pudding had been cleared, Mrs. MacArthur rose; with equal prudence, MacArthur did not let the port go round very long after dinner was cleared, and proposed their rejoining the ladies almost at once.

When they had come into the drawing rooms, several of the women had vanished, Miss Hershelm among them, Laurence was glad to see; Mrs. Gerald, on the other hand, coming up took him by the arm and declared her intention of presenting him to all the eligible young ladies of the company.

"For it is a great shame you should not be doing some girl any good," she said, "and it is really too bad of you; I am sure you could use some good company, and you needn't worry I will present you to anyone so poor-spirited as to mind a dragon. Miss Oakley, may I introduce to you Captain Laurence?"

Laurence managed eventually to demur, on the grounds of ineligibility and imminent departure both, and joined Hammond by the balcony, where he was speaking with another of the ladies: a Mrs. Pemberton, widowed on the very journey which had brought her to the colony, and only lately out of black gloves.

"I do not suppose we would have thought of it, save that Elizabeth—Mrs. MacArthur—is a friend of mine, from our schoolroom days," she said, Hammond having exclaimed over her having made so long a journey. "But having made your own home in so distant a country as China, can you be so surprised that others might wish to see more of the world than encompassed by a single parish in Devonshire, and six weeks in London? I was glad of the notion when she proposed our coming and taking up a grant of land; her husband would have had work for mine. But there is nothing for a woman alone to do here."

Except to marry again, she did not say, and her speaking look at the company—grown coarser by the moment, and more loud—made clear she did not see much to admire in the local prospects.

"You might return to England," Hammond said.

"And go back to Devonshire, and tat lace with my mother-in-law, while her pug snores at our feet," she said, dryly: it did not seem the sort of portrait which would appeal to a woman who had willingly followed her husband across the world to a half-established colony. "I understand you are gone away again shortly, yourselves?"

"As soon as we have our tide, and the wind is in the west," Hammond said, poetic but quite inaccurate, as making sail with a westerly wind from her present anchorage would serve better to drive the *Allegiance* onto the harbor rocks than to the open ocean. "But I do hope to return to England, ma'am, someday. I do not grudge my country any service, but I am not so peripatetic as that; and surely the delights of home must call still more to a woman's heart."

"And you, Captain Laurence?" she asked. "Does your heart yearn for a quiet retirement at the end of your service, and a house in the country?"

There was something a little mocking in her tone. "Only if there were room enough for a dragon," Laurence said, and excused himself to step outside and take the air: in the dark, with the lights of the house shining and the garden full of palm-trees and fruit bats obscured, he might have been at exactly that sort of manor, which he might indeed have imagined for himself, six years and a lifetime ago. He had given the future scarcely a thought since then, occupied excessively by an unexpected present; he was surprised to find he would now gladly prefer his isolate valley, with all its toil and inconveniences.

But the valley had been left behind: the cattle sold, or loaded aboard the *Allegiance* to feed the dragons; the pavilion roofless under the stars with its pillars sentinel over the half-grown sheaves of wheat. No caretaker could be found for so lonely a place; if ever they returned, there would be vines twining the pillars, and weeds and saplings thick in the fields they had so laboriously cleared.

If ever they returned. He turned and went back into the house.

The governor's mansion stood opposite the promontory housing the covert, around the bay, so the aviators and the soldiers had a sobering course of night air on the way back to their quarters. Some of the younger officers found the lights of the dockside taverns along the way a stronger lure than the quiet of their barracks, however, and eeled away in twos and threes; until Laurence was very nearly walking alone but for Granby. Rankin was on ahead, with Lieutenant Blincoln and Lieutenant Drewmore, and without need for discussion Laurence and Granby slowed their steps and turned off onto a more circuitous route, to stretch out the walk.

"No-one can say it wasn't a handsome way to see us off," Granby said, "although MacArthur might have been less festive about it: I am sure he would have wrung my hand with just as much pleasure if I had told him I was going to the devil; not to say we aren't."

"I think we must have a little more faith in Mr. Hammond than that," Laurence said.

"I've more in the Tswana," Granby said. "I can't imagine what he supposes we are going to say that will turn them up sweet, and they have some damned dangerous beasts: fire-breathers, and four heavy-weight breeds that we know of, and we know precious little. I would just as soon try farther north, and see if the colonials would hire out some of their beasts for fighting, if they have so many they are using them for freight these days."

He spoke with a vague disgruntlement shared, Laurence knew, by every aviator who had learned that the Americans had begun to raise dragons in so much earnest that they were bidding fair to rival British numbers, with a scant fraction of the number of men looking to fly them: it was deeply dissatisfying to those who had spent their lives in service, hoping for a rare chance to one day captain their own dragon.

"But much smaller creatures," Laurence said, "and without military training; there can be no comparison. You may be certain Napoleon will have shipped the most deadly of the Tswana, and as many of them as he could cram aboard his transports."

"Well, I will hope the three of us may make them take enough notice to bother listening, instead of just having at us straight off," Granby said, but pessimistically.

"I know Hammond is claiming there will be reinforcements sent to meet us from Halifax, or the Channel, but I will rely on that when they land before us yelling for cattle, and not an instant before.

"Anyway, I oughtn't complain about the Foreign Office's latest notion, when I am damned grateful for the consequences: it was enough to drive a fellow wild thinking of you and Temeraire thrown away in this wretched little port with that fellow Rankin yapping at your heels, and a crowd of useless layabouts besides. I don't blame you for chucking the lot of them and going into the wilds. Whatever are they about, now?" They had come at last in sight of the covert gates, and there was a commotion up on the hillside.

They found something of an uproar, overseen by four interested dragons whose heads loomed above the knot of men; Demane at the heart of it, Laurence rather despairingly saw, and an officer of the New South Wales Corps on his knees in the dirt before him with a bloody lip and wild-eyed alarm at Kulingile peering down.

"—outrage," Rankin was saying in great heat, "—will have his commander here in the morning, demanding an explanation—"

"I don't care!" Demane said. "And the only one who has been outrageous is *him;* I know you don't care a jot, so he is here and will stay here, until Captain Laurence comes back; and if he wants to get up and leave before then, he may *try,* and I will have Kulingile hold him upside-down over the cliff."

"But Roland, I am sure if Demane is angry with him, he has done something to deserve it," Temeraire was saying meanwhile to Emily Roland, with what Laurence could only call misplaced loyalty, "so there is no reason not to wait for Laurence to come back: he will certainly know whatever is the best thing to do. But perhaps you had better not hold that fellow over the cliff," he added to Kulingile, the first thing of sense in the conversation, "for you might very easily drop him, if he squirmed. If he should try and run away, you can just pin him down instead: only being careful not to squash him."

"You are all a pack of damned fools," Roland said, as furious as Laurence had ever heard her, "and if he weren't a coward, he *would* run, and none of you should do anything; there ain't any reason the captain ought hear anything about it."

Iskierka said, "Well, I would like to hear about it, as I am not asleep anymore; is there some fighting?"

"Oh, lord," Granby said, under his breath.

"I am here; what the devil is going on?" Laurence said grimly. "Demane, we spoke this afternoon, I thought, on the subject of brawling."

"I haven't!" Demane said; then realizing the bloody mess of his captive's face gave him every appearance of a lie, added, "Roland did that; only she would have let him off—"

"Because I didn't care to make a stupid great fuss of knocking down some drunken looby is no reason for you to put your oar into it; what bloody right do you suppose you have, pushing into my affairs?" Roland said. "Sir, pray don't give him any mind—"

"How was I to know, anyway?" the soldier blurted, from the ground, "—with her hanging about in trousers; I thought it was a get-up, for a joke."

"If it was, that wouldn't mean I wanted any of your grabbing, anyway," Roland said contemptuously, "and if you didn't know that, you ought have asked, first, if you mean to complain of me."

Rankin snorted. "Ah; I might have known it would be something on the order of this sordid mess. You may relieve yourself of your prisoner, Demane: no-one expects that the women of the Corps protect their virtue as if they were gentlewomen, and I can only imagine the ridicule with which any suit for breach should meet in such a case; or did you expect to be permitted to hang him for jealousy?"

"That is enough, sir; more than enough," Laurence said to Rankin, sharply. "And you: your name, sir, and your commander's," he said to the soldier, who a little belligerently gave it as Lieutenant Paster. "He will hear from me in the morning; I trust he will share my opinion of a man who cannot show decent respect either to a woman, or to a fellow officer."

Lieutenant Paster did not stay to argue, when Laurence had waved him off, but escaped down the hill at speed; Demane scowled, and the crowd began to disperse with the focus of interest lost.

"Sir, I don't need a fuss made," Roland said, coming up to him. "There wasn't anything to the matter—"

"If you please," Laurence said, forestalling her with a hand, and turning to lead her back to his tent, Demane following and trying to speak to her; Roland kept a determined shoulder to his face and ignored him coldly, while he protested that he had only done as he ought—

"That is more than I can say," Laurence said sharply, sitting at his desk. "Your first concern, Demane, ought have been for the reputation and satisfaction of the lady in question, neither of which can have been served by enacting a public scene in a temper—"

"*Thank* you, sir," Roland said, and glared at Demane with satisfaction.

"—I excuse it in the circumstances," Laurence added, "only as having proceeded from my own failing: the insult could not have been offered in the first place, had I done my duty and arranged for proper chaperonage. No, Roland," he said, when she began to splutter, "your duties must of course come first, but you are nevertheless a gentlewoman and the daughter of a gentlewoman—"

"I am not!" she said, indignantly. "I am an *officer* and Mother is—"

"If a man may be asked to be both officer and gentleman, so, too, may you, as far as duty permits," Laurence said implacably, "—The one does not preclude you from the responsibilities of the other; nor me from mine as your guardian, until you are of age. I will see to the matter in the morning."

"Now see what you have done," Roland hissed at Demane, and stormed out of the tent.

"Sir," Demane said in protest, "I didn't mean anything of the sort; it is not as though I would let anyone bother Roland—"

"*That,* sir, is not your privilege," Laurence said, "nor will be, unless Roland should choose to make it yours, with the consent of her family; until then, I will see to it you comport yourself as a gentleman, also. There will be no more of this running wild, and so far as you choose to press your suit, you will do so within bounds."

"But that is not—Roland and I—" Demane said.

"Has she made you any commitments, or given you license to consider her promised to you?" Laurence said.

"—No," Demane said, surly, "but—"

"Then let me hear nothing more of this," Laurence said with finality.

Demane stalked from the tent in as great a temper as Roland herself, and left Laurence with the very meager satisfaction of knowing he had faced up to an inconvenient duty, without the slightest idea of how to accomplish it. Hiring a satisfactory chaperone at all in the unsettled state of the colony would have been a remarkable task, much less finding one in the span of three days who would not balk at coming on a long sea-voyage and a dangerous mission.

And he could not leave Roland in Sydney; *that* would be to neglect his still-greater duty to see her formed into an officer fit to command a priceless dragon, the which could not be done without useful experience, even if accompanied by danger. She should have no opportunity to acquire any in a sluggish port, and still less under Rankin's command. In any event, that gentleman had made it perfectly plain he could not be relied upon to have any consideration for either Roland's training or her protection.

Laurence wondered doubtfully if perhaps he might find and hire some retired soldier, of advanced years, for the duty: the arrangement could not be called proper, and such a person could offer Roland none of that advice which Laurence vaguely felt was also the purview of a chaperone, unless perhaps the man had raised daughters? But it might do, in lieu of any better solution; and in the meantime, he realized, he should have to row out to the *Allegiance* and speak to Riley about Roland's quarters.

"Nothing particularly out of the ordinary," Laurence said, "but there must be a separate berth, and one for the chaperone."

"A lady?" Riley said, doubtfully. "Not that I don't see the need, of course," he added, "but Laurence, you cannot mean us to go carting a gentlewoman about to Brazil, with a war going? I don't suppose we have above three women on board, if you count Old Molly in the galley, and the gunner's wife, and her baby, which I don't think should count." And he looked even more doubtful at Laurence's proposed substitution of a retired gentleman.

Laurence was particularly grateful, now, that Riley had learned of the existence of female officers among the aviators; at least Riley did not need a long explanation. It was true Roland could not expect to enjoy the usual satisfactions of marriage and family, either, and perhaps nothing might truly apply, of the ordinary course of rearing a young woman; but Laurence knew very well what he would have thought of a sea-captain who let his young midshipmen run themselves into gaming debts or overindulgence in either drink or whoring; or otherwise render themselves wholly ineligible to a woman of sense and character. He did not intend to be guilty of the same, nor to allow a situation to persist which had already exposed Roland to insult.

"Even if I can only hire a maid, that would at least be something," he said.

"You had better consult Mrs. MacArthur," Riley said. "At least she can tell you how to go on, and perhaps put you in the way of some steady creature; if there is one to be had at such short notice: I think we will have our wind tomorrow, and the tide is at noon."

They went out on the deck, presently noisy with holystoning and stinking with fresh paint, the hands hard at labor under the watchful eye of Lord Purbeck, the first lieutenant; and Laurence thought Riley was right: a certain unsteadiness in the air, which spoke to old instincts.

"And if you do find someone, I can manage the berths, of

course," Riley added. "You haven't much crew among the three of you, and there is plenty of room in the bow cabins," these normally being intended for the use of aviators, aboard a dragon transport, and for a much greater number than the *Allegiance* would be shipping in this case. "I suppose my own mids may cut up a fuss if your ensign has a berth, if they aren't to know why; but they must lump it."

"That one source of difficulty, at least, I may remove," Laurence said, and shook Riley's hand before he went down to the ship's launch, to be taken back to shore.

He found Roland working, with short angry strokes, on oiling some of Temeraire's harness which had been neglected for lack of ground crew; she sprang up when she saw him. "No," Laurence said, "I have not reconsidered; however, I have also another duty, to which I trust you will not object: you have seen more than enough service to make midwingman."

The announcement mollified her a little, but she did say with hopeful cunning, "As midwingman I surely cannot need a chaperone, sir; and anyway, ought you hire one without consulting Mother?"

This reminder was as unnecessary as it was unwelcome: Laurence was awkwardly aware that he was by no means certain of Jane's approving the hiring of a chaperone. Certainly she herself had never had the benefit of one, and would likely abuse the notion as absurd. But neither did he think Jane would have approved of Emily's being subject to any unwanted attentions which she could no longer avoid through camouflage; and still less approve of Emily's engaging herself in any permanent attachment at so young an age.

"When we should again be in England, in her purview, naturally you shall not want for any other guidance," he said. "Until then, I cannot consider myself alone adequate supervision; have you never felt the want," he added desperately, by way of persuasion, "of some companion, to whom you might turn for—for advice?"

"Mother has told me all about that," Emily said with impatience, "and I don't mean to do anything stupid and put myself out of service for a year; whatever else should I have to talk about with some stuffy old woman who will sniff because I don't wear skirts?"

Laurence gave up the hope of argument, and contented himself with ordering her to see to the requisition of more gunpowder, for their incendiaries.

Chapter 3

⁂

TEMERAIRE COULD NOT PARTICULARLY REGRET seeing the small mean buildings of Sydney dropping away behind them, although Laurence and Riley spoke together so approvingly of the qualities of the harbor; that was very well, but it did not make up for the untidy appearance of the unpaved streets, which were too narrow besides, and the mud which was everywhere. And while he certainly appreciated all the goods which the sea-serpents brought, from China, he did not appreciate the extraordinary stench of the mash of half-rotten fish which they liked to eat; and he did not see why it needed to be kept in open barrels by the dockside. The wind was very nearly directly at their back, carrying the smell along to haunt them as the *Allegiance* traveled onward.

"I suppose they would not eat any of us?" Mrs. Pemberton inquired of Roland, hesitating at the base of the stairs up to the dragon-deck.

"Oh, they certainly would, if ever you gave them any opportunity," Temeraire said, peering down at her, "—They have no discrimination at all, I am afraid; but you see, they do not seem to be able to speak, so one cannot very easily explain to them that one ought not to eat people. If you should care to go swimming, you had better wait until we are at least a few days out."

The lady stared up at him dumbly. Temeraire had not precisely followed why Laurence had felt her presence necessary, and when he had asked Roland, she had said, "It is not, at all," in venomous tones; she now answered Mrs. Pemberton with faint contempt. "Of course none of them will eat you: she means you, Temeraire, and Iskierka and Kulingile, not the serpents."

"So I am afraid she cannot be very clever," Temeraire said to Laurence in an undertone, later that day, when they had come out into open ocean and Laurence had come up to the dragondeck again. "And you know, Laurence, I must say that I would consider myself equal to providing any protection which Roland should need, if only you had mentioned it to me; even if she were not of my own crew, I should consider it only my duty to Excidium, since he cannot be with us."

He could not quite suppress a hint of injury: in the interim Lieutenant Ferris   or Mr. Ferris, as he evidently was to be called— had explained Mrs. Pemberton's position to him, and Temeraire found himself in perfect agreement with Roland on the subject.

"In body I have no doubt of it," Laurence said dryly, "—in reputation, I am afraid you might have more difficulty: your opinion would not be solicited in the matter." He sighed and added, "She is a sensible woman, and not a coward, to have agreed to the position in the first place; I am sure she will soon understand you are no danger to her."

Several of the serpents had followed them out of the harbor, either for a frolic or in hopes of a meal, and played in the froth spilling out from the *Allegiance*'s bow, their sides gleaming in spray. No-one liked their company; aside from the smell, which anyone might have objected to, the sailors were very anxious over them and worrying they might at any moment attack. Which the serpents would not, of course, because they were too fat and well-fed; they had only to go back to the harbor if they were hungry. But the sailors were unconvinced and viewed the dragons as their only defense, so that if ever Temeraire tried to take a nap, the sailors were sure to make a great noise in the sails overhead, or send a cannon-ball rolling across the deck, or drop a coil of rope down upon him from aloft.

"I *might* be a danger to them, after all," Temeraire said, disgruntled, when a pailful of slurry had by supposed accident been allowed to pour down onto his neck after one of the serpents still following along in their wake had breached the water in a great curving iridescent leap, evidently to make sure he was paying attention.

Roland was now apparently too senior to wash him: instead Sipho was put to the task, along with a little creature called Gerry: the relic of a New South Wales officer and his wife who had both been carried off by some sort of fever, leaving behind the boy, not quite eight, with no family in the world within two thousand miles. Laurence had acquired him as a runner from Mrs. MacArthur, along with Mrs. Pemberton. "The price of her advice," Laurence said ruefully, but as far as Temeraire was concerned, Gerry was far more useful: his small fingers were much better able to clean underneath the scales, where some of the slurry had leaked unpleasantly.

He cried when brought up on the dragondeck, to be sure, but Roland abused him for stupidity. "I would have given a great deal to be taken on as a runner two years early, instead of only being put into school; what business do you have to be blubbing like an infant? No-one will ever think you worthy of having a dragon yourself, if you cannot properly appreciate the chance," she said.

Gerry sniffed wetly and said, "I do not want a dragon myself," which Temeraire could only approve: perhaps at last he might have another person in his crew who did not mean to go scurrying off to some other dragon, just when he and Laurence had got them trained properly.

"Then you are a great looby," Roland said. "Who would not like a dragon of their own, and be able to go flying and do their duty to England; and you the son of a soldier: you ought to be ashamed."

As Gerry's father had been an eager participant in MacArthur's rebellion, that late gentleman's commitment to country and duty was perhaps in question, but the argument at least distracted the boy from his tears. "I am not a looby," he said sullenly, and followed Sipho up on Temeraire's back, and by the time they had finished washing him was already reconciled to his new situation enough to go sliding down Temeraire's flank after.

No-one went pouring slurry on Iskierka, who slept in hissing, steaming state coiled along the front of the dragondeck; Temeraire regarded her with deep disfavor. At least Kulingile was being useful, and fishing: even if he did eat most of what he caught himself, that at least kept him from eating everything in sight at dinner-time, and looking wistfully over at other people's portions if one did not eat quickly enough.

"You needn't rock the boat so hard when you land," Iskierka even complained, when Kulingile had dropped back down licking his chops.

"You needn't make a noise about anyone else who is not lazing about quite uselessly," Temeraire said, "and that is very kind of you, Kulingile; thank you," he added graciously, taking the remnants of the small whale which Kulingile had brought back to offer around, though the edges were ragged and somewhat gnawed, and even these leftovers were more than Temeraire really wanted. He did not quite like to admit that he could not eat so much as Kulingile; it did not seem fair that anyone who had started quite so small and deflated should now be larger than himself, and very soon might even outstrip Maximus.

"I am not hungry," Iskierka said. "If there were any prizes in sight, that would be different, but there is no sense in flying around only for fish one does not want. Anyway you are not hunting yourself, either."

"I am guarding the ship from the serpents," Temeraire said, dignified.

*   *   *

The last of the serpents fell back to Sydney by mid-morning the
next day, and left the *Allegiance* alone and driving towards the
roaring forties: the water cold, dark iron-grey, and mazed with
greenish froth. Laurence joined Riley at the stern to watch them go,
through the glass: spined backs breaching the surface in glittering
curves up and down as they swam, until they reached the end of the
water stirred up in the *Allegiance*'s wake, and then plunged deep
and vanished.

From there on, monotony, of the sort a sailor loved best: a
steady knife-edged wind at their back, and the sun small and cold
white on the horizon for all but a few hours of the day. Laurence
woke each day to the holystoning of the deck, the round of the
ship's bells; sometimes in the first confusion of rising he wondered
why he had not been called for the morning's watch, and looked in
vain for a blue coat.

He could have wished only for a little more occupation: he had
grown used in the valley to have every day as much to do as could
be done, and found himself now unequal to the task of filling the
hours aboard a ship where he had no duty but to be a passenger.
Even his self-imposed duties as schoolmaster were usurped by Roland's chaperone, whom he could not deny was better suited to the
task than himself, having before her marriage served as a governess.

He had Granby for company; and might have had Riley, but
their relations had never quite recovered from the tensions which
had arisen on their journey to Africa. Riley's father was a slave-
owner in the West Indies; Laurence's own, Lord Allendale, devoted
to the cause of abolition: the voyage which led them past all the
wretched slave-port cities of that continent had left them con-
stantly rubbed against one another, and without room for apology.
Laurence could not open his real feelings on the subject of their
mission to Riley; Riley could scarcely avoid knowing what those

feelings were; they walked around each other with scrupulous courtesy, and spoke only of sailing, and the weather, and the life of the ship.

Laurence had the pleasure, at least, of going out flying with Temeraire: cold air brisk in their faces, clouds stinging with snow if they ventured south, and beneath them now and again great silvery schools of fish, or pods of whales or porpoises; occasionally the shadow of a handful of sharks. "I do wonder why they are not at all good eating when what they eat themselves is nice; it seems a waste," Temeraire said, as an aside, before continuing, "And I do not see why we should not do exactly as you propose, Laurence: after all, if the Tswana will take away the slaves anyway, the Portuguese may as well let them all go instead and not have all their cities destroyed, too."

"The Tswana cannot hope to raid all of Brazil," Laurence said, "not in time to rescue any of their people yet alive; if that is their only preoccupation."

He spoke cautiously but hoped otherwise: the Tswana had bent their wrath against even slave ports which had never shipped a single one of their own people, at great distances from their empire; that augured for a chance of persuading them to accept the offer which Laurence privately wished to make: a general liberation throughout the country, in lieu of having all their particular kindred returned.

This hope he did not intend to unfold as yet to anyone but Temeraire; Laurence could easily imagine Hammond's reaction. Wholesale abolition would scarcely recommend itself to the Portuguese, and might not satisfy the Tswana, either; but the mere possibility of engineering such a stroke demanded any effort in its pursuit.

"At least we must make the attempt; and if we had no other cause to come away, it must have been enough," he added.

"Certainly we must; and I am sure that the Portuguese will think better of refusing, if they do, when the Tswana have burned up a few more of their cities," Temeraire said blithely. "And I do not see that Hammond will have any reason to complain, if we should make peace as he wishes. Then we will go back to Britain and defeat Napoleon at last. Do you suppose that is a prize, Laurence?"

It was not: a whaler in the distance, almost certainly a neutral; too small to support Temeraire's weight, and undoubtedly only to be alarmed by such a visit even if they had been worth bespeaking for news. Temeraire looked around inquiringly; Laurence shook his head in answer; they wheeled away and flew onward without descending even to be seen.

The ocean was otherwise deserted and had been for weeks now; a few islands along their way, mostly rocky outcroppings of deserted volcanic rock half-eaten by lichen. The isolation, for lack of work, was more to be felt than in their valley; Laurence chose to feel it more. It was what he must expect, if he did not mean to subject himself to authority or ask Temeraire to do the same; if they meant to follow their own judgment. Laurence could not but look down half-rueful and half-amazed at the ship below, when they returned to her, and he saw in her the orderly decided pattern of his former life: an ordinary life, a comprehensible one.

He wondered suddenly at Bonaparte: at a man who would discard such a life deliberately, not under an inexorable press of duty or honor but only a flashing reckless hunger; at a man who could put himself outside the society of his fellows for such a motive. "I do not suppose anything will ever content him," he said to Temeraire. "What victory, what glory, could satisfy such a man? Although perhaps age may do what the mere turning of the world will not, and wear away the worst of his ambition."

"You may be sure that even if he were to grow tired of conquering and glory, that Lien would not; after all she will not be old for a very long time," Temeraire said darkly. "And anyway it does not seem to me we ought to only wait and hope: we had much better stop him ourselves, and be quite sure he cannot do any more harm."

"If Napoleon can seek to ascend all the thrones of Europe, I suppose we may go dragging them out from under him," Laurence said, although with some humor: descending alone from Temeraire's back to a ship on the far side of the world in the midst of a cold ocean, and setting his sights on the acknowledged sovereign of a great nation and the conqueror of half of Europe.

The table he returned to, that evening, was a slightly peculiar one, for Laurence and Granby had privately agreed they should treat Demane as if he possessed the rank to which his dragon entitled him, although neither his conversation nor his manners were suited to a seat near the head. But that was an evil often found in the service, in men without the excuse of tender years, and at least Demane might yet be worked on by admonishment and the embarrassment of finding himself under more observation than he had been used to, either as a runner or while deliberately ignored in Sydney.

But Hammond was an uncritical guest, and did not notice if Demane ate through four removes in a row in perfect silence or had to be nudged to make a toast; and his own conversation was more than adequate to fill anything lacking among the rest of the company. Four years as the chief British representative at the Chinese court had brought him some two stone in weight and settled his former driven confidence into assurance, but he was as pell-mell and passionate as ever when enlarging upon a subject close to his heart.

"By report, they have shipped two transports already, which remain in the harbor at present," he said, laying down biscuit crumbs to make the outline of Rio, and picking out the weevils. "The Tswana have evidently encamped within the ruins of the city."

"They cannot be much fonder of Bonaparte than of us," Granby said. "*He* hasn't outlawed slavery, either; are they really his allies?"

"I suppose one cannot call it an alliance, not in the real sense of the word," Hammond said. "You might better say they have given

him a truce, in exchange for reparations: but as his reparations involve shipping them across the sea to attack their enemies, which
are also his, there is very little to choose between the two. They
have not ceased their attacks upon the Spanish coast and the Portuguese, either," he added with a significant look at Laurence: such
attacks should certainly pose a danger to any troops which Britain
should land, as well.

"I don't suppose we might give them something more to think
about at the Cape?" Granby said. "Or closer to their home, anyway; the Med is a long way from the south of Africa, and I don't
suppose they can have an easy time of supply."

"The prospects of a new front in wholly unknown territory, for
uncertain gain, can have but little appeal," Laurence said. "We
knew nothing of the existence of the Tswana and their empire, and
the present evils of our situation are in no small order due to that
ignorance; how much more cautious ought we to be about ventur-
ing yet again past the coast of that continent, when we have already
certain proofs of their ability to maintain a significant force over so
great a distance."

He spoke absently, listening: above their heads, a change in the
rhythm of footsteps and voices on deck had intruded gradually
upon his awareness. There was no alarm, no beating to quarters; he
had no excuse for leaving the table, and had perforce to restrain his
curiosity until the meal had been cleared away, when he could propose coffee on the dragondeck.

Laurence put his head out of the ladderway and saw the sky:
curiosity was at once satisfied. Riley had been due to dine with the
gunroom that evening; he was already on the quarterdeck, directing the men: no frantic hurry, but a steady progress; the sails were
all being reefed. "We are in for a blow, I think; nothing to alarm
anyone, of course," he said out loud, cheerfully, before he added to
Laurence in an undertone, "The mercury would have run out of the
bottom of the glass, if it could; the dragons had better be chained
down sooner than late."

Laurence nodded silent acknowledgment and went to tell Temeraire he must endure the storm-chains which he so hated. "There is time for a short flight beforehand, if you should like," he added by way of apology, when Temeraire had flattened down his ruff in protest.

"I do not see why it must always be storming, when we are at sea," Temeraire said disconsolately, when they had gone aloft and seen in the distance the great billowings of red-violet and purple climbing the sky; the ocean had flattened to black.

He landed reluctantly prepared to submit; and then Iskierka said, "Well, I do not mean to be chained at all: whyever should I not just hold on to the ship, or if it is very bad, we may as well stay aloft," and Laurence realized in dismay she had never yet experienced a true three-days' gale, which should outstrip the endurance of any dragon even if the winds alone did not prove fatal.

"I suppose it is likely to blow too long," Granby said, looking inquiry up at Laurence, who slid from Temeraire's back and hastened to assure him of the necessity, as quietly as he could manage. Even so the sailors standing ready with the great tarpaulins and the storm-chains cast reproaching looks at him for inviting ill-fortune, which grew still more mournful as Granby began to argue with Iskierka, at a volume which could not help but carry across the ship.

Apart from a general deprecation of superstition, Laurence could not think that the storm building ahead of them required any additional invitation to be as thoroughly bad as could be imagined. Certainly the worse consequence would come from leaving Iskierka unconvinced and unprepared to endure the length of the confinement which the weather bode fair to demand. She argued the matter with Granby for the better part of an hour, while the shadow crept steadily nearer and Riley began to look anxious for the men being kept idle, and the dragons still unsecured. At last in desperation Granby said, "Dear one, we must have done: I will wear the coat if only you will do this for me; pray lie down and let them secure you."

This coat was a monstrosity of cloth-of-gold crusted with gem-stone beads which would not have looked out of place in the last century at Versailles; Iskierka had managed to arrange for its commission in India through Mr. Richers, Granby's new first lieutenant—subsequently much chastened by his captain—and Granby's flat refusal to be displayed in so much magnificence had since been a source of great and running dissatisfaction to her.

She pounced at once on the offer. "Whenever I wish it?" she demanded.

"So long as it isn't all wrong for the occasion," Granby said, hurriedly qualifying.

"Only if *I* may decide whether it is wrong or not," Iskierka said, and Granby submitted to his doom with resignation if not precisely with grace; in turn at last she yielded and stretched herself upon the deck, and allowed them to drag the netting over the massive red-and-black coils of her body, with the chains laced atop it.

Granby avoided Laurence's eye and went to stand in the bow while the process went forward. Laurence knew it ashamed him deeply to be forced to resort to bribery and stratagem to subdue Iskierka's temper to the needs of the service, and he could not have been comforted when Kulingile, who was of a very different and amiable temperament, said, "Oh, if you like, but how am I to go hunting?" when Demane asked him to lie down under the tarpaulins also, and required only the assurance that he would be fed if he grew hungry to reconcile him to the experience.

"It will not be at all comfortable," Temeraire said unhappily as he stretched himself out also, with more accuracy than pessimism: he and Kulingile would spend the storm lying to either side of Iskierka, whose inconvenient spikes made her more difficult to secure, as additional anchors for her bulk: subject as a result not only to the worse brunt of the storm but also to the perpetual emissions of steam from her body.

"We had better feed them up now," Granby said, returning, while the chains were made fast to the deck, and ropes thrown after them for reinforcement. The debate had consumed nearly all the time which remained to them of the unearthly calm, and now the swell began to slap rhythmic warning against the ship's sides. Even the hands who normally shied from any contact with the dragons were clambering urgently over the talons and scales to draw the bonds tight: the weight of the beasts could easily overset the ship, if they were not well-secured. "It can only help if they sleep away the first day or so, and there may be difficulties getting the cattle up on deck later on."

Temeraire was determined not to be difficult; he had seen Granby's crimson cheek, and Laurence should certainly have no such cause to blush for him, even if Temeraire disliked the chains extremely, more than Iskierka did, and therefore had far better right to ask some return.

"But I am not going to kick up a fuss, and make difficulties for everyone and the poor sailors, who will be working all the storm," Temeraire said, although he was sorry a moment later to have silenced himself a little too early: he would very much have preferred to have a proper meal, cooked through, but instead he could see a cow being hoisted out from the fore hatch, and the ordinary slaughtering tubs were out on deck, even as the first spatters of rain came down and rattled in them tinnily.

"And for that matter," he added sulkily, as the meat was served out, "Laurence has more right than Granby to wear finery; after all he is a prince *and* a captain, both, and Granby even has less seniority. So if Laurence does not choose to always be going about in his best robes," which Temeraire could understand: one did not wish to risk damage to anything so handsome unnecessarily, "I do not see that Granby is at all right to do otherwise."

Kulingile raised his head and put in, "Demane is a prince also," which Temeraire did not think was quite true, although he did recall Admiral Roland saying something of the sort to some fellow from the Admiralty who had objected to Demane and Sipho being his runners; but certainly it was not *as* true as for Laurence, who had been adopted with a great deal of formal ceremony. "And he does not wear anything particularly fine."

Iskierka bristled and hissed steam from her spikes. "Granby has *more* seniority, if one counts years as an aviator, and I am sure I cannot see any reason he should not be a prince, too, someday very soon." With this feeble rejoinder she put her head beneath her wing.

The rain had begun falling in earnest, an hour later; Iskierka, sheltered from the wind between them, was securely asleep and jetting out small puffs of steam regularly so that the drops collected upon the tarpaulin and set it sticking clammily to Temeraire's back. The raw cow sat unpleasantly in his stomach, and he was just contemplating whether it was worth sending Gerry for Gong Su, to perhaps brew him a bowl of tea, when Kulingile put his head over Iskierka's back and whispered, "Temeraire?"

"Yes?" Temeraire said, rather unhappily concluding that the wind and rain would spoil the tea before he could enjoy it, and then he should have wasted a bowl of their small supply: it was too dear for Laurence to buy in the quantities which Temeraire would have liked to drink.

"*Ought* Demane wear something more fine?" Kulingile asked, with an anxious note.

"Oh—" Temeraire said, and struggled with warring impulses, but justice decided him: he could not be reconciled to losing Demane and would have been very glad to have him back, but it would have been the meanest sort of trick to mislead Kulingile if he intended to look after Demane properly.

"Certainly one might expect the captain of a dragon of note to present a particularly handsome appearance, when the occasion demands," Temeraire said, therefore. "I will venture to say, he would do well with a better coat, at least, and he ought to have gold bars as Laurence and Granby do; you see that no-one thinks him a proper captain, without them."

"But where am I to get such things?" Kulingile said, and with a great rush of generosity Temeraire said, "Well, I will ask Laurence for you, as I am not quite certain; but if we were to take a prize," he could not help a wistful note in his voice, "and had shares, you would be in funds and could purchase anything you liked with them."

"Iskierka has many prizes, but we haven't?" Kulingile said, interrogatively.

"That," Temeraire said, "is only because she has been put in the way of them, by luck; you may be sure if ever a prize offered, I should certainly be equal to taking it, and I dare say," he added in fairness, "when you have been in a few actions, you should be sure of doing so as well; as long as you do not let yourself be shot."

"I don't think I should care for being shot," Kulingile said, and shook his head as a wave came rousing over the bow and went sheeting over them, cold straight through. "I don't care for this, either," he added.

"No," Temeraire agreed, hunching water off his shoulders, and huddled back down as the ship went bounding into a trench, a glassy wall of ocean rising sharply ahead.

The *Allegiance* was by no means the vessel one would choose for riding out a typhoon. "A wallowing bow-heavy tub with more sail than sea-sense; I would as soon cut my throat as try and make her mind," Laurence remembered hearing Riley himself say of her several years before, when the two of them had watched from the rail of the dear old *Reliant* as the transport attempted awkwardly to maneuver her way into Portsmouth: neither of them dreaming, at the time, they should ever be upon her in their present circumstances. Laurence had then six years of seniority on the post-list, and with an influential and political family and a record of distinction was marching steadily towards his admiral's flag, destined only for the most plum assignments; Riley his protégé and second lieutenant, with reason to hope for his own ship in the course of another five years with Laurence's own influence behind him.

That influence eradicated, Riley had been glad enough to take the *Allegiance* when she had been offered him. Now, of course, no more such criticism was to be heard from him or even tolerated in his presence, but it was not to be denied that her only virtue was in being almost too large to sink, which in the present circumstances felt more a gauntlet thrown to the elements, a challenge they looked all too determined to meet. Laurence recalled with no fondness their last experience of a serious blow: three days endlessly laboring their way up the crowded swells, doubting every moment whether the ship should reach the crest in time.

And though Riley had knocked some seamanship into all but the worst of the landsmen and gaol-birds, during the passage to New South Wales, there were a great many of the worst: dragon transports were not prized assignments, and Riley had not sufficient influence to preserve his best men from being pillaged away by senior captains. Laurence could not observe the workings of the resultant crew with anything like satisfaction; and yet he could do nothing to amend it but keep himself to the dragondeck or his cabin, containing any impulse to interfere.

"They have matters well in hand, I assure you," he said to Mrs. Pemberton that afternoon, remarks addressed half to himself, and regarded his cold dinner without enthusiasm by the dimmed light which filtered in through the windows: it was deeply foreign to sit to his meat while the ship's existence rose and fell without him.

But the storm did not run three days: it lingered for five, following them across the ocean as if by malice, without a single break in the weather long enough to sleep, and with a great many long enough to give them false hope that here, at last, had come an end. As the thicker darkness came to mark the night of the fourth day, and a fresh icy howling of wind swept over them from the south, Laurence went to Riley, who stood haggard and bloodshot by the wheel, and shouted in his ear, "Tom, do you let me send Lord Purbeck to sleep, and I will second you; when he is rested he may spell you in turn."

Riley nodded after a moment, dully; when Laurence went to him, Purbeck did not say a word to argue but only stumbled away half-asleep already. Laurence did not know the men very well: there was more separation than one might imagine possible aboard a single vessel between the aviators and the sailors, none of whom liked very well to share their ship with dragons. But he knew the *Allegiance* well enough by now to direct them, and pantomime served better than shouts, with the wind yelling in all their ears at once.

"Surely it must almost be over, now," Temeraire said, when Laurence came to speak to him briefly: the rain had lightened for a short while. "We might be let up, and stay aloft until the last of it has blown itself out—"

But he spoke low and hopelessly, enervated with fatigue and cold, and his eyes lidded down to slits; when Laurence said, "Not yet, my dear; pray have patience," Temeraire subsided without further complaint and ate the raw sheep, which was put into his gullet by hand: the galley fires were still out, for safety.

Iskierka, sheltered from the worst of the weather, was in high temper at the length of their confinement, and more difficult to restrain; if Kulingile and Temeraire had not effectively formed part of her prison by the weight of their bodies, anchoring the restraints, Laurence did not doubt she would have flung off the chains and likely cast the entire ship ahoo despite all Granby could do to persuade her to calm.

"Oh! Not yet? It will never end, and I will not stay here, I will not," she said, furiously, and began to try and throw herself back against the tarpaulin.

"Why are you making such a fuss?" Kulingile said drowsily,

and Laurence saw Demane say something in his dragon's ear; Kulingile yawned, and then heaved his head and one massive foreleg over Iskierka's shoulders and sighed out, pinning her to the deck with his weight.

Iskierka whipped her head around and snapped at his nose, hissing, but there was no satisfaction to be had: Kulingile was already gone back to sleep, his tongue licking the fresh sheep's blood from his muzzle in small darting unconscious strokes. "I will not," she repeated, angrily, but ceased to fight the chains; instead she flung herself flat upon the deck and glared fury at the clouds.

But by the next morning, even her spirits had been defeated by the ceaseless storm. She only gummed at the goat that was offered her, and left half of it in the tub; Temeraire ate nothing at all, and barely opened his eyes to acknowledge when Laurence came to speak to him. "They can't go on like this," Granby said to Laurence, meeting him below: Purbeck had slept a little, and was gone on deck again. "Perhaps we *had* better let them aloft for the rest? It can't keep storming forever, I suppose."

He did not sound very convinced, and indeed in the moment it seemed entirely believable that the storm would continue without end, that they sailed under judgment and deluge.

"I would not give anything for the chances of their keeping in company aloft in this cover, and we cannot arrange any sort of rendezvous; we have not the least notion where we are, nor will until we see the stars again," Laurence said.

"Then maybe Riley would let us put up a fire, and give them something hot to eat, if we were careful about it," Granby said. "It is bad when they are refusing their meat, Laurence; in cold like this, they ought to be eating more than their usual, even if they are not flying."

Laurence could not regard this suggestion with anything but dismay, but Gong Su, putting his head in—the aviators would never learn the polite fiction of failing to hear what was said on the other side of a bulkhead, aboard ship—made the suggestion that coals laid in the bottom of one of his great cauldrons would do to make some sort of hot soup, without the risk of open flame.

But Riley was asleep, and Purbeck would not countenance anything of the sort. "You might as well set the ship on fire to begin with," he said flatly, without even the little courtesy he ordinarily offered Laurence, "and save us wondering how long it will take; and you damned well shan't unchain them, either: we would be brought by the lee in moments if they went jumping around the deck. They must wait like all of us."

"If I were sure Iskierka would wait, I shouldn't ask," Granby said, with some heat.

"If she is run so mad she would sink us only to have a chance of drowning herself, you may say so, and I will run one of the bow-chasers up to her and we will put a ball in her head before she sends us to the bottom," Purbeck returned coldly; Laurence had to seize Granby's arm and draw him away.

Even when Riley returned to the deck, however, he was little more favorable to the notion. "I cannot see taking such a risk, in the least," he said, "and I wonder at your asking," he added, even his more generous temper worn away with weariness and the endless grating struggle to keep the ship afloat.

"I am tempted to tell Gong Su to go forward," Granby said angrily, as Laurence towed him back to the dragondeck, "and be damned to them all, talking as though we were asking for our own pleasure. The ship is meant for carrying dragons about to begin with; what else are they here for? Put a ball in her head, indeed; I would shoot him, first."

He did not even try to speak quietly, and besides the storm had altered their sense of volume, like deaf men raising their voices to compensate for their own lack; his words fell into another brief lull in the roaring tempest, to be carried precisely where they had no business to go. Riley stiffened; Purbeck looked disdainfully; and where the continuing storm might have shortly erased the memory under the pressure of necessity, in that moment abruptly the clouds broke, and the first sunlight in five days spilled down upon the deck.

"I do not see why anyone would ever choose to be going this way, when there are no prizes and such storms," Temeraire said, gulping toothfish while hovering mid-air; he was in no hurry to return to the ship, at all. He was sure he would not feel dry and warm again for weeks: the thin spare sun was not up to the task, for all it made a swath of bright colors hanging low among the horizon clouds, and he felt waterlogged to the bone.

Iskierka was farther aloft and flying in wild circles, breathing out flames and looping through the heated air to dry herself off. Temeraire would have been tempted to ask her to do as much for him, if it were not beneath him to be asking favors of her; and anyway, she was quite puffed-off enough for being a fire-breather without still more recognition.

"Are there any more of those?" Kulingile asked, swinging down to circle Temeraire, regarding the toothfish with interest. He had already eaten that afternoon a cow, two seals, and an entire pot of rice porridge which Gong Su had meant for all three of them and the leftovers for their crews.

Temeraire pointed him at the meager school of fish, although they were hardly large enough to be worth the effort even for himself. Kulingile swung back aloft to study the school from farther, however, and then made an efficient bite of them by diving and lowering his jaw directly into the water: dozens of startled fish went flopping wildly out of his mouth as he pulled back aloft, but enough remained for him to crunch in satisfaction, seaweed trailing out the sides of his jaws.

To lie upon the deck afterwards full and contented and unchained, with the galley fires going below for warmth, was in every way satisfactory, even though the swell remained high and at regular intervals waves crested up and flung cold spray upon them.

Temeraire propped a wing to shield himself from the worst, and curled his forelegs to make a space where Laurence might sit and read to him.

"I am sure it does not stop there?" Temeraire said, when Laurence had paused rather too long in the midst of a poem; Laurence did not continue, though, and when Temeraire peered down he found Laurence with his head tipped back limply in sleep against a talon, the book neglected and open upon his lap.

Temeraire sighed a little and looked, but Sipho was also asleep, huddled up against Kulingile's side under a scrap of tarpaulin, Demane beside him; even Roland, who might have been able to puzzle out enough of the characters to read to him, was drooping over her mathematics.

Kulingile sighed also. "I do not want to sleep anymore."

"I am not going to, either," Iskierka said; not even this declaration stirred Granby, lying in front of her in his splendid cloth-of-gold coat with his head pillowed upon a coil of rope. "I am sure there are no prizes worth taking near-by, but we might as well go look for some."

Temeraire could not find fault with this project; even Iskierka might have good notions now and again. "Only we must arrange a rendezvous first," he said, looking for the sailing master, Mr. Smythe, who might tell him the ship's heading, and other such things, which Laurence always asked for when he and Temeraire flew away from the ship for any great distance. Temeraire was not entirely sure how this information should guide them in returning, but perhaps Mr. Smythe could explain that as well, so he should not need to wake Laurence; there was no need to wake Laurence at all. Not that Temeraire thought Laurence would in any way object; only Laurence often did not think much of seeking after prizes, even when there was plainly nothing better to do, or at least nothing much better.

But Smythe was also not on the deck; only Lord Purbeck was on deck, and Lieutenant George standing at the helm with his head tipped aslant upon his neck, before he suddenly jerked straight again and blinked his watery blue eyes many times.

"I do not mean to wait; we can find the ship again without any of this," Iskierka said. "It stands to reason we only need to fly back the way we go, and then follow the ship's course from there; I can remember that without doing figures."

"I do not see how you can," Temeraire said, "when we will be over the open ocean, and you cannot mark your place by a tree or a building or anything of that sort; it would be very stupid of us to get lost, and likely have to spend hours flying about trying to find the ship."

"Maybe we had better not go," Kulingile said. "They are cooking something else for us, I think: that is a nice smell."

It *was* a nice smell—a roasting smell—beef searing over an open flame, somewhere belowdecks, and Temeraire inhaled with pleasure. He was not hungry at present, and he would not have pressed Laurence for more, when he knew all the cattle must be rationed against possible ill-luck fishing, but no-one would have said no to a treat like roast beef; if only Gong Su did not mean merely to turn it into a stew.

"I want the head!" Iskierka said, snaking her head over the rail to peer down into the forward hatch. "I have not had a roasted cow's head in ages: and you have both been on land forever and ever."

"It is not as though there were so many cows in the colony that we might have eaten them whenever we liked," Temeraire said, "and anyway we have all been at sea already for weeks; I do not see why you should have the head all to yourself. I would not at all mind a taste of beef brains-and-tripe."

"I will have a haunch," Kulingile said, "if they don't overcook it," anxiously; the smoke was growing a little thick.

Laurence jerked awake abruptly and came standing, the book tumbling from his lap heedless of Temeraire's protest. "What are they about, below there?" he said, and cupped his hands around his mouth and bellowed across the deck, "Fire!"

Laurence seized Granby's shoulder and roused him; together they plunged down the fore ladderway and into the ship's belly. More smoke was rising around them and wisping up between the deck seams, grey and bitter; men struggling past them to climb up out of the haze, red-eyed and red-faced and not merely stinking of rum but grinning with it, giggling, despite the dreadful danger of their situation. Laurence realized grimly they had certainly broken open the spirit-room: enough unwatered liquor to make the day's grog for seven hundred men over the course of six months, and every idler and waster of the ship's company like as not afloat with it, while the officers and able seamen slept off their exhaustion.

The galley floor was blood-slick with drunken butchery—two cows dead and spitted in their parts over open flame, flesh blackening; the fire had escaped to the tables, and was crawling along ropes. "Get to your pumping stations," Laurence roared, and caught a man out of the press: Yarrow, one of the able seamen and from Cheltenham, not ordinarily an unreliable man, but he had evidently also yielded to the temptation of drink: his face was soot-bruised and his eyes staring like damnation with the fire's ruddy glow cast upon them.

"To your station!" Laurence shouted at him, but there was no answering comprehension in that face; Yarrow only wrenched himself from Laurence's grip and back into the general mass of men, all of them maddened with liquor and fear.

Granby had pulled on his leather gauntlets and was tipping over the great cauldrons of seething salt pork to douse the cooking-fires: men screaming as the boiling water and fat ran down the smoking boards and over their bare feet. The fires were quenched, but a man howling in pain knocked over a burning table, and then he was struggling among the others and spreading fire from his clothing to theirs in the close quarters.

"Captain, Captain—" Darcy yelling—one of Riley's mids and only a boy, his voice still high and shrill, standing bare-legged in a white nightshirt with his yellow hair loose, visible in the light from the fore hatch. Past him Laurence glimpsed Riley, with no neck-cloth and his coat barely on, his mouth open but his shouts impossible to hear over the crowd and the fire, and behind him several of his officers in a wedge trying to force a path through the men to the galley.

Laurence had his sword on his belt: no use here. Granby stooping wrenched loose a plank from one of the tables and handed Laurence another; together they began to clout the drunken, maddened men to either side, and Riley at last won through with half-a-dozen officers. The cook's mate Urquhart, who had been induced to the butchery of the cattle, was cowering behind the stoves with his guilty knives; five of the ship's boys more enthusiastic over the meat than the grog had secreted themselves in a corner with a joint and were even in the midst of confusion still tearing away half-raw bites; two men who had been knocked down were now dazed enough to be compliant and not so drunk as to be useless.

With this undistinguished crew they set about mastering the worst of the fire: the men dragging over the bags of sand and the boys snatched from their dinner and set to pouring it in cupfuls onto anything which offered the least flicker; Urquhart cringing put out all the galley fires which were left.

He then lost himself slinking into the crowd and made his escape, perhaps hoping to have his sins forgotten if he could only get out of sight for a time; meanwhile hydra-like the little fires still crept along the deck, and the smoke clotted Laurence's nose and his breath; they stopped and wiped their eyes, steam of the cooking pots damp on their faces. "Laurence, Laurence," he heard Temeraire calling from above, the deep sonorous voice penetrating through the boards.

"We had better get back up where they can see us," Granby said hoarsely—no need to articulate for anyone the consequence of leaving the dragons to grow too anxious for their safety.

"Darcy, go along there and tell that tar-eating cawker Powton to beat to quarters, if he damned well cannot hear me shouting it; and if he has deserted his post, find a drum and beat it your own self," Riley said. "If I cannot have them pumping water, I would rather have the men at their guns than running wild all through the ship; we must get a little order here."

The boy scrambled up the ladderway even ahead of Laurence; he and Granby had barely gained the deck before the relentless drum-beat was pounding away and the officers all set up a shout, "To quarters, to quarters!" The effort did some good: sailors were not unused to smoke and disorder, in battle or in drill, and the familiar roll sent many of them, even confused with drink, running below to their battle-stations on the gundecks. But too many of the men less trained or less sensible were left shoving to and fro on the upper deck, to no end, and spoiling what progress could be made.

Laurence pulled himself out of the ladderway wreathed in smoke that curled and clung to his arms, and thrust away a pair of sailors wrestling with each other over an uncorked jug that spilled all its contents even as they fought. They reeled away from him, and then Kulingile reached down over the dragondeck railing and snatched them up in one great taloned forehand: Laurence looked up and saw him dropping the pair into an open sack made of his own belly-netting, pulled down loose.

"I thought it would help, sir," Roland called down: all three of the dragons were taking it in turn to pick off the worst of the drunkards, clearing the deck.

"Well done," Laurence called back, before he fell to coughing; he took one quick swallow from the rain-barrel to rinse his mouth, then with Granby joined the rest of the aviators in herding the worst of the drunkards forward to their doom, to be piled in on one another in the netting, a mass of arms and thrashing legs.

"Only be careful!" Temeraire called, not without cause: shot was rolling loose over the deck, knocking men off their feet and going overboard with gulping splashes, or tumbling into the hatches. The sailors had the advantage of liquored stupidity, which made them thoroughly unpredictable: careened into one another and pulled on the ropes, knocked over water-casks, slapped and shoved and yelled. The men on duty in the rigging, not drunk themselves and sorry for it, were jeering and throwing down handfuls of greasy slush scraped off the sails with indiscriminate aim.

The swell was not high—that was to say, not high for the Southern Ocean; only twenty feet—and the *Allegiance* rolled and pitched wildly from her crew's neglect. "Look out there!" Purbeck shouted, from the helm: one of the cannon had burst loose from its tackle, and as the ship heaved majestically over the next crest, the snub-nosed iron monster eased out of her traces and began trundling towards them at deceptive pace, wheels of the gun-carriage a hollow grumble over the deck.

Granby was trying to guide some men towards the reaching dragons: the carpenter and three of his mates, amiable drunks swaying deeply and keeping their feet only with the practiced balance of long-time sailors, arm in arm with one another and hiccoughing with laughter. The cannon slid into them sideways at the waist and knocked them over the barrel: expressions more of surprise than alarm as it swept onward with them.

Laurence had only time to seize Granby by the arm, and be dragged alongside with him by the inexorable weight: a corner of his coat was hooked over and pierced by the broken iron ring that had set the gun-carriage loose. Sliding over the deck behind the gun, Laurence managed to set his boot-heels to the railing and stop himself with a jolt as the gun crashed with ease through the oak. The cannon went over; the carpenters went, too, at the last yelling in fear as they fell. Granby screamed once, a shocked cry wrenched out of him, and his arm came queerly loose in Laurence's grip.

The fine silk slid through Laurence's fingers, embroidery snarling upon his rough calluses; the sun was in his eyes and dazzling on the cloth-of-gold. Granby had clenched shut his jaw, but his hand did not grip back, and he was sliding over the edge. Abruptly Ferris was beside them, dropping to his knees with a knife in his hands. He put it to the back of Granby's coat and thrust it through, ripping up, and the cloth sheared away.

Laurence tumbled backwards with Granby, who gasped only, very pale under his sunburnt color; the arm still hung limp when Laurence and Ferris had set him on his feet.

"Granby, Granby!" Iskierka was shrilling, leaning deeply over the dragondeck railing and reaching for the mainmast to support herself, trying to get to them: in a moment she would have clawed through the rigging.

Ferris called back, "I'll bring him to you, Iskierka; don't snatch at him or you'll jar his arm worse," so she subsided back in hissing anxiety; Laurence nodded to Ferris, who ducked under Granby's other arm and helped him across the deck.

There was no sign of the other men over the side; the ocean was beaten into a froth all around the ship. No more jeering came from the rigging. All the ship's officers and her Marines were now awake and on the deck, Riley calling orders from the stern and his servant Carver hovering behind him with a neckcloth flapping in the wind like a white banner, attempting now and again to dart in and tie it for him, over Riley's impatient jerked hand.

"Laurence, are you well?" Temeraire was calling, with not much less anxiety than Iskierka. Laurence wiped his streaming eyes. Smoke still seeped up from the creeping fire below, and Riley was sending the more coherent of the men down in groups under an officer, to go at it with buckets and pails; he needed hands now, and badly.

"I am very well," Laurence said, "and pray take those men in your belly-netting and go dunk them half-a-dozen times in the ocean; we will see if they can be sobered enough for work."

Then he was suddenly looking at the *Allegiance* as through a window of old mazed glass, green and rippled, with a sunset behind her: fascinated he watched her growing darker and more distant, red and gold color swallowed up by murk; he felt curiously light and free, like flying but without wind.

His head was dragged abruptly up through the water, the clear sun overhead a painful dazzle in his eyes and salt water choking his mouth; he vomited more onto the waves, and blindly clung where Demane put his hands, on a piece of driftwood—on a piece of deck planking, hot to the touch and still smoking from one corner—

There was no sunset. The *Allegiance* was shattered open along her stern: from the gundeck to the waterline a gaping mouth full of splinters and flames, and all her sails were ablaze.

"My God," Laurence said involuntarily; his voice was a raw croak.

"What happened?" Demane said, gasping for breath beside him, also holding fast to the plank as it bobbed in the waves.

A sudden roar and shudder shook the *Allegiance* again, and another eruption of incandescent fire burst from her side; Laurence pulled Demane's head down and ducked his own: in a moment a rain of splinters and ash came pattering over them, stinging on the skin.

The cloud passed. "But—" Demane said. "But—" He stopped.

Laurence looked up again. The flames inside the ship were dying as the waters rushed in over the broken planking. She was tipping backwards and up, the great fan-shaped dragondeck rising into the air. The dragons were circling overhead like ravens watching some great beast die, as she began slowly to sink down beneath the waves.

Chapter 4

TEMERAIRE DID NOT PRECISELY understand what had happened, at first—he had been skimming low over the water, soaking the drunken sailors despite their loud protestations, and then suddenly a great roaring and fire everywhere, a hundred times louder than Iskierka might have been. Burning scraps of sailcloth and wood were flung upon him, and when he pulled up into the air to look, he saw the flames rising from the deck.

"Is it a battle?" Kulingile demanded in high excitement, dashing over and dripping water onto Temeraire from the men crammed into his own belly-rigging. "Will we have a prize?"

"Well, I suppose we must have been attacked, but I do not see any other ship at all," Temeraire had said, deeply confused himself, and winged around the *Allegiance*, only then seeing the enormous gaping hole into the ship—and so very strange to see her cut open in such a way and look in at all the decks in cross-section, the lumpy white hammocks swinging from the rafters like the drawing he had seen once of silkworms in their cocoons, and the guns sliding out into the ocean with tremendous plashes. Casks and bales were floating everywhere, and the sheep had escaped their pen and were swimming away, bleating: many of them had fire caught in their wool.

"Oh," Kulingile said with interest.

"I am sure we oughtn't eat them now," Temeraire said, "this is not a time to be eating. And where is Laurence?" he added, and looked higher. The deck was littered with rigging and broken yards, the ladderways seething with fire and smoke, and bodies lay limp and strewn carelessly everywhere, bloody. Temeraire did not see Laurence anywhere, or any of his crew, and no-one answered when he called. "Laurence!" he cried again.

He flew around the ship again in perfect distraction—there were men in the water, but it was very hard to make them out, only little heads bobbing very much like casks, and they did not call out to him—why, why had Temeraire ever left the ship without Laurence? He had only meant to be gone a few moments—there had been no enemy in sight—what business did the ship have, bursting open in this way—

He jerked his head as something bright flashed in his eyes, and looking over saw Roland—Roland, waving at him wildly from the edge of the dragondeck. She had out one of his talon-sheaths and was reflecting the sunlight at him off the polished gold; she had been ducked underneath one of the tarpaulins. He stooped and snatched her up at once, and seized little Gerry and Sipho also while he was at it—he ought not have left any of them out of his reach at all, ever.

"Laurence?" he demanded. "Yes, yes, I see you," he added with impatience, taking up Cavendish, who was waving his arms frantically to be picked off the deck also: a midwingman of sixteen, whom Laurence had taken on for some inconceivable reason; who cared anything for *him*?

"I don't see the captain," Roland said, hooking her carabiners onto his harness, and reaching to help Gerry with his. "Leave off yammering, you damned drunken sots," she added, to the men clamoring from the belly-netting, as she climbed up past them, "or I will tell Temeraire to cut you all loose, and good riddance." Temeraire had quite forgotten they were even there. "Do you circle about, Temeraire, and go slowly; we'll all look, for him and—and for Demane." Kulingile was already flying in wide anxious rings around the ship, calling for Demane.

Iskierka came winging back to help look—she had Granby, latched on to her back; she had not lost *her* captain. And she had Ferris also aboard, even though Ferris was Temeraire's—but Temeraire could not be properly annoyed by that; there was no room in him for anything so small at the moment.

Gerry piped faintly from his back, "I see him! I see Demane, and the captain, too," and Temeraire plunged at once to snatch them both from the water, with the scrap of wood that seemed quite shockingly, painfully small to have been their only support.

"Give him here!" Kulingile demanded at once, hard on his heels and circling anxiously. "Demane, are you well?"

"He is too chilled to speak," Laurence said—at least, it seemed he said it; his voice did not sound at all like himself, very hoarse and grating, and he stuttered a little. "You must wait until he has warmed again."

"I've a tarpaulin, sir, if you will wrap up in that," Roland said, reaching up to help him and Demane step down from Temeraire's claw onto his shoulders. "And we might get some of our gear off the dragondeck, I expect, before she goes under: most of it was tied down."

Temeraire at first wondered what Roland meant; then he looked back at the ship. Water was pouring into the open hole, and the *Allegiance* was sliding slowly and gracefully beneath the surface.

"Oh!" he said, "but how are we to save her?"

"There is no hope of that," Laurence said, locking himself onto the harness with slow, precise movements; his hands were shaking. "Temeraire, I cannot shout; tell Iskierka and Kulingile to take up whatever survivors they can, and we will go after the supply: only you can hover over the ship."

Laurence was very urgent they should work quickly, but it did not speed matters at all that most of the sailors, quite stupidly, tried to swim away when Iskierka or Kulingile reached to pick them up out of the water. And they were able to get a few things only off the dragondeck—some harness and another tarpaulin, fetched by Roland hanging down on a strap from Temeraire's belly, with a hoist rigged up to get the things into his netting.

Gong Su had managed somehow to climb out of the belly of the ship, his boots tied together by their laces slung around his neck, with a thin oilskin pouch. He stood helping a still-drink-addled O'Dea balance on the ship's figurehead—a woman with flowing robes and also great feathered wings, which Temeraire had never seen before due to its ordinarily being hidden beneath the dragon-deck; she presently pointed almost directly into the air.

Gong Su pulled himself up Temeraire's side, when put onto the harness. "No, sir," Temeraire heard him say, when Laurence asked him about Fellowes, "I am sorry, but I did not see him; all the lower decks are full of smoke, and there are many men dead."

"It is only to be expected, sure," O'Dea said, and hiccoughed. "The judgment of the ocean—"

"Enough," Laurence said: that was all he said, but O'Dea subsided, abashed, and muffled his further hiccoughs into his hand.

"Should I try for some of those water-casks, sir?" Roland called up.

"Tell her no," Laurence said to Temeraire, "but you ought to drink whichever of them you can reach, yourself, and let Iskierka and Kulingile do the same; and you had better eat those sheep."

"Those fellows in the belly-netting will be thirsty very soon," Temeraire pointed out, "and so will you, Laurence."

"Let Roland light along a couple of canteens, and as for those bastards, they may go hang," Laurence said, and it was not only his altered voice which made him sound grim. "You must travel as light as may be, my dear: we will want land sooner than water."

An hour passed, dragging up supplies and a few more survivors from the ship, and then Iskierka was winging by. "We aren't pulling anyone else up," Granby called over wearily; his arm and his shoulder were bound up tightly against his body. "Not alive, anyway: the water is too cold. We had better go."

"Set your course northeast," Laurence said, "and keep as far apart from the others as you can and still be in sight of one another, so we may best watch for land; make sure Iskierka and Kulingile have lanterns for the night."

It was very strange and lonely to fly away from the remains of the *Allegiance* for good, out across the open ocean with no destination. She was nearly all beneath the water now and sinking more rapidly; only the dragondeck yet jutted out into the sky. The ship's boats were pulling away, crammed with sailors. They could not keep in company with them, of course; there had only been a brief shouting back and forth. Lieutenant Burrough was in command of the launch, and Lieutenant Paris, a boy of fifteen, in charge of the one cutter which had survived, with Midshipman Darcy to assist him.

"You do not see Riley anywhere, do you?" Laurence asked quietly, after they had spoken with the boats.

"No—" Temeraire said, after a moment. Riley had fed him that enormous red-fleshed tunny, three days after his hatching. Temeraire had never been quite so hungry ever in his life as those first few days, and Laurence had been asleep at the time—Riley had come down to the cabin with the fish himself because most of the sailors were too afraid—

"No," Temeraire said. "No, Laurence, I do not see him."

Laurence said nothing; when Temeraire glanced back, his face was set and grim, his eyes looking over the smoking wreckage distant; he only nodded, and turned to ask Mrs. Pemberton, "Ma'am, would you prefer to go in the boats?" She had been retrieved along with Mr. Hammond from the bow cabins: they had pushed out a window and waved her spare petticoat to attract notice, and been pulled up by a rope. "We can lower you down to them, and take off one or two of the men, if they are crowded."

"Thank you, sir; I should rather stay aboard," she said.

"You must realize," Laurence said, "dragons can stay aloft at most two days—perhaps three—"

"As I understand it, there is very little chance of a boat making landfall, either, from these latitudes," she said. "If it were done, t'were well it were done quickly, I think."

"Of course you are much better remaining with me than going in one of those boats," Temeraire said, swallowing a last morsel of raw mutton. After all, Lung Shen Li flew all the long way from China to the coast of Australia, scarcely landing along the way. Laurence might be pessimistic, but Temeraire was quite certain *he* was not going to sink in an ignominious fashion, without even a battle for excuse; he would certainly not drop before they found land.

"I still think we ought to pull her up," Iskierka grumbled, circling the tip of the *Allegiance* once more: all her prize-goods had been in the hold, and Granby's coat was entirely spoilt. That did not cheer Temeraire precisely, because one could not be happy that anything so very nice was ruined, or going to the bottom of the ocean for no-one but sea-serpents to enjoy, but it was something that Iskierka could not show away anymore, and meanwhile Laurence's own formal robes were safely aboard in their oilskin bag, with Temeraire's talon-sheaths for company; he could congratulate himself on having detailed Roland to keep them safe, and on the deck.

"We have already tried, when she did not have so much water in her, so there is no sense in imagining we will do any better a second time," Temeraire said. "We had much better go."

He put the sun behind him and flew.

Laurence looked around only once while the *Allegiance* dwindled away behind them, wreckage and flotsam spreading wide around her like the skirts of a court dress; the sharks were already busy in the water. It was a sorry, bitter end for so many good men: the worst saved and even now making moan in Temeraire's belly-netting, the best sent down to a silent grave trying to repair their folly, without even hope of glory for reward. Riley would be remembered as the man who had lost a transport on a cloudless day; if any of them lived to carry the report back to the Admiralty.

The weak sun, shrunken down and pale this far south, did little to warm skin and clothes waterlogged with salt, but Laurence was sorry to see it sinking, and still more sorry that the dragons had spent so much of the morning aloft in hunting and play.

They spread out as they flew; by dusk, Kulingile and Iskierka were specks to either side like distant sea-birds, growing faint to see as night fell: then there was only the small struggling glow of the lanterns keeping pace with them through the dark. They made not much noise besides the complaining from below, and even that died over time. The wind cut sharp and icy through the oilskins and tarpaulins on their backs, whistling, and the ocean muttered in low voices, patient.

"I am sorry we did not bring along some of the sheep with us," Temeraire said, yawning tremendously into the wind as the sun came up after only a brief night. "I would not mind another one now; it cannot be convenient to fish when I have so many people dangling off me."

He put his head down and flew onward. Laurence could not help but think how much lighter Temeraire would go without the men crammed into his belly-netting; it might mean as much as another day aloft. A thought rooted in darker sentiment, in angry resentment: *They have killed us.*

There were a few rocky atolls scattered across the Pacific at these latitudes; the chances of finding them with neither map nor compass were not to be counted, and if found, little hope of finding another within flying distance from there. These waters were not so hospitable they would sustain three large dragons for long, fishing in the same narrow space.

There was some better chance they would find instead a ship, which might be spied at even great distance by her lights—some lonely whaler plying her lines, or a clipper making for Cape Horn. But such a ship would offer no refuge for any of the dragons; they could only let off their burden, then drown having spent their last strength to rescue the men responsible for the disaster, who deserved better to end their journey at the end of a rope.

Laurence wrote a report as they flew, ten minutes at a time before he had to pause and warm his hands again, tucked inside his coat beneath the tarpaulin. If they did find any such refuge, the Admiralty should at least receive a full accounting, and know Riley had been neither a fool nor an incompetent.

> *He was betrayed, rather, by the Folly of foolish men, and the Evil of Liquor: when he and his Officers, who had put forth every most heroic effort and preserved the Ship throughout a Gale of terrific force and danger, over the course of five Days and Nights, were overcome for a little while by Fatigue; a great many of the less-skilled Hands, who were used more gently during the Crisis, in Shifts, than the Officers used themselves, seized upon this Opportunity to bring Ruin on all alike in their mad greed for spirits.*
>
> *I deeply grieve to communicate such a Loss to you, which must be felt all the Worse for its inutility, and the unwarranted Harm it must do to the Reputation of one of the most deserving Officers of my Acquaintance; and hope only that this letter, reaching you, may offer to you and to his son the Consolation of knowing any Ill-Report of him which may be bruited around shall be without Merit.*

He enclosed this more personal letter to Catherine Harcourt along with his report, folded within a square of oilcloth sawed away from the one wrapped around himself, and tied with a few scraps of fraying rope. He at least had little likelihood of having to face her in person with such evil news; which event would have been all the more painful for his doubts of her reaction. He hoped Riley would be mourned; Riley deserved to be mourned; Laurence was not at all certain that he would be. Harcourt had married him reluctantly and only for the sake of her coming child, who indeed had proved to be a boy, and she had shown only the greatest impatience since with Riley's every attempt to fulfill his duty to her.

"Roland, you will keep that by you, if you please," he said, and she roused from drooping half-slumber to take the packet and put it into her clothing, for safe-keeping. "I hope you will see the letter reaches Captain Harcourt, if you have the chance."

"I will, sir," she said, calm as though there had been any real hope of that; it was already afternoon, on the second day. The dragons had been aloft steadily for nearly thirty hours.

"I think there are some dolphins there," Gerry said, peering over Temeraire's shoulder. "Look, they are jumping."

Temeraire roused and abruptly dived, throwing all their stomachs into their throats and raising a yowling of alarm from below, which was silenced by the spray as Temeraire plunged into the pod and came away with three of the dolphins in his talons; he ate them with the efficiency of real hunger and without pausing in his flight, blood spattering back against his breast.

"That is very heartening, I must say," Temeraire said, licking his talons clean, when he had finished. "And I am sorry, but it is no use complaining; if you had not all run wild, you would not have had to be put into the netting, anyway," he added, to the unhappy sailors. "I suppose we have not had any sight of land?"

"Not yet," Laurence said.

Gerry's sharp young eyes caught a patch of foamy ocean, the next morning: only a scrap of reef some dozen feet from the surface, but that was something. Laurence signaled to Granby and Demane, and the dragons had an hour's rest, sitting perched on their hind legs with the waves washing over them; the sailors in the netting all pulled themselves up to the top and hung there to keep out of the water as best they could: they had by now given over complaining.

The dragons drooped half-sleeping. At last, Iskierka roused and said crabbily, "We may as well go on; there is no sense sitting here getting colder and colder," and shook the spray off her wings before leaping back into the air.

"Are you ready?" Laurence asked Temeraire.

"Oh, certainly," Temeraire said, although it came out mostly in a murmur; he stretched out his neck very far, crackling, and then one mighty heave propelled him aloft again.

The day crept away slowly, measured out in wing-beats; Temeraire did not bother to open his eyes very often, but only altered his course if Laurence touched him gently and spoke to correct their path. He startled awake once with cold water and yells, and jerked himself farther aloft: he had drifted so low a rising swell had struck him full in the face and run along his belly.

He would have liked to reassure Laurence that this had only been an accident—the result of a moment's inattention—not in any way a sign. He was tired, of course, but not nearly *that* tired; there was nothing for Laurence to fear. But somehow it was a very great effort to draw breath, and when he had drawn it, he preferred to use it for flying, instead; the air was so very cold.

Iskierka and Kulingile were also flying very low to the water—they were keeping in closer company now. Temeraire saw a spray rise up around Iskierka's tail for a moment; Kulingile was a little higher in the air, but gradually sinking also. Temeraire heaved breath again and roared—a paltry sort of roar, with nothing of the real force which he could put behind it; only a gesture of defiance, but it rang across the water, and Iskierka's head jerked up: she looked over and blew out a thin ragged stream of flame, in answer, and together all three of them beat back up determinedly.

Darkness crept up from the rim of the world, a long blue curving unbroken by anything which might have meant rest—no land, no sails, not even another reef. Temeraire did not really notice the night coming on; all the world had narrowed to the next wingbeat, and the next after that, cupping the air with each stroke and pushing it away, trying only to get enough room for a breath; trying only to draw enough breath for the next stroke. He could hear the swells breaking beneath him from his passage.

"Temeraire," Laurence said, and, "Temeraire," as though he had said it more than once already. "There away, two points to starboard, my dear." Temeraire turned and flew on; he was vaguely conscious that there was some movement upon his back, signals of lantern-light, and a few answering lights ahead, bobbing; then a blue light went hissing up from his back.

The painfully bright light flung out over the ocean for a moment, an island amid the dark, and with a final desperate effort Temeraire came over the deck and dropped down onto it—barrels and casks were hastily being cleared in every direction, and warm—oh, warm!—bodies coiling away to make room for him, and Iskierka, and Kulingile landing half on top of them both—Temeraire did not mind that in the least.

The men in the belly-netting were yelling protests and pleas. Temeraire caught Iskierka by the base of the neck and kept her from lying down upon her own load of passengers; there were knives and hatchets already at work, and the netting was coming loose, spilling men everywhere. They crawled feebly away, and Temeraire sank down gratefully; Laurence was climbing down from his back, Laurence was safe, and dimly as he fell asleep Temeraire heard him say, "We surrender."

Chapter 5

THERE WAS AN OPEN RAIN-BARREL directly before Temeraire when he awoke; he had not quite opened his eyes when he knew it was there—smell, a glimmer of light on water—and rearing up to throw off two of Iskierka's heavy coils he seized upon it and drank the whole off in one desperate gulping rush. Then he was awake—and *very* hungry, with his shoulders and wing-joints aching dreadfully, but awake, and he looked round and discovered he was being stared at in what could only be called contemptuous disapproval.

"I do not see what business you have, glaring so," Temeraire said, putting back his ruff and sitting up. "At least *I* am not all over feathers, or whatever those are," for the very peculiarly looking dragon was covered both body and wings in bright, elongated scales—or Temeraire thought they must be scales, but they had irregular edges, and were much larger and did not fit so neatly with one another as did his own. Anyway, Temeraire was larger, too, so there was no excuse; although he was unhappily conscious that it had been rather bad manners to snatch up all the water, without being sure there was enough for everyone else.

The strange dragon snorted, and said something back in a language Temeraire had never heard; then someone else said sleepily, "He says no-one who surrenders without even fighting, from only a little flying, should make much of himself."

Temeraire looked over at the young Fleur-de-Nuit lying on the other end of the deck, who had her large pale eyes half-lidded and shaded by her wing against the sun. "I am Genevieve," she added, "and that is Maila Yupanqui; he is an ambassador."

"Ambassadors, I have always understood, are meant to be especially gracious and polite," Temeraire said, eyeing Maila darkly. "What language is that?"

"Quechua," she said. "The Inca speak it."

The ship was the French transport *Triomphe,* fresh from the docks in Toulon and having just come around the Horn; she was sailing north, en route to the Incan empire, evidently with a project of alliance.

"I am sure it must be some mischief of Lien's," Temeraire said to a very disheartened Arthur Hammond—in Chinese, the only language in which they might have some privacy—when that gentleman had come up on deck. "But at least she is not here herself, and if we should explain all the circumstances to the Inca, I am sure they will think better of allying themselves with her and Napoleon: they cannot be pleased with him when he has been delivering strange dragons from over the ocean into their territory, or near it, anyway. Where is Laurence?"

"The French are not likely to give us an opportunity of making them any such explanations," Hammond said, seating himself on a coil of rope, "and Captain Laurence is belowdecks with Captain Granby and Demane: they are in good health. I am to inform you that they will each be allowed an airing once a day, in your sight, on the quarterdeck; so long as there is no gesture—no attempt—which might suggest a violation of parole." He spoke disconsolately.

"What is he saying about Granby?" Iskierka said, picking up her head, and when Hammond had repeated the intelligence for her in English, she hissed in displeasure. "I do not see we have given our parole at all; *I* did not surrender, and I am sure the three of us can take this ship, if we like: what is this nonsense of keeping my captain away from me?" she demanded.

"We needn't have let you land last night," Genevieve said, with some heat—she had been taught English, as well, it seemed—"and then you and your captains would be drowned. It is all very well to say *now* that you can take the ship: you ought have done it then, if you liked to try."

Iskierka snorted a curl of smoky flame from her lip—much to the alarm of the crew, whose urgent shouting she ignored—but there was no answering Genevieve's argument, however much one might have liked to do so.

It was hard to find oneself aboard a perfectly splendid prize, a French transport only just built, and not be allowed to take it when they could have. Besides Genevieve, who was not even fully grown, there was only a Chanson-de-Guerre named Ardenteuse, and a Grand Chevalier absurdly named Piccolo, both of them presently aloft overhead to make room on the deck for the visitors. Piccolo was flying back and forth over the ship and peering downwards narrowly, trying to see just how big Kulingile was—somewhat difficult as Temeraire and Iskierka were coiled up over him.

So that was three against three, or three against four if one counted Maila on the French side—he was disagreeable enough that Temeraire was perfectly willing to do so—and none of them able to breathe fire, or anything like. Oh! They would certainly have been victorious, in a fair fight; only it would not have been fair when they had just come from three days' flying.

Maila, watching Iskierka, said something to Genevieve without turning his head; she ruffled up her wings and answered him shortly, then after a second exchange she turned and said to Iskierka, "He asks if that is as much fire as you can breathe, at a time."

"Of course not," Iskierka said, and put her head to the leeward side and blew out a rippling streamer of flame which reached nearly the full length of the ship and shimmered all the air about it. "And more than that, if I care to," she added, with a flip of her wings.

This was too much for the sailors: a few minutes later the ship's captain, a M. Thibaux, mounted the dragondeck with lips grimly set and his hand upon the hilt of his sword, to express his objections to open flame aboard his ship. That was quite understandable, Temeraire felt, but the captain carried it too far, saying to Hammond, "I must beg you to convey to the beast, in whatever terms you think best, that her captain must suffer the consequences of her behavior—I would be sorry to have to execute such a threat, but monsieur, it cannot be tolerated; the next time, I will have him flogged."

"You will do nothing of the sort to Granby," Temeraire said indignantly, in French, "and if you should try, Iskierka *would* set the ship on fire; and I would not stop her, either."

"What is he saying?" Iskierka demanded, coiling up onto Kulingile's shoulders to peer down at the captain, jetting steam from her spikes. "Oh! Why do you all not speak so anyone can understand; what is it about Granby?"

"He says he would flog him," Temeraire said, still angry, "and I am telling him he mayn't at all: it is not *Granby's* fault," he added to the captain, "when your guest all but asks her to show away, and anyway she was perfectly careful." Not that Iskierka needed to be breathing fire all over the place, and ordinarily Temeraire would have been all too pleased to issue her a reproof himself, but he did not mean to yield any ground on this point.

Iskierka hissed in a dozen voices at once, from throat and spikes together; and woke Kulingile: he cracked a sleepy eye and rolled it upwards to peer at her as she jounced on his shoulders in fury, and asked, "Is there anything to eat?"

It was maddening to hear the rising uproar on deck, some two feet directly overhead, while powerless to have anything to do with it. "I suppose we may call it a blessing if *this* ship isn't sunk, when we are done," Granby said from the hanging cot where he lay, without opening his eyes; his face was drawn and deeply lined with pain.

Captain Thibaux had been everything gracious—had brought

his surgeon to see to Granby's arm, and his servant to give them an excellent dinner, though their hunger would have made it easy to do justice to one far inferior. But there was still a guard upon the door, four men well-armed and with a look of sturdy competence, and Laurence had no illusions as to their orders: the soldiers looked anxiously at one another, and above, as the noise of quarreling dragons grew all the louder.

That noise soon subsided, however, and shortly thereafter a tapping came on the cabin door.

"Captain Laurence, I regret we are fated always to be meeting in the most uncomfortable circumstances," M. De Guignes said. "Do you permit?" He poured: an excellent Madeira. "When this endless war is over, I insist that you shall visit me, and I may give you better hospitality, if God wills we should both be spared."

"You are very kind, sir; it would give me great pleasure," Laurence said, taking the glass with more politeness than enthusiasm; at present he could hope only that he would not be spending the interval in a French prison, with very little reason to encourage that hope. "I am afraid you might find Temeraire less convenient to host."

De Guignes smiled. "He should pose no more difficulties than my Genevieve," he said, touching with pride a small decoration upon his sleeve: the Legion de l'Aile, a singular honor lately created by Napoleon which came accompanied by a dragon egg and an endowment for the beast's future maintenance, together. Laurence heard this explanation in some astonishment, and later, when De Guignes had gone again, Granby coughed out a laugh from his cot and said, "Lord, trust Bonaparte to bring having a dragon into fashion: I suppose every one of his new aristos will want one, now."

"Mme. Lien has condescended to offer her advice on the most profitable of crosses to attempt," De Guignes now added. "Genevieve has now five tongues to her credit, and the last acquired after she was already out of the shell."

It had not before occurred to Laurence that Lien might improve the French breeding lines through such a mechanism: the Admiralty had rather congratulated themselves that Lien, being female, could only produce a handful of offspring for Napoleon's benefit. Laurence himself had strongly doubted she could be induced to do even so much, given her pride in her own lineage and disdain for Western breeds. Certainly the Chinese were acknowledged supreme in dragon-breeding techniques, but Laurence had imagined that these must be the province of some band of expert gentlemen very like those who served in the role in Britain and in France. But that was absurd, he belatedly realized: who better to direct the breeding of dragons than the dragons themselves, and if Lien had made any study of the matter, her knowledge would benefit the breeders of France far more than any individual contribution she might have made.

"The captain grants you should have the liberty of the quarter-deck from two to four bells of the afternoon watch, one of you at a time," De Guignes said, "and you will of course wish to see to the comfort of your men; I am desolate to inform you they must remain in the ship's gaol, in consequence of their numbers, but every effort will be made—"

"I understand entirely, and your assurances must satisfy me," Laurence said, interrupting: he did not much object if the rescued sailors were kept in chains and sustained on weeviled biscuit and bilgewater. "If I might solicit some better housing for our officers and crew, I would be grateful: I will stand surety for their parole, if they are willing to give it."

De Guignes bowed acquiescence.

He had managed to quiet the earlier uproar among the dragons—"Nothing to concern you, gentlemen," he said, "only the least of misunderstandings, owing to Captain Thibaux's unfamiliarity with the nature of dragons: he is new to his command, you see. But all has now been made clear: although I cannot *greatly* envy you, Captain Granby," he added in a touch of raillery, which Granby's set mouth did not appreciate.

"But sir," Laurence said, "I must ask you to confide in me: will we not overmatch your resources? Three dragons of heavy-weight class added to your complement—"

"We are perhaps a little incommoded," De Guignes said, "but I beg you not to fear: I have discussed the matter with the captain and our aviators, and I am assured we have no cause for alarm. The dragons shall take it in turns to spend some hours aloft, and by rationing and attention to fishing we will arrange to feed them all, if not quite so well as they might like."

"Everything is quite all right," Temeraire said the next afternoon, calling down to the quarterdeck—in English; De Guignes had very gently hinted that efforts at concealing the captains' conversation with their respective dragons might be taken amiss. "Iskierka is complaining of the seaweed—"

"As anyone would," she put in, without opening her eyes or raising her head, "—it is perfectly foul, and it is all great nonsense to say it is a delicacy in China: we are not in China, and I would much rather have a cow."

"Well, there isn't a cow for you to have," Temeraire said, "and I must call it the worst sort of manners to complain when we are guests."

"Seaweed?" Laurence said, puzzled.

"Ardenteuse has the net, you can see her there aloft," Temeraire said, pointing with his snout at the Chanson-de-Guerre flying alongside the vessel with a long rope dangling: shortly she pulled up a fishing net of fine line, full of dark green seaweed and wriggling silver bodies.

"They might pick the fish out for us, at least," Iskierka said, grumbling, "instead of giving it to us all mashed together. Besides, we are not guests; we are prisoners, since we have *surrendered*"— very sullenly—"so I will complain as much as I like."

"And it is not at all unpleasant to keep aloft for half the day," Temeraire went on, lordly ignoring her, "so long as one may come down and sleep later."

He made light of the difficulties, but there was an undertone of weariness in his voice which all the effort at cheer did not mask, and he put his head down and fell back to sleep even before Laurence had been gently ushered from the deck at the conclusion of his brief airing.

"It's not that they can't fly half the day," Granby said at dinner, having returned from his own outing equally anxious for Iskierka, "but not when they are to be half-fed, day-in and day-out; and this cold weather don't make it easier on them, either. I suppose it is still a long way to landfall?"

"Four weeks perhaps, if they are aiming for Matarani," Laurence said, an educated guess only: he barely knew anything of the Inca ports. They were notoriously unfriendly to sailors putting in at their ports in anything larger than a ship's launch, so any merchantman determined to trade was forced to anchor miles off the coast out of sight and ferry goods in by boat; and these on return often reported half their crews missing, lost to a fate whose horrors were only magnified for being unknown. Those boats nearly as often carried back chests loaded with gold and silver, in exchange for their goods, which caused the adventurers to persevere; but the Inca were not to be considered hospitable.

In any case, even if Laurence had known the coast as well as that of England, the French had not shown him their charts, and looking out the porthole at what stars he could see did not tell him precisely where they were. "We are out of the forties, at least I can say for certain, so will make worse time the rest of the way."

"Would you know when we are in range of land, Captain?" Hammond asked, dropping his voice confidentially, in a way Laurence could not like. "In flying range, I mean—and if we should be straining the ship's capacity—"

"We would nevertheless be bound by our parole to remain, unless the French should give us leave to go," Laurence said with enough finality, he hoped, to forestall any untenable suggestion: Hammond was a remarkable man in many respects, and Laurence had cause to be grateful for his gifts, but on occasion one might not be sure of him.

"Yes, of course," Hammond said, and sank back into his chair with a face like a sail with the wind spilling out of it, all gloom; in a moment he burst out, "They must have sent spies through Brazil—it is the only explanation; but how they should have persuaded the Inca—" and subsided; a moment later he was repeating, "I cannot conceive how they should have persuaded the Inca to open relations—"

De Guignes certainly did not mean to volunteer any information; however smiling his courtesies, it was plain he disliked extremely having encountered them, and meant so far as he could to isolate them from the life of the ship and in particular from his Inca passengers, if there were any: Laurence had so far seen none, saving the feathered dragon upon the deck. Captain Thibaux was more really welcoming, but as he could count on the captain's share of the head-price for three heavy-weight dragons and their officers, as well as for nearly three hundred sailors, he had greater compensation for his pain.

"No, Mr. Hammond, I have met none of the Inca aboard," Mrs. Pemberton said, when she was permitted to visit them, "although I have been made very welcome: Mme. Récamier has kindly lent me this dress, as I came away without baggage."

"Récamier?" Hammond said, puzzled. "Not of the salon, in Paris?"

"I believe she lives in Paris," Mrs. Pemberton said, confirming, "and several of her companions also."

"But," Hammond said, and fell into muttering confusion; Laurence could not deny he was as perplexed to find De Guignes carrying along half-a-dozen Frenchwomen of noble birth on a mission to a dangerous and isolate nation.

* * *

"I don't see why he must be so unfriendly," Kulingile said, meaning Piccolo, who was presently taking his turn to sleep, with his head buried beneath his wing so he would not see Kulingile flying overhead. It had proven necessary to the maintenance of harmony to have only one of the two of them on the deck at any time, once Piccolo had determined that Kulingile was indeed the larger. "It is not as though I were doing it on purpose."

"That scarcely makes a difference; it is not as though you would choose to be smaller if you could," Temeraire said. In all honesty he did not himself see why Kulingile needed to be quite so large, and still growing, when he had started out so small and from a stunted egg; it was a little difficult to adjust one's thinking.

But to be fair, Kulingile was not at all inclined to make a fuss: even though there was not enough to eat, he did not try to demand more than a proportional share, or filch some of the catch for himself the way Piccolo would if one did not make sure he was watched.

"I am not a prisoner of war," Piccolo had said over-loudly, when Iskierka had caught him at it the other day. "My captain did not surrender himself; this is our ship."

"It is all very well to make remarks of that sort," Temeraire had said coldly, "if you were prepared to defend them, but you know very well we cannot be having it out in the middle of the ocean. You may be sure there is not another transport about if we should lose this one, and if there were, there would be even less food to go around."

Temeraire did not like to remember those last desperate hours of the flight, drawing in a mist of salt with every too-short breath, his whole body growing steadily more heavy around him; it felt too like defeat. But there was no denying that he could not have flown much farther, with all the will in the world to do so. Nor could have Iskierka and Kulingile, of course; so it was not at all a weakness of his own, but nevertheless he had been forced to acknowledge what must indeed be a practical limitation upon almost any dragon.

He would have liked to question Lung Shen Li about her technique—perhaps there was some trick to a long flight—but after all, she did not have the divine wind, so he could not begrudge her a particular gift all her own. In any case, he now properly appreciated the absolute necessity of the ship to all of them, and so they must not quarrel; however much one would have liked to push Maila's nose in for him, with his constant airs and the shameless way he made up to Iskierka.

"Perhaps when we have made land?" he said to Laurence wistfully. "Not, of course, to violate parole," Temeraire added hurriedly, seeing Laurence's expression, "we would not really take the ship away; but only to make quite clear that if they hadn't our parole—"

But evidently this was not acceptable, either; although Iskierka snorted her opinion of that. "It is all stuff," she said. "Do you know that they mean to send us back to some breeding grounds in France, and put Granby and Laurence and Demane in prison, for all the war? We should not have any battles, or prizes, ever again; it is perfectly ridiculous to expect us to go along with it when we can roust them in ten minutes."

Temeraire could not disagree. He had already had more than enough of breeding grounds to satisfy him.

"And *they* know it, too," Iskierka added: which was perfectly true. Temeraire had made a point the other morning of exercising the divine wind against the ocean, to raise up a great wave. Of course he had raised it behind the ship and going away, but the bulk of it had been perfectly visible even from the dragondeck, Kulingile had assured him, and the roaring audible. Temeraire did not feel that had been excessive: he had not done it to show away, only to make clear how matters stood; and he had only made the effort once, while Iskierka shot off flames three times a day for no reason at all.

So he did think the French dragons could hardly help but see they were overmatched all around. "I suppose that is why," Temeraire said to Kulingile, referring to Piccolo's rudeness. "It cannot be a comfortable situation for them."

Ardenteuse and Genevieve had both been entirely respectful towards himself from almost the beginning, although Temeraire was a little displeased that they had assumed that attitude only when they had learned he was a Celestial. "Oh! Like Mme. Lien," Ardenteuse had said eagerly. "Only she is all white, like snow, and has the most splendid jewels, different ones for every day of the week—"

So it could not be called a satisfying state of affairs, in total; not by any means. "If only we had come across them sailing, when we had the *Allegiance* ourselves," Temeraire said.

"And we would still have had all the cattle," Kulingile agreed regretfully.

"But we are not at all planning anything," Temeraire protested, a few days later, when Laurence reproached him. "Indeed, Laurence, I would not do anything to dishonor you, I promise," except of course to preserve Laurence's safety, Temeraire privately amended.

He had learned his lesson in that regard when Laurence had been imprisoned for treason: the British had put Laurence into prison on the *Goliath,* supposedly safe; Temeraire had gone into the breeding grounds believing it; and then Napoleon had invaded and the ship had been sunk. And Temeraire could not find that anyone had given a single thought to Laurence's safety at the time—he had only escaped on the ship's boats because he had been helping them fight.

So Temeraire did not mean to trust any future promises of that sort from anyone; if the French should try and take Laurence away from him, he had already privately conceived of several stratagems which he might use to extract Laurence from their grasp. But there was no need to go into all of that, Temeraire felt, so long as the French did not do anything unreasonable.

"No," Laurence said. "No, you cannot be accused of anything like *planning;* there is nothing secretive or conniving in Iskierka's

announcing daily in full voice that she does not mean to be im-
mured in a breeding ground, or in your roaring up waves for your
own entertainment fit to sink the ship—" The wave had not been
nearly so large as all that, Temeraire wanted to argue, but it did not
seem the appropriate moment. "But neither are these gestures calculated to leave our hosts with any confidence in our respect for the
rules of civilized warfare, the which they have themselves so gener-
ously embraced in offering us harbor from a disaster of our own
making."

Temeraire did not think it was fair to call it their own making:
it was not his fault, or Laurence's, that the *Allegiance* had sunk.
But he did not argue: Laurence spoke too bleakly of the loss, and
Temeraire knew it had wounded him very deeply. Indeed he felt it
himself—it did not seem right that the *Allegiance* should be gone
forever, and Riley with her. The haze of the long, desperate flight
had left the sinking strangely uncertain in Temeraire's memory—
surely they would one day look out from a port, and see her coming in again.

"Of course no-one would ever dream of asking Captain Laurence to violate his parole," Mr. Hammond said, after Laurence
had been taken below again. "But as I think of it, there is no reason
you might not speak with the Incan beast—I cannot call myself a
proper scholar in the tongue, but I have made some little study of
Quechua—I should be happy to instruct you in what little I
know—"

"I see no reason why anyone would like to speak with Maila in
the least," Temeraire said, flattening his ruff as he looked up to see
the Incan dragon flying alongside Iskierka: the very stupid feathery
scales spread out wide when he flew, and shone gaudily iridescent
in the sun.

"If we could only form a notion of where their negotiations
stand," Hammond said, in a low voice, "it would be of the greatest
use—"

"What use will it be if we are only to be taken to prison?" Temeraire said.

"But by necessity we are first being taken to the Inca," Hammond said, even more quietly, "who might care to speak with us before they make any decision, so long as they know we are close at hand and empowered to make them offers."

That was a heartening thought: not *all* the Inca could be as rude as Maila, Temeraire supposed. "I suppose you may as well teach me the language," he said. "You can come up along with me when it is my turn to go flying next, and begin."

"Oh," Hammond said, and swallowed.

Quechua was not a very difficult language—very nicely regular, Temeraire noted with approval, so that once one had learned the rules, one could make further progress at a steady pace. "There are records of a great many more dialects, from the earlier colonial days," Hammond shouted through the speaking-trumpet—it was not really necessary to speak so loudly aloft, Temeraire could hear him quite clearly even if he did not yell, but Hammond could not be convinced of that—"but the Inca have imposed their own preferred dialect as a kind of lingua franca."

As for pronunciation, that was rather more difficult; Temeraire could not always be listening in on Maila's conversations with Genevieve, but he heard enough to know Hammond's left something to be desired. "You might bespeak him now," Hammond suggested, looking over at Maila, who was making a habit lately of flying close by whenever Temeraire went aloft—likely trying to show away, Temeraire thought. Not that Maila looked to advantage beside him, unless one was more fond of a flashy and vulgar coloration, ostentatious purples and greens rather than sleek and elegant black.

"I see no call for that," Temeraire said coolly. "We are sure to meet some other Incan dragons sometime, whom I am sure will be much better company."

"It is not as though you should have to translate between him and Iskierka," Hammond said.

"I do not see what that has to do with anything," Temeraire said. "I certainly do not care in the least if he does wish to speak with Iskierka; although he can scarcely have anything very intelligent to say, anyway."

"He gave me his share of the tunny, yesterday," Iskierka said on deck, later that afternoon, "and if he likes to talk to me, he may; I think he is perfectly polite."

She nodded to Maila, a gesture Temeraire felt was quite uncalled-for, and rather like fraternizing with the enemy; and to his indignation Maila puffed himself up and nodded back and said, "Madam—charming," slowly and carefully.

"Oh! So you can speak properly," Iskierka said. "Why haven't you, before?"

"Only a little, now," Maila said.

"He has been eavesdropping on my lessons," Temeraire said to Hammond, "in the most rude fashion, without showing the least consciousness after; I cannot think much of his manners at all."

"So he is learning English?" Hammond said, now whispering excessively low: nearly inaudible here on deck, where there were people shouting in the rigging everywhere to make it difficult to hear, when he *would* yell so frantically aloft. Temeraire flattened his ruff in annoyance. "I had thought older dragons could not, save your breed—how splendid that he can as well! Would he perhaps consent to speak with me, do you think—"

Temeraire did not see anything splendid in it, and in any case Maila steadfastly continued to ignore Hammond's overtures. One might have expected Hammond to have enough self-respect, Temeraire thought, to leave off his attempts, but instead Hammond insisted on shouting all the louder in his next lesson for Temeraire; and even though Temeraire tried to fly at a farther distance, Maila kept close after him, still listening in shamelessly where no-one wanted him at all.

"I think the day will be fine," M. De Guignes said to Temeraire the next morning, coming up to the dragondeck to breakfast with Genevieve.

Temeraire had just cracked his eye after a sleep not really long enough to satisfy. "Yes; it is growing warmer," he said drowsily, and then roused enough to realize that De Guignes had spoken to him in Quechua, rather than in French: rather a mean trick, he thought reproachfully.

"That is a pity," Hammond said, when Temeraire reported the exchange, "but I suppose we could not conceal it forever. Do you think you might be able to keep on, if they should keep me from going aloft with you? I might give Roland some notes on the language, to read to you—"

"You had much better give them to Sipho," Temeraire said: Roland was no great hand at studying. "But perhaps we had better stop, if the French do not like it; anyway I am sure I have learned enough—anyone really skilled at languages does not need to be always having lessons, to learn a new one," he added, looking coldly across the deck at where Maila was sunning himself.

But De Guignes did not make any objection, and after a few wary hours Hammond even set himself up on the dragondeck and began reciting aloud to Temeraire there, as loudly as ever he might, and enunciating his English words far more slowly and clearly than was at all necessary.

"I cannot make out the sense of their heading at all," Laurence said to Granby at their small table that evening: he could see enough of the stars to be nearly sure they were sailing northwesterly, for no reason he could imagine; as good as adding another week to the journey, at least, and worse if the ship should get herself becalmed—no joke to risk with seven heavy-weights aboard.

By Thibaux's courtesy, they had none of them been pillaged, so Laurence still had his glass; three days later, during his airing, it showed him a small atoll rising in the distance.

"Perhaps there will be some good fishing there," Granby suggested. "It would be worth giving up a week, to lay in some stores."

But the island, as it drew nearer, gave no evidence of particular fecundity: some green jungle carpeting a central peak, which could not be convenient to dig through; and the visible shore mostly black rock and sand through the spyglass lens: a scattering of palm-trees and scrub, sea-birds diving. There were some seals, but they cleared out with great speed after the dragons first set upon them, and did not leave behind enough numbers to make any landfall worth the while, Laurence thought. In any case he could not understand the French making so great a delay, when they might as easily have put the British dragons on shorter commons if they feared at all for their own beasts' health.

De Guignes joined him on the deck the next day, at the railing. "Ah, Captain Laurence, you see we have come upon this island," he said, clasping his hands behind his back and studying it meditatively: a black slash upon the ocean, with the dragons rising and falling over it in their hunting.

"Sir, I do," Laurence said, polite and baffled.

De Guignes nodded. "I am desolate," he said, "but here we must part, for a little while; I am assured," he added to Laurence's stare, "that there is fresh water—assured of it; M. Vercieux, the ship's master, has once before made landfall here—"

Chapter 6

$\mathcal{T}$HE SHORE WAS NOT MORE HOSPITABLE seen close up: the sand barely a crusting over a heart of hard, salt-pitted rock, and no animals to be seen but birds and small scurrying crabs that fled from the boats. De Guignes intended nothing heartless: the French landed for their provision several rain-barrels, in case the small stream should not be sufficient, and enough salt pork and biscuit to sustain the men at least for months; even a tub of preserved lemons.

"I hope you will not be excessively uncomfortable," he said. "I trust you will not, indeed; the climate, I think, is most tolerable."

He said it smiling, full of courtesy; but there was steel beneath, and Laurence did not imagine there was any use in Hammond's stammering, astonished protests. "Monsieur, we of course will return, in due course," De Guignes said, "on our way back to France: I beg you do not doubt it for a moment," and Laurence did *not* doubt it. De Guignes would be only too pleased to come back and retrieve a party of thin and demoralized men and beasts to be carried off to France as prize—however many of them had survived.

"But this must end our parole?" Temeraire said hopefully to Laurence, while they stood upon the shore watching the *Triomphe* haul her boats back aboard. "Surely we cannot be considered their prisoners anymore: they have let us go."

"I should not consider us as obliged to them further, no," Laurence said, dryly, "for what good that may do us."

A series of attempts, never flying more than a day out from the island, might hope to discover some other land in reach; and repeating the method even in time bring them to the continent—in theory. But the dragons had been stripped of harness and all gear; not a tarpaulin was left them. Even if they had wished to try such a blue-water crossing, there would be no way for the dragons to take more than a few men with them, carried in their talons.

"They have abnegated all their duty," Hammond said bitterly, watching the ship go. "Outrageous—without decency—"

Laurence could not so easily castigate the French, when the act might have been excused merely for the sake of their own beasts without the further provocation which had been offered them; and in a more cynical vein he could scarcely be surprised, either, that De Guignes had chosen not to convey them to the Inca. Maila even now looked wistfully back towards Iskierka from the dragondeck, as the *Triomphe* made sail and began to draw away.

They had been left a few dull-edged hatchets, which would serve to fashion some kind of shelter from the meager supply of wood; the salt pork might be eked out further with fishing, and perhaps some supply from the interior of the island, though Laurence doubted whether there would be much in the way of edible vegetation. He surveyed without pleasure the crowd of sailors, who, having made a muddy wreck of the basin where the stream emptied itself, had now disposed of themselves across the beach in sullen idleness, casting sidelong looks at the barrels and casks: Laurence did not doubt that but for the dragons there should instantly have been mutiny and folly along with it.

"Mr. Ferris," he said grimly, "let us have a little industry here, if you please."

He spoke preoccupied, from instinct; and then it was too late. Lieutenant Forthing was a competent officer and a sensible man; he had gone to New South Wales not, as had many of the other aviators sent with the mission, because he could get no other desirable post, but because as a foundling lacking all influence, he had little other chance of his own beast.

But this was little enough to put to his credit; and Ferris, meanwhile, had not by mere nepotism come by his original position with Temeraire. He had been made third lieutenant of a heavyweight stationed at the Channel as a boy of sixteen years, and since then had shown his worth across three continents and two oceans.

But that was not adequate excuse, Laurence knew. Forthing was not brilliant, but he was not short of courage or of sense, and he was first lieutenant; Laurence had made him so. That Laurence would rather have had Ferris in that place made no more excuse: officers not to his liking had been forced upon him before, and some of them the very dregs of the service, which Forthing was not; Laurence had never permitted his own disappointment to undercut the authority of one of his officers, and thus the chain on which all authority depended.

Never before: but now he had spoken; he had said, "Mr. Ferris," and given the direction to him; and Ferris could not be blamed—Ferris had likely thought as little as Laurence himself, before answering, "Yes, sir," and going at once to work which he did not need laid out for him: the sailors must be rousted from their beds of ease and set to clearing brush, the handful of surviving aviators—the only officers left among them—organized to supervise; small parties of the younger officers sent up into the interior to investigate what supply might be found.

All the work of command—work Ferris knew and had been formed for since his earliest years; work in which he would have been engaged but for a miscarriage of justice. But it was not his work, and Laurence ought not have given it to him. And no way now to easily recant—even more destructive if he had; as much as to say plainly that his first impulse was all for Ferris, and Forthing a poor second in his mind.

Instead Laurence said, "Mr. Forthing, you will oblige me greatly if you will go with Temeraire and look over our prison."

"Very well, sir," Forthing said, mingled relief and surprise in his looks superseding the first flash of dismay which Laurence's first command had produced; he was off to Temeraire's side at once, speaking loudly, "Temeraire, the captain wishes us to survey the island, if you please," before Ferris had even begun his own tasks.

"Yes, I heard; but Laurence, will you not come?" Temeraire said, looking over with a rather puzzled expression.

It was indeed a task Laurence would have preferred to undertake himself—aviators had no experience of surveying coastlines, and Forthing could not be expected to recognize a natural harbor or pick out dangerous shoals, beyond the most obvious. But to send Forthing aloft with Temeraire, Laurence himself remaining behind, was the one mark of trust he could offer which, in the eyes of the aviators, would outrank having put Ferris in charge of arranging the camp.

And to be just, this intelligence was unlikely to be of use. Laurence could not envision any way in which they could proceed, with their crew of disappointed drunkards, to form any boat more sophisticated than a raft; to set them to a little spear-fishing would be the apex of his ambitions.

"You will do very well with Forthing, my dear," Laurence said, "and I had best remain at camp at present; you may wish to delay if you see some chance of good fishing on the other side of the island, as well."

Temeraire did not quite understand why Laurence should have remained behind, when Granby was here also; and if he should have to go without Laurence, he would rather have had Ferris or Roland. Temeraire had not forgotten Forthing's behavior towards Laurence, when they had first been sent to New South Wales. Laurence might like to be generous; Temeraire was not so easily to be won over, and if he must grudgingly allow that Forthing had not been quite so useless as most of the aviators at the new colony, that did not mean Temeraire was enthusiastic to have him form one of his own crew.

Or, Temeraire thought, he might as easily have gone alone— more easily, in fact; he had to carry Forthing cupped in his talons, and it was not at all convenient to always be looking to make sure he had not dropped out; Temeraire was not aware of him in quite the same way as of Laurence.

"I suppose you may make notes," Temeraire said to Forthing, rather doubtfully, as they made ready to go; "but no; you cannot; we haven't any paper," so he had even less notion what use Forthing would be.

"I can sketch the outline when we have returned," Forthing said, a little doubtfully himself, but with an air of determination, "in wet sand."

He did also make a fuss of what ought to have been a simple circuit of the island, which was not very large—he asked Temeraire to set him down more than once, only so he could collect bits of one plant or another which to Temeraire's eye did not look any different from the ones on the original shore; and once in a sandy cove to collect up a truly enormous nest of turtle eggs. These he laboriously piled into his shirt one after another, wrapping each in leaves, while Temeraire had to sit three-quarters in the water being battened on by waves and mouthed at by the little sharks that lived in the cove; at least they were cleaning off the bits of seal meat which had clung to him.

"They are very good eating," Forthing said by way of apology for the wait, as he packed up the eggs, perhaps aware that Temeraire was regarding him with ill-concealed disfavor. That had nothing to do with it, however: it was a great deal more to the point that Forthing's coat had begun as a cheap and shabby garment, and was now both threadbare and faded from bottle-green to a drab greyish shade by sea-water and sun. His shirt, which it had formerly hidden from view, was worse—stained yellow at the neck and underarms with sweat and imperfect laundering, and the back mostly a mess of untidy darns done with thread of various colors.

He could certainly not have been considered a credit to any dragon at all, and Temeraire felt it keenly. One might excuse any number of temporary irregularities brought on by their trials, but Forthing might have had a better coat, or a decent shirt, to begin with; and he certainly might have trimmed his untidy hair or shaven his beard, which was inclined to grow in four or five different colors, off his very broad square jaw.

"We will want more of this sort of thing than we can get, I expect, before they come back," Forthing added, to Temeraire's censorious look.

"We are not going to just sit here and wait for the French to come back and take us off again," Temeraire said with some heat.

"Well—I don't see what else we can do," Forthing said. "We haven't any rope to tie ourselves on with, if you could even get anywhere from here flying."

"I am sure Laurence will think of something," Temeraire said; he had not himself, so far, but of course they had only just arrived. "This is just the sort of thing a Navy captain must deal with, you know, so Laurence is most fitted to work out precisely where we are, and what we shall do next; you see he knew at once what he wished us all to be doing."

Forthing had the gall to look unconvinced. "I don't see as being a Navy man will help him to get us off a deserted island in the middle of the Pacific a thousand miles from anywhere," he said. "If he were Merlin, it might be some use."

"Who is Merlin?" Temeraire asked, flaring his ruff. "I am sure he would not be any more use than Laurence, to anyone."

"I was only having a joke," Forthing said. "He's a wizard, but not really; it is only stories. There was a fellow would tell them to us, at the foundling house, to keep us quiet," he added. "About King Arthur, and all."

"You may tell them to me, then, as we go," Temeraire said, thinking Forthing might be a little useful after all: but Forthing looked awkward.

"Er, well, it is all early on," he said. "So they weren't very keen on dragons, at the time—" and it came out that this King Arthur and his knights had done nothing of real note but to kill innocent dragons all around Britain: almost certainly a pack of lies, as Forthing admitted they had not possessed even any guns at the time, and unpleasant lies at that.

"What *are* we going to do next, Laurence?" Temeraire asked, in a low voice, later that evening. Forthing had sketched out the lines of the island from memory, and not very badly; Temeraire had helped him. They thought the island was perhaps a mile wide at the extreme, mostly brush and scrub on the western side where the French had landed them, and a jungle-like growth over most of the eastern half; there were a great many little coves and inlets which they had not had time to investigate thoroughly.

"That rain-forest is promising," Laurence had said tiredly, wiping his brow; there had been a great deal of activity in their absence—lean-tos had gone up to shelter a supply of dry wood, and a cellar dug for the barrels of salt pork; the one cauldron which had been left them was boiling away ceaselessly to make their dinner—which had become breakfast when Forthing unloaded the turtle eggs. No-one else seemed to mind that Forthing's shirt was so wretched, although Temeraire inwardly writhed with embarrassment, and tried to keep himself between the scene and Iskierka's view, at least.

"There might be some fruit, at least; and better timber than what we have here," Laurence said now, yawning; he was leaning against Temeraire's arm, and his eyes were already closed. "We will send parties as we can; it is damnable not to have men one can trust."

"Oh, yes, but I meant, what are we going to do about getting to land?" Temeraire said. "We must find some way to get to Brazil, still; we cannot only wait here until the French come back and sail us off to prison."

"I will count myself delighted if we manage even so much," Laurence said; and then he was asleep, and Temeraire could not press him further.

It was an endless struggle to keep the men to their small ration, and could not have succeeded if salt pork were any more edible without its hours of boiling; in the third week, inspection discovered that the store of biscuits, weevil-eaten as it was, had been raided.

"It's a sorry mess, Captain, and it's certain we'll soon feel hunger claw at all our bellies," O'Dea said, reporting the destruction with an air of gloomy satisfaction, which Laurence would have been glad to think unwarranted but instead understated the case. Barrels smashed, one gone entirely, and nearly as much biscuit left to rot in the open air as had been stolen. That was worse than the mere theft: the rank stupidity which even an instinct of self-preservation alone ought to have prohibited.

"Enough left to live on, if we cut the ration in half," Laurence said, tossing aside a sprung board from one of the ruined barrels. "And if there is not another such incident of pillaging."

"We can't live on salt pork and crabmeat alone," Granby said, standing with him, pale and holding the injured arm clasped hard against his side. "There's no help for it: we'll have to keep a watch on it ourselves."

Laurence nodded. But there were already not enough aviators for all the tasks which a community of several hundred men required for its survival: too many of Granby's officers and Laurence's had been engaged belowdecks in fighting the fire, when the *Allegiance* had gone up. Besides Forthing, there was only Granby's second lieutenant Bardesley, a silent and sunburnt man brought on in Madras who had been fished from the wreckage; a few of their young midwingmen and ensigns, of whom Cavendish was the oldest; and Granby's harness-man Pohl: his ankle had been twisted a few days before the fire, and he had as a consequence remained on the dragondeck during the confusion, to the preservation of his life.

"Pohl will do it, and I'll take a turn myself," Granby added. "At least I can do that, if I am of precious little other use." He jerked his chin towards his shoulder.

They had no guns, of course, and no rope; nothing convenient to make a lash with, even if there had been a culprit or a dozen to single out. But any number of men had been on guard over the course of the week, and had opportunity to commit the crime themselves or allow others to do so. "And we cannot easily put a man on shorter commons than we already are," Laurence said.

There was only one other potential avenue of punishment—but Laurence would not ask that of the dragons for such a cause. Even if he had been willing to set them upon an unarmed man, fragile as a naked child before them regardless of guilt, and if they had been willing to be so set, the example would have been more maddening than salutary, he feared. The sailors already muttered among themselves that they should be fed to the beasts when the hunting had run out: the dragons were forced to spend nearly all the day flying out and back, to keep from stripping their fishing grounds.

"Soon I suppose we will have to eat sharks," Temeraire had said, dismally. "And it is all very well to say they can be excellent eating," he added to Gong Su, "I am sure of it, when they have been prepared properly; but we cannot carry any quantity of them back for you to cook for us, and eaten raw they are dreadfully gristly. But we cannot be flying much farther out, and still catch enough to make the flight worth the while."

This sort of conversation, overheard, did not reassure those same minds which thought to plunder the stores necessary for their own survival. Laurence supposed they would not have hesitated for a moment to throw their own fellows to the dragons, if thereby they might save their own skins, or for that matter obtain a cup of grog: which was the main subject of the daily reveries which occupied all their time besides the bare minim of tasks they could be chivvied into by the aviators.

There was not much necessary to keep the camp in good order: not much necessary, but what was necessary still was not done. Each morning saw the shore strewn afresh with driftwood and seaweed, palm fronds blown down upon them, the splatted excrement of the crying gulls objecting to the intrusion of so noisy a party into their domain. Laurence had given over trying to have the filth cleared away more than once every three or four days: instead they all kicked aside the refuse as they walked here and there, or slipped on it.

"If you will not work, you will not eat," he had told the men—the one threat which made for any work at all, and which could not be used without limit. A slight, stoop-shouldered midwingman of sixteen like Cavendish could not clout Richard Handes, a man of thirty and four with fists the size of melons and a mouth full of teeth broken in dockside brawls.

Demane managed to impose, when he needed to; which Laurence was certain must have been due to some ferocious quarrel carried on out of his sight, and Emily Roland might have managed a few at once on the strength of personality alone: might have, if Laurence had any intention of trying so dangerous an experiment; instead he took every opportunity to order her away from camp before sunrise, and watched closely that none of the sailors drifted in the same direction.

Laurence would have given a great deal for even one man among the lot whom he could have made bo'sun, but if there were any trustworthy men to be found, they had not put themselves forward. O'Dea and Shipley were not properly of the sailors: they were Laurence's followers, and O'Dea had enjoyed too well, during their stay about the *Triomphe,* making somber pronouncements on the demonic effect of liquor—a subject he was most qualified to speak upon, certainly—with imputations on the character of the sailors who had succumbed to its influence. His own culpability in that respect he protested vigorously: *he* had not been on duty, he was heard to say virtuously.

Shipley, meanwhile, had gown ambitious: he had begun to recognize, with so few hands among the aviators, that a man a little handy and willing might advance past his ordinary expectations. He had been a tailor, before some misfortune had led to his conviction and transportation, and with the loss of Fellowes had evidently formed the aim of making ground-crew master: they did not have harness for him to work on, now, but he made himself busy nonetheless, holding himself apart and lofty from the sailors. They were neither of them to be of use in bridging the gap.

The best candidate, if one were to be had, would have been Mayhew: an older man and one of their small handful of able sailors, who had at one time even advanced to the rank of master's mate before being rated for drunkenness, and might have been of some use. But he had breathed a great deal of smoke in his own escape from the wreck of the *Allegiance,* and yet coughed in a near-consumptive fashion; and in any case, he had made no push to fix himself in authority among his fellows.

So instead Urquhart and Handes were the most popular—had even been delegated to speak to Laurence, after the first week, with the sailors' grievances. "It is hard to be kept so short, Captain," Urquhart said, with a shifty and a sidelong look that said he did not like so well to be actually addressing Laurence, instead of merely muttering with his fellows. "—dreadful hard, after the troubles we have had; we hope you will think better of it—"

Laurence listened with a mouth pressed thin by wrath, until Urquhart trailed off sidling back and away as his words dried up. Handes, less perceptive, added with brazen insolence, "It is no good going on here as if we were all still on board, and high and mighty. The stores must be opened and shared out proper. We had better have mess twice a day instead of one, and the beasts might bring us a little fish, too, instead of eating it all the day by themselves."

The words alone were pure disrespect, if they had not also been foolish to an extreme; and to round them out with insult, Handes spoke while clapping one great fist into his other hand softly but in meaningful rhythm, as if he meant to imply some sort of threat: Temeraire was away hunting, at present.

But Laurence was neither slight nor stoop-shouldered, and he had once been a lieutenant—briefly and unhappily—under a hard-horse captain; he had never in his own command found it necessary to resort to similar tactics, but that did not mean he was shy of them. He bent down and seized a brand out of the fire and struck Handes in the belly to fold him over, and then again across the shoulders to flatten him to the ground.

"Stay there," Laurence said, savagely, standing over him, "stay there, Handes; I will not answer for it, if you should get up. By God, you may hope I will not think better of wasting the very air upon the lungs of a pack of misbegotten whelps of sea-dogs; I had as lief tell Temeraire to chase the lot of you out into the ocean for the sharks, and send you to join the better men who are gone before you. Get you both out of my sight."

There had been no repetition of this envoy from the sailors, and their industry had already been so bare that it could not be said to have slackened, but Laurence had no illusion that their feelings had altered. *Shared out proper* was euphemism: the men imagined, or at least dreamed, that there was some liquor hidden among the stores. There might have been: De Guignes had meant to leave them a supply of rum, but Laurence had without hesitation refused this particular generosity. He could scarcely have convinced the sailors of as much, however; to tell them that the offer had been made and rejected would be as much as to tell them it had been made and the results secreted somewhere for the private enjoyment of the aviators.

"That, as much as hunger, was behind this adventure, I do not doubt," Laurence said, making a tally of the damage. There were now fewer than two biscuits a day for each man, if rationed over four months: futile to hope the French would return any sooner.

"Well, don't look so glum, Laurence: perhaps there will be a plague, or some tropic fever, and kill off half of us," Granby said. "You don't suppose some ship will put in here? Some other ship, I mean."

"I cannot think it likely; we are too close to the continent and the island too poor," Laurence said. "A captain would likely seek a more certain harbor if desperate for resupply, and not waste the time otherwise. Nothing to count upon, at least. The dragons may sight one, more likely."

"And probably frighten them straight off, too," Granby said. "What are they doing now, do you suppose?"

He meant the sailors: farther down the beach they for once had stirred themselves to build up a bonfire and gathered around it; cocoanut shells were being passed around, and a burst of riotous laughter carried over the sand. "Oh, damn them all," Laurence said. "They have made a still somewhere, I suppose; that is why one of the barrels was taken. I ought have known."

"Can you brew liquor out of cocoanuts?" Granby said dubiously.

"That or they have found some other fruit which would serve them," Laurence said, "unless they are busy poisoning themselves; we will know in the morning. Yes, Mr. Ferris, we know," he added, as Ferris joined them gesturing over at the bonfire.

"One of the ship's boys told Gerry, inviting him to come along," Ferris said, "but only just now." And Gerry had evidently reported not to Forthing but to Ferris; Laurence privately shook his head.

"I don't suppose we can stop them," Granby said, looking over at their small band of aviators. "Not until the dragons come back, at least."

"And not then," Laurence said. "They will be all the more unmanageable with liquor in their bellies; we must let them drink themselves insensate if they will, and I only hope they will do so before they achieve some worse devilry."

"We had better get the rest of the biscuit and meat under some better cover instead," Granby said, and added, "See to it, if you please, Ferris—" to Laurence's dismay.

They worked all together the next few hours in the worst of the day's heat, digging a fresh cellar for the foodstuffs and lining it with palm bark and leaves, and carrying over what remained of the biscuit and pork. All the while the distant noise and celebration grew louder and more riotous: songs drifting over with the smoke, and also the smell of roasting cockles; the sailors had at least shown some industry in arranging their entertainment.

Meanwhile the aviators settled wearily on the sand, and Gong Su shared out their meager dinner: salt pork over long noodles made of pounded biscuit and seaweed, in a thin broth of pork and fish bones; this they were forced to slurp out of cocoanut-shell bowls, using sticks to maneuver the lumps of salt pork to their mouths. "Where is your brother?" Laurence asked Sipho, who was putting aside a bowl—was putting aside *two* bowls, Laurence noticed, and he added more sternly, "And where is Roland?"

"Demane has gone hunting," Sipho said evasively. "You know he is very good at it."

This was perfectly true, and did not satisfy Laurence any the better. Mrs. Pemberton had remained aboard the *Triomphe* as De Guignes's guest. Laurence had entreated the privilege for her, and could not have wished to subject a gentlewoman to the experience of marooning, but he felt it frustratingly inconvenient that the chaperone should be gone at precisely the moment her services would have proven of any use.

Demane and Roland did not reappear for hours, while the sailors' rout grew steadily louder and more turbulent, a quarreling noise: they did not have enough food nor liquor to content them. Scuffles broke out of the crowd, a few yells encouraging the brawlers as for entertainment; but in a darker spirit: a spray of blood bright on the sand, and ugly laughter. "Next pull is mine, lads," Handes shouted, grinning, as he pushed back towards the still; blood was on his fingers.

Laurence turned away, disliking even to look; and it was no fit sight for the young officers. "Gentlemen, I think we will send you into the interior for an hour or two—"

"No, sir," Ferris said abruptly, interrupting. "Look sharp, fellows," and he was standing up—a party of the sailors was coming towards them, dividing off the main body with a line of men trailing after, as though some rough beast reached out a paw; Handes was in the lead.

Laurence rose also, and found himself and Granby barred from the advancing men: Cavendish had planted himself directly before Laurence; Granby's ensign Thorne, only thirteen, was beside him; Bardesley and Forthing and Ferris had put themselves out front, and all in unison were herding them away towards a stand of scrub and thornbrake, with only Gerry and Sipho inside that protective circle with them: to be sheltered from harm as though he and Granby were children, Laurence thought, repulsed in every instinct.

The sailors closed in, loosely half-a-ring around them, eyes stained red and skin glazed with excessive sweat: their brew was not a wholesome one, and more than one man had vomit already in the corners of his overgrowth of beard. Their breath was so thick with spirits Laurence could smell it, even at the distance. Handes was smiling at him over Ferris's shoulder with a baring of teeth, gleeful and bloody. "Now, there's no call for arguing, boys," Handes said. "We don't mean any harm, only the captains will come along of us; and then I fancy we'll hear a different song from the beasts, when they are back."

"They'll disembowel the lot of you for the crabs, you ass," Granby said, "and like as not all the fellows who hadn't anything to do with it just the same; where do you even suppose you are going to put us?"

"Keep off, there," Bardesley said, sharp, and shoved away one of the sailors who was pressing in on him too closely.

The man crowded back in directly, and his fellows with him—a smothering weight drawing around them, and Laurence was pressed back against the crackling brush even as the young aviators fought to hold off the encroaching bodies. It was a queer wrestling struggle, an irregular pushing and pulling—when the sailors did try to strike blows, these as often landed only slightly and glancing, gone drunkenly amiss. It was nonetheless deadly serious for all that, and hideous. Disembodied hands came pushing through the human wall to clutch at Laurence's arm, drag upon his clothing, his belt: broken nails and hard-callused fingers caked with sand, which he could not join to any particular face or sentient will; he felt himself the subject of a blind and hungry urgency, groping after destruction with as much eagerness as if for life.

And over shoulders and heads he looked into eyes squinting and inhuman with that same mad urge; but it was there accompanied, Laurence thought, by fear: a fear he had seen sometimes in the faces of enemy soldiers in a desperate and impossible action; men who went to fight because they were in a mass of other men, forced to it, and knowing it a futile act; knowing they courted death for no reason. Only a few eager faces—Handes's eyes fixed on him full of delight and snarling—and the rest only men frightened enough they must act somehow, their wits loosened by drink.

The aviators had linked arms; they kicked and butted their heads at the uncoordinated assault, an ignominious defense, but the sun was dropping low, and soon the dragons would be— "Temeraire!" little Gerry cried: he crawled out from under their legs and ran out onto the sand, waving his arms, "Temeraire!"

There were three specks on the horizon, coming in: coming in swiftly, and half-a-dozen men broke away from the attack and fled, back towards the bonfire and the restless, watching mass of men. Another two followed, and soon the aviators would scarce be outnumbered by their assailants; Handes looked baffled. He struck abruptly at Cavendish—clubbed the boy's head aside and clawed, his fingers scraping over Laurence's cheek and tearing at the corner of his lip; he brought them away with bloodied nails, but he could not get purchase, even if Laurence could not strike back.

Handes fell back suffused with choleric red; his fellows were dropping back with him; and then they turned towards the brush at a crackle of branches: Roland and Demane were spilling out onto the beach, panting and in haste. They pulled up in dismay, looking at the sailors: and then Handes said, "He's captain for that big yellow one; we'll have him, anyway, boys—"

Roland shoved Demane back at the brush. "Run; run now, damn you!" she said, and stooping snatched up two handfuls of sand and flung them into the sailors' eyes as they came at her.

Sipho pulled his arms loose from the human chain and ran towards them; Ferris sprang after him. Handes had grabbed Roland by the arm and thrown her to the ground, and Demane was leaping on him: nearly a foot shorter and still slim as wire, but for once Laurence had cause to be grateful for his lack of gentlemanly restraint. Demane struck a clenched fist into Handes's belly, and an elbow at his throat; the fingers of his other hand went at Handes's eyes, and the big sailor went down choking, his breath suddenly a rattling wheeze, and blood was running down his face.

"I said to run!" Roland said, rolling up to her feet. "Get away from them, you ass; the dragons are coming." But the rest of the sailors were on them: some twenty men, and three of them seized Demane at once, heaving him up and off the ground. Roland dived at their legs, and managed to trip them; but one man booted her in the face and knocked her aside bloodied.

Ferris was there, trying to pull Demane free; Sipho had snatched up a dry branch and was beating one of the sailors holding him about the head. "Go, hurry!" Granby shouted at the other aviators; he had Laurence's arm. "We'll get into the brush—"

"What?" Laurence said.

"Go!" Granby said to them again, dragging Laurence with

him, over-riding protest: "No, damn your stiff neck; haven't you been an aviator long enough?"

Forthing had reached the sailors also, running hard across the sand; but he and Ferris were out in the open, and there were too many: another man seized Demane's arm and hauled him from under the pile of men; others were helping him, and the larger crowd gathered around the bonfire began to move as a body towards them.

"O God," Granby said, slowing to watch. The sailors were yelling in mad triumph as they began to drag a struggling Demane towards the bonfire with them. Sipho was trying to go after, but Roland grabbed him with one hand, holding him back; the other she had pressed up to her nose to keep the running blood from her mouth. Handes got up off the sand and stumbled after the rest, calling hoarsely with a hand clapped over his eye, "Wait for me, fellows—now we'll make the beast mind—"

Then he was falling to the sand and throwing his arms over his head: Kulingile was roaring, coming in over the water at full speed; roaring so it shook the trees, and his shadow poured over the bonfire like a flood.

It was over very quickly. Then Kulingile had Demane clutched in one talon, and lifting him padded away over the sand, saying, "Demane, you are quite well? You are not hurt?" He put Demane down for a moment only, and shook off a last dismembered arm before picking him up again and proceeding onward away; behind his lashing angry tail the fire had been scattered and crushed into ash, and bodies were strewn upon the sand; some still crawling, and moans carried over the sound of the surf.

The dead departed on a pyre built from the corpse of the bonfire and the palm-trees fringing the beach which had been laid waste. Most of the surviving sailors labored silently alongside the aviators to raise it, and the wounded were laid on makeshift pallets of grass, and bandaged with scraps. They had no surgeon among them, of any kind: Granby's new dragon-surgeon Mallow had been lost with the *Allegiance*, and Dorset had remained at the covert in New South Wales. Dewey, the former barber, only could do a little. There was for medicine only the dregs of the liquor.

"The biscuit won't run short, anyway," Granby said to Laurence, in a morbid humor. They were seated in state upon a few logs of driftwood, looking over the work going forward at a significant distance: the dragons were in no mood to let them go among the sailors, and the sailors were still less inclined to have the dragons anywhere near.

Temeraire had argued for keeping every last one of the aviators by his side: he could not see anything disproportionate, or for that matter out of the ordinary, in the scale of Kulingile's fury and the damage it had wreaked. "But Laurence, no-one could expect anything different," Temeraire had said. "I have never seen anything so brazen: even Prince Yongxing did not try and drag you away from me while I was looking on, as though I had nothing to say to it at all. I cannot reproach Kulingile in the least. Are you sure you had better not sit on the other side of me, where they cannot see you?"

Laurence was quite sure, despite the wells which Temeraire's restless clawing talons dug into the dry sand to be markers of his anxiety. But that was as much concession as Laurence could win: he and Granby remained a quarter-of-a-mile distant from the camp, with nothing to do but sit and be jealously guarded from a band of ragged and hopeless castaways by dragons the size of frigates.

Kulingile had gone still further: he had flown out to a rocky outcropping some distance out from the shore and sat there perched on his haunches with Demane held in his cupped talons; an occasional protesting noise might be heard from him, and he waved at the shore urgently once in a while, but Temeraire had firmly rejected the notion of going to fetch him.

"You could not wish me to be so very rude, Laurence," he said, "and anyway I am sure nothing could be more provoking at present; not that I could not fight Kulingile, but I do not in the least wish to do so." Meanwhile he had laid himself in a protective arc, and Iskierka had thrown several of her coils over his hindquarters, and so entwined the two had made a wall of themselves around Laurence and Granby.

"Lord, Ferris, you needn't look so sour," Granby added now, as Ferris trudged down the beach to report again. "I am sorry for the poor damned fools, but it's no worse to be dragon-clawed than hung at the end of the day, and they are man and all of them mutineers. Nothing much worse can have happened, I suppose, while we have been sitting here watching."

"Oh, can't it," Ferris said, losing in impatience the formal manner which was not so thoroughly seated in aviators under any circumstances. "There isn't any biscuit *to* run out: a couple of those big palms came down in the stream, and a corner of it has been trickling into the new cellar for the last four hours."

The cellar was two inches in mud stinking of spoilt salt pork: all the barrels on the bottom level mired deep. Ferris had already put some of the men to prying open the ruined barrels and shifting what biscuit was not soaked into new containers roughly formed out of palm leaves. Nearly half the already-inadequate supply gone: "We *would* starve, if Kulingile hadn't thinned us out," Granby said, dropping himself wearily back to the sand after he had peered down. "Or will we starve anyway?" he added, to Gong Su.

"I am afraid we may be a little hungry in two months," Gong Su said: by which he diplomatically meant, Laurence supposed, that by then they would likely be drawing lots for rations, day-to-day.

But not all of them: he would not starve, and not Granby, and not Demane; they could not be allowed to starve, or even go hungry enough to alarm their beasts. Laurence looked away, his fingers hooked into his belt and drumming on the dangling ring where the harness ought to have been attached; the French had taken that, too.

"Perhaps the dragons might take a whale," Granby said. "I

suppose one whale would set us up for another month, even if we will get tired of nothing but meat pretty soon."

"They are not likely to find anything but finwhales," Laurence said. "And not even a heavy-weight is going to bring one of those to shore: it can always dive away."

"Captain," Gerry said, running up to them, "Roland wants you: she is awake again."

Poor Roland was on a pallet set aside from the other wounded, and Laurence steeled himself to show no dismay: her face was swollen into purple grotesquerie, the lines unrecognizable, and her nose badly broken and imperfectly set. The sailor's boot had left her cheek torn open and the corner of her mouth; he was afraid it would surely scar. "Well, Roland, not too badly, I hope," he said.

"No, Captain," she said, the words coming slow and laborious through the slurring, "but Demane—Gerry says Demane is all right, but everyone is here—"

"Kulingile has gone broody and hauled him out on a bit of rock," Granby said. "Never fear, Roland, he'll do; when you are better you can walk out and hear him yelling if you like."

"I mean everyone else is still here, in camp," she said. "Did he tell you about the ship?"

"A ship?" Laurence said, at once eager and yet dismayed: by now any ship Roland and Demane might have sighted in the morning would be well away, in who knew what direction. "Where away?" he asked, already calculating in his mind—if he and Granby should set out at once, with Temeraire and Iskierka, what course would cover the best distance—

"The other side of the island, the long cove," Roland said, meaning a narrow twisting inlet which Forthing had reported from the aerial survey, which penetrated deeply into the interior: too impassable for dragons to follow very far inside the island.

"Well, that's a piece of luck," Granby said. "A ship really at anchor?"

"No, no," Roland said. "Wrecked."

*   *   *

There was no sense in beginning until the next morning, when Roland insisted she was well enough to show them the way, though Laurence would have spared her another day to recover. "Better sooner than late, sir," she said, and indeed if there were one point of agreement among all their party it was the desire to escape the macabre ruin of their shore encampment, with the ashes and smoke of the dead being carried ceaselessly upon them by the sea-wind.

If they had not had so many wounded, even the many practical difficulties of moving their remaining supply to some other beach would not have been permitted to stand in the way. During the night three more had died, others were beginning feverish, and they were all of them hungry and all badly parched: the stream now only sluggishly worked to refill the small basin which they had originally dug, where the dragons could drink.

Kulingile had come back to shore only once and during the night, as secretively as a dragon approaching twenty-six tons might be expected to manage, to let Demane get a canteen from Sipho.

"He won't listen to me at all," Demane said, gulping hurriedly in Kulingile's looming shadow: the dragon's body was swaying back and forth from the energetic lashing of his tail, and the spikes upon his shoulders were bunched and bristling. "He wouldn't bring me in until I started coughing I was so dry, and keeps too close a watch for me to swim to shore. Sir, we found a ship—"

"Roland told us," Granby said, "so don't fret him trying to get away. It's bad enough already: why the devil didn't you run for the forest when Roland told you? You and Laurence," he added, in some exasperation. "But at least it's not too late for *you* to learn better."

"Is she—" Demane said.

"Midwingman Roland will be perfectly well," Laurence said, flatly, "and we will discuss your excursion when circumstances better permit."

Demane darted a guilty look, and then Granby called, "All right, Kulingile, he's done; and we'll have a guard set when he needs to come for water next, only give us a shout."

Kulingile answered by snatching Demane away, but he settled back onto his rock more easily, and in an hour he had let Demane sit upon his back instead of clutched in his talons. Demane looked not much better pleased but sat watching them forlornly with his shoulders hunched against the cold water, which sprayed with regularity up Kulingile's haunches.

"I cannot quite like the notion of going away and leaving only Kulingile to watch over things here; he is too preoccupied," Temeraire said. "Not that I blame him in the least; only he might not think to keep a watch on my crew, at present."

"You cannot think me in any danger now," Laurence said: a more demoralized assemblage than the remaining sailors could not be imagined.

"I did not think you in any danger *before*," Temeraire said, "and plainly I was mistaken. It does not seem to me anything is so very different: Kulingile did not kill above thirty of those sailors, and they might as easily make another still, if you wish to blame it all on liquor; which I am by no means ready to do," he added. "After all, I have seen sailors quite drunk before, and they never set a ship on fire, or tried to snatch you; I am sure there must be something wrong with this particular lot."

Yes; but if there was, Laurence felt now he had encouraged it by his very despair of them: he had not wished to make anything of them, if anything might be made.

"Yet someone must go hunting," he said. "You and Iskierka and Kulingile have not been feeding so well you can go two days without anything to eat; and Kulingile will not."

"Then Iskierka may go," Temeraire said.

"I shan't, either," Iskierka said, raising her head bristling, but after some squabbling the matter was settled by lot: Granby drew a line in the sand and Temeraire dropped onto it a handful of pebbles—pebbles by his standards; each of them a boulder dredged from the ocean floor and roughly the size of a man's head—and then the results counted off: there were two more on Iskierka's side of the line than on Temeraire's.

"I am sure it might come out differently if only I tried again," Temeraire said, dissatisfied.

"Oh, I will not let anyone do anything to Laurence," Iskierka said impatiently, "and I will set them on fire if they should try, so you may as well go; you know they are more frightened of me anyway."

"I am sure I do not know why that should be so," Temeraire said to Laurence unhappily, before setting out, "but it is; what ought I do?"

"Nothing in the least," Laurence said, "when you consider—" and halted; he did not like to say, where Granby might overhear and be wounded by the justice of it, that any man of sense would be terrified of so ungovernable a temper as Iskierka's in command of so great a power of doing harm. "You must consider it as a compliment; true respect is to be preferred above fear, and to induce it a greater achievement than one which can be as easily credited to mere brutality."

Temeraire was persuaded to go; and meanwhile Laurence was forced to acknowledge the same criticism might be applied as well elsewhere. Where real mutiny was found—and while he would not give that name to the initial sin of running mad after liquor, scarcely so very unusual among sailors, he could give none other to the deliberate attempt to seize himself and Granby and Demane—where mutiny was found, there were sure to be bad officers at the root of it, he had always privately thought.

"It is not as though there had been anything to be done with the men, though, Laurence," Granby said, too easily dismissing the charge. "After all, what else have we to do but lie about?—and men who are working hard need more food and water than we could spare."

"Even so," Laurence said. "We ought to have imposed some discipline upon them, however high the cost; we might have known that men at once excessive idle and half-mad with fear could be relied on for the worst sort of starts: these are pressed men, not volunteers."

Only fifteen men, he felt, must be called mutineers: fifteen, that is, who were yet left alive. Handes, who in a more just world ought to have been first among the corpses and instead had taken scarcely any harm, could not escape the charge; nor had Laurence any desire to spare him, or the others who had been in the forefront. But the body of men might be spared: Laurence could choose to ignore that last general movement towards the struggle with the aviators.

"Mr. Forthing," he said, beckoning him aside quietly, "you will choose ten men from the sailors: steadier men, older men, who were not near the struggle; we will take them with us into the interior."

"Sir," Forthing said doubtfully, but Laurence was in no wise prepared to welcome discussion of the order, and his looks must have shown it; Forthing went.

In the same ruthless spirit Laurence left Ferris behind, and went into the island interior with less than three men he could have gladly relied on: Roland jarred painfully by every step, Sipho not yet eleven years of age and brought along to run back with tidings of distress if any should arise, and Bardesley, whom Granby had insisted on his taking—"If you mean for me to have Ferris here, you had better have some help."

Mayhew would come with them; he had held himself back from the worst excesses of the celebration, merely taken a cocoanut shell of the homemade grog and stood off in the shade of the palms with several fellows talking, which had spared him both a charge of mutiny and Kulingile's wrath. Laurence had no great reliance upon him, but something, he thought, might yet be made of him.

Forthing had dredged up also some men evidently chosen more for advanced age or a placid stupidity than any good qualities, and also Baggy: one of the ship's boys and so called because as a child of six, he had thought the ship was being boarded when Badger-Bag had climbed up the side in the ceremony of the crossing of the equator, and had leapt down from the rigging upon him, much to the distress of the ship's cook who had been playing the role, and the general delight of the rest of the crew. Baggy was now fourteen, and in the space of the past seven weeks had abruptly gone from a plump and nimbly scampering child to a gaunt-cheeked pole given to toppling over his own feet. He also blushed every time he looked at Roland, despite the bandage covering half her face—he had not much attention to give to her face—and blushed again when he met by accident Laurence's censorious eye.

"If I might be of use—" Hammond offered, tentatively; and remembering from five years gone a long grim night in a pavilion under siege, Laurence took him along.

The cove could not be approached from the air without doing such damage to the undergrowth, to clear a space for landing, as might easily send what was left of the wreck to the ocean floor. They were forced instead to go overland, hacking open the path which Demane and Roland had taken the day before: a meandering and mostly theoretical path, as they had not known their own destination at the time.

"We only meant to see if we could find anything to make rope with," Roland offered as they went, peering at Laurence out of her swollen-squinted eye to see how this was received.

"If you mean to compromise yourself sufficiently to impose upon me the necessity of requiring Demane to fulfill the obligation which his side of those actions imply on the part of a gentleman," Laurence said grimly, "you may continue in just such a fashion, Mr.—Miss—Roland."

"What obligation?" she said, in sincere confusion, and when he had clarified his meaning an offer of marriage said impatiently, "There's nothing to require: he already has, a dozen times. But it is no good anymore; you must see that, sir. I *had* thought—"

She stopped while they came to a particularly vicious stand of thornbrake, which she and Demane had merely squirmed beneath the previous day; while the men hacked away at it, she leaned against a tree and said softly, unhappy, "But now he has his own dragon. He can't be an officer of mine, when Mother retires and I get my step, and I can't ask Excidium to push off Candeoris after all these years,"—the Regal Copper who was the back center of the Longwing's formation, and his main defender—"even if the Admiralty wouldn't want Kulingile elsewhere.

"And it's not like you and Mother, you know," she added, unconsciously heaping coals of fire onto Laurence's already-burdened conscience. "The service is everything with her, and Excidium is next, so she doesn't mind; she doesn't want more than—" She shrugged in lieu of specification, with enough eloquence to make Laurence inwardly writhe. "But I don't want someone I *want*, if I can't be sure of seeing him one week in the year. What's the use of only having the right to be jealous?"

Laurence was left not knowing how to answer her; despite the separation that was the common lot of Navy officers and their families he could not persuade himself the circumstances were the same. There, one might have the assurance that only one party was gone abroad; the other remained and gave the home its character. Correspondence might be more or less reliably managed, and a wife could reasonably hope to see her husband for long stretches on shore, even if he were absent years at a time.

Aviators could take no such leave, even if they wished; dragons did not go into dry-dock. And Roland had the right of it: Kulingile would not be used merely defensively, if Laurence was any judge. He had besides the advantage of his immense weight the particularly vicious talons inherited from his Parnassian progenitor, and the spiked tail of the Chequered Nettle from the other side. He would surely in time be given his own formation, when the Admiralty had swallowed Demane as his captain, and the odds that formation would be assigned to the Channel were, Laurence thought, slim.

"None," Roland said despondently. "They'll want him at Gibraltar: I hear Laetificat's never gained back her weight, since the consumption, and she is sure to go to the breeding grounds soon. She's only been hanging on until the breeders got another Regal Copper over twenty tons."

The path had been cleared: she pushed herself up and went over to show where they might continue, through a curtain of hanging vines; her shoulders were stooped.

They came soon to a clearing with a fat gopher-like rodent hanging suspended in a rope-trap: Demane's work of the previous day, forgotten in the urgency of the discovery. No-one would have disdained a bite; it was cut down and taken along. The sound of the surf, which had been muffled away by the thickness of the jungle, became again audible as they continued; and then they came out onto an unpromising rocky beach, which curving plunged back behind a massive tangle of strangler vines that concealed anything behind them so thoroughly, Laurence could not envision how Roland and Demane had even thought to explore.

"There," Roland said, pointing where the sun gleamed on the picked-clean white of bone lying in a small pocket of sand; they clambered across the rocks and stood over the jumbled skeleton, in rags, disordered by the birds and lacking nearly all fingers and toes. The skull and one thigh-bone rested against a rock shallowly inscribed: HERE LAYS BASSEY AND GEORGE, GODE SHIPMATES, GOD HAV MERCEY.

"You can't say fairer than that," old Jergens muttered, one of the men Forthing had chosen; the low grumbling of complaint which had emanated from the sailors died as they climbed past the grave and lifted the vines to expose the rotting hull, and the jagged rock-torn hole.

She had certainly been a pirate: when they had cut away the growth and let some light into the hold, Laurence made his way ankle-deep in water and the remnants of assorted plunder: great gobs of whale oil floating around old barrels, burst chests of silk taken from some hapless East Indiaman. He ignored the furtive poking of the sailors behind him, as they followed him cautiously inside.

"Sir, if you would wait outside—" Forthing tried, looking at the beams phosphorescently green with rot. Laurence did not answer, but in the well-remembered crouch necessary to so cramped a vessel made his way towards the back of the hold, where the stores should have been, and stopping reached up to pull a corner of oilcloth wrapping away.

"Ah," he said: a coil of twice-laid hawser rope, the thickness of a man's wrist, lay dry and clean beneath.

It was no easy task to get the goods out: impossible to rig any kind of hoist or pulley from the rotten wood above, and the tide coming and going pulled at their legs even if they only stood in one place. More than one man fell, and came up pierced and bloody with splinters: when they at last emerged from the hold with the first bundles carried straining by four men apiece, some dozen sharks had come to look in on their efforts and were circling in the deeper water.

"Well, as long as they are here anyway," Temeraire said, and snaking his head out seized two in his jaws at once and lifted his head, swallowing down the thrashing grey tails: Sipho had run back to camp, and directed him. They could not risk his touching the fragile wreck, and the scrap of shore was not large enough for him to land, but he might cling to the shoals out in the water, and wait for them to finish bringing out the newfound treasure: rope and sailcloth and even some knives not entirely eaten by rust.

The sun was sinking low when they had carried out enough to merit loading him up: the men unwound one coil of rope, and set to sawing off a length to use to net up their takings for Temeraire to carry back to camp. It was a long and laborious task; while the men took the knife in turns, Laurence looked up where the stumps of the masts could barely be seen from between the vines, and below them the reflection of the sunset upon a pane of glass yet unbroken.

The vines offered no challenge to a man who had been used to go into the rigging since the age of twelve. Beneath a carpeting of moss and his cautious step, the ship's deck creaked but did not break, and he made his way to the small cabin behind the ship's wheel: odd to look through the stern window onto a garden view, with birdsong and tiny pale green curlers of vines coming in through the missing panes.

Whatever storm had driven the ship from anchor and onto the rocks had not left her captain time to knock down his things into the hold. The rotted remnants of a hanging cot were fallen to the floor, and a writing desk still locked lay in a corner alongside a guilty copy of *Fanny Hill*, which his experience of the midshipmen's berth permitted Laurence to identify by the much-faded cover. And beside them, still wrapped in oilskins, a sheaf of charts annotated in an old-fashioned hand. Whatever words there had once been were mere smudges now, but Laurence required none: only the scattered misshapen atolls drawn in. Each had surely been a refuge of pirates; they dotted the ocean like the broad-spaced paving-stones of an overgrown garden path, all the way to the continent; the last was marked not a hundred miles from the coast: the coast of the Incan empire.

II

Chapter 7

LAURENCE STIRRED AWAKE on Temeraire's back early in the morning hours, half-aware of something altered: and when he raised his head he could see as a faint jagged line the great Andean peaks standing on the horizon, lit from behind by the sun.

They had hop-scotched from one small island to another across several hundred miles of ocean. Laurence and Hammond sat aloft, tied on to the links of Temeraire's breastplate; a makeshift belly-netting of rope and tarpaulins slung below held the sailors, much to Temeraire's displeasure. But Kulingile had flatly refused to carry anyone but Demane at all, and as Iskierka made an inconvenient transport she had only been allotted the other aviators, a smaller group.

"Are you awake, Laurence?" Temeraire asked, glancing back as he flew. "Those mountains are very far away; where do you suppose we ought to land? And do you think they will have anything to eat besides fish?"

The coastline coming visible before them was a stand of rough brown cliffs that so far as Laurence could see through his glass supported only a barren desert plain: save for one green slashing line away to the north. "That must be a river there, I imagine, coming down from the mountains," he said, pointing Temeraire in its direction. "If nothing else we will be glad of fresh water."

There was more to be found as they drew near: the river and

ocean had together cut the cliffs down at their junction, and a large and prosperous fishing village had grown up around the river mouth where the access to the sea should be easiest. A great number of good-sized houses, thatched roofs high and deeply sloped, and even one larger structure of smooth stone; there were broad and stone-paved streets quiet even at daybreak but for the pale dots of cream and brown: grazing sheep, wandering freely.

"I hope the Inca will be gracious hosts," Temeraire said, looking on these last with an acquisitive eye as he swiftly beat on towards the coast.

"Pray remember, Captain—Temeraire," Hammond said anxiously, "Pizarro and his adventurers landed on this same coast, perhaps even in this very settlement—they, too, called themselves an embassy and accepted local hospitality, and then, of course—in short, we must remember we are not come to a virgin land, but one with cause for the deepest suspicion—we must exercise the greatest caution—"

Laurence had only the vaguest notion of the history of the conquistadors, a dredging from schoolroom days, but the story of Pizarro's gruesome end had been a favorite of the tutors whose task it had been to keep several young boys occupied, particularly when approved of as a morality tale by their father. "I trust, sir," he said dryly, "that though we are not a pretty crew, we will prove able to restrain ourselves from rapine and pillage; and I will go so far as to assure you of our not abducting and murdering the present Inca chieftain, should we encounter that person."

"I beg you will not joke upon the matter," Hammond said, without any marked decrease in anxiety. "If the Inca are indeed prepared to entertain negotiations—exchange ambassadors—if they are now at last willing to be persuadable, and the French have already made inroads—"

Hammond did not need to expound too greatly on this theme. Pizarro had correctly realized that he had discovered a great empire; he had written accurate and detailed reports of the excellent

roads, the wealth in gold and silver, the full granaries; he had recognized without any subsequent contradiction the value of the territory which he had found. His only error had been to mistake the
abundant dragons for feral creatures, spread wide for lack of
guns—an error disabused with marked speed and ferocity when his
last act of murder removed the one hostage whose safety had stayed
their retribution.

But his error had been only in favor of the Incan empire's might,
and since then some two hundred years had surely brought ad-
vances to their army and their nation; there was no question that a
French alliance with them could alter the course of the war.

"As little as I like to countenance any delay in our mission to
Brazil," Hammond said, "I cannot call it anything but Providential
that we should have the opportunity to intervene in such a negotiation, which but for the greatest good fortune we should have known
nothing of, and been unable to answer."

Laurence could not call it *greatest good fortune* to have lost the
Allegiance, or to be made prisoner and marooned; but he had no
argument with Hammond's conclusion: that they ought make every
effort to put Britain on friendly terms with the Inca, even at the cost
of delay. Yet without disagreement on this point, Laurence nevertheless could not care for Hammond's hinted suggestions of a covert approach.

"We will not avert suspicion by creeping past their coast stealth-
ily and falling upon their water or taking their game without invitation," Laurence said. "And both we must have imminently; I must
think it better to ask first, and hope we are met hospitably."

"As much as one can call it asking, when we appear with three
dragons in tow," Hammond said, dismally.

But there was no alternative. The pirates' map had not led them
astray, but many of the islands marked upon it had scarcely deserved the name, and certainly could offer no safe harbor. The two
weeks of their journey leaping from one to another, with only a few
string bags of cocoanuts and salt pork for refreshment, had not left

them in a condition to recommend themselves as guests, even while increasing their urgency to do so. Unshaven faces dirty and sunken-cheeked, ragged clothing and cracked boots: they looked very beggars, and were suitably perishing of hunger and thirst to match that state.

"I do not mean to steal anything, and I will just say a word in Kulingile's ear, and Iskierka's, so they shan't, either," Temeraire said. "But those sheep do look so very nice and fat: surely they can spare us one or two; or three, even. We might put that wall back up for them, that has fallen into the ocean, if they liked to be repaid; or perhaps if we should begin by doing it, they would feel grateful and inclined to be courteous."

Laurence examined the damage from aloft: a retaining wall around the grounds of the great stone structure, a low pyramid of broad stepped levels, and a portion of it had tumbled over as a single block now lying in the surf being battened on by the waves. "Where? Oh; yes, I see it—no, that is a house—" Hammond said, peering through the glass futilely, until he surrendered it again to Laurence. "It cannot but help to have some way to reconcile them to our arrival, I suppose—"

They signaled Iskierka and Kulingile on to a landing place a little south of the village, to avoid coming upon them in force, and Temeraire flew on. "Can you land on their beach, without disturbing those boats?" Laurence asked Temeraire, as they drew near: these were a handful of small craft drawn far up on the sand; Laurence wondered if perhaps a greater part of the village's fleet might already be out to sea.

"That would be a piece of good luck," Temeraire said, "if it means fewer men about whom we must persuade we are friendly, and not like those conquistadors; I will set down very carefully." He did manage to alight without causing harm to anything more than one large raft, which lying at an angle caught the draught of his wings and was lifted halfway into the water: but Temeraire hastily snagged it with one talon and drew it back up the sand without worse than a few gouges in the wood.

But no-one at all came down to the sand to greet them, nor even issued cries of alarm; at least none that could be heard over the sailors calling up, asking to be let loose from the nets. "Quiet there: I would as soon set loose a pack of wolves, before we have been made welcome," Laurence said. "If there is any man among you who is not afraid to come with us to make our introductions, he may come out: the rest of you must wait."

He untied the rope from Temeraire's breastplate and threw it out over the side; with one hand for the rope and another for Hammond's elbow, he climbed down.

"I'll go, sir," Baggy called out, in his wavering half-broken voice; Laurence took out Mayhew as well, ignoring that fellow's faint dissatisfied murmur, which did not quite reach a volume requiring acknowledgment: Laurence was determined to promote him, if he could, and regardless if Mayhew did not like it; a few more men volunteered themselves from curiosity, or a desire to stretch their legs.

"I do not see that I ought to only sit here while you go," Temeraire said, disconsolate. "After all, I speak more Quechua than do you, or anyone but Hammond; and my accent is better than Hammond's, too. Oh; with no offense meant."

As Temeraire was larger than any of the village houses, save the one ceremonial building on the hill, and the street would not have allowed his passage, Laurence could not endorse his attempting to come with them. "They can hardly miss seeing you from the village in any case," he said, "and your presence here must induce them to caution: I do not think we can be walking into danger."

"There is something wrong with my accent?" Hammond said, under his breath, as they left.

They scarcely seemed to be walking into any human habitation at all: they climbed the low sandy hill into the village, with Temeraire looming behind them on the shore, and came to the first houses without any sign of life. "Halloa," Laurence called, without answer, except one fat waddling creature which looked a cross between a lap-dog and a rat, which put its nose out of doors and came towards them with every overture of friendliness.

"A guinea pig, I believe," Hammond said, picking the animal up: it offered no resistance but snuffled at him curiously.

"Looks like good eating, that," Baggy said, making the creature the recipient of ever-as-longing a look as Temeraire had cast upon the sheep. "Which is to say, if they was to offer us some, I wouldn't say no," he added hastily.

"Can they all have decamped so quickly, without our seeing them?" Hammond said. "Perhaps we were seen on our approach—our lanterns?"

"No," Laurence said: there was no smoke of cooking-fires, and weeds grew thick in the street. "There is no-one here."

"I can scarcely credit that so prosperous a settlement should have been abandoned," Hammond protested. "Their herds—the boats on the shore—"

Laurence stepped to the doorway of the hut where the guinea pig had come, and looked inside: a few low pallets on the floor, empty, covered with blankets; some clay pots for cookery; a jug smelling pungently of liquor, when he bent over it. All the gently disordered air of a house lived-in, or only temporarily abandoned. Outside, on a wooden rack, ears of maize tied together by the papery husks were drying in the sun; picked at by birds, but far from stripped-clean.

They climbed up the road to the stepped pyramid: the earth around it had been turned a great deal on both sides of the pathway, and the mounds of dirt not covered over or laid smooth; only a few weeds had sprung up on most. The opening of the pyramid was a black empty mouth, waiting; Laurence stepped just inside, out of the sunlight, and waited for his eyes to adjust to the dark.

And then stepped back, quickly, putting his cloak over his

mouth. "Back to the shore," he said. "Put that animal down, Hammond; back to Temeraire, at once, and do not step off the path, or go into the houses."

"What?" Hammond said, even as the sailors began to back away. "What is it, Captain?"

"Plague," Laurence said. "Plague; and all of them are dead."

Temeraire was sorry for the people, of course, but as after all they had no more use for the sheep—which were not sheep, but another animal entirely, larger, with a long neck and meat not unlike venison, which Hammond called a llama—he did not scruple to enjoy them tremendously. Fish was very well and good, but one grew tired of it unendingly, especially when there was no chance of preparing it differently, either, and the sea lions they had taken on that last island but one were not really a sufficient change.

"You might try stewing a few of them for tomorrow," he said to Gong Su, gnawing clean a final bone, "and I would not mind some of that maize, either, did you call it, Mr. Hammond? It has a pleasant smell," emanating from the fire where a great many ears were presently being roasted for the men to eat along with a round dozen of the guinea pigs.

There were also potatoes—very peculiar in color, a lurid purple—which had come out of a great storehouse at the edge of the town. There were many other things in it also besides food: woven blankets, sandals, even several bronze tools whose purpose they could not make out: a long wooden handle with a blade set into it at the end, but it did not seem to be a weapon. "Something to do with farming, I suppose," Granby said, turning it over in his hands.

The bulk of the stores however were fish: dried fish, salted fish, fish, fish, fish. And there were not very many of the llamas at all left, when one considered them with an eye towards extended supply. "We had better start looking for some other town," Iskierka said, when they had done eating and looked over the remaining herd. "Those will not last for long, and I am d—d if I will eat more fish."

The men were very eager to be gone themselves, as soon as any other place could be found. "You had all three better go," Granby said. "I make no odds of anyone coming to a plague-ridden town, and if there is anyone left to object to our making free of their goods, there cannot be so many of them, anyway; we will do perfectly well, and you should meet the local beasts in force if there are any."

"I am not leaving Demane here with the sailors," Kulingile said, flatly.

"I will go hunting," Demane said, "and you will go find us somewhere to stay; I am not a child who needs to be always watched."

He stalked off; Temeraire thought it was rather hard on Kulingile, who drooped unhappily, but there was a great deal of sense in what Granby said. "And you would not want to bring Demane along the very first time to meet strange dragons, anyway," he said to Kulingile, which he meant as consolation, even though privately Temeraire would have preferred to keep Laurence with him also: he could not help but recall that in Africa he had also thought Laurence would be safe, and returned after only a day's flight to Capetown and found him snatched away by the Tswana.

"We will not go very far, either," he added.

There was at least no need to range widely over the ground: there was the river, and to either side of it a narrow green wilderness, and beyond that only a broad dusty desert; they needed only follow the course of the water. They did once come across what Temeraire decided on consideration was a road: the footpath itself was difficult to make out, certainly not intended for use by dragons, but it was marked very regularly with trees which could not have lined up in such a way by nature. It cut the river and continued on both north and south, which provoked some debate: Iskierka was for turning aside to follow it.

"It is built by people," Iskierka said, "so that must mean they go along that way, and where we find them, we will very likely find more llamas, and perhaps some other beasts."

"If they are travelers, they might go a very long distance without having any animals besides a horse, or something else to ride and not to eat," Temeraire said. "I cannot call it a good notion to go off into the desert when we do not want to be gone long. It is much more likely that we will find some people living along this river, if we only keep to it."

"But if they live along the river, they likely eat *fish*," Iskierka said, grumbling.

The expanse of green around the river broadened as they continued in the upstream direction. Kulingile was watching the progress of the sun by looking at the shadow of his wing, and wanting only to go back; but when Temeraire out of pity proposed his doing so early, Kulingile said low, "No; if I went back without you, Demane should know I had come to look for him; he does not want me back sooner."

"Well," Temeraire said, sorry, "we had better divide up and go separately, to cover more ground; then we can find something and all go back together, quickly." Kulingile brightened, and Iskierka was nothing loath, either; they agreed to find one another in an hour, and parted.

The hour was nearly spent before Temeraire gave up and turned back towards the river, for their rendezvous, and then stumbled quite by accident upon a sort of construction—an aqueduct carrying water northward, away from the river, and while he did not know its purpose it was plainly built deliberately, so he turned to follow its course and came with only a few minutes' flying out upon a broad field. In it a small dragon in green and yellow plumes was hard at work, dragging an odd contraption behind himself through the dirt.

The device, Temeraire thought, was made of six of the strange bronze implements they had seen, which had been somewhat clumsily yoked together; they were slung with ropes over the dragon's shoulders. A few men and women followed the dragon through the field, turning over the dirt that the blades had cut apart.

Temeraire paused hovering over the trees, but they did not look up, all of them too fixed and intent upon the earth beneath them instead, so he landed to introduce himself; and as he came down the small green dragon looked up, saw him, shrilled in tones of horror, and flung the entire bronze plow at his head.

"Ow!" Temeraire said, wincing away as the clanging mess struck against his breast and head. "You are not an eighth my size; whatever do you mean by—" but the dragon was not even waiting; it had seized up the handful of people in its talons and was tearing away into the air.

"Oh!" Temeraire said, outraged, and roared after him; the strange dragon only put on yet more speed, until he pulled up short mid-air just as suddenly, as Kulingile, lit golden by the sun, came flying over the tree-tops.

"I thought you were maybe Supay, or one of his servants," the small dragon, whose name was Palta, said absently, his impressed gaze still fixed upon Kulingile. But who Supay was, Temeraire did not know, and by *Supay* the dragon seemed to mean some sort of creature from under ground.

"I do not see how you can have thought any such thing," Temeraire said. "It sounds as though you had mistaken me for a bunyip or something like it, instead of a dragon, which is perfectly ridiculous."

"I do not mean to be rude," the little dragon said, ruffling his feathers up so that he looked nearly twice his size, "but you are all black and shriveled, as though you had been burned up, so I do not think it is as ridiculous as that."

That *was* rude, in Temeraire's opinion, and he was about to say so when Iskierka landed. "What are you all sitting about here for?

Have you found another town yet?" she said, and peered critically at Palta. "Is there anything more to eat near-by?" she demanded.

He did not understand her, of course, but Palta shrank back anyway from her outthrust head, wreathed in steam. "My fishermen have just had a very good catch of—" Palta began timidly when Temeraire asked.

"Whatever good is he, then?" Iskierka said impatiently. "Come along back to the camp, and we will find out more from this fellow instead."

"What fellow?" Temeraire said, and then discovered that Iskierka was carrying a man, whom she had evidently snatched up from somewhere: an old man, with very white hair and his skin deeply furrowed and brown with sun, and marks all over his face; and she had not even asked him if he minded.

"How could I have asked him when I do not speak the language?" she said, dismissing Temeraire's protests. He was quite sure that she had ought to have asked, and better still not taken him at all. "It is not as though I meant him any harm. We will ask him where we can find some better food, and then I will take him back where I found him—oh, somewhere back that way."

"I am sure she doesn't know in the least where she found him," Temeraire said under his breath, and then asked Palta. "I don't suppose you know him?"

"No, he is not mine; and you mayn't have any of mine, either," Palta said, putting himself anxiously between them and his small group of wide-eyed people. "If you try—"

"Pray stop that; whyever would we take them?" Temeraire said. "We are not trying to take you prisoner; we only want to know where we are, and how we can get to Brazil: we are not thieves." He paused, realizing Iskierka had already given him the lie. "Well; except Iskierka, but—you see—she does mean to take this gentleman back home, when we have asked him some questions," he finished uncomfortably.

Palta, unconvinced, was only persuaded to accompany them

back to the shore when Temeraire acceded to his demand that he should be allowed to send his handful of companions back to their home, first. Even so, he tried to keep himself in front while they left, as though he could stop Temeraire seeing which way they were going into the trees; and further insisted on waiting afterwards for a while also, until the sounds of their passage had entirely faded. He then wanted all four of them to go flying abreast and together, even though that was not convenient when Kulingile was slower than all of them, and Temeraire might have gone ahead.

The sailors had put up a makeshift camp with the goods out of the storehouse: several lean-tos and tents, farther up the river away from the village, and several cooking-fires, Temeraire was glad to see; the men were even singing a round of "Spanish Ladies" as they came in for a landing.

"Oh," Palta said, staring around the camp. "Oh; so many! Are they all yours?"

He was asking Kulingile, even though Kulingile did not understand him and could not say a word back. Temeraire snorted. "They are *ours*," he said, "although not properly the sailors: they are only along because we would not leave them to drown, and ought to be more grateful for it than they are. Laurence," he said, turning, "this is Palta, and that man is called Taruca: Iskierka snatched him, and I cannot find she asked him in the least."

They had made their camp upriver at a distance, but the temple on its hill threw a long shadow. The men went about with low voices, and did not even try to steal away to the village for looting, and Laurence did not say, even in a breath to Granby, what else he had seen inside the charnel-house pyramid: the sheets of beaten gold upon the walls, and the vessels of silver standing amid the silent decaying pallets of the dead.

The storehouse at least had offered a more modest scope for greed, and Laurence did not hesitate to order Forthing to share out the jars of local beer they found within: better the men should be drowsy and pacified than tempted to go prying about; he had no illusions about the sensible restraint any man of them was likely to exercise in the face of treasure on such a scale.

The dragons were not gone long, fortunately; although they brought with them fresh cause for dismay in the person of Taruca, and Iskierka was at once unrepentant and unable to say just where she had snatched him.

"He was alone, anyway," she said, "only sitting in the sun near an old empty house, and he did not even try to run away when I landed and picked him up."

"Oh, Lord," Granby said despairingly. "Of course he didn't, you lunatic beast: he is stone blind."

Taruca's face was marred with pockmarks, most nearly about his ruined eyes, but he seemed resigned more than alarmed by his abduction. At least, he was ready to accept their apologies and also a share in their dinner and a cup of the pilfered beer. "I thank you; that is refreshing," he said politely, without mentioning as well he might have that they were serving him from the stores of his own people. "But I am hearing the ocean: is this not Quitalén village? We must not linger here: the governors have banned men from the place while the unhealthy air remains."

"If I am understanding correctly," Hammond added to his translation, "the plague passed over not three months ago; and the—red fever?—a month later, which he says was worse."

"The measles?" Ferris suggested.

"Measles would scarcely be worse than plague," Granby said. "But there must be unhealthy air here; whoever heard of measles *and* plague, so close on one another; and smallpox, too, if this fellow's face is anything to go by. Pray ask him where we can take him home to?"

Hammond's imperfect knowledge of the language evidently gave him some difficulties in this communication: Taruca seemed perplexed by the question, and after listening in, the dragon Palta

looked sidelong up towards Temeraire in a cautious way and volunteered, "If you do not want him, I would be very happy to take
him myself: he could help attend the dead, and light work such as
that only; I assure you we would be very kind to him."

"We did not take him to make him a servant, to strangers,"
Laurence said when this was translated for him. "Mr. Hammond,
pray assure him we will certainly try and find his people, if we can;
at least Iskierka can give us the general direction. And if we do not
succeed—" He stopped: he had not the least idea what they should
do with the old man; they could scarcely leave him alone to his fate,
but to take him along away from his home and all his native society
seemed not much less cruel. "Ask him what he should like for us to
do," he finished, lamely.

When at last the offer was conveyed and understood Taruca
said, doubtfully, "Would you—you would take me home, to my
children? They are in the *ayllu* of Curicuillor, at Titicaca—you will
take me back to them?"

"I am afraid the precise meaning of the word is beyond me,"
Hammond added, to his translation. "I understood it to mean family, but that does not seem to be quite correct under the circumstances."

"In any case, tell him we will do so gladly," Laurence said, "if
he can direct us; where is it?"

"Lake Titicaca; that is in the highlands near Cusco," the dragon
Palta said, "and nearly two-weeks' flying in bad air; really you had
better leave him with me, as you don't want him yourselves."

"Two weeks' *flying*?" Granby said, dismayed, when Temeraire
had translated. "I suppose I ought to have expected you to have
seized upon a fellow whose nearest relations are on the other side
of the country," he added to Iskierka, "but what is he doing here,
then?" and meanwhile Hammond, as always fixed without any
evidence of mercy upon his ultimate purpose, raised immediate and
urgent objection.

"We cannot simply go flying about the countryside without

permission, at such a distance," he said. "Even if such an incursion were not to provoke a hostile answer—which, Captain," he added, "should scarcely permit us to be of any use to the poor fellow in any case—"

"You need not study to persuade me, Mr. Hammond; I agree we must first present ourselves, even as we are, to some nearer authority," Laurence said. "That, therefore, must be our next concern; afterwards—"

"Perhaps we may find some local traveling in that direction, who might take the gentleman with him," Hammond said, an optimism not much supported by the distances involved. Laurence was sure that unless such a lucky chance befell, Hammond would soon be arguing for pursuing the mission instead: and he was forced to admit such an argument would be cogent indeed, considering the loss of time a side journey of that distance would involve.

"Anyway," Temeraire said, turning his head to them after interrogating the little dragon further, "we may ask the governor what to do: Palta says his name is Hualpa Uturuncu, and he lives in a city called Talcahuano."

Chapter 8

"THE DISTANCE IS OF NO GREAT MOMENT," Governor Hualpa said, when Temeraire had explained their difficulty. "The theft, however, most certainly is."

They were all of them inside the ceremonial hall of the city, a splendid building many times the size of the pyramid which they had seen on the shore, although in the same style, with enormously broad stepped platforms made of great blocks of stone so snugly fitted one could only see the separations by looking very closely indeed. And inside, oh, inside! The walls were entirely covered with sheets of gold beaten thin and elaborately engraved, lit by many lamps and by windows cut in the roof, which allowed in great shafts of illumination when the sun was high enough.

One of the sailors had gone over to the wall and rubbed it, before being sharply called back to his place by Forthing: Temeraire had overheard him say, "Real enough gold, it is," in a low voice to his fellows, so it was not merely brass—even though brass would have been almost equally marvelous; Temeraire would not have argued with anyone who had proposed to offer him such panels made of brass, for his pavilion.

The setting made it only the more distressing to find themselves so unkempt and ragged. Laurence had held them back a day to scrub clean in the river and mend their clothes as best they could before entering the city and presenting themselves to Hualpa, but there was only so much one could do with cold water and a few bent needles. Temeraire had tried to persuade Laurence to wear his robes for the meeting, as Emily had those safe preserved, but without success; and no-one else had anything but what they wore.

He could understand, of course, Laurence's wish to share in the general privation, but when Temeraire had ducked his head under the lintel of the massive doorway and come inside, and his eyes had adjusted to the grandeur before him, he had regretted it all over again, and still more when the governor had come out to meet them: Hualpa was not so long as Temeraire himself, but not very much shorter, either, and his feathered scales ruffled up so wide about his neck and shoulders that he seemed somehow larger than he was.

In any case, his ornaments of office would have lent even a lesser beast enormous gravity: a band of gold was wrapped about the top of his throat, set into a woolen collar with a tasseled fringe in a bright green color which stood markedly against the deep intense violet of his scales, and enormous gold circles had been embedded within his ears, so they hung to the bottom of his jaw. Golden hoops pierced the lower edges of his wings, a form of decoration Temeraire had never seen before: remarkably handsome, he thought.

"Consideration must be given to strangers and guests who are unfamiliar with local custom," Hualpa continued, "but this is strange indeed: do you expect me to approve your behavior?"

He sat back on his haunches, the golden hoops ringing against the stone floor as he swept his wings down and onto his back in an elaborate movement: the emeralds caught the shafts of sunlight piercing the great room and flared brilliant green for a moment. "It is known that men from the sea are inveterate liars and thieves," he added censoriously, "and although I have heard arguments that this is from their being men of no *ayllu,* here you are all together, and brazenly you present yourselves in the court without even an attempt to conceal your crime."

"But the people were all dead," Temeraire protested. "The llamas were only wandering around perfectly loose—"

"Not of the llamas," Hualpa said, "of course you are welcome to the llamas, if no-one was herding them, and you were hungry: of the *man*."

"I had not understood they practiced slavery, in this country," Hammond said to Laurence rather anxiously, after Temeraire had translated his exchange, "but if it is the custom—if it is their law—"

Hammond might well express such anxiety, Laurence thought grimly: he could hardly name anything he would less desire than to hand a man over into bondage: whether owned by another man or a dragon scarcely made any difference. The great distance between Taruca's home—whence he had surely been taken unwillingly—and his present abode was now explained, and his resignation at the fresh abduction. A man once snatched into slavery might be indifferent to a change of master, and would scarcely see any reason to believe that any honest or merciful act should be the design of his new captors.

"Pray inquire of the gentleman," Laurence said, cutting Hammond's continuing murmur short, "why he was taken from his home: had he committed a crime?"

"I must remind you, Captain, that we cannot intrude our own judgment upon their practice in such matters—" Hammond halted, seeing Laurence's face, and turned to speak to Taruca, whose indignation when he had made out the line of Hammond's inquiry required no translation.

"What reason but that I had strayed too far, walking, from the protection of my own *ayllu,* and might be seized without retribution: indeed, why would anyone have wanted to, if I were a criminal and a thief?" Taruca said, and hesitated; then drew himself up proudly and added, "If more reason were needed, I am of the *khipukamayuq,* and have fathered three sons and seven daughters yet alive when last I saw them: and beside that I am marked, of course, which you do not need me to say."

Finishing this speech, his shoulders bowed as he said almost privately to himself, "Of course you do not mean to take me back," with a faded resignation. Laurence would have liked to reassure him more decidedly than he could, in the present circumstance.

Meanwhile the listening governor bent down and peered at Taruca with one slitted red eye. "*Is* he marked?" He lifted his head away again and shook it, setting the rings of his peculiar accoutrement jingling, and said to Temeraire. "So he has survived the pox? The matter grows even worse. You are sea-people: you have no *khipu* yourself for him to work with, and no other tasks suitable for a man of his years: what would you even do with him? And from what you say, you did not even offer a proper challenge."

"But we could not have made a challenge, even if we had wanted to," Temeraire said, "as I have explained Iskierka did not mark where Taruca was taken from very well: she did not know he was blind, and would not be able to tell us the way back. Anyway, we mean to take him back to his children, not to keep him to do work for us: and I think it is very unkind that he should have been taken away from them. If you mean to reproach us for taking him from his owner, that is scarcely worse than taking him from his family   "

Even before Temeraire had translated his own speech, Laurence had gathered its direction by the increasingly broad gestures of protest Hammond made, trying to catch his attention; at last Laurence laid a hand on Temeraire's side to interrupt him, and received an account of the conversation.

"You cannot so address the representative of a nation!" Hammond said, sharply. "Sir," he said, turning his head up towards the governor and shouting, "sir, I must inform you that this in no way represents the position of His Majesty—"

Governor Hualpa, who so far had taken no particular notice of the human members of their party, lowered his head to put that enormous red eye on Hammond, whose speech faltered a little, meeting it. "Why are you shouting at me?" Hualpa said. "The governor of men will not receive you, because your country-men have proven they are not to be trusted, and you would very likely try to take him prisoner for gold; you have no-one else to blame for that but yourselves. Are you trying to say that this dragon has no standing to speak for your party?"

This inquiry left Hammond agape and plainly reluctant to effectually supplant himself with Temeraire, as representative of their party. Yet if there were to be any hope of persuading the governor to permit Taruca to go free, without provoking grievous incident, some avenue of communication at least was necessary to them; Laurence took Hammond by the arm.

"You have yourself expressed confusion as to the means the French had found to open negotiations," Laurence said to him. "If the Inca *will* receive a dragon as ambassador, when they will not any man, the mystery is explained: you must not disavow Temeraire's authority, if you desire any chance of forming relations with them ourselves."

"Yes—yes, of course," Hammond said, reluctantly dragging, and at last conveyed the same to Hualpa, not without doing his best to extract from Laurence a commitment to make Temeraire say only what Hammond first approved.

"You know my own sentiments on this matter," Laurence said, while Hammond spoke to Hualpa, "and I am sorry—very sorry indeed—to learn that slavery is practiced here; but in justice to Hammond, we cannot hope to effect any change in their society, if we begin with antagonism; and indeed we are in poor circumstances to do so when our own nation can be reproached with its own share of barbarism in this regard."

"Well, of course I will be polite," Temeraire answered him, "but I must say it is rather much to be called thieves, only because we do not go about keeping slaves, and chaining them up, and selling them away from their families. It seems to me that it is only a compliment to them that I believed they were not slavers, either, and not an insult—"

"Not an insult!" another voice said, behind them, when Temeraire had turned to mention this to Hualpa; Temeraire looked over his shoulder to see that another dragon had come pacing into the hall: only a little larger than Palta had been, and in plumage entirely of green, "not an insult, when you talk as though I had treated him like a llama—chaining! selling! oh!"

The newcomer, a dragon called Cuarla, having bobbed his head to Governor Hualpa, proceeded to identify himself as Taruca's injured owner. "And it is not to be borne," he added, "that this burned dragon should be allowed to take him away: I am sure he *would* chain him up."

"I would not chain anyone!" Temeraire said, "and I did not take him, anyway: Iskierka did."

"What are you saying about me?" Iskierka demanded, rousing from her rapt contemplation of the wall; she had grown weary of the conversation, which she could not understand, and wandered off across the floor to go stare upon the panels. Several of the sailors were creeping along on her flanks and trying to use her to hide their attempts to break off small pieces; Ferris had every few minutes to go and chivvy several of them back into place.

"Nothing that is not the truth," Temeraire said, "so you may lump it; you did take Taruca, and this dragon is here to complain of you and make trouble for all of us because you did."

Iskierka looked Cuarla up and down and snorted comprehensively. "That little creature may complain of me all day if he likes; what does he mean to do about it?"

"Good God," Hammond said. "Temeraire, do not—"

"Of course I will not translate that," Temeraire said, with a flip of his ruff; he was not stupid, although he had to admit that Iskierka's remark, however unkind, was rather to the point. The snort, however, did not require any translation: even without an intelligible word said to him, Cuarla puffed all his scales out so as to make himself nearly twice his size—which still left him somewhat less than a quarter of Iskierka's.

"I will not have it," he said furiously, "I will not! I demand a challenge, if she will not give him back; *and* apologize; *and* give me one of her men, too; she ought not have so many if it only makes her greedy for more." And he glared at Iskierka with slitted fury.

Temeraire regarded him in some perplexity: surely he could not be a sensible creature. "He wants to fight you," Temeraire said, to Iskierka's demands for more translation. "No, I am *not* mistaken; and no, he does not think it is some other dragon he must fight; you can see perfectly well he is staring right at you, even if you do not know his language."

"Perhaps," Hammond said anxiously, "perhaps we might reconsider—Captain Laurence, it seems to me—the dragon seems very attached, and not at all likely to have mistreated—"

Overhearing, Iskierka swung her head around, outraged. "I am not going to *lose* to him."

"It can scarcely forward our cause for you to maim or perhaps even kill a native beast, after you have already begun by stealing one of his—" Hammond paused, and groped around for a word which should sound nicer than *slave,* Temeraire supposed.

"Enough," Laurence said, finally, while Granby spoke urgently to Iskierka, who huffed a little steam but subsided. "Temeraire," Laurence said, "pray convey to these—gentlemen—that we cannot see our way clear to handing over Taruca at present, as he does not wish it, but there can be no question of a battle: the governor at least, I hope, will not imagine that Cuarla has any chance of success, nor promote such an unequal contest."

But when Temeraire had tried to explain, Hualpa shook his head, the gold ringing like bells. "Of course Cuarla is not going to fight her in his person," he said. "What use would laws be, if that were the only recourse? We might as well be living without any civilization at all. No: if you refuse to return the man, and make acceptable restitution—"

"Well, we certainly are not going to give him any of our crew, only because we made a mistake; that is just nonsense," Temeraire put in; he did not feel any need to discuss that with Hammond, as it went nearly without saying.

"—then she must fight the representative of the state," Hualpa said, "and not merely the dragon she has injured."

"Oh," Temeraire said.

"I am sure I do not care in the least," Iskierka said. "I will fight anyone he likes; and it will serve them right."

That Iskierka was willing at any time to enter herself into a contest of violence was undisputed; but Laurence was no happier than Hammond to find them engaged in such an enterprise: aside from all the risks of failure, the risks of success were nearly as great, in its likelihood of provoking resentment and hostility.

"Sir," he said to Taruca, having recruited Temeraire to translate for him, "I must beg you to take no offense; but if Iskierka is to hazard her life for your freedom, I will know, first, that there is no better alternative than this challenge."

When Temeraire had explained, Taruca said, "What better alternative can there be? It is not Cuarla's fault, poor creature; he did not take me from hiding. He exchanged a young man to my last *ayllu* for me: I had no kin there, either, and the boy wished to marry one of the young women, so I said I would come. So now of course Cuarla has the right to a battle."

"Temeraire, you are certain he says he went to Cuarla by choice?" Laurence said, baffled. "Is it not his contention he was seized illegally?"

"I was, but that was many *ayllu* ago," Taruca said, quite evidently seeing no contradiction between his right to liberty and Cuarla's right to satisfaction, and puzzled that Laurence should even ask. "And you are not of my *ayllu;* you have no standing to demand that the champion of the state should fight for you."

"Have you no right to appeal to the governor yourself?" Laurence asked.

"He is a dragon," Taruca said with even more confusion.

"Then to—the governor of men?" Laurence said, a vague guess, and Taruca in some frustration raised his hands and let them drop again.

"What would I ask the governor? I have no complaint to make of Cuarla, to seek a different *ayllu* near-by, and I cannot live without any at all: I am blind, and I am too old. Besides, I was first taken in Collasuyo, a different province and a long way from here; even if I were a young man, chances are I would be snatched if I tried to walk the roads all that way alone.

"Why did you take me, and why did you say you would take me to my home, if you were not willing to give challenge? I am an old man to have my hopes raised so. At least when I asked Cuarla, and he refused, I understood: it is not in the natural order of things that a little dragon with a small *ayllu* should give me up. But you pressed me and I thought: you have three mighty dragons, and I can hear that your *ayllu* is large and full of young men; perhaps you could truly mean to be so generous. But it seems you only took me from my *ayllu* without any understanding of the law."

Laurence was silenced; he could not dispute the justice of Taruca's charge. And if they had not meant to keep him a servant, that was little excuse; Iskierka had still taken him for their own selfish benefit; and Laurence had no confidence that Taruca would not face reprisal from his owner, however previously mild, now that he had been so vocal about his desire to be elsewhere.

"Temeraire," he said finally, "pray tell the governor that intending no offense, we are sorry to have nevertheless given it; and that honor demands we see Taruca to his home. If by this challenge we can secure his liberty without further injuring relations between our nations, we will venture it, so long as Iskierka is willing."

"I might as easily fight, instead," Temeraire said, belatedly regretting having been quite so forceful about Iskierka's responsibility, when Hualpa explained that she must be properly attired to enter the arena, and some twelve young women he called mamaconas came out of a storeroom of the hall carrying together a golden neck-collar very like the one Hualpa wore, with the fringe splendidly woven of black wool. "After all, we are all of one party."

"As she is the offender, she must face the trial," Hualpa said. "Come: you may sit on her side of the court."

Temeraire sighed. "Yes, that is for you," he said, as the mamaconas brought the collar to Iskierka, who was eyeing it with wretchedly undisguised greed; she did not need to *advertise* their nearly destitute state. "And Laurence, the rest of us must go outside to the courtyard."

Which was if anything more magnificent than the hall itself: open to the sky and with two fountains at either end, and the dragon Iskierka was to fight at the other side, sunning himself on the hard stone: a sleek creature with long silver scales tipped with green, and enormously long black fangs overhanging his lower jaw.

"What dragon is that?" Granby asked, from Temeraire's back, where he had climbed up with Laurence to be carried to the stands. Temeraire regretfully recalled when that was Granby's proper place, and none other; that now Forthing occupied that position was too distressful to contemplate long: as though Temeraire had come very low in the world, from those first days.

"His name is Manca Copacati," Temeraire said, having consulted Hualpa, and settling himself upon one of the stepped platforms of the temple wall overlooking the long end of the court.

"Copacati?" Granby said. "The venom-spitters?"

Across the court, the silver dragon yawned enormously and

shaking his head spat once on the ground in the manner of an old
sailor clearing his throat: a thin greenish kind of ichor, which put
up small trailers of steam in the sunlight.

Iskierka, who had come out of a passageway yielding onto the
other side—and in Temeraire's opinion doing nothing short of
prancing—looked up at them over her shoulder and called, "Oh! A
real fight: Granby, are you watching? Is your view all it ought to
be? You might turn a little, Temeraire, so Granby can better see me
win."

"Damn her posturing; have they a surgeon, at least?" Granby
said.

"I am sure *I* would win, too," Temeraire said, under his breath:
and to sharpen his regret, the battle would not have been brawling
at all, but for an excellent cause, which Laurence approved.

"I would, too," Kulingile said to Demane, anxiously. "I am
much bigger than that dragon."

"*Cui?*" Hualpa said, gesturing, and some young men came
dragging a cart laden with hot baskets of delicious-smelling things:
guinea pigs, skinned, stuffed with a sort of nutty bean, and roasted:
and the baskets themselves made of maize husks, so one might pick
them up and eat the entire thing at once. Temeraire ate five for
consolation.

Granby, meanwhile, drank as many cups of the cloudy beer. Laurence could hardly chide him under the circumstances: an intermi-
nable wait while a crowd of spectators assembled with the air of
coming to see an entertainment, and at the other end of the court
the Copacati amusing himself by loudly recounting stories of his
former victories to his acquaintance sitting by his end of the courtyard. Iskierka demanded translations of these, which Temeraire
grudgingly provided; they made a narrative of maiming and destruction which even if exaggerated tenfold would have remained
upsetting.

Seeing Granby's distress, Hualpa said something to Temeraire which made his ruff bristle wide. "As though I would allow anything of the sort," Temeraire said, indignantly.

"What now?" Granby said, dully; he was bent forward against Temeraire's neck and had his forehead pressed against his good arm, against the sun which was climbing towards its zenith.

"He says that you should not be afraid, because Manca has an excellent *ayllu* and will take you into it, if he should kill Iskierka. But there is no need to worry: I have told him you would of course stay with me: and if that silver dragon should try to take you, *I* will fight him."

"Sir, I make noon," Forthing said, and at the same time Hualpa sat up on his haunches and shook his head in evident signal. The Copacati left off his conversation and turned to face Iskierka across the court, his feathered wings outspread with the tips brushing the ground.

Iskierka followed his model, drawing her coiling length beneath her and stretching wide her own wings, the membrane translucent in the bright sun and the color flat in comparison with the Incan dragon's long, glittering scales. "What effect do you suppose it may have, upon the beast's prowess; the feathers, I mean?" Hammond asked Forthing interestedly, tone-deaf to the situation.

"Well—" Forthing said, "they have a look of scales; I expect they may make it nastier to get at the wings if she goes after them, fighting—"

"She won't go after the wings," Ferris said, a little rudely, "unless she hasn't any sense. His neck is twelve points from the shoulder-joint, so he can look all the way round: if she closes with him there, he'll just turn his head and plant those fangs right below her breastbone: he won't need to be a Longwing for that to do the job."

Forthing said, "If she grappled; I don't suppose anyone has ever heard of clawing, on a pass—"

"Gentlemen," Laurence said, sharply, and they both subsided; Granby did not look much happier.

Perhaps another forty dragons had descended upon the temple and ranged themselves upon the steps of the pyramid: the largest four, who shared their level, all of them easily of heavy-weight class and ornamented with sufficient gold and silver to put a duchess to shame; but even these were accompanied only by a relatively few people, around whom they coiled their bodies jealously. When they looked, they looked not at Temeraire and Kulingile, but at himself and Granby and the others of their party, and there was an envious quality to the looks.

"Will you ask Hualpa whether there are an uncommon number of dragons in this city?" Laurence asked Temeraire, low.

"Certainly; this is the third largest city of Chirisuyo, and perhaps the eleventh largest in all Pusantinsuyo," Hualpa said—meaning, he clarified, the southernmost province of the empire, one of eight such provinces, and its second most populous part; a hasty sketchwork elicited that the imperial territory extended now to the neighborhood of the Straits of Magellan, since the reign of the last Sapa Inca but one.

"If half of the local beasts are here, which I must assume unlikely," Hammond said, "then in seven such cities—without consideration for the beasts which live in the more remote areas—"

His calculations were interrupted by all the dragons setting up a roar in full voice, Kulingile and Temeraire belatedly sitting up on their haunches to join in; before the noise had died away, the Copacati was launching himself aloft, and Iskierka shot after him.

Their first passes were mere flourishes: the Copacati darting in and back away at once, a baiting maneuver; Iskierka snapped her jaws at him striking-quick, but without much of an attempt to get near: only the clashing of her teeth chasing him back. Their shadows marked their positions upon the ground: Temeraire had gathered that the courtyard itself formed the boundary of their struggle, and leaving its bounds was tantamount to yielding; Laurence could see Iskierka casting a quick eye down to place herself, before she launched her own probing attack.

She looped towards the sun and went in high, claws out-stretched, and the Copacati was for a moment slow to react—"Bloody hell, it's a feint; damn you," Granby yelled up at Iskierka, "don't—"

Too late: she was plunging at the Copacati's exposed back, and as she descended the other dragon abruptly convulsed his body nearly in half, and so managed to flip himself to receive her with bared fangs already glistening. A low hiss of approval rose from the stands: the dragons sat up, anticipating.

But Iskierka had already begun to veer off from her straight-line course: the initial movements, Laurence realized, camouflaged by the sun backing her. Her back coils rolled, and their weight pulled her along; she fell away to the side and cleared the Copaca-ti's striking range: by feet rather than by yards, Laurence judged, peering through his glass, but good enough, then she was circling away again to the far end of the courtyard limits.

Willing to be even-handed in their evaluations, the spectator dragons hissed for her as well, with even louder enthusiasm; Hualpa said something to Temeraire. "He says this has all the makings of a really excellent fight, which honors the gods," Hammond said, "and perhaps it will end in—" He slowed and awkwardly finished, "in a death; but this I gather, Captain Granby, is a most uncommon occurrence."

"That *was* a nice piece of maneuvering," Temeraire said, rather grudging, "and his, also; but I do not think he can be classed with the very most dangerous sort of dragon. You saw, Laurence, that he did not even try to spit at Iskierka; which means he must have some limit to his supply, or else he might as well have had a go; or per-haps he must bite to have any effect, after all."

The Copacati was beating almost directly up and wagging his body as he did, offering his belly: a provocation which Iskierka was happy to answer. She barreled across the opening space towards him, jaws wide, and Laurence thought perhaps she meant to flame; but instead she veered off again short, angling low as she did, and let her hindquarters and tail with their bristling spikes go raking over his lower belly in passing.

The blow could only have been glancing; the Copacati shrilled with displeasure more than pain, and the watching dragons clicked their talons against the stone. "She has made the first touch," Temeraire translated.

"Huzzah," shouted one of the sailors, and the others took it up; several removed their shirts and waved them, in the nature of impromptu flags.

"There is no call for that, particularly when it is very early on," Temeraire said with a sullen air; the men paid no attention, but yelled more encouragement: "Go on, lassie!" bellowed one deep-voiced seaman, "go on, give him what-for!"

Iskierka flicked a pleased glance down, and even turned away from the fight and flew a low pass in answer along the stands, letting one wing-tip nearly trail the ground and stretching her length impressively. The wind of her passage kicked up dust and a clatter of small stones, so Temeraire snorted and raised up a wing protectively to shield them; this in no wise dampened the enthusiasm of the men.

"Keep your eyes on him, you wretched vainglorious creature," Granby yelled, but his objections were drowned out, and during Iskierka's distraction the Copacati had taken advantage to take on more altitude; he now circled far above, with full command of the field, and Iskierka was open to him below: his shadow on the courtyard only a small irregular smudge, and hers nearly full-sized.

Hualpa made a rough *tchach* sound deep in his throat, disapproving, and Iskierka was flying a little awkwardly, circling up and trying to keep her head turned on one side as she did, so she could watch the Copacati's flight. It was a crabbed position, difficult to maintain, and as they watched Iskierka plainly lost patience for it, shook her head vigorously back and forth, and threw herself instead directly into a climb.

The Copacati immediately stooped towards her, claws beneath

him outstretched: he had blown out his air, and his feather-scales were sleeked down, so he arrowed towards her with all his weight behind him, at a shocking speed. "Oh, oh," Kulingile said, and even Temeraire sat up with his ruff flattening; Granby's hands were bled-pale on the makeshift rope of their harness.

An impact on almost any point would surely fling her down upon the stone, stunned and easy prey for finishing, and Laurence could not see how she was to avoid it, save by throwing herself so wide she would fall out of the courtyard's bounds. And then as the Copacati came, Iskierka herself blew out her air, steam jetting in a frenzy from every spike, and dropped towards the ground with him instead of continuing to a meeting.

His speed was greater; in an instant he was alongside, and hissing struck, but she jerked her head aside and lashed him with her claws to keep him back; then they broke apart again: both dragons had to make their turn and beat back up, furiously gasping, to keep from striking the ground.

They rose through the lingering cloud of steam which Iskierka had produced, a glowing haze illuminated from above by the sun, and dispersed it. Trailing fog, both peeled away to either side and circled at their opposite ends, to catch their breath and look for some advantage, having had time to take full measure of one another now

And the Copacati had taken Iskierka's, certainly. He settled himself comfortably into his circling pattern, flicking his tail idly in a manner which suggested he was prepared to so remain for any length of time; he watched Iskierka, and his jaws were parted, but he made no move towards her. "Oh, damn him," Granby said.

This time he did not even have to offer his belly to entice her in. Iskierka, having circled half-a-dozen times, was already visibly grown tired of the inaction, and snorted her impatience. She broke her position, ceding the advantage, and began another pass at the Copacati. He completed his circle and seemed as though he would begin another, which would have left him coming out of the pattern just in time to meet her; but as she neared, he abruptly pumped his wings twice and shot forward with surprising speed, opening his jaws wide.

His head drew back on its neck, momentarily like a cobra ready to strike, and he spat: but even as he did, Iskierka coming to meet him opened her own jaws, and her flame boiled up out of her throat and seared the air between them.

The thin black stream of poison was caught and scorched, with a stench so powerful it reached the ground; an acrid black cloud rose up, and the dragons both wheeled back from it in either direction. The Copacati was reeling away while giving small cries of distress, black scorch-marks streaked over his face and forequarters, stark upon the silver scales. Iskierka did not give quarter, but circled back and pressed hard upon him, breathing another gout of flame from which he flinched sideways, and then another; and suddenly all the dragons were roaring once again, for the Copacati's shadow had slipped out of the courtyard, and fallen into the running stream.

Chapter 9

"MOST REMARKABLE," Hualpa said yet again, inclining his head in compliment while Iskierka preened; Manca Copacati was huddled sulking at the far end of the courtyard, with a handful of attendants washing down his hurts with water from the fountain, and applying some sort of ointment.

"After all, he did not know that she could breathe fire; it seems to me that is a slightly—a very slightly ramshackle sort of trick to use, to win. At least, it is not as impressive as if he *had* known—" Temeraire said; or rather, wanted to say; but in the end, he could not justify it to himself: too mean-spirited, and he had a horror of so appearing before Laurence. Instead he grudgingly said, "That was nicely fought," to Iskierka, in congratulations, and privately determined to himself that the next time they should have any call for fighting, he would show what he could do.

"Yes," Iskierka said complacently, "and I suppose they will know better than to challenge me in future; now you may tell that governor we would like to know the way to take Taruca back to his home."

This required a brief pause, for several large roasts were being brought out at that moment: llamas on spits, their fat still sizzling and dripping on the ground as they were carried in by young men staggering beneath the weight, and two extremely nice ones were delivered to Iskierka, who fell upon them at once.

"Hm," Hualpa said, gnawing on his spit thoughtfully, when they had eaten—it was made of some sort of interestingly flavored wood, which was very pleasant to have upon the tongue when the meat was done. "So you really do mean to give him away? I thought you were only saying so, as an excuse."

"Whyever would we have made up such an excuse?" Temeraire said. "It is not as though Iskierka—or any of us—minded fighting, if anyone wanted a fight with us."

Hualpa shrugged one massive shoulder. "You Europeans are always lying about one thing or another," an accusation which Temeraire did not think justified, and in any case, *he* was Chinese, "but if you really do not want him, he might as well remain here. I would be pleased to take him into my own *ayllu*, in fact. There is no sense in dragging an old man halfway across the empire just to leave him somewhere else."

"Indeed, Captain," Hammond said to Laurence eagerly, having overheard this suggestion, "you must admit there is a great deal of sense in what he says: and it is plain to see they have no notion of slavery, at least in the Western mode; there is surely no cruelty or abuse—"

"Sir," Laurence said, cutting him short, "will you ask the gentleman if he prefers to remain here, or be taken to his first-proposed destination?" and Hammond sighed even before he had put the question; Taruca had no hesitation in affirming his wish to be taken home, with an enthusiasm increased by his growing belief in its chances of being accomplished.

When Temeraire had made clear that they were quite firm in their intentions, Hualpa also sighed. "Well, as that is the grounds on which you accepted the challenge, I suppose the law is now with you," he said. "I will give you right of passage to Titicaca, then; and as long as you are there, you may as well continue on to Cusco, and see what the Sapa Inca will make of you: I have heard there are some Europeans to be welcomed there, presently, so perhaps it will be permitted."

"Is Cusco the capital, then?" Temeraire said. "Is it very far from Titicaca?"

"Two days' easy flying, I would call it," Hualpa said.

"*Oh*," Hammond said, and all the objections he had begun to make to Laurence abruptly fell silent.

"I wonder he should be so doubtful, when we have been laying ourselves all-out for his sake," Granby said, perhaps with a shade of resentment: he had gone all over Iskierka's head himself, by hand, making certain not a drop of venom had landed which might later roll into a nostril or an eye-socket or her jaws. "You would think he might believe, by now."

"I am grateful; but I have been stolen fourteen times, since this," Taruca said, touching his scarred face, when the question had been put to him. "But if Inti wills it, I will be glad to go home; if you *can* take me."

His latest cause for doubt was a merely practical one: the rope-and-sailcloth rigging they had put together would not do for very much longer. Shipley and all the sailors with any skill at needle-work had been at it daily, but by now it was more patch than original matter, and three weeks in unfamiliar high country would certainly be past its limits, unless they liked to risk plunging to their deaths upon the jagged mountain-sides of the Andes. But they had no supply. Hualpa had been generous enough to make them free of the countryside, hunting, but while there were enough llamas running wild and untended to feed the dragons to their satisfaction, there was no such easy source of leather: they had not even a single leatherworker left, of their ground crews, and the nearest thing was one old round-bellied sailor who vaguely remembered a childhood's apprenticeship to a tanner, of a few months' duration.

Gong Su had begun laying up stores as best he could lacking salt; Temeraire had knocked him down a large hollow tree, for smoking, and he had somehow managed to acquire a local tech-

nique of drying meat through observation and pantomime. Some
he also endeavored to exchange for sacks of dried maize. "I make
no promises that it will eat well," he said to Laurence, having organized several of the sailors to lug the sacks back to their ragged
little tent-camp on the city outskirts, "but at least we will not
starve."

But though their pile of llama hides rose, the best leather they
were able to produce was only a half-rotten scaly-natured material,
which stank queerly and gave no-one much confidence in its holding up to even the most sedate flight. "But sir," Forthing said privately, "I don't answer for the men if we don't leave soon: they will
be at the temple, the first chance they get. I have had to chase a
dozen of 'em down this week, and Battersea made it all the way:
was busy chipping away at the wall with his pocket-knife, when I
came on him."

Nor was this their only concern regarding the men: at the beginning of their third week of labor, Forthing came to report two
gone missing entirely, and four days later Handes disappeared as
well. "If it were him alone, sir, I would suppose he had run off,"
Forthing said, "but Griggs was not meant for hanging; and Yardley
is too damned lazy even to go after the gold unless someone were
marching him to it. What if they should have them here, those bunyips—" these creatures, native to the desert of the Australian continent, having been responsible for similar disappearances when
first encountered.

"This is settled country," Laurence said, "and I cannot imagine
Hualpa leaving us unwarned of such a peril, if it existed; nor such
incaution as the local populace show, about walking in the open.
No: I must assume they have been *stolen,* in the charming local
style," he finished dryly.

"And how the devil are we to find them, I would like to know,"
Granby added.

Temeraire was indignant and determined to pursue inquiries;
but without much success, until several days later Ferris came into

camp with Griggs, an awkward expression, and half-a-dozen men carrying baskets, which when he had gestured to have them set down proved to be full of excellent leather, thick and well-cured. "Sir," he said to Laurence, "I hardly know if you will think I have done well—I don't know myself—"

"Where has all this come from, Mr. Ferris?" Laurence said, putting down the lid of the basket.

"It is for Handes," Ferris said, "and for Yardley; payment, I mean. Or something like it, anyway: the land on the other side of that woods belongs to a dragon, and it seems he has a fellow there who can speak Spanish and a little English—ran with a missionary, a few years ago—and he crept over at night and persuaded them to go."

"Persuaded them?" Laurence said, in some incredulity, rising: Ferris flushed.

"Yes, sir," he said. "I have seen them—well, Griggs, here; Yardley I saw putting his head around a corner peering at me, and Handes wouldn't show himself anywhere as long as I was there. Griggs has thought better of it, but the others wouldn't come away."

Griggs looked uneasy and ashamed, and muttered when Laurence looked at him: "Which we were promised no work, sir," he said, "and a lot of gold, and women; but then I was thinking about my old mum and how she would manage, so—"

"Well, Mr. Griggs," Laurence said grimly, "I will not count you a deserter as you have thought better of it before we have left port, as it were; but you will not stir out of camp another instant while we are here. Mr. Ferris, pray explain yourself."

"Sir, I meant to round them up," Ferris said, "and I had words with that fellow, the missionary's guide, about what he meant by it, and how our dragons would take it; so then he said as they did not want to go back, it seemed hard on them to be dragged; what if we should take some gifts, in exchange, and let them stay: and he offered me the leather. And—" He paused, and then with a small helpless shrug said, "Sir, it seemed to me, what was the sense in bringing them back, when instead—"

"—we might sell them for our gain?" Laurence said. Ferris bit his lip and was silent.

"Laurence," Granby said, with another basket open and running the leather through his hands, "I don't mean to quarrel with you over managing the sailors, in the least; but I will say I would damned well rather have six baskets of this leather than Handes, any road; and I would call us lucky to find anyone to take him at the price. We might leave him, and fetch Yardley back?"

"I cannot disagree as far as Handes is concerned," Temeraire put in, nosing at the basket appreciatively, "and were we not going to hang him, when next we might have a court-martial? But Laurence, I do of course take your point: we cannot be letting strange dragons lure away our men, and think they may do so unchecked; very soon they should be coming after my crew. Perhaps I had better go and speak to this dragon: and if he would like to fight, I am sure I would be willing to oblige him."

Laurence ran a hand through his hair—already disordered in the day's work, and now certain to be more so—and stared at Griggs, with his lowered head. For a man to walk headlong and willfully into slavery, even under the most sybaritic inducement, was beyond comprehension; it was the same spirit, Laurence supposed helplessly, which induced men to yield themselves and their nation to the dominion of a Napoleon.

Handes, at least, could not be accused of yielding merely to folly and blind greed: he had his life to gain, and Laurence did not so love hanging men that he felt a particular eagerness to pursue the end at any cost. And yet Handes had more than earned the penalty—

"I am not suggesting we ought to let a condemned man run free," Granby said. "But he hasn't been tried yet, you know; and we are not properly his officers. A court-martial might let him off with a flogging, at that; it is the sort of thing the Navy will do once in a while, when there are aviators in the case: begging your pardon, of course."

"The Navy does not take so generous a view of mutineers under any circumstances," Laurence said. "And even so: there is a difference in allowing the man to remain behind and live to be of use to someone else—in some fashion—and accepting payment for him, as though we were prepared to sell our own."

"You might think of it as a dowry," Granby suggested, with a suspicious twitching around his mouth.

"Yes; thank you, John," Laurence said dryly.

He went with Temeraire to the neighboring estate—a large and prosperous farm, with more of the great stone storehouses visible in the distance at the end of the fields, and the residences a wide courtyard bordered around by more of the thatch-roofed huts. The dragon, a middling creature of some ten or eleven tons, was at that moment engaged in delivering a load of timber to the waiting hands of a dozen men evidently preparing to erect another of these houses. She put it down and hopped over to put herself between them and Temeraire, as he winged in for a landing.

"He says you are only going to kill him," Magaya said in great indignation, when they had confronted her, "and not even for some particularly special reason, such as a very important sacrifice; and no-one even does that anymore. It is a wicked waste, and I am sure the governor knows nothing of it; he could not allow it, if he did. I will *not* give him back to you: so!" And she flung back her head defiantly; although the effect was rather spoiled by her jumping back hastily when Temeraire frilled his ruff out wide and made a low, rumbling roar in his throat.

"I am sure I have never seen anything like the behavior of dragons in this country," Temeraire said, "it is beyond everything; first there is Palta, calling me a bunyip of some sort, and Hualpa saying we are thieves; and now you, stealing our people—"

"I did not!" she said. "They came to me! That is not the same at all—"

"*Stealing,*" Temeraire repeated, "and then brazening at me, as though you were up to my weight; I suppose because you think you can have a champion fight me in your stead—which might be tolerable if you were in the right, but you certainly are not; and in any case I could beat any champion who liked to try."

"My dear," Laurence said aside, laying a restraining hand upon Temeraire's neck, when Temeraire had finished translating this exchange, "I must remind you it is *not* stealing: these men are the subjects of the King, but even so do not belong to him, as property, and saving the obligations of their duty and the law have the right to dispose of themselves as they please."

"Well—yes, of course," Temeraire said, although Laurence could not help but notice that Temeraire seemed very willing to enter into the local notion of possession where it came to his crew, "but you see, Laurence, to her it is certainly stealing; that is, she meant to steal them and did not know they were not mine; so it does not make her less a thief, because they might not really be so."

"I *am* in the right," Magaya said meanwhile, in her defense, "because you have not taken proper care of them. If I were to start hanging my men from trees, and beating them, and keeping them at hard labor all the time, of course they would complain of me to the governor, and find someone who would look after them better: so of course the law allows for it."

"I have, too—" Temeraire began.

"You have not," Magaya said. "Why, they are all in rags, nearly, and not one of them has anything nice that anyone can see."

Temeraire flattened his ruff, and looked uncomfortable, and had to be pressed to translate this. "But that is only because we have had a very difficult journey," he said defensively, "and because I have Laurence's best things put safely by. Anyway," he added, "how should you know anything of the sort, if you were not watching and luring people away."

Magaya puffed up her neck and shoulder feathers and sank her head back into them in an attitude of embarrassment, giving something of the appearance of a huddled chick.

"So," Temeraire continued, triumphantly, "it is nonsense to say my men ran away to you: perhaps Handes did, but that is because he does not want to be punished for behaving very badly indeed; but Griggs and Yardley only came because you made them sneaking promises behind my back. It is not to be borne, and I am sure the law does not make provision for *that*."

"I do not admit doing anything of the sort," Magaya said, with dignity, "but even if I had, they would not have listened, if they were not dissatisfied. Anyway," she went on hurriedly, "as you are so upset, I see now that you do value them: but perhaps I might give you some more presents, instead?"

"There can be no question of leaving them behind, especially Yardley," Temeraire said. "They are the King's subjects, and members of our crew—"

"Oh, very well: but you might leave Handes, at least," she said. "You do not want him, after all; you only mean to put him to death. I could give you clothing, so your other men would not have to be so ragged—"

"Well," Temeraire said, and, Laurence was sorry to see, very enthusiastically entered into what he could tell even without benefit of translation was nothing less than haggling over price.

He eventually sat back on his haunches, satisfied, and Magaya smoothed down her collar of feathers in equal pleasure; she called over her shoulder to the watching workmen, and several of them trooped away to the storehouses: returning momentarily with many more baskets, of clothing and the leather sandals worn locally, of dried maize, and even one smallish one full of salt.

Yardley was brought out of one of the huts, and slunk over with a sullen and guilty air. "Sure I am coming down sick, sir, with that plague as killed all those people," he said, "so I thought I might as well stay here to die, and for them to give you goods for all the fellows—"

"That is enough, Mr. Yardley," Laurence said, putting a halt to this flow of excuses. "You are very fortunate indeed that Mr. Ferris found you; do you imagine that you would be permitted to live a life of indolence once we had gone, and the beast no longer needed to keep you seduced to hold you by her? I see no idle hands on this farm."

"Sure I don't mind work," Yardley said, outrageously, then added, "and she is the sweetest thing you ever saw, sir; as friendly as could be," which amazed Laurence for a moment, looking at Magaya with her eleven tons and viciously serrated teeth, until he saw in the doorway of the hut a young woman standing and waving cheerful farewell, all unclothed save a blanket wrapped around her and under one bare shoulder.

He shook his head. "Temeraire," he said, "will you find out from Magaya if that young woman has been made promises—if she expects marriage—"

"What do you mean?" Magaya said suspiciously. "You cannot have her!—or do you mean you *will* leave Yardley with us, after all?"

"No, no," Temeraire said, "I mean—Laurence, what do I mean?" he asked doubtfully.

"If there is a child," Laurence said, "there must be consideration for its care."

"Of course we will take care of it," Magaya said, when this was put to her. "The mother is in our *ayllu*, so the baby will be, too."

"Yes, but," Laurence began, "have her chances of marriage been materially harmed, by her—her congress, with—"

"Why would they be?" Magaya said.

"I am sure I do not know," Temeraire said, and looked at Laurence inquiringly.

"As she is no longer virgin," Laurence said in despair, forcing himself to bring it out. "And even if that dragon does not care either way, perhaps men will; pray inquire of the young lady, herself."

"Very well, but it seems silly to me," Temeraire said, and when he put the question to her the young woman blinked up at him and looked as perplexed as Magaya herself had. Laurence shook his head and gave up: the young woman plainly was neither friendless nor excessively sorry at the desertion; nor could he feel he was doing her any great disservice by taking Yardley away.

Of Handes, he saw nothing all the time, save perhaps a skulking half-crouched shadow the sun threw out from behind one of the storehouses, as though someone had hidden in the space between the wall and where the roof reached down nearly to the ground. Laurence looked irresolutely; he did not intend to make himself a prig, and he felt all the compulsion of their dire need and the mercy of leaving Handes behind, and yet there was everything to dislike in the principles of such an act, if not the practicals.

"I do not think there can be anything really wrong in it," Temeraire said. "Magaya seems a decent sort now that she has come around to behaving better, and I am sure she will take excellent care of Handes: which is more than he deserves, anyway. Besides, Laurence," he added, "you have just said yourself that the King's subjects have the right to do as they wish, so long as it is consistent with their duty: Handes wishes to stay here, and it seems to me even if he did not wish to do so, one might consider it his duty to do so, since we will come by so many useful goods, in consequence."

"It is no free man's duty to allow himself to be sold into slavery, in a foreign land, no matter how good the price," Laurence said.

"It is not *exactly* slavery, though," Temeraire said. "You would not say that *you* were a slave, after all, only because you are mine."

It was some time since Laurence had considered himself entitled to *demand* Temeraire's obedience, which otherwise might have enabled him to explain the contradiction easily; and on the face of it, he realized in some dismay, the relations between captain and beast could with more rationality be given the character of possession by the latter, than the former.

"I dare say," Granby said, when Laurence had laid this insight before him that evening, while all around them the camp bustled with activity, as the new harnesses were stitched together under Shipley's busy and strutting supervision. "At least I am damned sure Iskierka would agree with you on the subject; pray don't say it so loud. This wretched country cannot be a good influence: we may count ourselves lucky if Temeraire don't go home thinking dragons ought to have men and not just votes."

Chapter 10

❦

$\mathcal{H}$OME AND ENGLAND seemed very distant in the morning, when they came into the foothills of the great clawing peaks of the Andes, serrated and blue-shadowed where the long swaths of snow lay on their sides. The river divided into a hundred little tributaries trickling down the mountain-sides as they climbed, and by evening the dragons were landing in a high meadow gasping for breath. They had made scarcely ten miles if their progress were to be measured as a line drawn on a map, Laurence thought, and more than a hundred straight up.

He stumbled himself, climbing down from Temeraire's back, and they were all of them short of breath and queerly sick with some miasma of the mountain air. A few of the men fell over heaving like bellows, and lay where they fell.

Laurence walked to the edge of the meadow where it ended in cliff to breathe deep of some cleaner air and pull it into his lungs, and found he was looking down at a series of terraced fields: man-made yet lying fallow; maize plants struggled with weeds and tall grasses for dominion, and even a few tools lay half-buried in the greenery, abandoned.

All the rest of that journey had the same quality, as though they walked through a stranger's unattended house, neither host nor servants there to greet them. They saw once in a while dragons, some even laboring in the fields and others carrying loads of timber. Only once in the first few days did they see any human life: a couple of young girls sitting in a field with their arms wrapped around their knees, watching over a great herd of grazing llamas in a high valley.

They threw a swift startled glance up at the strange dragons and dived for cover into a nearby cave little more than a crevasse in the rock, too narrow for any dragon to reach into, and rang out a clanging bell for alarm. "Pray let us continue on," Hammond shouted anxiously in Laurence's ear, "as quickly as may be; there is nothing served by offering even the appearance of provocation—"

"We might have stayed and had some of those llamas, fresh," Iskierka said, later that evening; instead they had come to ground in another abandoned field with a storehouse, and she was eating a porridge of dried maize flavored with the smoked llama meat which Gong Su had prepared.

"It is truly wonderful, the quantity of supply which this nation has provided along its roads," Hammond said, inspecting the storehouse. "I believe we have seen not fewer than six to-day alone; do you agree with me, gentlemen?"

Gong Su also was interested in the construction of the storehouse, and when he saw Laurence looking, showed where his attention had been drawn to its design. "It must work excellently, for draining the rainfall: certainly this food has not been stored recently, but very little is spoilt."

Easy, also, to build up great stores when so far as they could see there were few to consume them. There was something strange and sad in the dragons tilling the great fields, to raise crops which no-one would eat. The handful of beasts to which Temeraire spoke looked at the two hundred men and more aboard with eyes at once eager and resentful: and many offers were made him.

"There once were more men," Taruca said, when Laurence questioned him. "Many more: my grandfather told me there were so many that only half the *ayllu* had even one dragon among their *curaca*—" by which word he seemed to mean the chiefs of each clan. "It was a great honor to persuade a dragon to join one's *ayllu:* a great warrior might win one for his kin, or a skillful weaver."

"So you see, Captain," Hammond said, listening, "I was not at all wrong: it is *not* slavery, in the ordinary sense."

"It was not, in those times," Taruca said. "Why does a dragon wish to say how a man shall live his life? The honor of the *ayllu* was the honor of the dragon; its strength her strength; they did not govern. But then the plagues came: and men died, so now nearly all the chiefs of all the *ayllus* are dragons. And they are grown anxious, and do not like us to go anywhere; and rightly when they steal from one another."

There were people, of course: the country was not deserted. As they came northward into the more populous regions, men might be seen openly upon the roads with llama pack-trains, and dragons in a particular blue fringe flew the route. "She says they are watching the roads to make sure there is no theft," Temeraire said, when one of these had stopped them in their way and demanded that they land in a deserted valley, and show her their safe-conduct from the governor.

All three dragons were inclined to be offended by her intrusion, as she could not have weighed above two tons: to Laurence's eye she was smaller than the little courier Volly. She did not seem to care that she was dwarfed by them, however, and when she saw the men were most of them in native dress—courtesy of Magaya's gifts—she insisted on having every last one paraded before her, so she could assure herself of their indeed being all Europeans. This caused some difficulty, as they were not; and aside from the handful of Malay and Chinese sailors who made her most suspicious, several of the British men were tanned too dark and were forced to disrobe to reveal their natural color; and then Demane and Sipho and the three other black men among the crew, she suspected of being made-up in reverse fashion.

"Demane is *mine*," Kulingile said, when he felt she had looked too long. She only ruffled her feathers up and back at him in answer, still peering closely, and he reached the end of his patience. Sitting up, he spread wide his wings and threw out his chest: he had always before been remarkably even-tempered, and not often given to parading himself, but he had despite all their privations continued to grow, and when a dragon of nearly thirty tons chose, he could no more be ignored than an avalanche. The patrol-dragon gave a hop sideways, startled into looking up at him, and he threw up his head and roared.

Kulingile's voice had remained thready and piping, but his roar shared no such qualities. It did not have the same eerie and particular resonance as the divine wind, but the noise was shocking nonetheless, sourced in so vast a pair of lungs, and at such a near distance. Involuntarily many of the men covered their ears, and when Kulingile leaned forward, the patrol-dragon skipped prudently back still farther, made some hasty remarks about being satisfied, and scurried into the air.

"You did not need to make quite such a fuss," Temeraire protested, his ruff flattened backwards. "She might have been more polite, of course, but she was very small: it is not as though she were really any threat."

"She was not so small she is not bigger than Demane," Kulingile said, which was inarguable, "and those dragons are quick, too; what if she had snatched him up, and I could not have caught her? Anyway," he added, with a worrying rumble, "I am done with swallowing insults."

"I hope he does not mean to be quarrelsome," Laurence said to Temeraire, troubled, that evening when they had made their camp; Kulingile had retreated from all their company and was brooding over three slaughtered llamas. "He has never before behaved so—"

"I expect he is still distressed," Temeraire said. "I will confess, Laurence, I am not wholly easy in my own mind, either, where the sailors are concerned. How much more dreadful it must be for Kulingile when they actually laid hands on his captain; and I must say, Demane might be kinder," he added.

Laurence considered at first whether to apply to Roland, to speak with Demane, but realized they were no longer sitting together as had been their habit: she was putting Gerry, and Baggy with him, to mathematics, the first time Laurence could recall her ever showing the least unforced engagement upon any sort of schoolwork. The torn skin of her injury had mended as well as might have been expected, and she had only a tracery of thin lines crossing her cheek and a crook in her nose to show for it now, which she disdained to conceal: instead she had plaited her hair still more severely back.

Demane meanwhile sat a little distance away from her, just past the limits of intrusion, and watched her broodingly; he broke only now and again to pass a suspicious gaze over the sailors, particularly Baggy, who came in for his coldest looks. Roland steadfastly refused to meet Demane's gaze all the while. So Laurence could not ask her to breach a silence whose cause he could only approve, if she had taken his last advice to heart, and meant to add a proper distance, however inconvenient that might prove in this particular circumstance.

Demane's temper could not be said to have improved with her reproof, if reproof there had been. "I don't mean to be always sitting in a basket, being watched," Demane said, shortly, when Laurence spoke to him directly of Kulingile's distress, without taking his eyes away from Roland. "You do not hang back, when there is fighting, even when Granby says you ought," which was a shot that went home too well. Laurence had often been reproved for hazarding himself further than his duty might allow, as an aviator, and had never yet been able to make himself cleave to a practice which, in a Navy officer, must have instead borne the name of rank cowardice.

"There is a distinction," Laurence said, "between seeing one's duty differently, and neglecting it. To render your beast unhappy merely for the sake of demonstrating an excessive independence, with no pressing cause, can only be called the latter."

"You shall not lecture Demane," Kulingile flared, raising his head abruptly from where he lay, having overheard. "He is also a captain, and I am larger than Temeraire; you do not outrank him."

"Oh!" Temeraire said, indignantly rousing in his turn, "I call that nice, when you should not ever have grown so large if I had not carried you halfway across Australia, and shared my kanga-roos when you could not fly yourself; and anyway even if Laurence and Demane are both captains, Laurence is the senior."

"No, he isn't," Kulingile said, "for he was not a captain, when Demane harnessed me; he had been dismissed the service."

"That," Temeraire said, "was only in the nature of an inter-lude; it does not signify."

"It does, too," Kulingile said, "for Caesar told me, in Sydney, that the captains are all on a list, and one's name goes on it in order; so Demane is ahead of Laurence on it."

"And Granby is ahead of them both." Iskierka smugly flung her own fuel on the fire, and with Temeraire's ruff bristling out fiercely, the three looked likely enough to come to blows in a moment.

"Captain Laurence has been restored with seniority!" Ham-mond cried, rising from his own place by the fire to break into the looming quarrel, and added urgently when the dragons had looked over, "And if I am not mistaken, Captain, that dates from your having made post, in the Navy."

"So Laurence *is* first, and by a great margin," Temeraire said, with intense satisfaction, and Kulingile looked at once mulish and sullen: so matters had only been worsened, and over a mere trivial-ity. Laurence had not troubled himself to inquire regarding his place on the Admiralty lists: even more meaningless than his polite fiction of a reinstatement.

"Regardless," Laurence said, "Captain Demane, I do offer you my apologies; it is perfectly true that I spoke as I ought not, to a fellow captain: interference is not allowed in the Corps, and for good cause; I hope you will allow me to cry your pardon."

"Oh," Demane said, blankly: wind spilled out of his sails. "I don't—yes, sir, of course?" he finished uncertainly, and then looked at Roland, who hastily averted her own gaze. Gong Su called them to dinner then, interrupting. But when they had eaten, Demane strode over with a determinedly casual air to sit with Kulingile after all; he slept between the dragon's forelegs rather than going out with his sling to forage as had been his wont, the previous nights of their journey.

Laurence was prepared to find a handsome settlement at Lake Titicaca, from the quality and regularity of the roads and the general excellence of the construction, but his expectations were inadequate for the vista, when they at last saw the blue haze of the water: some distance from the shores, a great city was laid out before them, centered on a raised plaza dotted by immense carved figures, and surrounded by curious fields carved into rows flooded with water.

"Is that your home?" he asked Taruca, as they drew near. "There is a city of red stone—"

Taruca shook his head. "No, that is Tiwanaku; but there is no-one who lives there now," and as they flew past, Laurence saw that the broad roads were deserted, and the great temple, for so it seemed to him, stood empty; the fields were fallow and dry.

They continued to the lake: or the inland sea, Laurence might as easily have called it, stretching enormously wide and cupped by mountains, and of a piercing and almost unnatural shade of blue. There were villages scattered about on the lake islands, and the largest of these supported more than one settlement and was nearly ringed round with the cultivated terraces.

Taruca directed them towards the island's southern end, where a broad hillside cut with terraces rose up from a series of storehouses at its base, and at the summit a great courtyard where a truly immense dragon slept: longer than Kulingile even, and perhaps near him in weight, although that was difficult to tell beneath the feathery scales; she was burnt orange and violet in her markings, but the scales were faded along their length and nearly grey at the tips, and her eyes, opening as they landed before her, were filmy with age.

Four other dragons took to the air from other points around the lake directly they put down, and came winging over: all hatchlings of her get, Laurence gathered from the debate which followed between the dragons. "We are *not* here to steal anything, or anyone," Temeraire said, exasperated at last, "indeed, if anything we are here to give you someone back: here is Taruca, who asked us to bring him to you."

"Taruca was stolen eleven years and three months ago," the ancient dragon said, "and none of my hatchlings could find him; what do you mean, you are here to bring him back?"

Taruca waved an arm from Temeraire's back, and called, "I am here, *curaca;* I am here."

The dragon's enormous head swung around towards him, and she reared up her forequarters with an effort to lean forward and sniff at him. "It *is* Taruca," she said, "it is—how dare you take him? I will call the law upon you at once, if you do not give him back."

"We *are* giving him back!" Temeraire said. "That is why we are here; I have already told you so."

The exchange was prolonged for several minutes more by mistrust before at last Curicuillor both understood and believed that they truly meant to give Taruca back, and without any recompense. The final resolution was indeed only achieved when he had been helped down from Temeraire's back and guided over to her, and she had nosed him over thoroughly to make sure of him.

"Why, your nation has been unfairly maligned," she said at last, settling slowly and painfully back onto her stone bed. "You must forgive an old beast her confusion: but indeed I cannot recall a more astonishing example of generosity to mind, from all my days. Taruca returned to us, after so long, and when we had quite given up! We must celebrate, and we must do you honor: we must feast all together, and give special thanks to Inti."

"Yes!" Iskierka said, with enthusiasm, when Temeraire had translated the offer: they had flown the last three days with no sign of an untended herd, and they had been obliged to ration even the dried meat.

Though hastily assembled, the dinner was splendid indeed: a tender and pleasantly gamy sort of llama, lightly grilled, and five kinds of fish; with this masses of potatoes and of maize, roasted and salted and heaped with melted fat. Great cauldrons of soup were brought by one of the dragons, full of lumps later revealed to be frogs, nevertheless delicious; and were accompanied by the whole fried guinea pigs that so delighted Temeraire and the other dragons.

Besides the four dragons who had already swung over, three more came, each carrying a sizable clan, and two more dragons alone, evidently younger beasts.

"Yes; we have prospered," Curicuillor said, with pardonable pride as she swung her faded vision over the extent of her sprawling clan. "I have given my offspring each two families, when they had grown wise enough to have charge of an *ayllu* of their own; and if they have done particularly well, I have let them have more." She sighed and rearranged herself for more comfort, scales rasping faintly over the stone. "And I will do so again, soon. I am not one of those greedy clutching creatures; I will not need so many people to look after when I have gone to the other world."

So she said, but a certain reluctance in her tone made Laurence skeptical of her claims, and her foreleg curled in jealous protection around Taruca. He made no objection, however, but sat with beatific expression holding on his lap one of his great-grandchildren, a child too young to speak and sucking thoughtfully on a rattle, made of gold and which would likely have fetched a thousand pounds at a low estimate, despite the toothmarks.

"I am endlessly grateful to you, Captain," he said, when Laurence and Hammond had opportunity to speak with him, albeit over Curicuillor's foreleg. "I did not believe truly until I heard the voices of my children: but you have brought me home. This is my daughter, Choque-Ocllo," he reached out his hand, groping, to a matronly woman sitting beside him. "I have been telling her of your wish to see the Sapa Inca."

Choque-Ocllo nodded to them equably, and said, "I do not see why it should be impossible to arrange. It has been a long time since Atahualpa, after all, and those were plainly lawless men. Your king has sent a great *ayllu* to speak for him, and you have proven that you are men of a different character; it is only fitting that the Sapa Inca should receive you. Although it is unfortunate you have no women with you; that girl cannot have had a child yet."

Hammond looked confusion at Laurence, but bowed and said, "Madam, the rigors of so great a journey and a sea-voyage are sufficient to bar our subjecting a woman to them without cause; I hope their absence will give no offense, as I assure you no lack of confidence in our hosts is meant."

"Offense?" she said. "No, none at all; but that is not the same as letting you see the Sapa Inca. But I am sending a message with you—my son Ronpa there is weaving it already, you see—and my father will add his personal testimony; if they will not let you see the Sapa Inca directly, at least the governor of Collasuyo—that is this province—will see you, and he is high in the councils of the Sapa Inca."

The message was a peculiarly knotted cord, which Taruca called a *khipu,* from which long strands descended in colors; the young man was expertly forming the cord from a heap of yarn, and tying knots in irregular distances. When he had finished, he passed it along to Taruca himself, who despite his blindness ran his fingers over the cords, consulted once or twice as to the color of various strands, and then swiftly knotted on another sequence.

"Yes, here you can feel the words," Taruca said, putting Laurence's hand on the knots. "Some young people these days put markings on paper instead, the way you Europeans do: it is quicker, I imagine, but the old ways are best when it is information of any importance. What if it should get wet, or be torn; or chewed by insects? You could not rely upon such a thing."

"I only wish there were some way to inquire, without giving offense, what standing his daughter has to send such a message," Hammond said in an undertone to Laurence back at their own seats, irresolute as he turned over the mass of the knotted cord in his hands. "Are we carrying a note from a family matron, a noble-woman, or—" He shrugged helplessly.

"Any note of introduction must be an advantage," Laurence said, "regardless; and sir, you have only to look about you: this is no private householding, but a great estate. You may surely ask the population of the place."

When Hammond did inquire, of Choque Ocllo, several of the dragons put up their heads at once and answered before she could— evidently with slightly different numbers, which produced an argu- ment among them; while they quarreled, Choque-Ocllo said, "Some of them do not like to count children until they are old enough to walk: it distresses them too greatly to lose any. But in all the *ayllus* which have at least one chief of Curicuillor's line, there are a little more than four thousand people: that, of course, is why other drag ons will come here to steal men, sometimes; and you would be wise to keep a close watch on your own party yourselves."

"Do they come so very often?" Temeraire turned to ask Curicuillor, having overheard Laurence's conversation: it occurred to him, cast- ing an eye over his crew and the sailors, that it would be as well to organize some more systematic guard, and to know just what sort of threat they faced.

"Things are better now than they were, before the patrols were formed. But still it is not as it was when I hatched," Curicuillor said, wistful. "There was no stealing then: if a man from another's *ayllu* wished to marry one of my women, he would come, and I would send a gift back; or if one took a particular fancy to a person, one would merely try and persuade them to come and stay. Why, I found a young girl once in the mountains, with a splendid voice, in an *ayllu* only of people with no dragon at all; so I took in all her *ayllu* with her and they were so very happy to come—but she died of the spotted fever, a hundred years ago."

The dreadful decimation of the last two centuries had altered the circumstances: dragons whose entire *ayllu* died would steal others to replace them. "And of course they will particularly try for those like my Taruca," Curicuillor said, nosing at him gently, "for anyone can see he will not die, at least of the pox.

"And there are laws in place now," she continued, "against the practice; but even so some dragons will sneak about and try to steal men from very far away, so they will not be tracked down and caught: and then we cannot even find them, to challenge or to take them back."

"And the Sapa Inca will sometimes take men and move them about, if one beast has very many and another beast has lost all of hers," added Churki, one of her younger offspring, with a faintly resentful air, "and there is no refusing: otherwise we would have even more than we do."

"Ah, well," Curicuillor said, adjusting a few of her coils and resettling, "you cannot expect someone to go on if all their *ayllu* are dead, as though they were some savage beast in the wilderness; of course they will go raiding, then, if some measure is not taken."

When the splendid dinner had been cleared away, at Laurence's prompting Temeraire asked her for further direction. "Cusco is there," Curicuillor said, showing him the way upon a wonderful map laid out in a courtyard of her home, a sort of model made of gold and gemstones, showing all the surrounding countryside, "and also we will give you another safe-conduct which you should wear upon your breast: it may help to reassure the guards as you approach the city, despite your appearance."

Temeraire flattened his ruff; there was nothing in the least the matter with his appearance, in his opinion.

"And if you like," Curicuillor added thoughtfully, "when you have concluded your business there, you might come back; or for that matter not go at all, as all this business of foreign wars sounds foolish to me. It is easy to get excited over fighting, but that is not mature behavior: you ought to be ready to fight if you must, to defend your *ayllu* or to expand your territory so they may prosper, but not just to be making noise for the sake of it. Why, here you are with nearly two hundred men, all of them of an age to sire children, and only two little ones; which is no wonder when you have no women with you."

"Oh," Temeraire said doubtfully. It struck him as uncomfortably remarkable. here he was across a great ocean from China, and yet this dragon who was plainly very old and wise—even if one occasionally had to repeat things several times over before she would believe them—was of nearly the same opinion regarding fighting as his own mother, Qian. He had almost convinced himself that in this one respect, perhaps the Chinese practice might be considered inferior to the West; but to have it echoed so forcefully and independently here on the other side of the world undermined his conclusion.

"We do not miss having women about," he said, "that is, wives, which is what I suppose you mean; I should be perfectly happy to have more women like Roland about. But I have not thought of Laurence marrying." He did not see why it should be at all desirable.

"How are there to be children, otherwise?" Curicuillor said, in a faintly exasperated tone. "I hope you do not set your heart only on one person. What if he should die with no children at all, because you are wanting all his attention: then you will be quite alone and it will serve you right, for not planning."

Temeraire did not see why Laurence should die, at all, but he was uneasily aware that men did do so, quite often; he thought of Riley and was silent.

"Well, you are all very young," Curicuillor said with a sigh. "I do not know what things can be like in your country, when hatchlings your age have already an *ayllu* of their own. You *are* of an age to be fighting, but so you should be with the army, and not responsible for others; it is no wonder to me that we hear such strange reports of your men."

Heaving herself up, she padded down to the edge of the water. When Temeraire came up beside her, she shook her head out towards the far side of the lake, where a handsome clear white beach stood out from the trees. "I have meant to have Churki begin there with her *ayllu,* when a few more children are born," she said, "for then we should command this part of the lake on all sides, and it would take a very brazen thief to make an attempt at us then. But there is no need to wait. Why do you not think better of this war of yours? You and your friends might stay: I will exchange with you, so you will have enough young women to start some proper families, and we will have new blood, so it will be good for all of us."

"They do seem to arrange things better, here," Kulingile said wistfully. They were sitting on the beach watching: one of the younger dragons was digging out a new terrace into the hillside with a party of a dozen young men and women, who were spreading out gravel of many shapes and dirt in layers to fill the space as he carried over loads of each. When the dragon had finished depositing the final layer, he settled to earth and a couple of the young women who had been sitting on the side climbed onto his back with a basket of large silver hoops, which they had been polishing all the morning, and put these back into place along his wings.

"I had much rather have Granby than a dozen other people, even if they were splendid about polishing jewels," Iskierka said, "but they do seem to have heaps of treasure here; and I should not mind for Granby to have children."

Temeraire did not say so, but he felt quite strongly that he *would* mind, if Laurence were to be very occupied with them.

"We shan't stay here, of course," Iskierka continued. "That would be great nonsense when there is a whole war going on in Europe, which we can go back to; but we might as well trade her some of the sailors for women. *That* seems to me very sensible: I do not see why we haven't more women in our crews to begin with."

"Well, I do not, either; Roland is particularly clever, and can be trusted with anything, even jewels," Temeraire said. "But it is the sailors' duty to remain with us and help to fight the war; and we may not trade them because they are not our property."

"I don't see why not," Iskierka said, "if they want to stay; which they do, because I heard Granby telling Laurence that it would be a job to keep from losing half the men to desertion with women making calf-eyes at them, and silver cups on the dinner table."

"But in that case the women very likely should not like to *come*," Temeraire said. "In any case, I do not think Curicuillor should like us to carry them away, either. It is not much to say, she will trade them to us if we stay here, where she can see them anytime she likes: that is not really like giving them away."

"Oh, well," Iskierka said, giving up the scheme easily. "I suppose I will wait until we are home: then I will find some young women for my crew, and to have children for Granby."

"You would not like to be always having children, would you, Laurence?" Temeraire asked that evening.

"I beg your pardon?" Laurence said, and when Temeraire had explained Iskierka's plan was quick to assure him that he had no such desire. "I would hope," he added, "that she means to consult John's wishes before proceeding with this design; if there were any grounds for such hope."

The men began to make ready to depart, the next morning, and

Temeraire flew from their encampment in search of Curicuillor to make their farewells: she was back in her courtyard half-asleep, with a group of women around her weaving industriously: beautiful cloth in bright red and yellow, which Temeraire could not help but look over with an appreciative eye: not silk, but it looked nearly as fine.

"It was too much to expect that you should have so much sense, at your age," Curicuillor said regretfully, when Temeraire explained they did not mean to stay. "But still, you have been very kind, and behaved much better than I would have expected when you are so young and from an uncivilized country. I will send Churki with you, to introduce you at the court.

"And Choque-Ocllo has given you a *khipu,* although even so I cannot say if they will let your men see the Sapa Inca," she added. "Men and women have such short memories: but *we* have not forgotten the dreadful way Atahualpa was murdered. My own mother was alive at the time: three roomfuls of gold and silver were delivered in ransom for him, yet even so those evil men pulled him out into the great courtyard of Cajamarca and put a cord around his neck, and before anyone understood what was happening, he was strangled. Pahuac was watching all along. He threw himself off the mountains with his wings closed, afterwards, for letting it happen; after he had killed them all, of course."

Temeraire hunched his shoulders up in horror. He had seen a hanging once, at the Channel: the traitor Choiseul, who had nearly abducted Captain Harcourt and passed secrets to Napoleon; and it had been carried out in front of his beast Praecursoris, also. But at least he had done something to invite his fate: they had not given heaps of treasure, and then been murdered out of hand.

"I do not see how Pahuac could have expected any such thing to happen: no-one could," he said. "Those men must have been quite mad: certainly Laurence would never do anything of the sort."

"Yes, but it is not every dragon who has the responsibility of protecting the Sapa Inca," Curicuillor said. "Pahuac ought to have considered their being mad, and intervened sooner: but he was too afraid. That was not long after the pestilences first came, and so many were dead; he was ready to give over everything only to protect Atahualpa.

"To be fair," she added, "those men had no dragons with them, so plainly even in your own country they were not worthy of being taken into any dragon's *ayllu*: low peasants, or even thieves or murderers, I suppose."

"Well, most men in Europe are not in any dragon's keeping," Temeraire said. "They are afraid of us; and also there are too many of them, and not enough of us, I think. In Britain there are ten million people, Laurence says: there was a census, in the year one."

She had been lying at her ease, until then, her eyes half-lidded and drowsy even while she spoke; but at this she raised up her head quite wide-awake; and even the women hard at work interrupted their own conversations to stare. "*Ten million men,*" Curicuillor repeated. "Ten million? Is Britain a very large country?" When they had worked out the relative sizes as best they could from Temeraire's memory, she sat back on her haunches. "Ten million, and in so small a place: there are scarcely three million in all Pusantinsuyo, these days."

She bent her head low and was silent for several moments, desolately; her plumage flattened to her neck. Then she said to Temeraire, "You may tell them that, when you have come to Cusco: I am sure it will make them more likely to let you speak with the Sapa Inca. Ten million men! If only we had so many!"

Laurence could not be sorry to leave again, despite the unquestioned generosity of Curicuillor's hospitality; he could not think her influence on Temeraire and the other dragons an unqualified good, in further encouraging them to embrace the local mode of thinking; and apart from this consideration a stay of any duration would surely have resulted in the rapid diminishment of their force. During the night three men had tried to creep away, and when the dragons were at last loaded for departure, Laurence was forced to ignore that another two had managed to desert despite all of Forthing's best efforts, or there would have been no departure: in the time spent finding them, others would have run.

"Laurence," Temeraire said frowning, when they put down for water a few hours later, "there is something wrong: we are short two men."

So Temeraire had noticed two missing, out of nearly two hundred, when he had never before been so particular about passengers; there had of course been his favorites, among his crew, but until very lately he had rather disdained the sailors than valued them.

"Well, I do not *much* mind," Temeraire said, when Laurence had persuaded him that they could not return and hunt for the deserters, "as they are not properly my crew, and I suppose we should have to give them up anyway when we come back to Britain." He made this a question, and looked at Laurence; when Laurence had affirmed it, he sighed. "Do you think, Laurence, we shall receive a full crew again, when we have got back? It would be nice to be properly scrubbed, as a regular matter; and to have my harness better arranged, and looked-after."

He was reconciled to the loss further when he considered that Curicuillor had provided them with an abundance of supply, and even made him a present of a pair of silver hoops, which Laurence with difficulty dissuaded him from having pierced through his wing-edges. "They would likely catch, in battle," Laurence said.

"I am sure I could avoid that," Temeraire said, "but it is quite true that only one pair would not be very impressive. When we should take a prize next, perhaps we may get a few dozen, and then it will be something like."

"Something like a Covent Garden dancer," Laurence said to Granby, with a sigh.

"You shan't complain to *me*," Granby said, with some justice.

The spring was cold and delicious, and they flew the rest of that day over a rolling grassland peopled with roving herds of wild vi- cuña and a handful of villages: Churki led them on, and the patrol- dragons made no attempt to check them. She had the same orange-and-violet plumage as her mother, and if not quite as large, still more than a respectable match for any Regal Copper: a beast of some twenty years' age, she had informed Hammond. "I was with the army, until last year," she said, with her gaze fixed on him in what could only be called an unsettling way, "and I won many honors: then I came home to learn good management from my mother before she goes to the other world. I am ready for an *ayllu* of my own, now. Very soon I shall begin my establishment."

She paused and then added, "Do I understand correctly that you are not properly of Temeraire's *ayllu*, yourself? And not Iski- erka or Kulingile's, either?"

"I must be flattered," Hammond said to Laurence, "but I hope it may not be considered neglect of any possible service to our country that I do not pursue the offer; I doubt very much she would be willing to come back with me, if I did."

"I might put it to her," Temeraire offered. "Curicuillor was very impressed that we should have so many people in Britain, so perhaps Churki would consider it after all."

"Oh, ah," Hammond said, in some alarm: he had still a faintly green cast from the day's flying, and no desire whatsoever to belong to a dragon.

The next day at morning, Churki suggested he should accom- pany her, flying; and when he feebly demurred she nosed at a tall stand of green-leaved shrub and said, "Brew those leaves fresh, in- stead of those strange dried ones you carry with you, and you will feel better; or take a handful and chew them."

"I trust she would know if it would poison me," Hammond said doubtfully, and carried a sample to Gong Su for his opinion; Gong Su nibbled and spat and shrugged.

"It is always safer to boil, first," he said, and when brewed the tea had a peculiar but not unpleasant flavor; by the end of the day Hammond had drunk seven cups, and would certainly have been dead if it had possessed even the most mildly toxic character.

"It is quite miraculous," he said that night. "Do you know, Captain, I have not been ill even once all the day: I feel myself as I have not since we left New South Wales, and I have been shipboard or dragon-back every day. I feel wonderfully clear-headed, indeed; I am willing to declare that it outstrips tea in flavor and in healthful effect, both."

Their flight the next day brought them to a deep river valley that Churki called Urubamba, and from there they followed the river upstream through deep gorges. They were descending now, the highest mountains behind them, and more roads and villages scattered beneath their passage, until coming around a narrow pass within the river gorge they saw an immense bridge of rope, stretched from one peak to another.

It was heavily laden: three horsemen leading their beasts, and a train of some dozen llamas behind them, and a large party of men walking—or rather clinging to the sides. The bridge was swaying not only with ordinary use, but towards its destruction: the thick ropes were fraying, and even as they approached a piece of matting fell away towards the river, decomposing into its component sticks.

The horses were blindfold, to be led across more calmly, but they were already uneasy with danger; as they scented the dragons on the wind, they went mad with terror and began to rear and struggle against all handling. If there had earlier been any hope of the party's clearing the span before all the structure came down, there was none now, and scarce moments to disaster.

Temeraire dived at once; the men on the bridge pointed at him and cried out, shouting, but he passed them and hovering bore up underneath the main portion of the bridge as best he could. "A little farther to port," Laurence called to him, already unfastening his own harness-straps, "and if you will shift backwards, the weight will lie across your hindquarters. Roland, light along that spare harness, from below; we must get those horses hobbled before they fling themselves over."

He pulled himself up onto the bridge ahead of the party, Forthing and Ferris scarcely a step behind, and they together managed to calm the lead horse, if *calm* were the word for it; they had nearly to bind it into immobility and bodily drag it, and as they hauled the snorting and terrified creature its saddle-girth burst. Saddle, blankets, harness, all fell away and jouncing off Temeraire's hip-bone tumbled down the gorge and were flung from side to side in their descent, the stirrups clanging, until at last they vanished into the cataracts below.

Even with Temeraire supporting nearly all its length, the bridge felt alarmingly fragile: a motion not unlike the crow's nest on a windy day, save it had not the solidity of aged oak underfoot and thrice-laid hawsers in arm's reach. Laurence managed to draw the plunging horse along its length—a stallion, he noted with some irritation, and no wonder the beast could scarcely be managed—with Ferris lashing its hindquarters unmercifully, until at last it was got up onto the far bank and he left Forthing to secure it to a nearby tree.

He climbed cautiously back out upon the leaping bridge, and offered a hand to the man lying prostrate and clinging to the matting, white-faced; what use, if the bridge were to fall apart around him, Laurence did not see. "Get along, there," he said, pushing him along the length, and turned to the second horse: but the poor animal's frenzy had overcome it. In its mad kicking, it had put one leg clear through the matting, tearing its own flesh against the sticks, and even a glance showed there was no hope: blood pouring freely, and bone showing white from fetlock to hock.

The man at its bridle had seen as much; he drew a pistol from his waist and threw Laurence a swift unhappy look, found no reprieve in Laurence's nod, and clapping the gun to the animal's head put a period to its misery. "Temeraire," Laurence called up, "can you take this carcass off?"

"Not very easily, I am afraid," Temeraire said, craning his head about, "but I had a llama this morning: Kulingile, would you care for it?" he called: the other dragons had withdrawn to the far side of the gorge, and perched themselves where they could upon the bare stone.

"*Arrêtez, arrêtez!*" the handler said, pointing to the fallen animal's belly, which Laurence only then saw was grossly distended with pregnancy; as they watched a tiny hoof might be seen pushing out from within as if in protest.

"What the devil does he want to do, cut it out in mid-air while we are all hanging fire?" Ferris said: he had clambered back out to Laurence's side, and the bridge yet undulated beneath them like a blowing veil.

Kulingile came off the wall of the gorge and sweeping low took the dead horse off in one massive talon, and laid it in the same pass upon the far side; Demane slid down his shoulder and was by the side of the carcass in a moment, knife out, to slice open the belly. The handler looked long enough to see that Demane knew his work, then turned back to the last of the horses; with his assistance and that of the third horseman, they had the beasts off at last, and in the meantime the llama-train and their handlers had retreated to the other side of the gorge.

The little foal had been extracted from the body of its dam and was tottering feebly on stick legs; the handler had wiped it gently clean. "What does he mean to feed it?" Demane said, frowning, but the third animal, another mare, was not much less forward in pregnancy as well. Though she seemed justly perplexed to be applied to by a foal before having given birth, she did not make great objection, and shortly the small animal was suckling energetically enough to give hope of its survival.

"*Mille fois merci,*" the handler of the horses said, coming away

from the nursing foal to seize and shake Laurence's hand vigorously.

"*De rien,*" Laurence said, bowing politely, and then belatedly
realized they were speaking French: and also that his hand was
now all over blood. The horseman noticed as much in the same
moment, and in some embarrassment left off his clasp.

"Do you mean to tell me," Granby said, when Iskierka had
landed—they were encamping for the night only a little way off
from the men they had rescued—"that we have just been risking
our necks to save a French baggage-train?"

"Yes," Laurence said. "They are on their way to Cusco overland, following De Guignes: he and his embassy are certainly there
already."

"And a baggage-train of gifts, I have no doubt," Hammond
said, "meant for the Sapa Inca: those horses are breeding stock."
He spoke half-reproachfully, as though he blamed Laurence for
having rescued the Frenchmen and their goods. "And here we look
little more than beggars."

"As we have none to give, sir," Laurence said, "let us hope instead that the ruler of a mighty nation will not be so easily swayed
by trinkets and gifts."

"Let us hope that without them, we will be admitted into his
presence at all," Hammond said.

Chapter 11

CUSCO STOOD IN THE BOWL of a mountaintop, cupped round by jagged short peaks, green and mossy, and overlaid with a veil of clouds. The city from aloft had a curious and peculiarly deliberate shape: a lion in profile, its head an immense fortress of carven stones built upon a hill, and the city its great body, lying alongside the banks of a river and formed of many large houses of fine construction, many with deeply sloping roofs thrust high into the air, of thickly layered thatch. The buildings were established in groups around courtyards: in several of these dragons lay sleeping, in others sitting alert and watchful, all of them in an array of brilliant plumage and adorned in gold and silver, so a faint chiming might be heard even from aloft.

So far as Laurence could see, there were no hovels, not even smaller houses, and no sign of any market within the proper bounds of the city: these practicalities seemed to be constrained to villages that huddled around the city walls in clusters, along short and well-used roads.

Several dragons in the ensign of the patrol came winging to meet them, long before they had reached those walls: the patrol-beasts flew in rings around them peering at Temeraire's safe-conduct, and exchanging a yammering conversation with Churki. They were at last escorted—whether as guests or prisoners was difficult to ascertain—towards an immense raised plaza, directly to the north of the river, plainly of ceremonial function and which would have admitted even a small army of dragons.

"We are to stay in the *kallanka* there to the side," Churki informed Hammond, indicating a great covered hall alongside the plaza. "The other foreigners, they say, are on the other side—"

"The other foreigners?" Hammond said. "De Guignes is here, then?"

And as they landed, across the plaza Laurence could see Genevieve asleep beneath another covered hall, the Fleur-de-Nuit's immense lamp-eyes lidded down to pale slits.

The patrol-dragons settled down around them as they landed, with an air of intending to remain; Churki held still more discussion with them, and at one moment turned and hissed something aside to Hammond, who started and then said to Laurence, "Pray, Captain, shall we let the men down? Churki is of the opinion that— that it cannot but convey our peaceful intentions, when they have seen us disembark—"

From his awkward looks, Laurence doubted whether Churki's exact meaning had been translated, but Temeraire was distracted at the moment by low argument with Iskierka on the subject of the ornamentation of an immense temple visible a little to the southeast: "Laurence," he said, swinging his head around, "do you think that can really be gold, there on the *outside* of that building? Surely no-one would put gold out where it might be rained upon, and dirtied."

"You had better apply to Churki, for an answer which might have some authority behind it; it may be gold leaf only," Laurence said, doubtful himself: certainly the frieze looked golden, but it seemed implausible. "Mr. Fer— Mr. Forthing, I think we will let down the men, if you please."

The disembarkation of nearly two hundred men certainly had an effect: as the belly-netting was let down and the sailors gratefully spread out to stretch their legs, and set up a clamoring for beer, the patrol-dragons stretched out their necks to peer at them with interest and low murmurs of appreciation and, Laurence thought, perhaps of envy. In any case, they looked on Temeraire and Iskierka and Kulingile with a less suspicious eye.

"Yes," Churki said, "now they begin to believe me, when I tell them you brought back one of my mother's own stolen ones: they thought I must be mistaken somehow. And of course they are very impressed; you see, there is no reason for you to be distressed that the French are bringing horses and jewels; what is that, to what you have brought?"

Temeraire added to his translation, "I have no notion what she can mean; surely she sees we are quite destitute," and asked her.

Churki shook her wings out, with a great jingling noise. "Why, all these men, of course."

"Mr. Forthing," Laurence said, as they began to lay out pallets and rig a few rough tents for more shelter against the cool mountain air, "you will post a watch of trusted men, and let there always be an officer on duty with them, if you please." A guard which he meant for protection in all directions: Laurence was unpleasantly certain that Hammond would not have scrupled to exchange even two hundred men for any advantage he might gain thereby over the French, in establishing diplomatic relations with the Inca.

The letter, or *khipu,* had gone to the authorities; Churki also left them, to convey her assurances to a more significant representative. But the day wore away around them without an answer, and meanwhile across the plaza they saw the great French Grand Chevalier Piccolo make a landing accompanied by several Incan dragons who bore many slaughtered llamas in their talons, to share out as a repast with Genevieve.

"I would not mind a llama," Kulingile said, watching intently. "Mayn't we go hunting? It is getting late."

But Hammond would not have any of them leave, before some authorization came; he was not without justice anxious should any of the dragons, flying alone, provoke a local beast to challenge their presence in the heart of the empire. He was still more adamant when Churki at last returned, to inform them that their messages had gone home, and some representative of the court would shortly come and see them: "We cannot fail to meet them in whatever state we can manage," he said, and would have the dragons line themselves up, and arrange the men in ranks around them, dispersed in such a way as to suggest their numbers were even greater than they were.

"You might put on your robes now, Laurence," Temeraire suggested, egged on by Hammond's enthusiasm; Laurence could only with difficulty divert him to the task of assuring his own appearance: the talon-sheaths were brought out, and the breastplate polished, and under Roland's guidance a party of the sailors were formed into a line to carry water from the great fountain at the center of the courtyard to the dragons, and pour it over their backs.

"For I cannot but agree with Mr. Hammond that we must present a respectable appearance, if we can," Temeraire said defensively, when he had roared in a small way at a few of the sailors who had unwarily expressed objections to being put to this labor, "and I am sorry to say it, but for that we can only rely on Kulingile and Iskierka and myself; there is no denying we have a very strange look, as a party, with all that Curicuillor was kind enough to do for us in the article of clothing. You would not wish us to give this Incan nobleman a disgust of us, Laurence, surely; and are you certain you would not consider—"

Fortunately, before Temeraire could renew his efforts to push Laurence into the robes, Churki said, "There: he comes now, and look, it is a lord of the Sapa Inca's own *ayllu,* himself; did I not promise, Hammond?"

Temeraire sat up sharply, arranging his wings against his back, looking around the empty courtyard as vainly as the rest of them; then he looked aloft and said, "Oh: not him again?" and drooped his wings, as Maila Yupanqui descended into the square before them.

"I do not see why you insist on being so unfriendly," Iskierka said, and made rather a spectacle of herself in Temeraire's opinion nodding to Maila, who simpered back at her even while he answered Hammond's shouted inquiries.

"There is certainly some official who might meet with you, if you wish. Perhaps the political officer for Antisuyo: you wish to travel through the jungle, do you not, to this country of Brazil?"

"Yes—yes, of course," Hammond said, darting a cautious glance at Laurence, "but naturally as I am here, as representative of His Majesty's Government it is incumbent upon me—it would be inexcusable—not to make my bows to the Sapa Inca: to convey His Majesty's affections and to bring greetings from the ruler of one great nation to another; and information regarding the present circumstances of the war in Europe—"

"Well, you are a man," Maila said dismissively. "It is not yet clear to me such a meeting must be necessary. But," he turned to Iskierka, "there is no reason *you* might not visit the court, and be presented: the Sapa Inca has heard of your victory in the arena of Talcahuano, and is most eager to see you: the great Manca Copacati has not been defeated in battle in twenty-three years, and all would know how it was done."

Temeraire flattened his ruff in indignation: as though he would not have defeated the Copacati himself, without any difficulty; and as though he were not the senior dragon of their party—

"Of course I will come," Iskierka said, preening in the most absurdly self-satisfied manner, "and meet the Sapa Inca, and I would be happy to explain how I won: it was a great battle, of course, and he was a very dangerous enemy, but that is nothing to *me*. Will we go at once?"

"But—" Hammond said, "but—"

"There is no reason to wait," Maila said. "The court is meeting now: the Sapa Inca will be glad to see you, if you can come."

"What are you doing?" Temeraire demanded. "Mr. Hammond, you surely cannot allow her to go and speak for England—"

"Whyever not!" Iskierka said. "If the Sapa Inca does not want to see you, most likely because you want to speak of tiresome things like trade, and politics, and everything dull, why should I not go instead; unless you mean for us all to sit here and watch the French go back and forth to the court."

This argument, Temeraire was distressed to see, struck Hammond very forcefully: he said to Iskierka, "You must understand that you must in no wise represent yourself as speaking for His Majesty's Government, without approving even your particular turns of phrase with me: and your first objective must of course in all things be to persuade the Sapa Inca to see me, as His Majesty's representative—"

"Yes, yes," Iskierka said, with a flip of her tail. "Pray lead on," she added to Maila, who inclined his head and leapt aloft, while Temeraire stared after them in astonished betrayal that all the order of the world had so upended itself.

"She will not persuade the Sapa Inca to do any such thing," he said stormily to Hammond, "she will not even try; she will only come back and lord it over us that she has been to the court and we have not: you must see that is perfectly clear. Oh! To send Iskierka on a diplomatic mission—one would think you had never met her, nor spent ten minutes in her company; I dare say she will lose her temper, and start a fresh war for us."

"You speak as though I had made a deliberate choice," Hammond answered, with some heat, "when I should be inexpressibly delighted to have any other avenue of communication available—any other intermediary but a dragon as ungovernable in temper as she is unconcerned with the good opinion of anyone; and the instant such should offer, I will seize upon it at once with the greatest satisfaction; on that you may rely."

*   *   *

Granby was if anything less consolable than Temeraire. "Laurence," he said, "if that lunatic beast of mine should go into a fit and insult the Emperor, or set fire to the palace—"

Laurence would have liked to reassure him with more honesty than platitudes; but he could not but share the liveliest alarm at any mission which should rest upon hopes of Iskierka's good conduct. "You may comfort yourself," he said at last, "that she comes to the court with a reputation which must inhibit any offhand insult from being given, having defeated a champion of so much note."

"Unless some other beast takes it into his head to challenge her," Granby said, "from revenge or ambition. Put someone on watch, would you? I will be on fire with anxiety until she comes back; and if anyone else comes near, let me know and I will go and hide until we know she hasn't started a war."

Kulingile only was content. Maila had granted them the liberty of the local herds, Demane had gone with Kulingile hunting, and they had brought back nine llamas, which already were roasting on spits under Gong Su's supervision: there were extensive roasting-pits behind the hall, evidently intended for the purpose of feeding assembled crowds, and a great supply of llama dung for fuel. Laurence only hoped this profligate hunting would not invite reproach; but when Shipley called, "Captain, there are some fellows there, and I think they must be coming to us," and they espied a small party of men approaching their encampment from across the plaza, Laurence felt they had entirely too many just causes to fear.

But when the men drew near enough to be recognized, De Guignes was in the lead, escorting on his arm Mrs. Pemberton, and he brought her to their camp with a smile at once polite and peculiarly forced, for all his usually impeccable courtesy. "I am delighted to see you all so well!" he said. "I will not pretend," he bowed, "that I am not surprised: but I am filled with admiration for your ingenuity. You must tell me how it was managed, when there is leisure; and I trust that your sojourn was not so uncomfortable as to create any lasting spirit of resentment between us."

Hammond's expression conveyed without words that the spirit of resentment was alive and well; Laurence answered more politely for their party, and added, "And I am indebted to you, sir, for having given Mrs. Pemberton your protection: indeed, madam, I would ask on your behalf if he would extend that protection a little further, as we are not—"

"But of course—"

"Captain, if I might—"

"No, I thank you," Mrs. Pemberton said very decisively, cutting short Laurence's question and De Guignes's immediate response, and Hammond's own interjection as well. "I have felt my own lapse of duty most keenly, gentlemen; and while I hope Miss Roland will pardon my having deserted her so long—" Miss Roland's expression made it abundantly clear she would more easily pardon the desertion than the reverse. "—I cannot allow it to continue.

"Thank you, M. De Guignes, for your generous hospitality, and pray give my thanks again to Mme. Récamier for her kindness, and the gift of the dress," she added, holding him out her hand, marshaling somehow in the midst of an open plaza and surrounded on all sides by ragged soldiers all the authority of a chaperone thirty years older delivering a set-down in the midst of St. James.

De Guignes took his dismissal in reluctant part, outdone only by Emily Roland's visibly truculent looks; but when he and his men had made a few more polite remarks, they at last retreated to their own distant encampment on the other side of the square, leaving Mrs. Pemberton to stand in place, incongruous in her neat gown and gloves and calm looks, until Laurence had arranged her a seat contrived from a coil of the belly-netting, with several of the local capelets thrown over it for upholstery.

De Guignes had brought her to Cusco with his party. "And regrets it now extremely, I should say," she said, when she had seated herself. "He was not in the least enthusiastic about permitting me to rejoin you, and I believe if I had not witnessed your arrival directly with my own eyes, he would have been as glad to keep the intelligence from me as long as he might."

"I should be sorry to imagine M. De Guignes would ever behave so little like a gentleman," Laurence said, startled by her condemnation of one who, it seemed to him, had only intended to assure her comfort.

"Oh, I do not say a word against him, Captain, I assure you," Mrs. Pemberton said. "He *has* let me go, after all, and one cannot really blame him for regret in the present circumstances; he scarcely can rely on my discretion."

"Certainly not," Hammond said with enthusiasm, "of course not; how should he expect that a subject of the King should keep his confidences, in any matter that concerned her own nation; madam, pray tell me: have the French been admitted to the presence of the Sapa Inca, themselves, or only their beasts?"

"Not all their party," Mrs. Pemberton said, "but yes: they are at court every day—"

"Every day!" Hammond cried, dismayed. "Good Heavens: we must find a way to persuade them to let us in; Captain Granby, you must exert all your powers over Iskierka—you must convince her to promote an invitation—"

"Sir," Mrs. Pemberton said, "I have been invited to come again tomorrow, myself; I would of course be happy to—"

"What? You have met him?" Hammond said. "How was it arranged, were—"

"Her, Mr. Hammond," Mrs. Pemberton said.

"I beg your pardon?" Hammond said.

"The Sapa Inca is a woman," Mrs. Pemberton said.

The Empress, Mrs. Pemberton was able to explain to them, was the widow of the previous lord, and the daughter of the one before him. "So far as I can tell," she said, "he died of the pox. As she herself had by then already survived the illness, while he kept his sickbed she took on the role of intermediary and spoke for him to the court; and he seems to have taken an unconscionable deal of time dying. They have a most peculiar custom of preserving the dead here, instead of a proper burial, but I gather *his* remains are not fit to be seen, and have been sequestered away instead under a shroud."

"Properly gruesome," Granby said. "And when she couldn't prop him up in a corner any longer?"

"By then, I gather," Mrs. Pemberton said, "she had persuaded the chief dragons of the court that a woman was better suited to the role of empress: where it would be the duty of a man to go forth and lead the army, she might remain at home under their protection. The argument has carried a great deal of weight with them."

Laurence asked, "Ma'am, how certain are you of this intelligence?"

"Perfectly certain," she said. "I have had most of it from the Empress herself, or her handmaidens: she speaks French already, and has asked me to tutor her in English."

The Frenchwomen whom they had seen aboard the *Triomphe,* it transpired, were here for no lesser purpose than to carry on negotiations with the Inca on De Guignes's behalf. "And if possible to persuade her to see him, but so far they have in this respect been unsuccessful. I have been made a member of their party, and welcome to join them in their regular attendance at court, but I have not," Mrs. Pemberton said, "been privy to all their conversations with the Sapa Inca: and the ladies are far too shrewd to allow their intentions to slip in mere gossiping. You can imagine better than I, sir, what terms they are likely to have offered and to seek."

"An exchange," Hammond said thoughtfully. "I should not be in the least surprised if they proposed an exchange—of people, I mean, for dragons; I am quite sure Napoleon would be delighted to receive a number of beasts in France at the price, I suppose, of the population of his prisons. But I am sure he would also settle for a mere vague agreement of friendship—a truce of sorts—*he* does not require an ally on this continent, when he is already delivering the Tswana here by the boatload.

"Perhaps they are here only to prevent our acquiring one—? Only," he paused, and gnawed absently upon his thumb a moment, "only, would De Guignes come on so incidental a mission? And bind himself to a dragon for its sake? No—! Blast."

He muttered to himself in this vein for several moments more; Mrs. Pemberton listened until he ran down again and had turned away from her to his teapot, for a fresh cup of the coca tea; then she said calmly, "I will see what I can find out in more earnest, sir; and present Miss Roland to Her Majesty tomorrow morning, with your permission."

The steaming cup in his hand momentarily forgotten, Hammond looked up doubtfully at her and then at Emily Roland, who stared equally doubtful back.

"We cannot suffer by having another pair of eyes and ears admitted to the Sapa Inca's presence," Mrs. Pemberton pointed out. "Miss Roland and myself will extend whatever offers you might wish to Her Majesty, Mr. Hammond; and I am sure we should be glad to do our very best to accomplish whatever you would like."

"What I would like," Hammond said to Laurence several days later, nearly pulling upon his hair: all efforts at obtaining his admission to the Empress's presence had failed, "what I would like, would be the liberty of carrying on my own negotiations, without recourse to intermediaries: untrained intermediaries! A violently quarrelsome dragon, a governess, and a fifteen-year-old girl! And I must credential them—I hope no-one in England may hear of it."

"You may at least comfort yourself that the French can be only a little better prepared than are we, for the circumstances of such a negotiation," Laurence said.

"Can they not?" Hammond said. "*They* at least have known what to expect—they have surely been sending spies over here through Brazil these last two years. We already know that Mme. Récamier is here on their part; I thought she loathed Bonaparte, but I suppose she loves an opportunity of intrigue on such a scale enough to compensate. And at least De Guignes's beast has not taken it into her head to form a distaste for the foremost Incan dragon."

Laurence could not dispute the justice of this last complaint: Temeraire and Maila Yupanqui were only just short of daggers-drawn with one another. There would have been every cause to despair of progress, indeed, if Maila were not more than ready to be pleased by the rest of them, most notably Iskierka, to whom he applied regularly for private conversation, on the excuse of continuing his efforts to acquire English.

"I am sure I do not see any reason why Iskierka must put up with being annoyed," Temeraire said.

"*I* am sure I cannot name a single other advantage we have to hand," Hammond said, "so you will oblige me by not interfering."

So Temeraire remained resentful, and grew only more so when Iskierka landed shortly thereafter and announced, "I have been out flying with Maila: he has shown me a mine where they take gold directly out of the ground; cartloads of it; and he tells me they could take still more than they do, but they do not have so many hands as they need for the work, as it is only men who can do it properly."

"Laurence, do you suppose there might be a mine of that sort in England?" Temeraire asked him in low tones, shortly after his scornful dismissal of Iskierka's report had provoked them to a quarrel which left them sitting at opposite ends of the hall. "Or perhaps in our valley, in New South Wales?"

"I cannot think it at all likely," Laurence said. "Gold mines are not a common occurrence; from what we saw on our journey across the Australian continent I should think the country might more likely have opal mines."

"Oh!" Temeraire said. "Like those stones which they sewed to your robes? That would do splendidly; I would rather have opals than a like quantity of gold. Laurence, *will* you not wear your robes, perhaps to walk across the plaza, where you might be seen?"

Laurence only with difficulty made demur, on the grounds of the occasion lacking sufficient importance, but that afternoon Iskierka landed and announced triumphantly, "Well, I have arranged it all, as perfectly as any of you might possibly have wished: the Inca will see you, Granby!—oh, and you and Laurence may come as well, Temeraire, if you like."

Temeraire was inclined to be indignant at this offhand invitation, but then he brightened and said to Laurence, "So you shall put the robes on, now; and I am sure the Inca will see at once that you are the senior officer of our expedition."

"Pray be certain not to move towards her uninvited," Hammond said anxiously. "Not without very plain invitation—and if possible, avoid any nearer approach at all, indeed—save, of course, if you should gather the impression such avoidance might give offense—"

"I don't see why you oughtn't go, instead of me," Granby said. "I am no hand for diplomatic affairs; and if they still have their backs up over their quarrel with those Spaniards two centuries ago, surely they would rather have an ambassador than an officer."

"Of course you must go," Iskierka said, overruling all objection. "You are my captain; naturally she would like to meet you."

"We cannot say—perhaps there is some particular favor in their society, some distinction, conferred upon military men—certainly their chief men are generals, and soldiers," Hammond said. "We cannot take the risk; certainly we have been particularly favored to receive any invitation whatsoever—Mrs. Pemberton assures me De Guignes has had none, so far as she knows, and he must be quite wild about it. Captain Laurence, you do recall—no approach unless you are very clearly beckoned—"

"Yes," Laurence said, grimly folding back the sleeves of his robes. "I recall."

Their introduction took place at a hall which faced upon another great plaza called the Cusipata: Iskierka led them on proudly and descended at nearly the far end of the long courtyard so their approach might have the best effect, in defiance of Hammond's advice. Under the roofed building, a great dais stood awaiting them: a stepped platform with a low stool set atop it, and enormous plates of gold affixed to every side all around.

Maila Yupanqui and three other great beasts were disposed about the dais in heavy coils, the burnished shine of the metal gleaming out only here and there between their bodies; they shifted in restless anxiety, and all their heads weaved in the air. Laurence might almost have called it an absurdity, to have four immense dragons watching himself and Granby with so much cold anxiety, and with not half so much attention on Iskierka and Temeraire; but the tense suggestion of waiting violence leached any quality of humor from the circumstances.

Two rows of guards stood also to either side of the dais, armed with swords and muskets—of Spanish or of Portuguese make, Laurence judged, and likely traded for at the coast, or from Brazil itself—and wearing a sort of armor made of thick wool; which might have been merely intended to add to the imperial state, but the atmosphere conveyed was not one of formality but of an armed camp, and the unfriendly looks bent upon them would have been merited more by assassins than by honored guests.

The Empress sat upon the stool on the dais: a tall and slender woman with incongruously broad shoulders, she wore a deep scarlet turban with feathers thrust into it, bound in gold, and her very long black hair hung down in plaits clasped with gold and emeralds; her garments were of wool of extraordinary fineness, splendidly woven in small patterned squares of bright colors, and ornamented with jewels. As they neared, Laurence saw she had also a scattering of pox-marks over one cheek, which had been brushed with gold dust and shone in the sunlight that spilled down from the ceiling in great shafts.

"Laurence, only look at the fountain," Temeraire whispered: a great leaping construction, the basin all of solid gold catching sunlight, so the water as it leapt seemed to have caught fire; also carved and set with gems: and to either side of them the walls themselves were sheathed in gold.

Temeraire and Iskierka seated themselves in leonine fashion, though Maila and the other Inca dragons, six in number, remained on their haunches, and there was a tension in their limbs which suggested a readiness to spring. "We shan't make a fuss about their behaving rudely," Temeraire said to Laurence, in what was likely intended to have been a whispered aside, "because they are so very nervous; but pray do not be the least worried, Laurence, for if they *should* attack us I shall certainly not allow any harm to come to you; if I had the least doubt on that subject we should not have come."

Laurence sighed: there was a firm insistence on this final point which he did not think boded well for Temeraire's complacency, in future, when duty should compel him into danger. He halted where they stood and bowed to the Inca, who looked at them with a thoughtful expression: not a particularly handsome woman, and made less so by the scarring, but her eyes were exceptionally dark, and a shrewd calculation looked out of them.

"I am Anahuarque Inca, and I welcome you to Pusantinsuyo," the Empress said, in English only lightly accented, and then changed to surprisingly excellent French to invite them to be comfortable; woven cloths, thickly padded, were brought and laid out on the floor for them to sit upon.

"At least that makes it plain enough how near to approach," Granby muttered to Laurence, very gingerly lowering himself onto one of the blankets; and then started: the Empress rose from her throne and descended to the floor of the hall, and even as her warriors and her dragons stirred uneasily, she seated herself on another woven cloth not five paces distant.

"Are you comfortable?" she asked, looking at him with an attitude of curiosity. "This is the custom of your people: to sit while you talk?"

"Oh, er," Granby said. "Well—thank you, yes, most comfortable—"

"And the conditions of your journey? The roads were in good repair, and the storehouses full?" she inquired.

Granby threw Laurence a desperate look, but she was too clearly addressing him directly. "Yes, ma'am—Your Majesty?"

He would gladly have stopped there, but Iskierka put down her head and nudged him, hissing, "Say something more, Granby: why are you being so stupid? She will think you are not clever."

"I am not in the least clever, in conversation, and less so in French!" Granby answered her with some heat, and groped about feebly for something to say. "The storehouses are remarkable, Your Majesty," he added. "We scarcely had to hunt along the way—oh, hell," he said, reverting to English and muttering to Laurence, "ought we admit to taking from them all along the route?"

"I am glad to hear it," Anahuarque said, however, without any sign of objecting to their pillaging. "The harvest has been good in the south, so I hear; I believe you have said it was so, Ninan?"

She repeated this question, directed to one of the hovering warriors, in Quechua: the gentleman in question, a tall and fiercely glaring young man, whose hand rested on the butt of a pistol thrust into a sash at his waist, started and answered her after a moment. She turned back to French and asked Granby about his satisfaction with their quarters; then discussed the weather and the approaching change of season, in each case weaving her own attendant men into the conversation.

Laurence, who had been used from childhood to hang his head from the banister overlooking his mother's political dinners, even before he had been old enough to join the table, realized in short order there was no accident in the seeming banality of the conversation, but rather a masterful degree of management. He might have blamed it on Anahuarque's being hampered by speaking as she did in a tongue other than her own, but this would have more naturally led to stammering and pauses; of which there were none.

As the conversation continued, and poor Granby bore the brunt of it, Laurence looked closer and saw the warriors around her throne were plainly not mere guards. Several of them were older men, others visibly battle-hardened; and all of them adorned both with large disks of gold embedded in their ear-lobes, and woven and fringed turbans which he began to think denoted perhaps nobility, or military rank. And the suspicious looks these men cast were not confined to Granby and to Laurence: they scowled at one another with equal fervor.

"She is playing Penelope's game, I think," Laurence said to Granby, when they had at last been dismissed the Empress's presence and landed at the hall again. "She is being pressed to take a consort, who surely would seek to assert his authority direct; and she is playing her rivals off one against another."

"And we are as good as a circus for distraction," Granby said. "She can't have had the least wish to speak to us for any other reason, when all she did was ask me about the weather in England, and I can scarcely tell you if it is summer or winter there at present. Laurence, she will keep us all here dancing attendance endlessly, along with the rest of those fellows, if only we give her a chance."

"Yes," Laurence said, and added to Hammond, who had been waiting to meet them, "but I think we can at least give you this assurance, sir: I do not think she can intend any serious alliance with France, at least not one which would engage her to commit any portion of her forces. She cannot afford to raise one of those men above the others; if she makes a great general, or allows any one of them to build repute as the foremost warrior of her realm, she at once puts herself in that man's power."

"Unless," Hammond said bitterly, "she puts into place a counterbalance," beckoning them inside the inner chamber.

"What do you mean?" Laurence said. "Have you heard something?"

This last was addressed to Emily Roland who yet wore the gown which Mrs. Pemberton insisted upon, for their visits to the women's court, so they had come straight from there: Roland would otherwise have immediately cast it off for her uniform. Mrs. Pemberton stood in the corner of the room chafing her hands over the small brazier of coals, almost wringing them in an uncharacteristic betrayal of anxiety.

"Yes, sir," Roland said. "The Empress wasn't at court this afternoon, for she was meeting you, and so none of us had anything to do but sit and watch her ladies weave; and then that French lady, Mme. Récamier, blabbed a bit to one of the others: 'Yes, poor Josephine; but not quite so poor as she was. she has got Fontainebleu, and not *him*.' "

"What?" Granby said. "What the devil does that mean?"

"It means, Captain, that Napoleon has divorced Josephine at last," Mrs. Pemberton said. "He is at liberty to wed."

Chapter 12

"IT IS NOT REASONABLE," Temeraire said to Iskierka, "that Napoleon should also try to become Emperor of the Incas; one would think he might be satisfied with France, not to mention Italy and Prussia and Spain, and all the other places which he has conquered. It is quite outrageous; and I suppose that fellow Maila has been encouraging them, or else they should never have come here with him: I hope you do not think so much of him now."

But Iskierka refused to acknowledge the very dire situation, and was only quite dismissive. "I am sure the Inca is not going to marry Napoleon; why would anyone marry Napoleon, when we are going to beat him? You do not need to worry. Although," she added, "you all *have* made a great muddle of the negotiations. It is just as well that I am here. I am sure the Inca would not have had anything to say to any of us, otherwise."

"She is quite absurdly partial, only because Maila is so very impressed that she fights so well, and can breathe fire," Temeraire said to Laurence, "which is ridiculous in itself: they have fire-breathers here also."

"Rather small creatures, from what we have seen; and with limited range, my dear," Laurence said. Temeraire sniffed; he did not see why that should alone make so great a difference.

"If she should have any intelligence to suggest the Inca will not marry Napoleon—" Hammond began. "If, perhaps, Maila might have conveyed privately—" He glanced at Laurence and added hurriedly, "Not to suggest she should violate a *true* confidence, but any suggestion—any cause to believe—she would need only hint—"

"I am quite certain she has no such thing," Temeraire said, and stalked away to the courtyard and went aloft to go and take a couple of vicuña for dinner; when he had brought them back, however, Gong Su was already occupied: Maila had sent over a brace of pigs—real pigs, which had been acquired from trade with the colonial nations—as a gift; and Iskierka was sitting in the courtyard watching Gong Su roast them on spits, with an expression that one could only call smug.

"No, thank you," Temeraire said coldly, when he was offered a portion.

"I will take them, then, if you don't mean to eat them," Kulingile put in.

"You may do whatever you like," Temeraire said. "I will wait for my own catch to be ready, if you will be so kind, Gong Su; that pork does not look particularly fresh, to me."

"It eats excellently," Kulingile said, crunching through a rib cage; Temeraire settled himself upwind of the smell of roasted pork, and ignored the general feasting.

"I hope," Hammond said, "I hope, Captain Laurence, that we will not have any trouble. Any open quarrel must be dreadfully prejudicial to our cause. Churki has assured me that in a challenge, even victory on Temeraire's part—which we must of course hope for if matters should come to such a pass—would scarcely leave us the better off than an ignominious defeat: Maila is not merely respected, but considered the guardian of the royal house, and any injury even to his pride would be widely resented."

Laurence looked soberly out at the courtyard: Maila had come again, and was speaking with Iskierka at the far end too quietly to overhear, their heads intimate and conspiratorial; and Temeraire was sitting nearer their hall with his head raised haughtily, hearing Sipho recite some poetry to him. Or at least pretending to do so: his head was tilted ever so slightly at an angle calculated to give him the best chance of overhearing the distant conversation, and when Sipho paused for a question it was several moments before Temeraire looked down and replied.

"I cannot easily answer you, Mr. Hammond," Laurence said. "I should not have said that Temeraire's affections were engaged in such a way as to enable Iskierka to cause him pain; even now I must believe that it is his pride which is wounded, more than his heart."

"The cause matters very little," Hammond said, "if it should lead to the same end; the question is only whether you can restrain him; for I must call it increasingly evident that restraint will be called for."

Laurence disliked that he was not sure of his power to do so, and disliked still more discussing the subject with Hammond; he excused himself and stepped outside, to join Granby in his usual haunt of late: sitting in what might have been a casual manner upon the roof of the hall, which offered him an excellent vantage point over the city: as dragons came and went, he sketched them and made note of their points in a crabbed and awkward hand which contrasted peculiarly with the precision and clean lines of his sketchwork. His left arm was at last out of its sling, though it still gave him some pain; but he could now rest it atop the sketchbook to keep it in place for his work.

"I have two new catches so far to-day," Granby said, showing Laurence the results: one middle-weight beast marked as being all over yellow with green eyes, and a small, bright-eyed creature with a wingspan twice its length, which according to his notes could play the flute. "What? Oh—that says, *fly backwards*," Granby said, when Laurence asked a translation. "I have never quite seen the like: she pulled up mid-air and went back on herself as easy as winking. That makes twenty-six distinct breeds," he added, "and I have seen another half-a-dozen new beasts come and go, also."

They looked back at the courtyard, where Iskierka and Maila continued their tête-à-tête, and Temeraire his sulk. "I do not suppose, John, that you have any notion how seriously Iskierka has engaged herself with Maila?" Laurence asked him.

"No; and I wonder at it, for ordinarily she will brag of anything and everything to me, at all hours of the day," Granby said. "I will try and get it out of her, if you like; but don't let Hammond fret you to pieces. There shan't be any fighting over her, much though she would like. She has been chasing Temeraire for a year and ten thousand miles or thereabouts without much luck; I expect she is only trying to annoy him into it, instead, and sees this fellow as a handy way to do it.

"You might try and persuade him instead," he added. "I don't mind saying it would be a great thing for the Corps, if we *could* get an egg out of the two of them."

Laurence demurred at doing any such thing: if he could recognize the desirability of the mating, he felt still more strongly the very great officiousness of interference in such a matter; and even if Temeraire's attitude towards the proposals of England's breeders had at first been less outraged than flattered, he had lately been given a disgust for the business through excessive solicitation. "And in any case, if Temeraire should apply to her, at present, and find himself rejected—whether for Maila's sake or as mere stratagem on Iskierka's part—it cannot ameliorate the situation; indeed it must provoke a still more passionate feeling on his part, as regards setting himself against Maila."

"Well, I don't count on her doing any such thing," Granby said, "if only he gave her a little encouragement; but I will have a word with her, and see what she is about; not," he added resignedly, "that I expect to be able to persuade her to do anything differently, if she is determined to go on playing cat-among-the-pigeons, but at least you can whisper a word in Temeraire's ear, and maybe that will settle him down."

He stood to call to her; but before he could do so Iskierka had gone aloft again with Maila, and Temeraire had abandoned his fiction of disinterest and looked after them with his ruff alarmingly wide.

"If I may say so, Captain, I would rather propose a cooling draught," Gong Su said to Laurence, who had approached him to prepare a consolatory dinner of some unusual style, to divert Temeraire's attention. "The local peppers are excellent, but not to be recommended in the present circumstances. I am afraid her excess of *yang* makes Iskierka a difficult companion for Temeraire, from time to time," he added, with delicacy.

"I see he is tolerably transparent," Laurence said.

"If you will permit me," Gong Su said, "I will see if I can invite his attention into a more calming direction," and he shortly enlisted Temeraire's aid in fetching a great block of ice, cut from the peaks which overlooked the city, and then a bar of iron. This Temeraire and Kulingile laid upon the ice block and drew along its surface to shave a great heap of soft ice into a waiting trough; meanwhile Gong Su had prepared a syrup of some kind in his great cauldron. When he judged the ice sufficient and the alarmingly green concoction had cooled, he directed the dragons to pour it over the shaved ice.

"Oh!" Temeraire said, lifting his snout out of the resulting heap, "oh, it is splendid beyond anything, Gong Su; I might eat it forever." Kulingile did not interrupt his own ecstatic consumption long enough to compliment the receipt; but when he had finished he settled back on his haunches and sighed with wordless delight.

"I am afraid we could not reserve any of it," Temeraire informed Iskierka, with an air of smugness, when she returned that afternoon from yet another excursion, "for of course the ice would not stay; it is a pity you could not have any."

"I will have it sometime, I expect," Iskierka said, dismissively.

"All right," Granby said to Laurence, "I am going to have it out with her. I should not have thought it out of the ordinary if she had snatched Gong Su and stormed off to fetch more ice at once, even if she were only gone for pleasure; and if she did mean to be prodding Temeraire, she would be mad as fire to-day."

"I do not care about a sweet; I am concerned with much more important matters," Iskierka said, when Granby had asked her. "As," she added, with a sidelong look at Temeraire, "it seems to me others ought to have been; *I* have not neglected our mission, and meanwhile you are all doing nothing but wringing your hands, or making some treat, selfishly."

"Oh!" Temeraire said, "as though you were really negotiating anything, when you are only busy making up to Maila—"

"I have been carrying out our mission!" Iskierka said. "The Empress only wished to see Granby because of *me*; if it were up to you, I dare say she *would* marry Napoleon. Maila has told me she thought of it, and the French have made her a great many promises."

"What? And you have not said a word, all this while—!" Hammond said. "Do you know anything of their offers? Would their marriage give him in any way charge of their army in some fashion—of the aerial forces? But surely she must go to France, if she accepts him—would she install some governor—"

"No, no! I would have told you, if it was of any concern, but you may stop fretting; she will not marry him at all," Iskierka said, and jetted some steam, smugly. "She will marry Granby."

"What?" Hammond said.

"What?" Granby said.

*　*　*

The only ones at all pleased with the situation were Iskierka, and Hammond, who once past the initial shock urged them to take no hasty measures. "After all, we must have some alternative to offer them," he said. "If the Sapa Inca indeed is willing to consider—"

"Damn you, Hammond," Granby said, "don't you see Iskierka must have lied her tongue black to bring this about? You don't suppose the Incan Empress wants to marry a serving-officer, or that her people would let her, if they knew; she is not proposing some little fiction like you arranged in China, which everyone can forget as soon as the ink is dry on the paper."

"We know nothing of the proposal, or what obligations have been assumed on our behalf," Hammond said in placating tones, putting a hand upon Granby's arm earnestly, "and just so we must go carefully until we do understand, or risk giving offense. I hope," he added, "I am sure, Captain Granby, that my knowledge of your character is not mistaken: you would not refuse to undertake any singular duty, for your country, which only you could perform—"

"Laurence," Granby said, calm with horror after Hammond had eeled off with some excuse, "that damned diplomat and my thrice-damned dragon are going to marry me off to an Empress if they can do it: they are *both* run mad."

Laurence hardly knew what to say; with all Iskierka's assurances he hardly believed it could be possible, until Temeraire landed in the courtyard, bursting with fresh indignation. "For I have spoken with Churki," he said, "who has spoken to the other courtiers; and she says it is all a-hum: the Inca has not promised to marry Granby at all."

"Oh, thank Heaven," Granby said.

"She is only *considering* it," Temeraire went on, "and—"

"The devil she is!" Granby said. "What has Iskierka told them, about me? Does Her Majesty know I am the third son of a Newcastle coal-merchant? What is she thinking—"

"Oh! The Inca does not care for any of that, at all, Granby," Temeraire said. "She is thinking that if she marries you, Iskierka will have eggs for them, and the next Sapa Inca will have a great dragon who breathes fire: *that* is what she has promised."

Which to Granby's dismay rendered the arrangement more plausible by far: Britain itself had all but emptied the treasury to purchase Iskierka in the egg, and a nation so dependent on aerial power to preserve its sovereignty against the hunger of its neighbors would surely crave even more a fire-breather on such a scale. Though there were some native beasts which possessed the ability, they were small and their flames of a different variety altogether: low and coming only in short bursts, burning cool red and fading quickly; their value was more domestic than military, save as a distraction and a weapon in close quarters.

"You needn't be dog-in-the-manger, either," Iskierka said to Temeraire, when they confronted her. "I have said I will have an egg by you; and I will, too, but first I will have one by Maila: and I am sure you haven't the least right to be jealous, when you have been shy all these months, all because you are afraid you cannot."

"I am *not* jealous, and I am especially not afraid; I do not want to have an egg by you," Temeraire said, "in the least."

"That is nonsense," Iskierka said, "why wouldn't you? And Granby will be an *emperor*," she added, and jetted so much steam in her delight that with the sunlight reflected off the wall-panels of gold, she was wreathed in a wholly undeserved gauzy halo of light.

"This certainly alters the complexion of the situation," Hammond said thoughtfully, when informed. "I confess I had been concerned regarding what obligations she might have established—what promises might have been made—but if we are quite certain she has so far committed only herself, in her person—"

"And *me*," Granby said, sharply.

"Yes, of course," Hammond said, with a look which said plainly he did not care two pins for that.

Further inquiry determined that Iskierka's promises had not been quite so scanty as that: she had airily assured Maila of the British gladly sending tens of thousands of men to repopulate the *ayllus* of many an Incan dragon; with vague hints that the sailors daily on display in the courtyard might themselves be delivered to the dragons of the court. But in doing so she had offered nothing to which Hammond greatly objected; indeed, Laurence thought Hammond would gladly have put the men up on a chopping-block and auctioned them off to the highest bidder.

"Of course their feelings must be consulted in the matter, Captain, but if there are men who *wish* to make their home in such luxurious circumstances," Hammond said, "—who wish to serve their country in such a fashion—I can see no real objection. In any case," he added hastily, "that, I think, is not truly the appeal of Iskierka's proposal: you see, Captain Laurence, you were correct. For all her delay, the Empress must marry, and if she were to marry Napoleon, she must go to France: a nation torn by revolution and in the midst of war. I think the consideration must weigh with the dragons of her court greatly."

"Which is as much to say," Granby said, "that if she marries *me,* she shan't be going anywhere; and I am meant to live out my days knocking around a palace. You might *ask,* Hammond, or at least make a pretense of it."

"Captain Granby, I beg you do not refine on what we must as yet consider a most remote possibility," Hammond said, beginning to sidle out of the hall in what could not be called a subtle manner. "Pray excuse me: I will just have a word with Iskierka—" and was gone.

"I think we must soon wish you happy," Laurence said dryly to Granby, who stood flushed with choler, "with such enthusiastic matchmakers taking your part."

"There, Captain Granby, sir," O'Dea said in comforting tones, from where he had been sitting by the communal fire enjoying a tot of rum and very likely some eavesdropping, "sure and there is no harm in marriage, after all: though it all must end in a vale of tears, there's naught better to be looked for in the ash of this sad and worldly life: why not."

"Damn your impudence, O'Dea," Granby said. "Whatever do you know of it?"

"Why, and I've buried four wives," O'Dea said, and raised his glass in the air. "Katherine, Felidia, Willis, and Kate: the loveliest women ever to grace the earth, for to take pity on an old wretch like myself, and may the Good Lord be looking after them even now in his marble halls among the saints; although true enough there's no certainty of salvation."

He drained his tot and wheedling the other men at the fire said, "Come, lads: give me another drop if any of you have it to spare, a man needs a little heart in him when he thinks on love long gone."

"Then there's enough heart in you to dwell on the wreck of Rome," Granby said, and stalked away.

That night Granby came to Laurence's chamber, and knocking quietly asked him to go out. They went together through the courtyard and ascended the terraces that mounted up the hillside, silently; at the summit they looked down upon the broad plaza circled by the blue-gas lamps, and the orange glow of firelight out of the windows of the hall. "I suppose I am a fool; it didn't occur to me at first any of it could really be true—still less that Hammond could really mean it to happen, and now—" Granby stopped.

"I scarcely know how to counsel you," Laurence said, troubled; he had been no less reluctant to make himself over to be a pawn in Hammond's negotiations in China, even if they had ended greatly to his advantage; and the present arrangement should mean a far greater upheaval for Granby.

"It's worse than that," Granby said. "Laurence, I can't marry her. I know I ought to have spoken at once, and not left it so late; but there—it would scarce have made much of a difference, when Iskierka has kept the whole matter under her wing so long to begin with. Anyway, I couldn't—cannot—tell Hammond. I won't trust him so; but if I don't tell him, I don't know how to—what to—" He cut off the uncharacteristic stammer, and ran his hand down over his jaw, pulling it long and frustrate.

Laurence stared. "Are you already married?" he said, doubtfully.

"Oh! Lord, if only I were," Granby said. "My sister wanted to settle one of her friends upon me; if only I had let her arrange it! Not even Hammond could ask me to become a bigamist, I suppose. No, Laurence—I—I am an invert."

"What?" Laurence said, taken aback—the practice was scarcely unknown to him, coming from the Navy; he had known several fine officers addicted to the crime, their failing common knowledge and quietly ignored; but he had always understood it to stem from the lack of opportunity of a more natural congress, which could not be said to be the case for an aviator.

"Well, I don't know what the cause of it is, but it hasn't anything to do with opportunity; for me, anyway," Granby said shortly, and they fell silent.

Laurence did not know what to say. He had never suspected Granby of being even ordinarily unchaste; and belatedly realized that in itself was evidence. "I am very sorry," he said, after a moment. "—very sorry, indeed," feeling the expression inadequate to the confession.

"Oh—" Granby shrugged, with one shoulder, "in the ordinary course of things, you know, it scarcely makes a difference. I have never seen the use for an aviator of battening on some girl who like as not cannot say boo to a dragon, and leaving her to sit in an empty house eleven months in twelve for the rest of her life, while you live in a covert with your beast. And for that matter, I had as soon have a little quiet discretion with another officer, as make my way in the ha'penny whorehouses outside the coverts like other fellows do." He jerked a hand, as if to fling away the notion. "But now—this lunacy—"

"Ah," Laurence said, braced himself, and asked, "*Can* you not?" steeling himself against the indelicacy of the question; but after all, on the Navy side he knew of at least Captain Farraway: eleven children, one for every home leave since his marriage, and his pattern-card wife unlikely to have strayed at all much less in so precise a fashion; so plainly it was not impossible as a matter of course—

"I can manage *that* if I must, I expect," Granby said. "I would have to try and put myself out to stud to provide for Iskierka soon enough anyway. But once or twice is not the same thing as marriage. She must resent it; the Inca, I mean, and why shan't she say 'off with his head' if she don't like it?"

"If she should not learn—?" Laurence offered. "Not that I would counsel you to dishonesty," he added, "but if it is no barrier to your duty to her—"

"It won't do," Granby said, bluntly. "Not that I would make a cake of myself, any more than I ever have, but I don't undertake to be a monk the rest of my days, either. I would try and be discreet; but it is more than I expect that no-one should find out and blab to her: I shouldn't be just some aviator, that no-one cares about, but the husband of their queen."

Laurence said slowly, "And yet—she cannot be looking for affection of the ordinary sort which one might hope to find in marriage. For that matter, she must know soon enough if not already that Napoleon has divorced another woman for her, one whom he married for passion; and she herself is a recent widow. Her marriage must be an act of state, rather than a personal gesture; I cannot think she would take it as an injury in the same manner as might a woman entering into the marriage contract under the more ordinary circumstances."

"Laurence," Granby cried, with a look of reproach, "I should not have said a word to you of any of this, if I had been set on fire and dragged by wild horses, except that I hadn't the least notion how to get *out* of the thing without help; and now you are as much as telling me you think I ought to go through with it."

Laurence, sorry, said, "I would say, rather, that I do not know how to advise you," but in truth, he could not claim Granby's confession had successfully overcome his uncomfortable consciousness of the advantages of the match—or more to the point the deadly disadvantages of the alternative. It only increased in great measure the pitiability of Granby's situation, without making Laurence able to feel in earnest that it was not Granby's duty to allow the arrangement to go forward, if it might be achieved. "This alone does not seem to me a greater bar to your marriage than must be all the other obstacles: the difference in your station, and the uncertainty of the local politics; the ruin which it must make of your career—"

Here Laurence trailed off: for he himself *had* ruined his career, to carry out what he felt his duty; and Granby, who had looked away, knew it: Laurence's own actions spoke too loudly of the choice he himself would make.

"It is not, of course, your duty," Laurence said.

"I beg you consider whether it is not your duty," Hammond said, when they had come back into the hall: he had been lying in wait for them, or very nearly, at the door. "Of course there is no question of imposing the match upon you unwilling," he added, "none at all—"

If this were true on Hammond's part, a large assumption, it was certainly *not* true on Iskierka's; she dismissed Granby's protests one and all, even the last desperate attempt, when he corralled her in private, out of earshot of everyone else but Laurence. "Of course I know that you are not fond of women, in that way," she said. "I am not stupid; I know that you and Captain Little were—"

"Oh, for the Lord's sake, will you not be quiet," Granby cried, scarlet, and looked sidelong at Laurence in misery.

"Well, why did you speak of it, then?" Iskierka said reasonably. "*I* did not raise the subject: Immortalis told me we mustn't do so, although I don't see why; it is not as though I would allow anyone to arrest you, no matter what. But here it cannot signify—Anahuarque does not want you to be in love with her, only to make eggs, and be Emperor. I will ask Maila if you like, to be sure there will be no difficulty about it, but there shan't be."

Granby made plain to her that he did *not* like, in the least; but between her relentless determination and Hammond's coaxing, he was chivvied along in a manner which could only inspire sympathy, rather as watching a stag harried by a pack of hungry wolves. He was at length persuaded into allowing himself to be formally presented to the Empress as a suitor, in a ceremony of Maila and Iskierka's joint devising.

"Which, Captain Granby, if it achieve no other good, Maila tells us will induce them to allow me into her presence," Hammond said, "which must at least advance my ability to negotiate to our advantage—"

"And to my disadvantage," Granby said to Laurence, with more grim resignation than real protest; and he said, "I don't suppose any of us have a clean neckcloth between us? I must at least try and not look like a scarecrow, I guess."

Temeraire could not feel that Laurence had taken a proper view of the situation. While of course no-one could like the Sapa Inca to marry Napoleon, it seemed to him quite unreasonable that poor Granby should be sacrificed to avert it, especially as he disliked it so. Someone else might marry the Empress, since after all she did not care and only wished for fire-breathing eggs from Iskierka, in what anyone of sense would call a great lack of judgment. Iskierka might stay with Maila, since she liked to—no-one very much wanted her, anyway—and Granby might rejoin Temeraire's own crew.

He had hinted at the idea to Granby—not in a direct way, for Iskierka was sure to be unreasonable about it, and after all Temeraire did not mean to be rude—or to behave as though he wished to steal Granby; he did not. Only it seemed hard that Iskierka should be permitted to take Granby away from Temeraire in the first place, *and* make him wretched, *and* keep him forever in this far-away country, however much gold they did seem to have lying about everywhere.

But despite the gold, Granby had indeed said dismally, "I would give a great deal this moment to still be a first lieutenant, and nothing to worry about except whether I should ever get my hands upon an egg: what my mother will say when she hears of this, I don't like to think."

Which response, Temeraire felt, quite justified pursuing his notion of an alternative. "I suppose *you* would like to stay here, and marry the Sapa Inca, and be an Emperor?" he inquired of Forthing, experimentally.

"Catch me," Forthing said, snorting.

Temeraire sighed; he would have been just as happy to leave Forthing behind, as not. But he had to admit it would not be a reasonable exchange. Indeed, he had been forced twice this week to check Forthing pretty sharply: he had gone far overboard, in his attempts to prepare for this absurd and unnecessary ceremony of presentation.

"The Empress has not thought anything wrong in Granby's clothing so far," Temeraire said, "and if his boots are worn-out, he has those sandals, so I am sure you need not go to such lengths and spend so much leather on making new ones.

"And neither do you," he added reproachfully to Ferris: who had just returned from the market at the outskirts of the city, with two alpacas laden with beautifully woven green cloth: he evidently thought to use this to make new coats for all the aviators who should be participating in the ceremony. "Where have the funds come, for all of this? For we have had none, before now."

"Oh—well—" Ferris said, evasively, "—there are those stones, which Maila gave Iskierka."

"She has not traded them for your getting ordinary cloth," Temeraire said, with increasing suspicion, and swung his head around to count the sailors where they lay in the courtyard drowsing: he was sorry to say it, but he did not entirely put it past either Forthing or even Ferris to have allowed one of the men to sneak away to another dragon, in exchange for more bribery; a practice which Temeraire did not mean to continue. Laurence disapproved, for one thing, and aside from that, while the sailors were not very good, and he did not consider them his *crew*, exactly, certainly he was responsible for them.

He saw now that it must be a very poor sort of dragon who would only concern himself with one person; of course Laurence outweighed in importance all the rest; and his officers and crew after, when he had got a ground crew again; but that did not need to be the limit. Temeraire saw no reason he might not undertake to look after more men than he could carry at one time, if Curicuillor and her offspring did as much; and indeed one might say that Temeraire's own uncle was responsible for all China, in a way, as he was the Emperor's dragon.

In any case, Laurence had been working on the crew's discipline, and they were rather better, especially now that Handes was gone: they grumbled a little, but did their work, and when Ferris had put them to the new supply of fabric, they even proved able to turn out perfectly serviceable coats, after one remaining threadbare garment had been sacrificed to make pattern-pieces from. So Temeraire did not mean to let them be traded away, particularly in such a cause; and he kept a close and watchful eye on all of them.

"And one of them *is* missing," he said wrathfully, the next morning, "Crickton, and where has he gone, I should like to know at once, pray," and it transpired that Crickton had grown enamored of a serving-girl who lived in the estate of the governor of the eastern province.

"He hasn't *gone*," Ferris said to Laurence, hurriedly, when Temeraire had called him to account, "he is only *visiting* her, for a little while; I didn't think there could be any harm in it."

"Oh?" Laurence said, grimly.

"Well," Ferris said, "it is hard on the fellows, when there are no ladies on the town, as it were; and I gather, sir, it is hard on the women hereabouts, also, for they cannot get married outside their own *ayllu* without a great deal of trouble, in negotiations—"

Crickton had evidently been trying several nights to sneak away, to visit the lady—on the basis of little more encouragement than smiles, from the doorway of the great hall where she lived— and had been caught in the act by Ferris. "And I represented to him, sir, that it could not be his duty to go away in such a manner; he proposed that he should only have a visit with her, and return; and the steward of the estate thought fit to send us a thank-you—"

"For his providing stud services," Laurence said flatly, and Ferris looked at first abashed, and then shrugged wide.

"It is not as though we don't ourselves, sir," he said. "If one has a dragon, I mean."

Laurence looked rather troubled, and later said to Temeraire, "My dear, I hope you do not wish for me to—that is to say, I cannot feel—barring marriage, I should not be prepared to—"

"Pray do not think of it, Laurence," Temeraire said at once, reassuringly: he understood exactly Laurence's concerns. "*I* should never demand that you marry where you do not like, only to be an Emperor; and as for children, I had much rather have a properly trained crew. Anyway," he added, "perhaps Admiral Roland will have some for you, since Emily must go to Excidium; now that I think of it I cannot feel it quite fair that I must give her up with no return, just when she is all trained up and ready to be a splendid officer."

Laurence did not seem entirely consoled by their conversation on the subject; and Crickton was allowed to remain with his paramour, for no good reason: Temeraire would have been quite happy to send back the cloth, and fetch Crickton back; and if the steward had objected, he was thoroughly in a mood to defend his rights. But while barring any further such arrangements, Laurence would not reverse this present one, as the cloth had already been cut; so the coats were made.

And then Forthing did not wish to be outdone—although why he should object when the final aim was so little to be desired, Temeraire did not see—and Shipley was very ready to please an officer by setting the sailors to sewing up the scraps into a few additional garments. Forthing had steadily applied himself to learning the language—Temeraire now bitterly regretted offering any tutelage on the subject—and somehow managed to exchange these in the market for a very handsome length of red woolen cloth, which was made up into a cloak for Granby. Forthing even had the temerity to propose that some of the opals from Laurence's robes should be transferred to make an ornamental border upon it.

"Some display would be most suitable," Hammond began, and was silenced only by Temeraire's coldest look and his flat refusal to allow any such *mutilation* to be considered.

"Have done; you have made enough of a guy of me," Granby himself said, with impatience. "You are as bad as her," meaning Iskierka, who was meanwhile prancing about looking unbearably self-satisfied, and making eyes at Maila every minute of the day: Temeraire would have thought not even for gold would Iskierka have handed Granby over to someone else, to marry; and Granby did not even want to marry the Sapa Inca.

"You might at least wait for nicer weather," Temeraire suggested, as a last resort; but not even Granby agreed on that point.

"Let us get the meeting over with; and I hope to God she thinks better of it," he said, and two days later at morning their party was assembled in the Cusipata courtyard: the twenty aviators all in their fresh coats of green and their white trousers scrubbed and lemon-bleached and mended; Hammond in his handsome brown coat which did not show the stains of travel, and his sash of ambassadorship; Mrs. Pemberton in her black dress; and Granby undeniably splendid in the red cloak. Temeraire had not even the consolation of seeing Laurence in *his* finery: the robes remained in their box, and Laurence wore only one of the new coats and patched boots.

"I cannot outshine Granby on such an occasion," Laurence had said; and Temeraire supposed it were just as well: if Anahuarque were to take it into her head to want Laurence instead, that would have been quite dreadful. Of course, Laurence would have made a splendid Emperor, but Temeraire was not Iskierka, to all but sell Laurence into marriage in such a manner, only to advance his rank.

"And wealth," Iskierka said, "for Granby will own *all* of this, you know," under her breath, indicating with the avaricious sweep of her gaze all the great hall of the Empress. For the occasion the walls had been specially burnished and all the silver polished bright, and great lanterns had been hung even though it was still daylight, only to make the metal and the gemstones shine all the more brightly.

The Inca herself wore a gown of surpassing magnificence, which Temeraire could not deny might even rival Laurence's robes for elegance and splendor: it was woven of yellow and red and even threads spun out of gold, so that it sparkled in the light, and on this occasion she wore a crown of gold and silver, with the gorgeous plumes clasped within it at the top.

"That was my notion," Iskierka whispered to Temeraire, who heard her out unwillingly, "they had no crowns here, but I told Maila that the monarchs of Europe all wear them, and he was in perfect agreement with me that it was an excellent design; so he has had one made for the Inca; and Granby shall have one, too, when they are married: and they are going to have thrones, also, only those take longer to be made."

"They are not married yet; nothing has been settled," Temeraire said to her, coldly; but it was a poor rejoinder, and she justly ignored it: the Sapa Inca did look at Granby with an acquisitive eye, while her courtiers looked at him sullenly, and Maila simpered at Iskierka and ruffled his feathers up along his shoulders and made a general spectacle of himself.

"I will be sure to tell her, Captain Granby," Hammond said in a low voice, as they approached, "that you have no interest in governance—that you would not seek to interfere—?"

"Yes," Granby said wearily, "you may tell her I will be a proper lap-dog, and let her have her own way in everything, and not do anything but sit next to her and nod when she pokes me; and you may as well remind her if I ever do care to do otherwise, I still shan't be able to, as I don't know ten words of the language yet and likely won't put a sentence together for a year to come."

"Captain Granby begs Your Majesty's pardon," Hammond said, "that his lack of skill in the language bars him expressing his gratitude for the honor which you have done him, by this invitation; and wishes me to convey to Your Majesty—"

He went on in this perfectly untruthful vein, with which Anahuarque seemed quite well-satisfied; Temeraire looked away to watch instead the traffic of dragons coming and going among the great stepped terraces and high roofs of the city, laid out before their present vantage point, which if less remarkable was at least less dreadful than the debacle in progress before him; and for interest there were three dragons coming in from the south, two rigged out with elaborate streaming banners of great size.

Then Temeraire sat up sharply: the banners were the tricolor, and the dragon in the center was white: "Laurence!" he said, interrupting Hammond, "Laurence, Lien is coming; and those are Flammes-de-Gloire beside her."

Chapter 13

*I*T WAS NOT HIS FAULT, of course, but Temeraire conceded that his announcement had disrupted the ceremony beyond repair: the dragons of the Incan court were all sitting up and watching the oncoming dragons warily, paying Hammond's attempts to resume his speechmaking no attention, and Maila had reared up on his hind legs and put a foreleg on the Inca's podium as though he meant to snatch her up and go at once.

Temeraire could see Genevieve go up from the hall where the French were quartered, with Piccolo and Ardenteuse on her heels, to join the approaching party: and then all six dragons circled together overhead and descended one after another into the royal court, Piccolo unsubtly crowding against Kulingile's shoulder to make room for Lien to come down.

She was looking splendidly, Temeraire could not help but reluctantly acknowledge: besides the immense diamond upon her breast, which caught the light of the lamps, she wore also a sort of gauntlet upon each foreleg—talon-sheaths tipped in rubies, joined by delicate lacy chains of silver to broad cuffs set with diamonds, which were in turn joined to another set of cuffs above her elbow-joint set with sapphires, so that she wore the colors of the tricolor herself. She wore no other harness, and carried but one rider—

The French dragons all bowed their heads low, and the men aboard their backs removed their hats; De Guignes slid from Genevieve's back and knelt, as Napoleon dismounted from Lien's back, stepping easily down onto her proffered foreleg, which she then lowered to the ground.

He took De Guignes by the shoulders and raised him up, kissed him on either cheek, and said in French, "Best of emissaries! You must not be offended that I have come myself, any more than are my Marshals when I come to take the field; some battles a man must win himself. This is the Empress?" And when De Guignes confirmed it, Napoleon said, "Then tell her, my friend, that I myself have come! And hazarded my own person, to show her the honor which I and France mean to do her, if she will come and grace our throne."

If the Inca's dragons were inclined to resent the intrusion of the French party into the ceremony, and Napoleon's disregard of their protocol, his very temerity seemed to carry fortune with it: De Guignes was heard out, and the ruffled dragons gradually subsided on hearing Napoleon identified and his flamboyant message translated. Certainly there was enough courage to impress in the act of delivering himself into the power of a foreign sovereign; although Laurence noted that the two Flammes-de-Gloire bore each of them more than a usual complement of riflemen, all wary-eyed and with their guns ready to their hands.

A murmuring ran among the Incan dragons; even Maila looked uncertain, and abruptly Anahuarque raised a hand, and her court fell silent. "Tell the Emperor we welcome him to our court," she said. "Such a great journey must have left him fatigued: you shall go and rest, and we will dine all together this evening, to celebrate the opening friendship among all our nations."

Hammond translated this excessively optimistic speech for Laurence's benefit, as the Sapa Inca turning spoke low to Maila, with a hand upon his muzzle. She then stepped into the dragon's grasp; with one final look at Iskierka, he went aloft and carried her from the hall, while the other dragons swept away the rest of her retinue in similar fashion, and left the courtyard to their foreign guests.

Napoleon did not immediately depart himself, either: he turned smiling to the Frenchwomen who had been serving as De Guignes's deputies, and kissed their hands; and not content with stopping there came towards them, exclaiming, "Captain Laurence! I hope I find you in the best of health." He greeted Hammond and Granby on De Guignes's introduction with a similar warmth, which disregarded all the just cause any Briton had to resent both his general overarching ambition, and most egregiously his late invasion of England, which had been only just thrown off two years before at the dreadful cost of Admiral Nelson's life and the loss of fourteen ships-of-the-line, and twenty thousand men or more.

Laurence answered his inquiries with all the reserve which he could muster; Napoleon disregarded the latter, and pursued the former with unexpected intensity: before the onslaught of questioning Laurence found that he was saying more than he meant, about the peculiarities of the interior of Australia, and the sea-serpent trade established with China; at the description of which Lien might be seen to flatten her ruff back against her neck disapprovingly.

"I expect she does not think China ought to engage in commerce with foreign nations," Temeraire said when they had returned to their own quarters, "just as she thinks Celestials ought not engage in battle."

Hammond had managed to extricate them from the Emperor's company with excuses barely short of outright rudeness; and when he had been set down fell to anxious pacing in their hall, muttering to himself, and packing coca leaves into his teapot. "Pray have a care not to disarrange your appearance," he added, raising his head. "We cannot be sure when we will be summoned to dinner, and we must be ready; they are certain to have plans—offers to make—oh! The wretched timing of it all. Has Maila come to see Iskierka?"

"We have scarce been back here in the hall five minutes, so no, he hasn't. And it is a sorry state of affairs," Granby said to Laurence, dropping himself to the floor with a sigh, and no care for the beautiful red cloak which crumpled beneath him, "when I must cheer Napoleon on, and hope that he outdoes us all: but my God, I think I have never been so happy in my life as when he landed."

Temeraire could not be pleased to see Napoleon, and still less Lien, but that did not mean feeling the least unhappiness at the oversetting of the ceremony. He felt Iskierka had deserved any amount of discomfiture. He flattened back his ruff as Maila came winging down to the courtyard to see her, and threw a scornful look her way. "I *hope*," he said loudly, "that no self-respecting dragon would abase themselves, by pleading with the representative of a foreign nation, only from disappointment."

"Oh!" said Iskierka, "I do not *plead*, with anyone," and Temeraire had to do her justice: she received Maila very coolly, and only grew more so when he began to sidle around talking of Napoleon's dramatic arrival, and how it must alter their immediate plans—how the Flammes-de-Gloire had been demonstrating the range of their own fire-breath, that afternoon—how Lien was a most unusual beast, and clearly blessed by the gods because of her remarkable coloration—

"You might try your luck with *her*," Temeraire said, not even bothering to pretend that he was not listening in, "perhaps *she* will have eggs for you; but I should not expect it, myself."

Maila huffed out his neck-collar feathers and said, "Lien has explained she is not able to have eggs, with a dragon so distant from her own ancestry—that Celestial dragons cannot be crossed with other kinds. She does not wish to waste our time, or else she would be honored; that is why she has brought the fire-breathers, who are two dragons of her honor-guard. They will remain here, if we wish it, to form closer ties between our people."

While Temeraire reeled back into silence, appalled, Iskierka snorted. "If you think a couple of ratty French beasts are as good as *me*," she said, "only because they can breathe a little fire, then you are welcome to their company: I have better things to do with my time than to make a push for anyone, much less anyone so un-discriminating."

"I do not!" Maila protested. "I do not think them your equal, at all: that is why I am here. I am only warning you. You must come and speak to Anahuarque; you must persuade *her*—she must marry Granby, and send this foreign Emperor away, not marry him and go across the ocean."

"If you ask me," Temeraire said, his tail lashing violently—he had been deeply agitated since Maila's visit, and Laurence had not yet had any opportunity to pursue the cause—"he is not interested in you and your eggs, after all; he wants only to keep the Empress locked up safe here in the mountains, and not let to do anything: and I am sure he will want to do the same with Granby, too."

"He is, too, interested in my eggs," Iskierka said, flaring, while Hammond urged their immediate attendance on the Inca: Maila was prepared to arrange a private audience at once, informally, for them to plead their cause.

"There can be not a moment to lose—the dinner this evening may decide everything, and in any case De Guignes may already be making them proposals by some other channel," Hammond said, very nearly trying to drag Granby out the door, or push him, all while straightening his cloak and ignoring Granby's half-attempts to thrust him away. "We *must* go, at once, at once."

The conversation was thoroughly one-sided. Granby retired to the background with relief, after the first presentation, while Hammond flung himself into the breach wholeheartedly. But Anahuarque only listened impassive while Hammond tried one avenue and then another. He hinted at the dangers of the ocean crossing—spoke of the revolution in France, and the execution of the King and Queen—listed all the many nations which had lined up to oppose Napoleon's ambition, never acknowledging that of these, Spain had all but fallen, Prussia had been defeated, Austria had accepted truce, Russia only watched from afar—

He ran down at last, and Anahuarque still said nothing, but only watched them with her dark, thoughtful eyes: her silence a deliberate thing, it seemed to Laurence, designed to invite Hammond's very torrent of words, and all the intelligence which he might thereby deliver even unintentionally.

Laurence rose and said quietly, "Madam, we cannot know what will sway your decision, so I think we will take our leave of you and give you time to consider. I would only say, if you permit, that the Emperor is a prodigiously gifted man"—he ignored Hammond's sudden frantic twitch of his sleeve—"prodigiously gifted man, who has turned those gifts to the evil service of ambition. There are no bounds to his appetite for the conquest and subjugation of other men, and whatever aid you choose to give him you may be certain will be turned to those ends, regardless of the misery and privation the pursuit will bring upon the world."

He bowed, and turned to Temeraire, who was waiting to lift him up. "That was splendidly said, Laurence," Temeraire said, as they flew back to their courtyard in company with Iskierka. "I am sure it must decide her for us: no-one could like to help Napoleon fight still more wars; not that wars are not exciting, but it is unreasonable."

Laurence shook his head; he did not know, himself, anything more than that he had at least spoken the truth. He looked at Mrs. Pemberton, who had accompanied them; she said after a moment,

"I would be more sanguine, sir, if she had not also seized herself a crown—but on the other hand," she added, "I think she has not much desire to share it."

The feast was a deeply peculiar affair: French and British soldiers seated across from one another, mostly unable or unwilling to communicate with one another except by scowling; the Inca's generals on the upper and lower ends of the square joining in, more universally; the dragons seated behind the men murmuring to one another while they ate their roasted llamas. Even Hammond and De Guignes seemed thrown off their stride by the situation, with its equal shares of high tension and silence, and the only person who gave evidence of being thoroughly comfortable was Napoleon himself.

He had evidently studied Quechua to a little extent, and forged ahead in using his handful of words despite what Temeraire said scornfully to Laurence was a dreadful accent and no grammar whatsoever. He paid a relentless court to the Empress, though seated at several removes from her stool, and took advantage of a rather rude question from one of the warriors seated by her side as an excuse to sweep the cloth before him clear and demonstrate upon it the victory of Austerlitz, with pieces of potato to represent the battalions. Even Laurence could scarcely resist leaning in to hear this narrative; he thought ruefully, in his defense, that with all the just resentment in the world no military man could fail to be enraptured, until one considered the dreadful toll of life, and the consequences to all Europe.

Anahuarque, meanwhile, said very little; she gave Napoleon brief smiles, for encouragement, but as he spoke to the warriors of the battle, Laurence looked to see her eyes intent upon the Emperor, and surprised a look of cold and determined calculation in her face. She glanced back at Maila Yupanqui, who was coiled and brooding with his head laid beside her stool, and laid a hand gently upon his jaw; she bent and murmured to him, some reassurance perhaps for all the foreign men gathered at her table, and his ruffled feathers smoothed after a moment down against his throat.

"Well," Granby said, fatalistically, as they left the table, "at least there's this: she'll only marry me if she *wants* someone who will not give her any bother; maybe I can even leave, in a few years."

"If you have already given her a child; two or three, ideally. I hope your family are productive?" Hammond said, as they walked; only as an aside: he was sunk in gloom, and did not even notice the wry looks which his remark provoked.

"I don't think anyone should say I had an excess of sensibility about the matter," Granby said, which Laurence thought rather understated the case, "and in any case one could not worry over-much about a child with, as far as I can see, a dozen nursemaids over ten tons in size; beyond the usual line, that is; but it is over-much for Hammond to talk of my qualities as a sire in that way, as though I were a horse."

"I am sure it was just Lien's excuse," Temeraire said, "and not true in the least; I do not believe it for an instant that Celestials cannot breed."

"If you say so," Kulingile said equably. "I don't see it matters much," which Temeraire could not agree with; but then, Kulingile was rather young, and did not yet think of eggs as desirable things. He did not appreciate properly that Temeraire's own egg had been so valuable a prize that Laurence's two-eighths share, as captain of the vessel which had seized it, had bought the splendid breastplate of platinum and sapphire which Temeraire yet wore; and that Iski-erka's egg had commanded a hundred thousand pounds in gold coins—of course, no-one had known at the time what her personality was to be, and Temeraire had been thought only an Imperial rather than a Celestial dragon. But that only went to show how very important eggs were: no-one in Britain would give a hundred thousand pounds for Iskierka to-day, he was quite sure; except perhaps Hammond at the present moment.

"It is just chance," Temeraire said uneasily, "that I have not yet had an egg—"

Iskierka, who was watching narrowly across the great courtyard, where the lamps showed Maila sitting outside the French hall and speaking with the Flammes-de-Gloire, snorted over her shoulder. "After all that noise you made, of having to do your duty by all those dragons in the breeding grounds which they put you to? And that was years ago: by now there would surely be news, if any of them had got an egg by you."

"Well, if Lien is telling a little of the truth, perhaps it is that I have not tried enough with the right sort of dragon," Temeraire said, "for they were forever putting me to only the most docile beasts—not," he added, "that they were not perfectly pleasant creatures; but they had none of them been particularly remarkable, in battle, and many of them were only middle-weights—"

"You do not need to hint," Iskierka said, with a huff, "although it would serve you perfectly well if I did not care to anymore; but I *will* try now with you, if you like, and Maila can wait," she added, in a rather venomous tone, "as he likes to go sit and make eyes at the Frogs."

"I was not hinting—" but Temeraire shook out his ruff, and hastily said, "—oh, never mind; very well," when Iskierka bridled up, with a martial light in her eye. Privately even he might admit that it would be something, to have an egg with both the divine wind *and* breathing fire. He bent his head, and surreptitiously polished his breastplate; it was too bad he had not insisted on his talon-sheaths for the ceremony earlier, he belatedly thought; only he had not felt like putting his best forward on what had been such a dismal occasion.

"Come on, then," Iskierka said. "I should like a snack first: I saw a herd of those wild llamas moving on the plain to the south, yesterday, and I dare say they are still there; and there was a nice private little valley just up the mountain-side from there."

"Those *were* tasty," Iskierka said, licking her chops: when they had finished hunting, Temeraire had persuaded her to heat up a few rocks with her fire; he had piled them into a pit with the llamas and buried them along with a pleasantly aromatic shrub and a bit of water from a salt spring, so that when they had finished their business, the llamas were cooked and ready to eat.

"And we shall see," Iskierka continued, "about the egg. It does not seem to me there was much to it, and I am sure for my part at least, everything will go smoothly. I have been ready this age: if only you were not always so difficult."

"As though you had any business accusing anyone else of being difficult," Temeraire said, but without much heat; the llamas had been excellent, which he considered a triumph in his first attempt at cooking anything himself. And after all, no-one could deny that Iskierka was an impressive dragon. Her spikes had even not been so very awkward as he might have thought, although requiring some ingenuity in maneuvering.

It was nearly morning: a certain pallid quality to the sky behind the mountains ahead of them as they flew back to the city, Temeraire carrying a couple of extra cooked llamas, which he meant to show to Gong Su for his approbation. "What is going on, there?" Iskierka said suddenly, as they drew near: there were many dragons gathering behind a wall of the great city fortress, and also soldiers in their woven armor with swords and musketry, forming into lines.

"Wait: this way, we mustn't let them know we have seen them," Temeraire said, nipping at Iskierka's wing, and they darted back out of sight behind a curve of the mountain-side. Temeraire set down his llamas. "Wait here—oh, pray stop grumbling; if you should let off any steam or fire, they will certainly see you at once."

"I do not care, in the least," Iskierka said. "What are they about? Of course they are making an ambush," she added impatiently, "but on us, or on the French?" She stretched out her neck to peer at the gathering force.

Temeraire went aloft, careful to keep the gradually lightening sky ahead of him, and studied the scene: the British enclave lay to the east of the soldiers' position, the French to the west; both in striking distance. The Inca's soldiers were carrying shields covered splendidly in silver, and one of these caught the rising sunlight and gleamed painfully bright out of the terrace for an instant as Temeraire looked.

"On us," Temeraire said to Iskierka, as he dropped down to seize his llamas again: they might need the food, he thought. "They are going to attack us; we must fly at once."

III

Chapter 14

᳖

$\mathcal{T}$HE WATERFALL WAS NOT WIDE but very high, crashing noisily down over its long and broken cliff wall, and so muted the labored panting of the dragons as they slept a little; the high canopy of jungle trees provided them cover. Kulingile's golden scales they had slathered over with mud, and Temeraire and Iskierka were not in much better case: branches thrust through their harness-straps all over their backs, and vines strewn liberally atop, the better to camouflage them against the relentless pursuit.

A host of small dragons, lightning-quick, had chased and harried them near three hundred miles already in little more than a day and a night and a day, although they had not traveled anywhere near that distance in a straight line: their course had been desperately zig-zagging and convoluted. If they paused, or tried to engage, the small beasts fled before them: to carry the news of their position back to the larger dragons who hung back, waiting and reserving their strength to come directly upon them.

Already they had just barely evaded several close engagements with various Incan aerial battalions: six dragons of heavy-weight size and thirteen of middle-weight, who skillfully attempted to surround and bring them down. Only Kulingile's massive size had enabled them to escape the first: he had put his head down and bulled through the hemming line of dragons, not one of them less than twenty tons. Temeraire and Iskierka had darted out after him, then turned with their greater maneuverability to claw and lash the enemy long enough for Kulingile to get away into the cloud cover, where they followed shortly after.

The Incan dragons pressed the pursuit without excessive risk, cautiously: all the advantage of time was on their side, and knowledge of the territory. With every moment of flight, Temeraire and Iskierka and Kulingile grew weary, and their strength waned.

There had been no time either for provisions or sensible assembly. The two llamas which Temeraire had brought back from his hunting had gone down Kulingile's gullet, while the men were hurried into belly-netting without even the opportunity of putting on harness; at least four had been left behind, Laurence thought, having evidently sneaked off on night excursions. He was only consoled that their fate would not be as unkind as it might: they should certainly be welcomed into some dragon's *ayllu* in their persons, despite any political differences with their nation, rather than flung into a prison from which there would be little hope of extrication.

The force which had been assembled to seize them—with, he could not help but believe, the aim of securing the dragons as prisoners and perhaps for breeding, as well as delaying any report back to Europe—had come on them even as the sun rose. The few minutes of warning which Temeraire and Iskierka had brought proved, just barely, enough; they went aloft pursued by the first roars of challenge, and flung themselves into a mist-shrouded gorge, flying desperately east into the mountain fastness.

The day had worn away; night brought no relief, for a handsome half-full moon shone on the ice-sheathed mountain-slopes, and there were dragons among the pursuit who seemed able to see them in the dark. But at last Temeraire, flying in the lead, had broken out onto the eastern side of the Andes, and they fled down the slopes into the seeming endless jungle which rose impenetrable and green at their base.

Here they had found enough concealment for a few breaths, a little sleep; a few swallows of water might be cupped from the steady rivulets which trickled down the smooth bark of the trees. Already a light misting rain had fallen twice, in the half-day which they had spent in hiding. But they could not hide for very long with three such beasts among them; Laurence watched the sun creep over the sky, through the dappling leaves, and hoped only that their shelter would serve them until the night.

Hammond, shaky and green from the speed and unsteadiness of their flight, was folding together with trembling hands a few of the coca leaves, which he had stuffed into his pocket as they fled: he put the leaves into his mouth to chew, as they could not boil water for tea. "It is an outrage—a betrayal of all common principles regarding the sanctity of ambassadors—" he was saying, a variation on a theme which he had not ceased to develop since their pell-mell departure.

"If they take their notion of principles from the example which the Spanish made them, there is not much to wonder at," Laurence said, controlling irritation; he would have been glad of a cup of tea himself, and more grateful yet for one of strong black coffee; instead he cupped water in one of the broad, dinner-plate-sized leaves which hung vinelike off the tree, and poured off the trickle into his mouth.

"We must rather consider our course of escape, and our direction," he said, and bent to sketch out the shape of the continent roughly in the dirt.

"To Rio, of course?" Hammond said, as though it were merely a matter of choosing their destination. "Now there can be nothing worth delaying for; we ought make all speed possible."

"Well, we can't: it is asking for disaster to go haring off through the jungle with no water to speak of," Granby said. "Laurence, I don't think we have much choice in the matter: this tree-bark dribble will do for us, but not for the dragons. There might be a hundred streams flowing under the leaves, but they won't do us any good if we can't see them from the air. At least if we hold by the mountains, we are pretty sure of seeing some run-off every day."

"And more likely to be seen in turn," Laurence said, "by our pursuit. But I do take your point: if we should keep to the trees by day, and put our heads north by night, towards Venezuela—"

"No, no," Hammond cried. "Gentlemen, we *must* go to Rio. You have not considered, perhaps, the increased urgency of our mission. With the Sapa Inca having decided to throw her lot in with Napoleon, Brazil is now beset on all sides. You must recall the Prince Regent of Portugal is there, and all the royal family. They must be warned—warned, perhaps rescued; they do not as yet know anything of their danger. I must insist upon it, in my authority as ambassador: I hope you will agree I do not exceed it, in such a cause."

"If he can't marry us off, he will murder us, I suppose," Granby said to Laurence under his breath. "Had we better make for Venezuela, and then circle back to Rio along the coast?"

"We should lose six thousand miles on such a journey," Laurence said, "and no guaranty of supply along the way, in any case."

They bent their heads over the dirt, trying without much hope to plot a course more direct across the jungle: they scarcely knew where they were, so even to begin was difficult, and at Granby's insistence had to allot full half each day's flying for finding water. "And that I would call ambitious," he said. "In any case, we mustn't go so far that we could not fly back to some decent water within a day."

"Well, it will have to do," Laurence said finally, when they had at last agreed, and they made their uncomfortable damp beds on the ground to take a little more rest before nightfall; but twilight had only just begun to descend when Demane was shaking Laurence awake.

"The monkeys have gone quiet," he said softly. Laurence sat up listening, but the waterfall covered any sound of wings. They sat together a moment, squinting upwards: then a groan of rustling branches, and a great orange-feathered dragon's head thrust down and whispered in Quechua, "Hammond? Are you there?"

"What?" Hammond said, staring up, and Churki landed among them, ruffling up her plumage to cast out the leaves and twigs which had been caught betwixt the feathers.

"We must leave at once," she said. "The *tumi* patrols are out after you, and beating the jungle near-by: I have bribed a lieutenant to let me rescue you, but he cannot keep them off for very long."

When they demanded explanation for her having gone to treasonous lengths in their interest, "How can you call it so?" she protested. "It is my duty. After all, I did not know the Sapa Inca was going to choose to marry your enemy when I asked Hammond to join my *ayllu*. What sort of creature would I be if I did not do all in my power to protect him, only because it has become inconvenient?"

Of course, her preferred notion of that protection was that Hammond should return with her, to her mother's territory. "For the Sapa Inca will not mind at all, I promise you," she added persuasively, "and my mother will give me more people to join the *ayllu*: you may have three wives all your own, if you would like."

"I call that justice," Granby said to Laurence, with a great deal of enjoyment in Hammond's discomfiture, even as they directed the urgent retreat: all were piling aboard the dragons in great haste, men scrambling to tie themselves to the harness while Forthing and Ferris pushed the clumsier among them back into the belly-netting.

Hammond struggled meanwhile to dissuade Churki, edging close to Temeraire as he spoke: a certain frowning gleam in her eye suggested temptation to snatch him away in disregard of his wishes, when they were so plainly misguided. Until at last he hit in desperation upon the notion of adding, "And you know, I cannot desert my family: why, I have eight brothers and sisters, with any number of children themselves—there must be three dozen by now—"

"Oh!" Churki said. "Why did you not say so, at once? *Dozens*, and in that uncivilized country of yours, with no dragon to look after them. Of course we must go back to them." She ruffled her feathers high. "I do not like getting in the way of the *tumi* patrol, of course; I am sure it will make trouble for my mother if it is known. But she will understand, when I can send her word."

They were aloft scarce twenty minutes after Churki's warning. Full dark had fallen, and even as they rose they were attacked by a patrol: five dragons, striking out of the dark, all with small spear-shaped heads and dark green feathers cropped short. They were middle-weights at most, each not a quarter of Temeraire's size, but they made up for that in numbers and in night-vision; their coloration made them nearly invisible against the night, and plainly the hazy moonlight which came through the clouds was sufficient to enable them to see.

The green dragons were making low calls to one another, in almost chirping voices. "Do not roar," Laurence called urgently, as yet another of the dragons came darting into the fray from up ahead, slashing at Temeraire's flank in passing as it winged to join the other five in harrying their flanks. "Temeraire, do you hear me? The jungle must be alive with these beasts; if you should roar, you will draw them upon us in a cloud: we must get ahead of their line before you roar."

Temeraire flicked his ruff in acknowledgment; he was flying and fighting at once, and Laurence had all the pain of feeling himself and his crew useless in their present circumstances: they had neither guns, nor incendiaries, nor even flash-powder, which might have allowed them to be of assistance against enemy beasts, and could only cling on and hope they did not obstruct Temeraire's own efforts.

"Mr. Ferris," Laurence called, leaning over, "do we have that netting—the rope and sailcloth netting, have you any of it left, below? Light it along, if you please—"

"Aye, sir," Ferris called, and came clambering up Temeraire's side with a rope lashed around his waist, a tether to the heavy entangled bundle; Forthing and Roland and even Hammond joined their hands to the cable, and they drew it up, brine-stinking cloth and half-rotten rope. Laurence hacked apart a portion with his sword, Roland setting her knife to the sailcloth: she and Ferris and Forthing, aviators all since childhood, managed to take and keep their feet long enough to heave it out as one of the green-feathered dragons swung close to Temeraire's hindquarters, and the mess billowed open, descending, and settled on the dragon's head.

The beast squalled, muffled and surprised, and fell away clawing blindly at the unexpected attack; it ran into a second beast and fouled her flight for a moment, but this one squirmed loose and plucked away the ragged cloth, throwing it out over the trees. It sank, a momentary flash of pale cloth, and vanished away amid the trees behind them.

The effort won Temeraire only the briefest respite, but at least it was something. Laurence sawed grimly away at the rope with the dulled edge of his blade, and they managed to try a second time, and a third, but by then the green dragons had grown wiser. Three more of them had joined the pursuit by now; Laurence looked again where the moon made a glowing patch of haze in the sky: they were being herded back westward, and the dragons' chirping calls were growing more energetic.

Iskierka also had not loosed her flame: as much as lighting a beacon of invitation to the enemy; but the enemy dragons evidently already knew to fear it, anyway. She bore the brunt of their sweeping attacks, one pass after another which only her maneuvering enabled her to avoid; and even so she was clawed and bleeding from a dozen small wounds. She hissed in fury as another pass caught her along one shoulder, and turned to lash out reprisal at the smaller beast: the green dragon fled and was caught only a glancing blow, feathers bursting loose, but the effort left an opening which the enemy were too numerous to miss.

Two of the dragons flew at Iskierka's head, one from either side, beating their wings furiously to obscure her vision; a third, the largest of the enemy, lunged at the side which Iskierka's strike had bent into a wide and open curve, unprotected by the chainmail which was her usual battle-gear, and savaged her with tooth and claw both, opening the flesh to the air.

Iskierka roared in agony, and turning blasted flame at the dragon who had already lifted away, too late. Her head was wagging back and forth in pain; and Laurence could see a line of steam in the air where her blood ran freely away. Then he heard Granby crying out, "Sear the wound! If you go down, it doesn't matter, Iskierka; sear the damned wound, or I swear to you on my honor I will jump anyway—sear it at once—"

He was standing on her back, harness-straps hanging loose save one that he gripped in his hand. Iskierka cried out in protest, and then bent her head back and breathed fire upon her own side: flames coruscating up and over her hide, washing down her length as she flew. Laurence saw Granby and Bardesley silhouetted black against the yellow-red banner of fire for a moment, then the night was pitch-black, darker for the moment of light, and he did not know what had happened to them.

He blinked away the dazzle of the light: Kulingile had ranged himself alongside Iskierka, trying to shield her wounded side with his bulk, and Temeraire was racing to her other side: but behind them, the enemy were gathering together for another run at her, one which should surely bring her down. Their light chirping voices rang clear, incongruous and dreadful as they arranged themselves for the strike and came, arrow-shape formation, towards them.

Laurence felt Temeraire gathering himself, drawing in the great breaths one after another which expanded out his lungs, and yet something different: when Laurence put down his bare hand, he felt nearly a drumming tension to the hide. The enemy dragons were coming, swiftly; then Temeraire turned and roared: but not once only; he roared, low, and roared again, and a third time, and only with the fourth rose to that shattering, terrible sound that was the divine wind.

The very air seemed to shake and howl, rushing away from

them; the rain-mist boiling into tight spindled clouds. The first dragons of the formation were pulling up, beginning to pull up, as the ripple struck, and Laurence saw blood come bursting from their noses and their ears.

The three dragons foremost in the formation fell from the sky without a sound, stone-dead; Laurence heard their bodies crashing through the branches below. Others, too, were falling, thrashing in mid-air, choking on blood; and only the hindmost beasts survived, sheltered by the bodies of their fellows: survived, reeled back, and fled away into the night, shrilling out their horror.

Chapter 15

❧

*T*HEY WERE PURSUED NO LONGER. That night they lay exhausted amid trees that towered away from a strangely dim and barren jungle floor populated by ferns and the decomposing bodies of fallen giants, suffering the yelling resentment of the monkeys and of astonishing birds plumed in colors Laurence had scarcely seen in artifice much less nature.

The next morning they buried Lieutenant Bardesley there, in a grave as deep as Temeraire's claws could open. There was no avoiding the funeral, as the ordinary course of putrefaction seemed accelerated by the damp heat and luscious verdure all around: though Mrs. Pemberton had sacrificed her petticoat and Emily's to make a shroud, by first light the corpse was crawling with ants the size of grasshoppers, whose jaws left angry bites as they were beaten away. They did not open the shroud to look on his face before they laid him to rest.

Iskierka's wounds had not mortified, cauterized as they had been by her flame, but a strange feverishness set in by the following evening: the steam which ordinarily issued from her spikes dried to a bare trickle, and her eyes were glassy and bloodshot nearly to black. The heat of her body was become intolerable for close quarters.

"She must have water, and soon," Churki said, after a sniffed inspection of the injuries, and with a decided air. Laurence had known dragons of more years—Messoria, of their formation, and Excidium—but these had been raised in the British fashion, to obey rather than to command, where Churki seemed to take a certain precedence as a matter of course: she was of course eldest of the dragons by far. "Where do your family live, Hammond? We must determine the best course to reach them."

When Hammond had, with a certain degree of duplicity, explained their desire to reach Rio and thence to take ship for Britain, she looked at Laurence's sketch of their proposed route and shook her head, ruffling. "This will not do very well: guessing at water is not sensible. We must go to the Ucayali and follow it to the sea."

They were no longer pursued, though they did little to conceal their passage. Three more days of flying under Churki's lead brought them to the river she had described: sluggish-brown, enormous, swollen with all the ice-melt of the Andes.

"If it is not the Amazon, it must yet come out at the ocean," Laurence said, shading his hand to look down along its length while Iskierka crawled into the river and submerged herself; crocodilian animals with long snouts swam away resentfully, and she rested her head upon the bank and closed her eyes as steam curled up and away from her back where the water lapped against the scales.

The river swelled ever further as they followed its course northward and it met new tributaries until at last the whole mass of it turned east, away from the mountains, and they began the long and grindingly slow journey to the coast. The country was not unpopulated: native tribesmen looked in on them now and again, mostly from the other side of the river, but these vanished as quickly as they came if ever Laurence tried to hail them, or even if Temeraire called out a few words in Quechua. Of dragons they saw only a few small feral beasts, and those by accident: Iskierka was in the river again, preferring to half-paddle herself along than to fly, and so Temeraire and Kulingile had gone off to hunt meanwhile; Iskierka came around a curve and startled three little dragons the size of Winchesters, sharing a meal of a peculiar long-snouted piggish creature on the shore.

She was barely a head in the water at the time, and the dragons stared in curiosity; then she reared up partway on the bank and demanded, "Where did you find that, and is it any good?"

Yet three-quarters and more submerged, she nevertheless outweighed all three of them together; the dragons went into the air as though fired from a cannon and fled, leaving behind their dinner; this proved their only encounter, save for glimpses at a great distance of small beasts flying away. "Oh, well," Iskierka said callously, and devoured the remnants without a pause, gulping them down with swallows of river water.

"What have you been eating?" Kulingile inquired, on returning: their hunting efforts had so far yielded only some smallish red deer, which did not answer very well to satisfying the hunger of three large dragons, one of them convalescent, though Gong Su did what he could to stretch them.

"I don't know; they wouldn't stay and tell me," Iskierka said drowsily, already half-asleep on the shore and resisting persuasion to continue any farther that day.

In the middle of the night, Laurence woke to her groaning and an acrid stench: she was vomiting heavily into the river, and sank miserably back on the shore afterwards gone limp. They went nowhere that day, and when Temeraire managed to return with a couple more deer, Gong Su insisted on their being boiled nearly to inedibility. Iskierka's misery carried the day for him, but the dragons were not enthusiastic about the resultant meal, and neither were the sailors, although by then they were glad enough for anything to eat.

The jungle miasma lay heavily upon all of them. Hammond was also queerly feverish and short-tempered, and so, too, several other men, including Ferris; Laurence feared the beginning of some tropical fever setting in among them. He himself was almost perpetually in a sweat, the woolen clothes suited to the high mountain fastnesses of the Inca were become a prison for all of them, but the viciousness and size of the insects prohibited all but the most insensible from exposing any unnecessary part to the air.

"Well, and it is an evil part of the world we have come to, Captain," O'Dea said, expressing a general sentiment, after a few more days: Temeraire had woken them all with a shattering roar of protest, and shaken off three bats which had latched on to him, in the dark.

"They *bit* me," he said; as improbable as the accusation was, investigation turned up small leaking wounds upon his flank where the bats had clung and fed, so it seemed, upon the blood; and several more of them were discovered on all the dragons.

There was something especially horrid in feeding this species of hunger, but the bats were no more to be escaped than the mosquitoes, though Granby slept on Iskierka's back and woke several times throughout the night to chase them off with his one good arm; and their bites offered a similar kind of discomfort, growing hard and swollen and hot to the touch after a day.

The half-healed injury which Granby had taken to his arm, in the sinking of the *Allegiance,* had been aggravated and all earlier progress lost in his being flung from Iskierka's back to the limits of his harness-straps, leaping to escape the flames. Laurence looked at it grimly, in the light: the elbow grossly swollen and bruised purple-black, and the hand dangling useless. They had no surgeon; only the former barber Dewey, who had been pressed into the *Allegiance* out of a dockside carouse, and his only contribution was to offer, "Why, I can have it off easy as you please, sir, if the little miss will lend me her knife; and someone can find me a bit of drink to steady my hand," which made Roland glare.

"Wrap it up tight for me, Laurence, if you please," Granby said hastily, "and let us see what a few weeks will do: it does not pain me over-much—" this last delivered while he was clammy-cold and pale with agony; but Laurence was in too much doubt of the wisdom of the arm's removal to argue for its being endured: the shoulder which seemed the real seat of the injury could not itself be taken off.

Four days later, the arm looked yet worse: a bluish darkening beneath the skin from elbow to fingers, and Granby could not close his hand. The shoulder at least seemed a little recovered, and when palpated the flesh of the upper arm yet felt warm; but in the morning there was a feverish heat growing above the elbow, and the engorgement of the blood vessels creeping upwards.

"Had it better come off?" Granby said, looking at Laurence's face.

"I think it must," Laurence said grimly, and Dewey, coming to inspect his field of work, patted Granby's shoulder.

"Never you fear, Captain; why, I have had off the arm of a fellow twice your size in under three minutes; although I do not have my saw." He took the knife which Roland silently proffered him, her irritation at being called *miss* now subsumed in anxiety, and carried it down to the riverside to sharpen against the stones of the bank.

"Laurence," Temeraire said, peering over, "whatever are you about? Surely you do not mean him to take off Granby's arm, for good? Iskierka is asleep: I am sure she ought to be consulted on the subject."

"*That* is all I need, at present," Granby said, under his breath. "Let her sleep, if you please, and Laurence, I would be glad of something to bite on."

Laurence nodded, and rose to call Forthing and Mayhew to assist him with holding Granby down; abruptly from the bank came a shriek, and he turned to see Dewey being dragged into the river headfirst, a pair of massively wide crocodilian jaws clamped about his skull. They all stared, horrified; three more of the creatures erupted from the water, seizing on flailing arms, legs, and wrestling over the body with terrible strength: before even Temeraire could act, the water was running red, and his lunge pulled out only a headless corpse, lacking also a leg, with a crocodile dangling still clenched upon the other.

"Oh!" Temeraire said, furious, "oh, what do they mean, *eating* him!" and plunged his head savagely into the midst of the still-frothing waters: he came up with three thrashing beasts, each perhaps a ton in weight, and holding them in his jaws cracked them with a sound not much less dreadful than Dewey's own death-cry.

He flung them down, and went again into the water, and again, until he had piled up a dozen carcasses; by then the rest had slunk beneath the surface and glided prudently away.

"There," Temeraire said, panting, "they will think better of it, next time," and Laurence had not the heart nor the stomach to argue with his estimation of the animals' intelligence: in any case the men would certainly think better of going anywhere near the riverbanks without great care.

Iskierka had been roused by Temeraire's frenzy; she sat up and yawned and said, "Whatever did you do that for? They are not good eating; but I will have a couple, if there is nothing better," and several of the men crept away into the trees to be noisily and emphatically ill.

The crocodiles were abandoned uneaten; but the slaughter forced their immediate departure, as the scavengers of the jungle were too enraptured by the immense feasting prepared for them to delay: the monkeys were not afraid of dragons, and neither were the beetles. Granby said uneasily, "I will have to make the best of it," and wrapped his arm up against his waist once more before he pulled himself one-handed aboard Iskierka's back.

Laurence had grown used to the tremendous speed at which dragons consumed the miles: fifteen in an hour at a steady enduring pace, and as many as two hundred in a day, with no obstacles to be surmounted or roads to clear and no dependence upon the wind; but their passage through the jungle was more akin to the slow creep of a ship through the doldrums, being towed by her boats: Iskierka could not fly for long. She leaned heavily on Kulingile and Temeraire, who took it in turn to brace her up, but even they could not support her massive weight very well or for any real length of time. Granby drooped upon her back; she drooped in mid-air, and often came down to rest in the body of the river and moved along like some vast steaming river snake, paddling herself along.

The heat was tremendous, and the air of the jungle close and thick around them when they flew low, or crept after Iskierka in the river. Hammond urged speed, and looked piteous for it: he mopped his brow with shaking hands nearly every minute, and slept fitful and feverish; the other men had by now most of them recovered, but Hammond had never given the impression of particular resil- ience, and their journey had strained stronger men to the limits. But there was no speed to be had: all energy, it seemed, had been wrung out of them.

Mrs. Pemberton, in her long black dress, was an improbable and lone figure of civilization amid their increasingly ragged num- ber: she managed by dint of quiet but firm requests of a few well- chosen men—those not so tired as to refuse to move but disinclined to argument or quarrel—to every evening arrange a small separate campsite and fire for herself and Roland, and even hot wash-water.

They dragged themselves slowly through the jungle, until Lau- rence dreamed one night of gulls crying, and woke to hear their voices: when Temeraire went aloft there was a cloud of them wheel- ing and circling in the distance over the great mouth of the river where it met the open endless ocean blue: they had come to the shore of the Atlantic.

Iskierka lay down in a tidal pool and shut her eyes; Granby was lifted down from her back and carried into the shade of palm-trees. Temeraire and Kulingile went out into the ocean, and did not come back for a full day and night; Laurence had begun to fear in earnest when looking out over the waves, under his shading hand, he saw the strange apparition approaching: a vast misshapen creature with four wings and no limbs.

"Clear the shore, there," he called, when they came closer; and in exhaustion the two dragons set down their prize: a true monster of the deep, a blue whale not perhaps fully grown, but even so nearly larger than them both together.

" 'Twould bring twenty thousand pounds rendered down, I expect," one of the sailors, an old whaler, said in hushed tones, as they sank a sharpened spear into the blubber and cut away to find it nearly a foot deep. Every man had a slice, and Iskierka ate a good two tons of the stuff; Temeraire and Kulingile had already eaten.

"I killed it with my roaring, when it came up for breath, and then we took it in turns to keep the whole above water while the other ate," Temeraire said, drowsily, while Laurence stroked his muzzle, "for we thought that should make it easier to carry back: but I do not mind admitting to you, Laurence, that I rather worried it was too large even so. Oh! I am very tired."

In the morning, Iskierka finished another meal of whale meat and blubber, and roused enough from her torpor to say peevishly, "Where is Granby? Why is he not with me?" and then she saw him.

"If none of you are going, I am," she said fiercely, when she had overcome her first confusion, after Granby did not answer her: his eyes were heavy-lidded and far-away, lost in fever and in pain. "He must have a surgeon: he *shall* have a surgeon; you will put him on my back at once."

There were seven other men burning with fevers and the mortification of small wounds, mere scratches acquired in passing which had at first gone unnoticed, until they had gone quickly to rot; two had already been buried. Laurence had not yet decided to press forward, undecided as to the greater evil: he had seen enough men die, at the surgeons' hands, not to easily take on the risk of moving Granby only to deliver him into those hands, even if any skilled man might be found near-by.

But Iskierka's determination followed on the bleak acknowledgment there was scarcely any risk to be run, anymore. Gently they bundled Granby onto a stretcher made of branches and woven vines, and covered him with tented leaves against the sun. "I will go and hang on to him, sir," Roland said, and not even Temeraire protested her climbing aboard Iskierka's back to help keep Granby shielded and in place.

They turned southward, and came within a day to Belém: the small city huddled down behind its walls, and bells ringing out wildly in alarm as the dragons came into view. "Pull up!" Laurence shouted, realizing too late: the inhabitants saw only four dragons of enormous size, with no uniformed troops and no flags, and of no easily recognizable European breeds: Temeraire was Chinese, Iskierka Turkish, Churki Incan, and Kulingile a fresh cross and wholly unfamiliar. "Temeraire, pull up, and make Iskierka do the same: they will fire on us in a moment."

Iskierka thought only of Granby, at present, and was diving for the city square: Temeraire plunged beneath her, and bodily heaved her up and out of range even as pepper-guns spoke by the dozen; the thin black clouds spread like a pall over the city's walls, and then the narrow, long-throated cannon roared out at them and the small barbed balls flew.

But the town was better armed than generaled: the first spurt of firing died away, and a second did not come for nearly ten minutes, and was flung in their direction despite all the dragons having withdrawn beyond the range; when this had finished, Laurence touched Temeraire, and they dived forward into the square, where a regiment was trying to form up with what looked to be half the soldiers missing.

"Stop that," Temeraire said angrily, in French, "we are not here to attack you, at all: we are British, not the Tswana, and we are here to help."

* * *

"I ought to be more grateful," Granby said, "seeing how I have had one close-run thing of it after another, and I amn't in the ground yet; and I don't mean to complain, but what a nuisance it will be," answering Laurence, who had complimented him on the progress of the healing stump. The relief of their proving friend rather than foe had spurred a spirit of generosity on the part of the city, improved by Hammond's presenting them to the local governor in the light of saviors who had come to assist against the invasion; Laurence suspected he had not yet mentioned the altered circumstances in the Incan empire. An excellent surgeon had been provided, along with enough strong spirits to render Granby still more insensible than his fever; and several religious were now nursing him day and night.

"I know fellows go up and down well enough regardless," Granby added, "and I suppose I can get a hook, so pray don't listen to me; meanwhile, we had better be going, hadn't we? I can't make out all of what they are saying, here, though I made my Spanish tolerably good when I was stationed in Gibraltar, but it seems pretty clear we are needed in Rio yesterday if we are to have any hope of finding the Regent there, anyway."

"We will not go for a few days more," Laurence said quietly; Granby was still pale and fever-hectic. "Temeraire is working with their local priest, and several of the traders, to plot us a route: we will save the time twice over, in not having to hunt after water as we fly."

"All right, then; and tell Iskierka to behave herself, and I will creep out onto the balcony again to-night," Granby said, and let himself sink back against the pillows, his eyes already closing; Laurence pressed his good shoulder, and went out to be pounced on for information by an anxious and fretting dragon.

"I am glad you killed so many of those dragons," Iskierka said to Temeraire, when Laurence had given her his report, and gone to speak with the surgeon about some point of the surgery, "very glad; only I wish I had done it, and perhaps I will go back and do it now. If Granby should not get well, I shall, too."

"That would not be in the least sensible," Temeraire said, "for we were fighting them in the dark: you will never recognize the particular dragons in question, and it is not as though all of them had an equal share in the assault upon us: I dare say there are a great many of that sort of dragon who never heard of us at all. If you would like to blame someone, you had better blame the Inca; or even Napoleon, for I suppose the Inca set the dragons on us for his sake. Anyway you are still not well, either: have some more of this cow."

Iskierka ate, if sullenly, and Temeraire bent his head over the map which Sipho was drawing up, according to his instructions and what Temeraire had gleaned from the various traders who had been marched unwillingly up to him for questions.

Iskierka swallowed the haunch and said, "That whale."

"Yes?" Temeraire said, absently.

"May I have it?" she said, and leaned over to nudge Kulingile. "And your half, also."

"Can I have the head of your last cow?" Kulingile asked, opening an eye.

"Yes, all right," Iskierka said, and pushed over the cauldron in which it had been stewed.

"If you like; but what do you mean to do with it?" Temeraire said. "It is nearly half-a-day's flight away from here, now; and I suppose the meat cannot be good anymore, as we did not preserve it."

"I don't want the meat; I want the blubber," Iskierka said, and insisted she did not care that the blubber would surely have taken on all the flavor of the spoiled meat; which Temeraire did not understand in the least, until she came back again at the end of the next day, stinking and sooty and triumphant, and fell upon her share of the provisions which the town now daily made them.

"Granby has asked for you twice," Temeraire said, reproach-fully, and flattened back his ruff, "and you might sit downwind; what have you been doing?"

"I have been rendering down the whale," Iskierka said, tearing at her sheep, "for some of those traders: one of the sailors showed me how to go about it, and now I am rich again; and I am going to buy Granby a golden hook."

"One might think she would be above trickery," Temeraire said to Laurence, "not, of course, that I begrudge Granby anything at all; but it was *my* whale: mine and Kulingile's, and she might have said so if she knew we might get gold for it."

He could not stifle resentment when he saw the result, and had to watch as Granby came down from his sickbed at last several days later, to be presented by Shipley—whom Iskierka had re-cruited as her deputy in the matter and was all smiles in a fine suit of black cloth, bowing as he held out the box—with the truly splen-did hook: shining gold on black velvet.

"It will be too soft for use, you know," Granby said, when he could speak again, "so we will have to put it by for special occasions—"

"Not at all," Iskierka said, "for I thought of that; and so they have made it out of steel, really: it is only gold on the outside; the rest of the funds went for the diamonds."

"Yes; I see," Granby said, staring at the shining faceted gems which gleamed all around the base of the hook in even rows.

"Put it on, at once," Iskierka said, audibly hissing steam in her excitement, and then Granby put down the lid of the box and said, "No."

Temeraire raised his sullen head, blinking, to watch as Granby said, "No. I am done with this, Iskierka, do you hear me? I am done with being dragged about, and made into what a lunatic might call a fashion-plate, and *married off*—"

"But you are not married, at all—" Iskierka protested.

"No fault of yours if I am not," Granby said, which was very true, "and I dare say if I let you go on as you have been, you will try again, soon enough as you have found some princess or duchess or other lying about—" Iskierka twitched in what Temeraire could only call a guilty fashion. "—and I shan't put up with it anymore: you aren't fresh out of the shell any longer, and we are going to have a little more sense. Or you may take your leave of me, and find a captain who will swallow all your starts, and let you do just as you like—"

"Never, never!" Iskierka said, bristling wildly. "Oh! How can you be so cruel, when you must see very well that I am only thinking of you."

"What you mean is, thinking of how you can show me off to your best advantage," Granby said bluntly, "which isn't the same thing, at all."

Iskierka coiled on herself uneasily. Temeraire felt a smart of anxiety for his own part: but, he told himself, it was not at all the same thing, to wish Laurence to be recognized for his own abundant merits; and after all he did not insist on Laurence's wearing his robes, but only proposed it, now and again, when it seemed to him most appropriate, and when Laurence's natural modesty should from time to time require a push to overcome.

"Well, I *mean* to think only of you," Iskierka said in her defense, "and surely you must like to have splendid things, and have everyone see how particularly important you are—"

"The most splendid thing I am ever like to have," Granby said, "is a Kazilik dragon, dear one. All I have ever wanted is to call myself a captain, in His Majesty's Corps, and if you should manage to make me into a lord or an emperor or a rajah, I shouldn't know in the least what to do with myself."

Iskierka grumbled deep in her throat, but said grudgingly, "Well, if you very much dislike the idea of being a prince, I suppose I will give it up; but you do want a hook—"

"I should be very glad of a serviceable hook, of good steel, with no gewgaws to catch a blade upon in battle," Granby said firmly, "and as for the rest of the money, we will put it to provisioning, as the whale was caught for all our benefit," which Temeraire brightened at, as repairing the injustice of Iskierka's selfishness. "And if you should ever take another prize in future," Granby concluded, "we will put it into the Funds."

"What are those?" Iskierka said.

"Oh—stocks and so forth," Granby said vaguely, "investments; I dare say when we have come to England I can find a man of business to manage them. I should much rather have the money in the five per cents than wear it in my sleeve."

So when they left, two days later, they left at last decently equipped again: trousers for all the aviators, and boots—if these did not fit exactly right, they were still closer to proper uniform than before—and at least a shirt for every man. Temeraire rejoiced in four rifles, acquired triumphantly by Roland through an intense bout of haggling, and still more that he had proper riflemen again: Laurence had plucked up Baggy to take one, swearing the boy in as an ensign, and Ferris had one as well. And by Laurence's order, the spare gunpowder was poured out and stored in small powderhorns, which might even be used as incendiaries in need.

The harness was repaired also; when at last it was buckled on again, and the men had climbed aboard in an orderly fashion almost like a proper ground crew, Temeraire breathed deep in satisfaction. "All lies well; and how wonderful to feel myself properly rigged out again, Laurence," he said, looking over his shoulder as Laurence settled himself into place.

"Yes; I will be glad not to feel so wretchedly useless, when next we are in battle," Laurence answered, with satisfaction of his own; and Temeraire noted with pleasure that he and all the crew had carabiners again, which should be far more reliable in keeping them safely aboard.

"I ought to ride with Temeraire," Hammond said, trying to sidle past Churki, who was insisting on his riding on her back, alone; she had nothing but a light neck-strap for harness that he might use to secure himself. "If we should encounter any of the Tswana, in the air, I ought to be on hand—"

"We will all keep in company," Churki said, "and Temeraire is a fighting-dragon: you are not a soldier, and therefore should not be aboard a beast who must go into battle if it offers. I can much better keep you safe as an ambassador ought to be."

He yielded without much grace, but consoled himself with a handful of coca leaves: he had found a fresh supply, and they had quite restored him to health. "Pray do keep in mind," he called to Temeraire, "that if we *should* meet the Tswana, you must wait for me to bespeak them: we cannot have any more of this excess of independence."

"I call that unfair," Temeraire said to Laurence as they went aloft, "when it is not my fault that our negotiations in Pusantin-suyo did not work; *I* did not try and marry Granby to the Empress."

Mrs. Pemberton joined Hammond on Churki: offered the opportunity to stay and await a ship for England, she had refused. "No, Captain, although I thank you for the offer," she said. "But I should consider myself poor-spirited indeed not to see my charge through to the end: it is only now, after all, that we have arrived at our original destination."

They made their approach to Rio directly from the north, cutting across a great swath of jungle; and as they drew near they began to be flying over broad cleared estates, green and full of peacefully grazing cattle. "I think perhaps we cannot have heard truthfully, about the destruction," Temeraire said, swallowing another bite of delicious beef, when they had stopped short of the city to eat well and restore themselves. "Everything seems in order to me here, and we are very close to the sea again."

But "There is no-one tending the herds," Laurence said quietly, and asked him to circle around south, so they might approach the city unnoticed, sheltered from view by the Corcovado hill. That next afternoon they came at last into sight of the beautiful harbor of which Laurence had spoken so often, and all the city laid out below.

"Good God," Hammond said; they were all silent. In the harbor, a great dragon transport even larger than the lost *Allegiance* was riding at anchor, and a host of smaller vessels around her: six light frigates, bristling with guns. The tricolor snapped gaily from their masts.

All the rest of the city was a ruin of shattered houses and deserted streets, blackened by fire, with perhaps a dozen dragons of varied size nesting in the rubble or perched on some of the wreckage like crows. Some of them were eating cattle, and others lay watchful and huddled around a sort of encampment of tents and sheds which had been erected in one cleared section of the city near the docks.

"They are not all heavy-weights, anyway," Temeraire said, although privately—he did not wish at all to convey alarm—but privately, he did think it would be rather difficult for even the four of them to manage so many, in a single fight, even if Churki should decide to fight with them; there *were* at least five heavy-weights among the enemy; and Iskierka was not yet quite well. "Although that red-brown one looks as though he might come up to my weight—"

"Kefentse," Laurence said. "His name is Kefentse."

Chapter 16

❦

"I AM GLAD TO SEE YOU WELL, Captain Laurence," Mrs. Erasmus said—or rather Lethabo, as she informed him she had resumed her childhood name, from before her abduction. Indeed there seemed nothing left of the subdued, silent woman Laurence had first met on the way to Capetown. She now wore the elaborate Tswana dress of patterned cloth, and much gold jewelry bright against her skin, but these were mere externals: the true distinction lay rather in the stern carriage of her neck, the severely pulled-back hair which disdained to hide the scarring upon her forehead, and her direct look.

"But I hope you are not come as an enemy," she added, bluntly.

She had returned hence with Kefentse to direct the search for more Tswana survivors among the slaves on the estates. Brazil had been the destination of nearly all those slavers who had preyed upon the villages of the Tswana before the Tswana's armies, being roused, had struck against the slave ports of Africa and stifled the trade. She herself had been brought here as a mere slip of a girl, abducted from her home and sold into bondage; only great good fortune had preserved her to obtain her freedom and eventually return to her homeland. Yet there could not be any great number of similar survivors: apart from the hideous toll of the ocean crossing in the foulness of a slave-ship's hold, those who lived to reach Brazil would for the most part have been set to hard labor clearing the deadly jungle or harvesting cane.

"You must know you are being used, by Napoleon," Laurence said, "to an end which would see more and not less of the world reduced to a subjugated state; indeed he has reinstated slavery, rather than forbidden it, in the territories of France. Can you have found so many survivors of your own particular tribe, with this assault, as to justify the toll in life among the innocent?"

"There has been no slaughter," she said. "We did not burn the city: the Portuguese did that themselves, in their panic, while we stayed upon the mountains and made our demands for the return of the stolen. We took the city only after they had fled it. As for the survivors, you may come and see for yourself."

With a word to Kefentse, she guided Laurence and Granby and Hammond down to the encampment and through its cramped and narrow lanes, which housed to his surprise many thousands: men, women, children, dazed with both destruction and liberation. "Some are the descendants of those stolen," she said, "and do not remember their home in Africa."

"And others," Granby said to Laurence in an undertone, "haven't anything to do with the Tswana at all, I imagine: those dragons don't seem likely to me to be so very particular about who they have found, so long as they have found someone." He started guiltily, seeing Lethabo's eye upon him overhearing.

"But he cannot be wrong," Laurence said to her, when they had gone back into the dockside house which, being one of the remaining standing buildings, served presently as her headquarters. Supplies of foodstuffs and clothing salvaged from the wreckage filled the rooms, and they sat among barrels of salt beef. "I can scarcely believe that so many would have been taken before provoking that answer, which your dragon country-men have made, of smashing the slave ports; and you yourself have told me that not one in ten could have survived this far. The greater share of those you have rescued cannot be of the Tswana."

"If it were so," Lethabo said, "and yet they claimed ancestry or some distant memory, would that be less true than the rebirth of our ancestors as the dragons who guard us?"

He did not know how to answer her: she had been the wife of a missionary and, he thought, too good a Christian to believe in that superstition; she saw his confusion and shook her head. "I do not call that a lie," she said, "which when believed is true; and I think God loves justice better than the letter of the law. You will forgive me a moment."

She rose, for another four survivors had that moment come rushing into the house: a man and a woman with a child in arms and an older one clinging to her hand. They looked with fear over their shoulders at the middle-weight dragon who had deposited them before the door; in contrast the beast stood outside hunched down and peering in after them, with a hopeful air.

Lethabo spoke to them in Portuguese; Laurence could not follow the conversation, but saw them grow gradually calmer, and then uncertain, looking back at the dragon with doubt writ on their faces. At last Lethabo went to the table before the windows and opened a great ledger in which names were written in two columns: she paged through it and found the name *Boitumelo* solitary on the left, and read it aloud to them.

The man repeated it slowly, and looked a question at the woman; she looked at the children, and in a moment repeated the name also. Lethabo nodded, and wrote in the right-hand column; then took them outside to the waiting dragon, and spoke with the creature in the language of the Tswana. Laurence went to stand by the doorway, and heard her tell the dragon that the man was likely the grandson of Boitumelo, and this his family. The dragon bugled joy and answered that he had thought so: there was a decided likeness, in the little boy; and he put his nose down to the older child, who after a moment tentatively reached out and gave it a pat.

In a little more than a quarter-of-an-hour, Lethabo came back inside: the new arrivals had been seen off to shelter in the settlement by one of the women assisting her. She raised an eyebrow at

Laurence, who stood looking over the ledger. "Do you have any other quarrel with my work?"

"No," Laurence said quietly, as she shut the book again, "none; save to wonder how you will take so many home."

"The French have promised to sail us back," she said, "and then return for more: we were brought from Africa in smaller ships; on these great transports near one thousand can sail, and in better comfort, with the peace of knowing they go to freedom and not to slavery." She nodded at his look. "And on their return the ships will bring back still more dragons, yes. Of course they are using us: and we them; this is no true alliance, and our King knows better than to trust Napoleon, but we have had not much opportunity to choose our allies in this cause."

"Would you prefer others?" Laurence asked outright, ignoring Granby's startled look, and Hammond's barely restrained flinch of protest.

"Perhaps, Captain," Lethabo said, "and I think we must have others, if we are all not soon to witness the very slaughter of which you first accused us."

"Captain," Hammond said at once, as they left the headquarters and began the walk back to the city's edge, where Temeraire waited to carry them up to their encampment on the hill, "of course our engaging in a direct action on behalf of the colony is presently somewhat impractical—"

Laurence exchanged a look with Granby, whose face showed what he thought of this as a description of a confrontation between three dragons and near two dozen.

"—but I feel I must remind you that the Portuguese are our allies, and invaluably so—even this very moment British soldiers may be landing on their soil—and I cannot countenance any arrangement which should damage our relations with that nation."

"I hope to do no such thing," Laurence said.

"Sir, you will forgive me," Hammond said, "but as a point of law, these men and women you see thronging these alleys are escaped slaves—the legal property of landowners subject to the Portuguese Crown: in the—the tacit encouragement, the, I must say, near *endorsement*—sir, you did not at any moment take pains to establish the rights of the—of the owners—"

Laurence stopped in the lane and took Hammond by the arm and turned him forcibly to look: children played in the street building toy forts from shattered bricks, women sat together with their washing; a scene which might have belonged to any village, despite the framing ruins. "Mr. Hammond," Laurence said, "if you came here with the purpose to render thousands of human souls into bondage, for the mere worldly profit either of landowners or of nations, then you brought the wrong man to assist you; and I think, sir, you well knew as much, when you solicited that I should come."

"Oh—" Hammond tried to draw away, uncomfortable and without much success. "Captain, I speak here of sovereignty—the necessity of balancing—I must assert that we will not secure the liberty of these men and women, if you begin by giving offense to the Portuguese Crown: in breaching the subject of negotiations with the Tswana first, without reference of any sort to the wishes of the prince regent, you have usurped his authority—"

"If you can envision a solution to the present difficulties faced here by the Crown which does not entail coming to terms with the Tswana," Laurence said, "then I beg you to enlighten me; and likewise if you imagine any circumstances where the Tswana should agree to affirm the rights of slave-owners. But otherwise, you have heard Lethabo's account of the circumstances, and unless you doubt her veracity on no grounds whatsoever, in my opinion there is not a moment to lose."

Lethabo had explained that in the wake of the burning of Rio, their demands having gone unanswered, the Tswana dragons had swarmed out over the nearby countryside and among the nearest estates, snatching up slaves and carrying them back to the city. Rumor had soon outrun their work, and many more slaves as well had begun to flee their masters, and to make their way to the city in hopes of liberation.

There had been no direct battle offered, no extensive engagement: the Tswana were too anxious to avoid any injury coming to the slaves, and the few confrontations with local militia had quickly been resolved in their favor, their having early on seized or ruined nearly all the available artillery. At first the Tswana had carried on their rescue with impunity, but some of the colonists, fearing both the loss of their property and the direct attacks which had not yet come, had hit upon a dreadful solution to forestall them. The slave-owners had made some number of their slaves hostage and penned them into barns or small buildings on their property, which they now threatened to set alight if ever the dragons approached.

This tactic had, in the near term, established a stalemate: the Tswana had confined themselves to snatching only slaves they saw in the open. But their anxiety to protect their kindred warred with their impatience, and the stalemate would not survive for long.

"Yes," Temeraire confirmed, as they flew back to the camp. "I have been speaking to Kefentse, and he is firmly of the opinion that they must attack regardless. They have been quite at a standstill for two months now, and the hunting is getting thin if they avoid the estates where slaves are held. They do not all agree with him, of course. Dikeledi—she is that middling pinkish dragon with the horns, whom you have seen, flying—Dikeledi has not yet found any survivors of her own tribe, and so she refuses to countenance the risk."

She was less willing to be deceived than many of her fellow-dragons; having lost her village only a few years before, one of the last struck, she insisted on recognizing the survivors in their persons, rather than accepting others as their descendants to renew her lineage. She was not one of the larger beasts, but had nevertheless

enormous consequence among the Tswana for her skill and maneuverability in the air, and, Laurence gathered, was held to be the re-
incarnation of a priestess of great renown.

But Temeraire reported the general opinion had begun to turn
against her: the other beasts were grown angry and brooding over
the hostage slaves, whose treatment they feared; particularly after
the attempt at starving out one of the plantation owners had ended
in horrified failure when he began to starve his slaves in turn.

"A bloodbath on all sides is certain to ensue," Laurence said,
"if we cannot forestall it; therefore, Mr. Hammond, you will oblige
me with rather less concern for the injured sentiments of our allies,
and more for the swift advancement of a truce which should preserve their very lives."

The Portuguese government had retreated to a fortification in the
city of Paraty, near the limits of the day's flying range of a dragon.
Temeraire flew in under a somewhat ragged British flag which had
been dug out from the rubble of the city and provided by Lethabo,
despite which their approach met shouts and ringing bells of alarm
and assembling troops. Temeraire pulled up and hovered out of
range of the guns, while Gerry vigorously hung out the colors and
made the handful of appropriate Portuguese signals which had
been cobbled out of the collective memory of the aviators, none of
whom had ever served very long as signal-ensign.

These were received doubtfully below, plainly occasioning a
great deal of discussion, until reply came some quarter-of-an-hour
later, and they were bidden to land in the face of a bristling defense:
all the guns which the Portuguese yet held, and their crews sweating at the touch holes with the match smoldering.

"You will go aloft again when you have let us off, Temeraire, if
you please," Laurence said, with an eye on those nervous hands.
"We can have no reliance on the judgment of those men: keep out
of range until they have recognized our party."

"Well, I will: but only just out of range," Temeraire said uneasily, "and if there is any difficulty, I am certain if I should come at them from the flank, and roar at the proper angle, I could roll up all those guns at once."

Laurence shook his head, privately: he had not yet thought over all the consequence of the amplification of the divine wind, which Temeraire had achieved on Lien's example. Though she had formerly disdained direct action in battle according to the Chinese tradition, her reluctance had not survived the immediacy of threat to Napoleon's person; and Laurence had no doubt that Napoleon would bend his every wile towards persuading her to unleash so astonishing a weapon in his service in future. That it might be put to use so devastatingly on land, and not merely at sea, made her even more dreadful a danger.

But now he slid from Temeraire's back into the courtyard, and helped Hammond to climb down before Temeraire lifted away; he turned to meet the dubious eyes of a sweating Portuguese officer in the uniform of an infantry captain, who brightened as he saw Laurence's green coat and gold bars. He nodded with enthusiasm, and said in broken French, "Ah, you join us! We are overjoyed, pardon—" and turning waved back the guns, and the soldiers fell with expressions of relief out of their ragged square.

Messengers went running into the main building of the fort, which showed recent signs of repair: fresh masonry and paint unmarked by weather. They were kept standing, and Laurence used the time to study the walls: not much use, he thought, against the Tswana; not up to standing against even a middle-weight.

At last Hammond elbowed him and bowed, as from the fortification issued a party of men, with one corpulent man uniformed and beribboned in the front, and Hammond greeted him in his native tongue and then continued in French to say, "And I beg Your Royal Highness will forgive our delay in arriving, occasioned as it has been by difficulties beyond our control; and permit me to introduce to you Captain William Laurence of His Majesty's Aerial

Corps," before he whispered urgently and unnecessarily to Laurence, "Pray make your bows, sir: this is the prince regent of Portugal."

"We will certainly take back Rio, very shortly," Prince João said, "when our forces are well-gathered: from Mexico we have already a dozen beasts, whom even now you can see at maneuvers—"

He waved a hand at the window of his office which looked out upon a valley below, meaning by this a handful of small feral-looking dragons. "One generation at most out of the wild, if that, sir," Ferris said to Laurence in an undertone, as he peered out the window. The beasts were none of them bigger than a Greyling, and certainly to be rolled up by any one of the Tswana dragons, who were the product of dragon-husbandry at least equal to that of the West and raised on a diet of elephants.

"And we await any day the advent of more beasts: it is not Napoleon alone who has transports, after all. Your dragons shall be of great assistance, but as for truce: no! We will never yield—"

"Then, sir, you have not attended to our report," Laurence said bluntly, while Hammond blanched. "As we speak Napoleon is securing not merely alliance but direct allegiance from the Inca, whose empire now abuts your own realm so nearly as to intrude upon its claimed boundaries; shortly he will be there upon your flank, not with a handful of dragons imported from overseas, but with the vast and organized aerial legions of that nation."

"Captain Laurence," Hammond said desperately, "I think you forget yourself—Your Highness, I hope you will forgive—"

"Mr. Hammond, I forget nothing," Laurence said, "but I will not stand by and serve as audience for a venture so ill-advised as to wreck all hopes of the preservation of this colony: if that, Your Highness," he added, turning back to the prince, "and not some temporary victory is your desire, you have only one real avenue which I can see: not merely to make peace with the Tswana and send them hence, but to persuade them to settle here among you."

Laurence chose abruptly to make the proposal, fully expecting the astonished silence which it won him: he could not deny it sounded even more mad when said aloud than when it had first occurred to him, looking upon the French transports in their harbor, the ten thousand refugees and more in the city. The calculation of voyages and time which should be required to send so many back to their home in Africa had struck him with great force. If the Portuguese were persuaded to yield up their remaining slaves, the numbers would swell into impossibility; add to that the hazards of the crossing, and the Tswana could not so easily return home as they had come. Which likely had been Napoleon's design: he meant Brazil to be besieged a long while.

"Sir," Laurence added to the staring expressions, "you must recognize you have no other prospects of a defense against the Inca; not in time. If you should acquire a handful of dragons from overseas, those beasts are stolen only for a little while from the war in Europe. Even if victorious here, which can by no means be relied upon, they must return in short order. In the Tswana, you have at hand a small army of dragons already skilled in aerial battle, attached by the bonds of natural sentiment to a portion of your citizenry, and able to remain and at once begin to breed up beasts of battle-weight."

He went to the window, and flinging it open called out, "Temeraire! Will you be so good as to join those dragons, there?"

"Oh, if you like, of course I will," Temeraire said, raising his head from the ground, and peering in the window: his great gleaming blue slitted eye filled the glass, and sent half the men in the room startling out of their chairs and back. "Only I thought I should spoil their maneuvering."

He lifted away from the courtyard where he had been napping, with a leap that rattled the curtain-rings, and in a moment was among the little dragons. They left off their practice and swarmed around him clamoring in excited voices, which carried even up to the window: in their relative proportions not far short of sparrows circling some great beast, a lion or a bear, to which they could pose no threat. Laurence turned from the window to the prince.

"Your Highness, you can see your recruits will never make a dragon who can stand against a heavy-weight," Laurence said. "The most skillful breeding program should require decades to achieve such an end. Even if by some method we should drive the Tswana out of your country, do you imagine Napoleon will give you that length of time, before he falls upon you from the west?"

Poor Hammond was much to be pitied, Laurence thought ruefully while he spoke, as being a very unwilling accessory to perhaps the most outrageous speech which likely an ordinary serving-officer had ever made to a ruling sovereign; he looked increasingly more dazed with horror even than distressed.

"Where I am mistaken, or my arguments ill-founded, I am ready to be persuaded," Laurence added, "and I hope I offer no willful defiance: but neither I nor Temeraire nor any dragon of our party will lend ourselves, in the present circumstances, to a project of attacking the Tswana: an endeavor as sure to lead to disaster in its success as in its failure."

When he had issued this flat ultimatum, there was not much other discussion to be had: dismissed with some abruptness, Laurence made his courtesies and departed. Hammond remained, at the prince's command, and Laurence did not try to persuade him otherwise. He could well imagine that conversation: the prince should certainly inquire as to the extent of Laurence's influence upon the other aviators of their party, and Temeraire's upon the other dragons, information which Laurence rather wished Hammond to convey than to conceal.

"I will not urge you to act in any way contrary to your conscience; I would reject any such suasion on my own part," Laurence said to Granby, when he had returned to camp; and with a look he extended the scope of his words to Demane, who raised his head from where Roland was sketching for him on paper the outlines of a maneuver for a heavy-weight beast: he had suddenly of late grown surprisingly intent on furthering his education as an aviator, and now in every open moment was to be found harassing the senior officers for any scrap of knowledge.

"I am not going to attack the Tswana to help these slave-takers," Demane said flatly, recalling to Laurence that Demane's own people had suffered similar insult at the hands of the Dutch settlers of Capetown, if not abduction from their native country. "I would as soon fight with them, instead; why shouldn't we?" he demanded, to Roland's sitting back on her heels outraged. "Kulingile and I aren't going to fight Temeraire or Iskierka, but I don't mind attacking the Portuguese, if they should start the fighting."

"Oh! As far as that goes, I will say that I shouldn't mind it, either," Temeraire said, overhearing. "While I do see that it would be quite inconvenient that the Portuguese should be beat, since they are helping us against Napoleon otherwise, perhaps the Tswana would agree to help us against him instead: and I should just as soon fight *with* Kefentse. Even if he did snatch you, that time," he added to Laurence, "he has very handsomely apologized for that, and explained the misunderstanding. And one cannot really blame the Tswana for being so upset; they have the far better cause, it seems to me."

"I suppose that is a call for me to ask Iskierka," Granby said, "but I know very well that she will be perfectly willing to fight anyone whosomever. Well, if it helps you make them see sense, I will go as far as *saying* I plan to be sitting on my heels; but Laurence, I can't give you my word: there are those reinforcements to think of, which Hammond claimed would be sent us from the Channel. I didn't believe that they would ever arrive, when I thought we needed them to make any sort of go of things here; but now that they would be inconvenient, I think we must expect them at any moment. And if they do arrive before you have talked all these fellows round to this scheme of yours, and there are British dragons going into battle, I am not going to watch them square off against the Tswana while I sit here and twiddle my thumbs. Thumb," he added, rueful.

Laurence nodded silently: he wondered, himself, if he could under such circumstances remain a mere observer, without doing whatever he could to persuade Temeraire to join the battle; it could scarcely be borne.

Hammond returned later that afternoon and began a determined pursuit of private inquiry with Granby; who eeled away from him energetically as far as he was able, until finally cornered just before the dinner-hour: Hammond went away from the conversation dissatisfied and anxious, to be taken back to Paraty by one of the Mexican couriers.

"Well, he has made me commit myself," Granby said, sighing as he swung a leg over the planed log which made one of their benches and dropped himself unceremoniously into his seat: they ate in the open air, their handful of tarpaulins gone for shelter from the sun, and very little cover otherwise. They had established their camp in the hills a little distance from the coast, to avoid the eyes of the French sailors and also their guns, and without relief of wind coming off the water or any shade from trees which had long since been felled to put up the city, the tropical sun was punishing.

"I only hope you shan't get me dismissed the service, Laurence," Granby added, reaching across the table, and then winced for the indelicacy: poor Ferris had flinched, and now sat staring down at his trencher of flat wood.

Laurence looked at him, soberly: he could not see another course, but impossible not to recognize that he could scarcely have prejudiced Ferris's chances of reinstatement more effectively. There would be no triumphant return from this mission; at best they might preserve the colony against immediate destruction. Hammond's offer of his good offices, such as they were, would not likely survive Laurence's recalcitrance; and this entire action, working as it must to remind their Lordships of Laurence and Temeraire's general incorrigibility, would not incline them to mercy for his former first lieutenant.

"Of course, we would have the devil of a time going after them in there, to begin with," Granby said that evening: they had climbed up to the summit of Corcovado together under the cover of darkness, to spy upon the Tswana in their nightly conclave: the dragons huddled in a circle with the Tswana warriors and councilors forming an inner ring around a low fire: their shadows stretched away long like the spokes of a wheel. Out in the harbor the lanterns of the French ships were glowing out a misplaced constellation on the water, and the light here and there shone on the iron of their guns.

"But I don't know what we will do if they *do* go after those plantations," Granby added: while the deliberations were at too great a distance to be followed, Dikeledi's head flung back in loudly hissing distress boded ill for their direction. "Do you think there is any chance the regent will go along with you?"

"I hardly hope so far," Laurence said, tiredly. "At best, he may think on his danger from the Inca a little more, and seek out some truce; but he has a thousand slave-holders clamoring against any arrangement to which the Tswana would consent. And very likely he only thinks me a peculiar sort of lunatic."

"Well, at least Hammond will have given them a better notion of you—or a worse notion, I should say," Granby said, lowering his glass. "They haven't a prayer against the Tswana without us, if they only have a short one with."

"Granby!" Iskierka hissed up the slope at them, stones rattling away as she clawed partway up. "We must go at once: there are dragons coming towards our camp, from the south, at least five of them."

"I oughtn't have opened my mouth," Granby said; Laurence gripped his arm at the elbow, over the thick straps which bound on the hook, and together they scrambled down into Iskierka's reach to be put up onto her back. She leapt into the air with a mighty heave, and Laurence felt the rumble of her ceaseless inward workings beneath his legs like the grinding of a millstone as she drew up her flame, preparatory.

"Hi," Granby said, thumping her in the shoulder with his fist, "that's enough: those are *our* fellows, most likely, and you shan't go flaming them only because they will make matters difficult. I don't suppose their captains would love us for it," he added over his shoulder, "but do you suppose Temeraire could talk the beasts round?"

"I think there is every likelihood of it," Laurence said, as they closed in: Temeraire was on his haunches roaring out in greeting, and there was scarcely any mistaking the silhouettes of the approaching dragons: Lily's wide-stretched wingspan, and the vast and impenetrable shadow which was Maximus's bulk.

Chapter 17

MAXIMUS WAS BEING PERFECTLY UNREASONABLE about Kulingile, Temeraire was sorry to be forced to admit. Not that Temeraire did not understand his point of view, but after all, Kulingile had not chosen to grow so large; there was no sense in putting one's back up. "And if I have grown used to it, after having been there when he hatched as quite the scrawniest thing imaginable, you cannot very well complain," he added.

Maximus grumbled, deep in his belly, and said, "Oh, well, if he is a friend of yours," and Kulingile rather uncertainly said, "Would any of you like some beef? Gong Su has just stewed a few of them—" which thawed him further.

"I am glad he is not mean, at any rate; not to be swallowed, if he were," Maximus added to Temeraire, swallowing instead an entire cow. "And," he added afterwards, cheered, "I rather think I have an edge on him in wingspan; I am almost sure of it."

Temeraire was sure of no such thing, but prudently did not say so; everything went off reasonably and in the end they all settled into camp together with no outright quarreling. So there was really no reason for Berkley to be so distressed.

"Those damned blighters back at the fortress wouldn't mention there was a beast of thirty tons sitting here at your back, would they," Berkley said to Laurence, as he sat down at last: flushed through and downing a mug of grog which he now accepted, still breathing heavily. "No, it is all, 'Laurence and Temeraire are up to their usual starts, go and talk sense into them.' What have you done this time? That young whelp of an ambassador back at Paraty looked like to have an apoplexy when we told him we didn't undertake to do any such mad thing; as if there were a chance of success, either. I suppose being dismissed the service *once* is not enough for anyone, ha ha."

"The Admiral told us you had been reinstated," Lily said to Temeraire, "but why are we not fighting: I thought that was what we were all sent here for?"

"I shall explain it all to you," Temeraire told her and Maximus, "when we have all eaten, and slept: perhaps we ought to go and get another whale, so as not to have the bother of hunting for a few days."

"No," Maximus said decidedly, crunching the cow's skull between his jaws, "no whales! If I don't eat fish for a month it will not be too long: they did not have *any* meat on that ship. No fresh meat, I mean; it was all dried and mixed in with that porridgey stuff you gave them a notion of, and if we wanted anything better, we could go roust it out ourselves."

"Don't listen to him," Messoria said, as she ate her portion more sedately, "there were half-a-dozen cows aboard only for him; but he *would* eat them all, nearly right away, and then it was complain, complain, complain, all three months of sailing."

"I don't see what is the use of saving them to get thin and tough, at sea," Maximus said, injured.

Temeraire said, "Well, tomorrow I dare say we will find some more cattle, and I do not mind letting you eat my share to-night: how happy I am to see you all!"

There was something so very comfortable about having Maximus and Lily back, and all their formation also: Messoria and Immortalis, Dulcia and Nitidus, so that around the fire there were a great many voices, all friendly; and together they could certainly have stood against nearly anyone. There were of course still more of the Tswana, and anyway Temeraire did not want to fight them, but it was much pleasanter to think that they *could* fight, if they wished to, or if anyone offered them an unacceptable insult.

"Anyway it was still better than staying at home in England. It has been all watching the Channel, day and night," Lily said to Temeraire, tipping her head back daintily to swallow the last haunch of her cow, "and not a single engagement; the French dragons have nearly all gone away, to Spain or to the east, and it is only a few unharnessed beasts who fly patrol along their coast now and never come across. So tiresome, but when we thought we might as well help Perscitia, with the pavilions she is building, everyone grew stupidly upset."

"Dug out half the best quarry in Hertfordshire," Berkley said to Laurence, "and tore up four dozen oaks in the Midlands."

"So they sent us here," Lily went on, "and we did not mind going; but now we have eaten, and I want to know what we shall be doing here? And why are you shy of fighting those other dragons, if they are the enemy?"

"I am not *shy* of fighting them," Temeraire said. "Whoever said so? Only, they are not the enemy, in my opinion; they are those dragons we saw in Africa, and they are only here because they are trying to find their crews again: or what they call their descendants, who were taken for slaves."

"Those dragons who took Catherine from me, that time?" Lily said, with a cold yellow gleam in her eye.

"You will meet Kefentse tomorrow," Temeraire said hastily, "and I am sure he will apologize, just as he has apologized to me. Anyway, the real enemy are the Inca, and Laurence is sure that they will overrun this colony if we do not persuade the Tswana to stay and protect it."

"So that part is true?" Captain Harcourt said to Laurence, her face baffled. "Hammond began to say you intended something of the sort, before he understood we weren't going to oblige him, but I thought he must have muddled things up: not that I am in a hurry to go roaring in when we are outnumbered three to one, but where do the Inca come into it, at all?"

Laurence briefly acquainted them with the disastrous success which the French had found in the Incan empire, and Temeraire added, "We did try to stop it, of course: but she would marry Napoleon, for all we tried to warn her against him."

"Small wonder," Berkley said. "I'm only surprised you didn't have to flee the country with a horde of dragons on your tails."

"Well, we did," Temeraire said. "—It was not in the least amusing; so I don't see why you should be laughing," he added, rather nettled.

"I would beg pardon if you deserved it, you great lunatic of a beast," Berkley said, still snorting in what Temeraire felt was a most undignified way.

Harcourt and the rest of the formation of course had come direct from England, with all their crews, which overran the previously orderly camp in the usual haphazard manner of aviators; but they had also brought supply: guns, and powder, and chainmail armor to spare; and to the endless satisfaction of the sailors several casks of dark rum. Grog was served out with haste, and exchanged for fresh meat and fruit, while a comfortable bonfire was arranged for the captains, and the dragons laid down split logs around it.

While the preparations were under way, Laurence and Granby together described more fully the course of their unfortunate negotiations. "We cannot be certain," Laurence concluded as they seated themselves, "but the Empress would scarcely have committed herself so fully as to order an attack upon us if she had not resolved upon the marriage: we must assume if it is not yet accomplished, it soon will be."

"I suppose there is not much chance we could catch them this side of the Horn, if we set sail at once?" Little asked, sitting down beside Granby and handing him a mug of grog. "If he has lingered over the wedding-ceremonies, perhaps." Laurence exerted an effort of will not to permit himself a look at Granby's face: he would not have known of the liaison, save for Iskierka's indiscretion, and so he *would* not know of it.

"If we did manage to find them in the middle of the ocean, I don't know what we'd do with him," Granby said. "Two transports at least, if not another ship, and trust the Incas to cram every dragon aboard that they can."

"Well, so far we're even," Sutton said. "Captain Blaise has the *Potentate* waiting off the coast, and I presume the *Allegiance* is hereabouts somewhere?"

Granby stopped and looked at Laurence, who also was halted by surprise: but of course his report to the Admiralty was still in his writing-case—and his letter to Harcourt very likely still in the courier bag aboard the *Triomphe,* De Guignes having in courtesy accepted the duty of posting it. Even if that had been handed on to some French courier or frigate by now, Harcourt had been at sea for months now: she could not have received it. The evil news must come to her now, fresh and with no warning.

"Gentlemen, you will excuse me a moment; Captain Harcourt, may I ask the favor of a word?" Laurence said, at least hoping to give her a moment of privacy, but she stood up and looked him in the face and said, "Laurence, Tom is not dead?"

He looked at her helplessly; there was no help to be had or given. "Forgive me," he said. "I ought to have realized I had outrun my news: the *Allegiance* was lost in the forties, after a five days' storm."

"And he wouldn't come away?" she said.

"I beg you not to assign to him any such willful act of self-destruction," Laurence said. "He was to my last sight of him engaged in the most vigorous efforts to rescue the ship from disaster, which until those final moments not the most cautious observer would have considered without hope."

She nodded silently, and stood there a moment austerely pale and still; her long face had lost its youthful flesh in the crucible of the service and of childbirth, and her hair was pulled back into a severe plait. "You will pardon me, gentlemen," she said, and walked away from the firelight alone.

Her slim silhouette remained dark on the edge of the camp a long while, with only Lily's head bent down to her side, offering comfort. Laurence sat up by the fire, waiting, when the others had withdrawn to their tents; thinking she might wish to question him further as to the circumstances: if he could give her little satisfaction, there was no-one to offer more. But when she returned at last with reddened eyes and her skin blotted in places, and sitting down picked up her cup, she did not ask him anything; she only said, "What a dreadful waste; and oh! whyever did I let you persuade me to marry him? His brother is dead, too, and now that harridan will be after me day and night to let her keep little Tom."

Laurence gathered that by this she meant Riley's sister-in-law, who was surely anxious not only for her nephew's education but for the fate of her three daughters, left with only meager portions. After the baby, the estate would devolve upon a distant cousin who could scarcely be expected to have much consideration for their future, or for the comfort of the widow.

"And he is welcome to the whole kit, as far as I care; do you know little Tom can already climb the harness from belly-netting to the captain's seat, all by himself?" Harcourt said, with a pride which Laurence could not wholeheartedly approve in the case of a three-year-old child. "I have begun to take him up with me: I am sure he will get a dragon even if I cannot persuade Lily to consider him, after all; how I should *like* not to have to bother with another."

The advent of the formation, killing Hammond's last hopes of bringing pressure to bear which should force Laurence into a nearer compliance with his wishes, at last broke the hanging stalemate.

The regent yet refused to meet with the Tswana directly, an attempt at preserving his royal dignities, and delegated the conference to several of his noblemen headed by one Dom Soares da Câmara, a gentleman who spoke proudly of holding some thousand men, women, and children as chattel; and meanwhile the Tswana general Mogotsi who had charge of their forces bore rather a contemptuous look when he came into the main fortification at Paraty, which was too small to have allowed the entrance of dragons.

Laurence could understand only some words of what the general said aside to Lethabo, but gathered the meaning: a sneering at someone who had not a single ancestor worthy of rebirth. Mogotsi's dismissive flip of a hand at the feral dragons outside, hanging well back from Kefentse, required no translation whatsoever. The subsequent negotiations were carried on with a degree of hostility better merited by open warfare: which several of the Portuguese negotiators, slave-owners themselves, seemed if anything to be making an attempt to provoke.

"It must be their only hope of preserving their estates, of course," Hammond said distractedly as he paced the small anteroom to which they had retired for a brief respite, "their only hope—at least if there is a war, there is some chance of victory—indeed I am most impressed with the forbearance of that general; one would not expect it of a military man—"

Laurence, who had listened to Lethabo translating and picked out whatever he could, did not think that Mogotsi had needed to exercise so much restraint as Hammond would have given him credit for; and suspected that some remarks on the other side which might have given the Portuguese noblemen some excuse for ending the discussion had similarly been left out.

The chief Portuguese negotiator only snorted, and returned to his own occupation of glaring at Laurence; under his urgent whispers, Hammond had thrice renewed his attempts at remonstration, since Lily and her formation had arrived and put a period to his hopes of obviating any need for Laurence's assistance. These attempts—cajolery, threats, insults, appeals—had not been crowned with success, and at last Hammond had given over and turned his efforts to persuasion of the regent, instead, to make some at least temporary peace.

That it should be temporary was certainly the second hope of the Portuguese negotiators. But in the night, one of the little dragons came darting into the courtyard; his courier-rider dropped off panting, and ran in to convey the news that another French transport approached the harbor: with another nine Tswana dragons who had already left the deck and come to join their fellows on the shore.

The negotiators, roused in the early hours by the news, huddled murmuring and grim together until dawn brought Kefentse back, and the discussions resumed. Having given over the notion of preserving their slave-holdings for the moment, the Portuguese now began to argue for the manumitted slaves remaining on their estates—plainly, Laurence thought, with an eye to reversing that manumission as soon as circumstances might permit it, if not rendering it a mere fiction to begin with.

Lethabo listened, spoke with Mogotsi, and then turning back said, "You have torn kinsmen from one another; this cannot be allowed. Where they do not desire to return to their homeland, however, they may be reunited with their ancestors upon the estates."

Laurence doubted extremely that the Portuguese negotiators, wearing self-satisfaction in every line of their faces, understood that by *ancestors* the Tswana meant the dragons; nor did he enlighten them when afterwards Soares da Câmara bragged to his fellows in the next recess.

"You see how they swallow the least gesture," he said. "We ought to have met them across the table before: these savages have no understanding, no sophistication; they can easily be led if only one should satisfy their primitive impulses. They have learned that to be a *slave* is undesirable; very well, we will let them call themselves free; what does it matter, if they do not refuse to live in service to their betters, as some instinct of wisdom must lead them to accept? Even if a few thousand of them decide to brave the passage again and go back to Africa, we will scarcely be the losers when one considers the rate at which presently they flee their appointed places, knowing they may escape to the beasts."

Hammond looked uneasily at Laurence, perhaps wondering how much he understood and whether he would object; Laurence said nothing, and only glanced across the room at Lethabo, who looked back and met his eye with the faintest suggestion of a smile.

"Well, I hope they *can* be persuaded to remain, most of them, now that you have arranged handsome estates for them all to live on," Harcourt said, surveying Rio from the heights: the city had grown a little cramped with another five heavy-weight Tswana dragons trying to clear themselves room in the center, and a scattering of middle-weight beasts debating over the other corners. "If we do have to send them by the *Potentate,* we will be sitting on our haunches here ourselves for another year; or likely three: one trip won't be enough to get the half of them back over."

"They can't much like the idea of going back crammed aboard the hold very like in the way they came, and so they would be," Warren said, "for if dragons go along, it will be no end of work fitting enough provisions for them all. If it can even be done: I would not wager on getting more than five hundred passengers aboard at a time, myself. Look sharp, there!"

This exclamation was provoked by the approach of one of the larger Tswana dragons, who abandoning her attempt to make herself comfortable in the ruin of the city had gone aloft, and now came towards the mountain. She had not sighted them, however, or at least paid them no attention if she had; she landed clutching onto the cliff face and began to scratch at the wall experimentally, as though to work out its composition.

Evidently satisfied, she turned her head down and roaring

called to her fellows, a few of whom left off their own efforts and joined her in examining the stone. One of the smaller beasts made a thoughtful chirruping noise and darted away, returning shortly thereafter with one of the stolen cannon. From this they stripped away the wheels, leaving only a portion of the wooden housing, on which they seized; the barrel was set against the wall, and the larger beasts began to take it in turn to hammer the length into the rock. The smaller ones held it in place, and when it had been sunk halfway in began to twist and rock it; shortly they had burst out a small pattering avalanche of rock. It bore a strong resemblance to the work Laurence had seen once at the Tswana city of Mosi Oa Tunye, where the dragons carved immense living caverns out of the walls of the waterfall gorge.

By the next morning, the space was large enough for one of the smaller beasts to climb inside and sweep out debris; by that night, two of the larger dragons settled down therein to sleep. "Well, at least *some* of them are making themselves at home," Sutton said, as they checked upon the progress, but when Laurence returned to the negotiations and spoke with Lethabo, she shook her head.

"Kefentse will stay, and so will I and my daughters, for we have no other kinsmen remaining back home: but that is not true of many of the dragons," she said.

Fortunately Lethabo had been more generous to those beasts whose kindred had been wholly decimated, those same being more willing to accept refugees of doubtful lineage; and those dragons were willing to remain rather than risk the dangers of the crossing. But a dozen of the beasts still had villages and kin waiting for them in Africa, and insisted on returning at once, with almost two thousand men meant to accompany them: a company the size of a small army, and if anything more difficult to provision.

"Whatever fine language the Portuguese choose to write down in those papers, Captain, does not very much matter to dragons," Lethabo had said to Laurence, as they had left the negotiations. "You know it, and so do I. No agreement will hold which does not satisfy them. But this truly is our price: all the slaves freed and re-united with their ancestors, and transport back for those who wish to go. If you cannot do it, we must yet treat with the French, and then, if the Portuguese will not free their slaves—"

She spread her hands eloquently, and Laurence nodded.

"We could send the men by other boats, smaller ones—frigates, or a good-sized merchantman?" Warren proposed now—Laurence flinched a little at hearing him call a frigate a *boat*—but this sugges-tion Lethabo rejected out of hand: the dragons would not again be parted from their descendants.

"Well," Granby said, looking down past the harbor, where the two French transports rode at anchor, their colors bright from the masthead in the sun, "there is nothing else for it, but how can it be done?"

Chapter 18

⁘

"IT SHOULD BE EASY AS WINKING, if we wanted to sink them," Captain Warren observed: and a mere bombardment with boulders, carried one after another from the shore and dropped from on high, would indeed have sent the transports to the bottom of the ocean in no short order—where, of course, they would be of no use whatsoever in getting the Tswana home.

To take the great vessels, preserving them in a useful condition, was by far a more difficult problem, and not least because the French had been alive to the danger of just such an impulse on the part of their uncertain allies. The transports themselves were heavily armed, and bags of caltrops hung from the yard-arms above the dragon-decks in such a way that they might instantly be spilt across the planking, their iron teeth being large enough to prevent any dragon from landing easily upon the ship while offering only a little difficulty to the sailors aboard.

Meanwhile the frigates in their company were too small for any but Nitidus or Dulcia to land upon: fast and maneuverable and armed for the most part with a few heavy snub-nosed cannonades which would certainly be turned at once upon any dragon who tried to descend upon the transports: they were close enough to make a directed attack practicable. Laurence could spy among their complement as many as four gun-boats apiece, each armed with the long, narrow-barreled guns which threw the small barbed cannonballs.

"The gun-boats will be in the water five minutes after the alarm is sounded," Laurence said, peering at them through his glass, "if the crews know their work; in ten minutes, otherwise, and we shall hear from the guns directly after; and the cannonades. We cannot keep the dragons on the decks under that degree of fire."

"And even if we do manage to hold the deck, the French will have hulled the ships so wretchedly we may as well sit in harbor the next three years, for all the good they will do us: they will never make the long crossing," Sutton said.

"Yes; we must do something about those gun-boats, first," Harcourt said, rolling out a sheet of smudged parchment, and taking a scrap of charred wood from the fire to sketch upon it the outline of the harbor. "If we can keep them pinned down, somehow; then take the transports quick as quick can be, if they aren't to spike the decks against us—if we can only give those frigates a proper fait accompli, they shan't hull us, unless they mean to sink all their own crews."

"There's another difficulty for you," Warren said cheerfully. "Who's to sail them? We shan't; and the *Potentate* can scarcely let us have enough men to sail *two* transports more across the ocean and to home. Your bag of sailors will do some good, Laurence, but—"

"They are much improved," Laurence said, "but I would not trust them to sail a dinghy rigged fore-and-aft across ten miles of calmest sea without trained officers."

"Pray let us worry about one thing at a time!" Harcourt said. "If we do manage to cut them out, we ought to be grateful enough to have any other difficulties to work out."

"I do not quite see how it is to be done myself, Laurence," Temeraire said over his shoulder as the blue-black ocean streamed away beneath them. The weather was all that it should be for flying, clear and not too hot, and he could not help but spiral in mid-air for sheer delight: the difficulties of taking the transports should surely, he thought, be overcome; one could not let that worry one on a day like this.

"I am still on the shipping lanes, I hope," he added, peering down: he did not understand how Laurence managed to be so certain without an elaborate consultation of his compass and the stars where in the ocean they might be; they had left behind land some two hours ago.

"You are," Laurence said, "and if you will bear two points to starboard, that is a whaler, I think, and we may hope one of ours; or an American—at present I would be glad to take a dozen sailors out of an American, and damn the provocation."

Temeraire would have been equally glad, so long as Laurence was satisfied that the act could be justified, and he put on as much speed as he could: but when they came nearer, she hung out Dutch colors to meet their own Union Jack. Laurence swung down by a rope to the rigging, and climbing to the deck met with her captain while Temeraire hovered above her.

He climbed back up alone, without taking any men out of her, so it was not a mere ruse; Temeraire sighed, but when Laurence had reached his back and clasped the carabiners on again he said, "South-south-west, my dear, there is not a moment to lose. Captain Hoerug tells me they spoke the *Dapple* this morning: a forty-eight and a crack frigate, and if we can catch her before she goes beyond our range, we will have our men."

Laurence scoured the ocean with his glass, and put every one of his small crew to the same task in all directions: a flash of light off a window, the gleam of a lantern when twilight came on, anything would do; and finally near the limits of the range he had privately defined to himself, Baggy called down uncertainly, "Captain? Is that her, there-away; I think I see a flash, maybe."

Dapple sent up a blue light as they neared, and seeing their flag hung out her colors, an unsuspecting welcome: her captain would not expect to be pillaged from aloft, of course. Laurence did not recall who had *Dapple* presently; there had been a vast and somber reshuffling in the wake of the disaster at Shoeburyness, and he climbed down preoccupied with working out how many officers she might be able to give him. Only when he was on the deck, amid the familiar life of a Navy ship, and found himself asked for his name, was he recalled abruptly to the awkwardness of his position. To most officers of Britain, he was yet a condemned criminal and a traitor: his reinstatement would surely not yet have made official news.

"Captain William Laurence," he said, "of Temeraire," and saw the starts of confusion in the younger officers, the whispers traveling hastily to enlighten those unfortunate enough not to recognize their names; and the looks thrown skyward into the dark, where Temeraire's black hide was only a shadow against the sky.

The ship's third lieutenant, a young man scarce twenty years by his looks, had been directing the men into throwing out the pontoon-decks by which they could have offered a dragon a landing place. "Hold there, if you please, Mr. Rightley," he said, and looked at his captain.

"Captain Adair Galloway," that gentleman, of an age with Laurence, said slowly without offering a hand, "and sir, I believe I require some explanation."

"You shall have it, sir," Laurence said, "but it must be brief: I am sorry to come to you with such demands, but I must have every man you can spare; and if possible some you would find it hard to part with." He saw his words travel the deck with even more astonishment than his name; and Galloway looked still more bewildered. Laurence knew him by name and a little by reputation: a stickler, and his ship looked it; fresh from the Atlantic crossing and on the verge of a run at the Horn, her paint gleamed new-bright and her brass shone warmly beneath the lanterns; her officers were every man of them in uniforms that would have done justice to a dinner-party, and there was a sense of quiet order in all the lines of the ship.

She was, in short, run along the methods he would once have preferred himself, Laurence realized, rueful and aware of his marked trousers, his dull and unblacked boots, his yellowing linen. However, there was this absurdity in his favor: he had four years on Galloway on the post-list; he had seniority. "Shall we go inside, sir?" he said. "Temeraire would be glad of a short rest, if you can give it to him; but we must be aloft again as quickly as we may: there is not a moment to lose."

With few alternatives, Galloway showed him into the stern cabin, and shut the door on his interested crew; Laurence knew, of course, that if not every ear on the ship would be pressed directly to the door, they would still hear the conversation repeated soon enough. "Sir," he said, "I hope you will pardon my forthrightness, but I would address your hesitation at once: I am restored to the list as of 11 November in the last year. But my personal circumstances are of little importance. There are two French transports in Rio: we mean to cut them out, and we have ten dragons to do it with; but I have only two hundred men for prize-crew, and not an officer among them."

Temeraire hovered impatiently, until the pontoon-deck had been tied down at last: it was not very large, and he had to let himself down very cautiously with his belly quite full of air to keep from swamping it entirely. "There; that will do," he said, swinging his head round to the ship's railing: a line of staring sailors backed hurriedly away, except for one young officer who blanched but kept his place.

"Thank you: although pray secure that third line a bit better; that knot is very ugly and is sure to slip in a moment: it would not be in the least pleasant to have this come apart beneath me, and I suppose I should have to pull on the ship to get out of the water again. How many of you do you suppose will come with us?" he asked, unable to resist inquiry.

He did not receive any answer but stammers until Laurence came out with the captain, who looked very displeased, but nevertheless gave orders for forty men to embark, and four of his officers. For the officers, Laurence had Gerry sling over some carabiners and spare harness, and Temeraire put them one after another onto his back, beginning with the third lieutenant, Creed, and ending with a midshipman of fifteen named Wren. The men reluctantly climbed into a makeshift sack upon the deck, which Temeraire himself drew up and stuffed into his belly-netting, where the sailors might climb out of it with some awkwardness but reasonable security.

Forty men more! Temeraire thought triumphantly as he lifted away. Though of course these new recruits should soon go into service aboard the transports, and would thus pass from his purview, the sheer number seemed quite an achievement however transitory; and anyway perhaps they would *not* be able to take the transports, in which case they might remain with the other sailors as a part of his extended crew, after all.

So he was perfectly satisfied, when he came to camp and let them off; and having eaten an excellent meal of roasted cattle stuffed with the sweet ripe banana fruit he fell asleep until roused unceremoniously several hours later by a shove. "Ow," he said, opening one eye, "whatever is that for?"

"This is no time to be sleeping," Iskierka said. "Get up and help me stop this nonsense: they mean to go take those ships without us."

"I am sure you have just misunderstood," Temeraire said, sitting up yawning. "Lily and Maximus would not—"

"Not *them*," Iskierka said impatiently. "Granby and Laurence!"

Midshipman Wren sat in the front of the boat softly mouthing the time; the sound did not reach the stern where Laurence sat, and the oars dipped silent into the water and rose out again smooth, scattering only a few drops over the waves in their swift arcs before they dived again. Lieutenant Creed sat in the stern of the boat immediately to port, his thin face just visible by its pallor of excitement. He could not fail of being made post for this, of course, if they succeeded: a boy of twenty, to take into charge a transport; the sort of leap of fortune men dreamed of in the Navy.

Or, as O'Dea had gloomily observed on their embarkation, "As like we will end by feeding all the monstrous serpents of the deep, Captain." Laurence glanced to starboard: Granby's boat there, rather a tub, which had been acquired from a fisherman down the coast and laden with a heap of chainmail; past him Harcourt's boat. Laurence had made a vague gesture at trying to dissuade her coming; but they were cramming aboard every last man down to those who could only dubiously lay claim to the name—even young Sipho, clutching the signal-rocket intently—and she scornfully disdained the attempt. When he turned away subsequently, Roland's eye had met his with a martial light; so there he had not even tried, but contented himself with assigning her to take charge of the second of the boats assigned to lay on the chainmail: at least she would not be on deck until the end.

Their flotilla in miniature crept mouse-softly across the harbor towards the towering bulk of the transports: the *Polonaise* and the *Maréchal*. For illumination they had only the moonlight above and the bonfire in the city behind them where the Tswana had gathered for their usual nightly conclave: its noise carried louder over the water than the noise of the other boats, and the glare, Laurence hoped, would dazzle the eyes of the look-outs.

As they drew nearer, Lieutenant Creed looked over at Laurence and nodded, and his boat split away towards the *Maréchal,* drawing half-a-dozen of the others along in its train. They had drawn alongside the *Polonaise,* and Laurence opened up his glass and looked: the officer of the watch was down near the stern beside the wheel, the hands on deck made sleeping humps amid the cannon on the quarterdeck, and the lookout in the near crow's nest yawned against his arm: a ship in harbor, at peace.

Laurence nodded to Seaman Ewyll, waiting in the prow: a sturdy if stolid young man, who flung up the rope with its grappling-hook. It clanged against the rail as it seized on, and they all held still, waiting; not a breath misted the air.

The alarm was not called. Ewyll swarmed up the knotted rope, another five tied at his waist, and he flung them down quickly to the other boats: by the time Laurence made the deck, there were two dozen men already aboard the empty dragondeck, crouching low beside bales and casks, and the seven Frenchmen who had been sleeping on the deck were trussed like roasts with rags stuffed into their mouths. Ewyll and Wren were climbing into the foremast rigging after the suspended bags of the caltrops, with Captain Little and Captain Chenery gone directly after them, easy in the rigging from long mid-air experience aboard their dragons.

Laurence leaned over the side: Granby waved up from his boat, which having sent off half her men now rowed away around the other side of the *Polonaise,* where she faced the *Maréchal,* and began the critical work: they flung up ropes to men on deck to be looped over the railing, and began to draw up the chainmail netting, pillaged from the dragons' equipage, to lie over the portholes of her guns. Laurence turned away, and leading the assembled men soft across the dragondeck halted near the stairs leading to the main deck: a man lay snoring wet and thickly beneath them, mouth hanging slackly open.

Mayhew looked at him; Laurence nodded; Mayhew and another sailor, Todd, slipped barefoot down to the main deck and around back of the stairs, and Mayhew stopped the snoring man's mouth, pinning him down by the throat with his other hand. Laurence, looking through the steps, could see the Frenchman's wide starting eyes ringed with white as he struggled against Mayhew's broad hand; Todd lashed his arms to his body with rope and tied him at ankles and knees, swiftly, and they shoved him behind a stanchion and cleared the way.

Laurence crept down to the main deck, nearly on his toes, glad of the thin battered wreck of his boots. He counted off eight of the men for the fore ladderway, now almost directly before them and unattended. They seized one of the water-barrels and wrestled it on top to block the way, and hovered by it with their pistols and their knives and their cutlasses, whatever weapons they had contrived to conceal about their bodies.

The open deck now stretched away, and the watch-officer, an unlucky young lieutenant, was turning from his desultory conversation with the helmsman and coming towards the prow along the leeward side. Laurence waited, and waited; he wished to give the men in Granby's boat as long as he could, and the men in the rigging: even half-a-minute might have invaluable worth in the present circumstances. The watch-officer paused mid-decks and looked over the rail—he was inspecting the hull, which Laurence had noted in climbing up was indeed badly barnacled: she would have benefited from a thorough scraping.

The French officer straightened again and came on, humming with an occasional stifled slide towards whistling. He stopped again, squinting out to sea—he was looking at the *Maréchal,* which stood between them and the shore, so that the bonfire in the city illuminated the crouching shadows of the line of men stealing across her deck.

"Britain!" Laurence bellowed out, at the top of his lungs; the young French officer jumped undignified, turning, drawing his sword, but three of the sailors were on him; he went down at once. Laurence could not look to see any more: he was running towards the aft ladderway with another eight men behind him, and they clapped another barrel over the opening just as faces appeared below, staring up alarmed.

"*Alarme! Alarme!*" the boy in the crow's nest was yelling, and the hands on deck were starting up out of their sleep: starting up and meeting swords and knives, many of them. But one man heaved himself up enormously tall, overtopping six and a half feet with arms like a bear's: he shouldered aside the waving cutlass of the *Allegiance* sailor who stood in his way, snatched up with both hands a cannonball from one of the caissons on deck, and turning smashed the British sailor down with it. The cannonball rolled away, leaving a trail of blood and brains, and the Frenchman had the cutlass in his hand: he threw himself over the barrel of the neighboring cannon and cut down another man.

Laurence had the water-barrel at his back, which shivered with the rhythmic thumping from below as the men tried to come up; and French sailors were rushing at him across the deck. He fired both his pistols: one man down, another winged along the arm; then it was sword-work and awkward in close quarters: he planted his boot-heel in one man's belly and thrust him away, jerked free and slashed down at another who was grappling at his sword-arm. Blood spurted hot from the man's cheek onto his coat sleeve, and Laurence smashed him across the face with his fist, clenched around the blade-hilt.

The man clutched at Laurence's sword-arm, dragging it down with him as he slid to the deck, and the enormous Frenchman was charging. Laurence struggled to wrench loose his arm, to meet the swinging overhand stroke of the cutlass descending. The blade came on a mere shadow in the dark, a smattering of rust like black pits on the surface, and Laurence put up his arm to meet it sacrificially to keep it off his skull; then the Frenchman was crumpling onto him a heavy dead weight.

Laurence heaved off the corpse and looked past him in surprise: Gong Su was drawing a long knife from the Frenchman's side, so sharp barely any blood clung to the blade. There was blue light shining cold off the metal and casting a strange grey color over his face, and a hissing streak overhead: the signal-rocket had gone.

That meant they were fighting aboard the *Maréchal* also: they had been made, and now the next ten minutes, perhaps not even so many, would determine the fate of their venture. If the deck could not be held, on either ship; if the frigates were already awake and launching their boats—

And then Temeraire was roaring: impossible to mistake, as though the world itself were shattering, and Laurence felt even the great mass of the *Polonaise* go rocking as the ocean unsettled around her. Away across the water he could hear cries of alarm, and rattling thumps as of a hailstorm, if hail were made of solid rock and the size of a man's head: the dragons were dropping bushels of rock upon the frigates, going after the gun-boats where they were lashed to their trestles.

Laurence could not spare time to try and see, through the dark, whether the stroke had gone home; behind him, the water-barrel which held down the ladderway hatch was growing suddenly light: the men below had sprung out one of its slats, evidently, to drain it empty and allow them to push their way to the deck. "Hold it down, Wesket," Laurence shouted at one of the sailors, and moved to protect the man's back from the French as they came on.

Then the *Polonaise* rocked again as Temeraire landed on her deck: rearing up he tore the French colors from the mast, and roared again: even most of the British sailors flung themselves flat on the deck in horror at that noise, and Dulcia came darting in amidships and managed to plant herself somewhat precarious along the larboard rail, from whence she began to pluck one Frenchman after another off the deck, and hurl them out into the ocean.

"Laurence!" Temeraire called anxiously, and caught sight of him then: all the way at the far end of the ship, near the stern ladderway, and quite surrounded by Frenchmen—even if most of those were presently lying prone upon the deck for no reason which Temeraire could see. Temeraire snorted reproachfully: so much for promises of caution or of hanging back. "Dulcia!" he called to her. "Pray will you look after Laurence: I must go aloft again, for there are another four frigates to manage."

"I will; is Chenery there?" she called back, while obligingly lunging out across the deck and seizing a couple of men in her jaws, to throw them overboard, who had risen to their feet and approached Laurence.

"He is, here in the rigging," Temeraire said, after a quick glance, "and shall I bring him to you, now?"

"Here now, I can get myself across the deck of a ship, I hope!" Chenery said, looking up and wiping sweat off his brow. "Just you take these caltrops, will you, and heave them over."

"Oh; I will use them instead, I think," Temeraire said, seizing the makeshift sacks which Chenery and Little had made, tying up the corners of the caltrop-sheets. He carried them away into the air, and flying over to the nearest frigate, which was bringing her guns to bear on the deck of the *Polonaise*, he called, "Iskierka!"

"I am busy!" she called back, from the frigate which she was circling: she was breathing flame past the rigging, to the leeward side, and yelling at them to strike their colors.

"You are not, you are only trying to show away and take *another* prize," Temeraire said, "when you know perfectly well we are only trying to take the transports, and all we have to do with the frigates is to keep them off until the transports have struck: now pray fire these for me, as I drop them."

"Oh, very well; if you will come back to this one, after, and tell them in French to strike; I do not think they can understand me," she said, flying over to him: he shook the caltrop-sacks open, and she blazed away at them mid-air, so the iron tips of the things were half-melted as they fell down upon the deck of the frigate, and all the gun-boats, and so became stuck on to the wood. Temeraire hovered, watching in satisfaction: the crews had dived away to avoid the rain of smoking-hot iron spikes, and now could not easily manage their boats.

He looked up sharp, however: there was a fresh roaring, around the other side of the second transport, but this time of guns and not of dragons: and Maximus was bellowing in pain.

Temeraire leapt into the air: one of the frigates which he had thought disabled by the rocks had managed to turn broadside to the *Maréchal*'s dragondeck, and had all-too-cleverly reserved her fire until the moment when Maximus had landed to take off the caltrops: all her guns had gone at once, and poor Maximus had been exposed quite: a gaping rent showed in one of his wings, where the membrane hung loose as a piece of cut sailcloth, and he was bleeding black from shoulder and haunch and side. The *Maréchal*'s foremast also had been badly shattered, and splinters stuck porcupine-like from his head and neck: he swung his head back and forth with his eyes shut tight, bellowing, and meanwhile the frigate was surely reloading all her guns.

But even as Temeraire flew towards them, Lily was already at work: she dived low and spat a long running stream of acid along the deck, directly above the sides which faced the *Maréchal,* and cries rose up with the hissing steam as the droplets ate their way down into the gundeck and spattered the crews. Temeraire came following in a rush, and roared up the ocean furiously: the frigate reeled away on a great twenty-foot swell, and the second broadside erupted only stuttering, to hurl the cannonballs into the ocean some ten yards ahead of the *Maréchal*'s keel.

"There!" Temeraire said, triumphantly, and then cried out himself, shuddering, and nearly dropped into the sea: there was a dreadful burning pain just beneath his wing-joint, so that to stay aloft was agony with each stroke; he cried out gasping again, and abruptly Kulingile was there beside him, to take his weight, and saw him down to the deck of the *Maréchal* beside Maximus.

"But Laurence," Temeraire said, gulping a breath, "Laurence—"

"*He* has not got himself shot," said Gaiters, Maximus's surgeon, who was laboring away urgently and with his arms bloodied to the shoulder, "so just you hold still there, until one of us can come and look at you; for God's sake," he roared up at the young ensign who was temporarily his assistant, and attempting to assist him in stanching the wounds, "pack that sailcloth in harder; stand on it, if you have to."

"I am not going to sit on deck while we are still fighting," Temeraire protested, and craned his head around to look at the injury— perhaps it was not quite so severe as all that, and he might—"Ow!" He stopped: even turning so far was dreadfully unpleasant; he could feel the hooks of the ball tearing at his flesh. "Maximus, are you very badly hurt?"

"I am sure I will be perfectly stout when they have patched me together," Maximus said, with a grunt. "I should not have roared at all, only it took me by surprise."

"You will be stone-dead in an hour if we do not stop this blood, so you will shut your eyes and keep quiet, damn you," Gaiters said furiously. "Where is that fire-breather? Why don't she make herself useful: I will need this cauterized, as soon as I have dug out this ball—"

"Ough," Maximus said—not really a complaint, Temeraire thought loyally; it was only a startled noise—as Gaiters very nearly put his head into Maximus's side, and came out dragging the great iron cannonball with him in both hands, hissing himself in pain: it was still hot, and he dropped it on the deck and rolled it away over the side with his foot.

Iskierka landed, in answer to their signal, and heated the iron bar which Gaiters held out to her with tongs; Maximus reared up his head and yelled—not even the most loyal interpretation could call it anything else, sadly—as it was clapped to the wound, sewn up already with catgut.

But even as the wound was seared, the ship shuddered beneath them with the rolling thunder of the guns, and Temeraire looked anxiously out towards the *Polonaise*, where Laurence was still fighting. Although Lieutenant Creed and his party had so far also managed to keep the French penned belowdecks, there were still nearly six hundred men aboard, and those had gone to the gun-deck, instead, and now were taking aim at the other transport's deck to save her from their own fate.

But Granby's men and Roland's had done their work: the chain-mail netting hung over the sides of the ship, and if it did not stop the balls it dragged them down so they went splashing one and all into the sea; only a couple from the end reached the other ship, and splintered away a portion of her dragondeck.

Berkley stood up from Maximus's head, and climbing down heavily to the deck banged his big gauntleted fist down on the planking beside the fore ladderway. "Is your captain down there? We have the deck; you can see your fellows are all ahoo; now say you strike, or I will let you up, and the dragons can start knocking you overboard like ninepins: but I will damned well have an end of it."

Chapter 19

"I DO NOT WISH IN THE LEAST to diminish your very just sense of accomplishment, Captain," Hammond said to Laurence, looking out from the promontory at the two transports, flying British colors and supporting at present three and four dragons respectively: the rest being engaged in shepherding anxiously the boats which were ferrying over their recovered kindred, or bringing themselves the sacks of grain and dried salt beef which should sustain them over the six-week journey to the coast of Africa: in a species of justice, perhaps, they would disembark at the ruins of Lunda, that same port which had seen so many of them first pressed into bondage.

"Not in the least," Hammond repeated, in dismal tones. The *Potentate* could also be glimpsed, at a fair distance but coming in: she would be at anchor before sunset, Laurence judged, and they would begin their own process of provisioning her for the journey back to Portsmouth: one which Hammond certainly could not anticipate with any sense of pleasure.

No good would come him from the report which the Portuguese ambassador should make of him: at best, Hammond would figure as an ineffectual nonentity; at worst, as deliberately conniving at Laurence's insubordinate maneuvering, and the latter was more likely: to do him credit, with the transports acquired, Hammond had devoted his energies to winning over sufficient support at the Portuguese court for the negotiations to see them grudgingly accepted.

And Hammond could not rely on any leavening of success to gloss his supposed misdeeds. The Admiralty would make hay of the cutting-out of the transports, but the Foreign Office would not care much for that in the face of the devastating news regarding the Inca, and to hear that yet another great power had aligned itself, willingly, with Bonaparte: to hear that Britain stood now alone.

"And whatever am I to do about the beast? It is very well and good to say she is not mine; if she persists in following me, she may as well be mine, and I cannot find that any of the dragons have the least sympathy, or inclination to chase her away," he added, in some exasperation. Indeed Churki's attachment showed every sign of tenacity, and Hammond's attempts to dismiss her were met with the amusement of a parent retrieving a wayward child.

"She can't very well follow you over-sea," Chenery said.

"Can she not?" Hammond said bitterly. "I have already over-heard her discussing arrangements with Temeraire: she means to provide so many bullocks, in exchange for her passage; and how is she to be got off the ship once she has landed on it?"

"But Laurence," Temeraire said, when Laurence had at Hammond's plea spoken with him, "I cannot see any reason why Churki should not come back to England with us: you have said very often that the Admiralty is always quite desperate for new dragons who will fight. She was an officer in the Inca army, you know: no-one could argue she does not know how to go about it, and she has promised she will, if she is given her own crew."

"My dear, she is a subject of an empire which must now be inimical to our own," Laurence said. "If she aids us, she is a traitor; if she does not, she is our enemy."

"It does not seem to me treasonous," Temeraire protested. "After all, it is not as though she were going to fight Incan dragons, her friends perhaps; she will be fighting the French, and she says the Sapa Inca marrying does not make Napoleon *her* Emperor. Anyway," he added, "I cannot see myself being so dreadfully rude as to

shove her off: she is not so big that she will make things uncomfortable, and she is so much older than any of us except Messoria."

"So I am afraid I can offer you not much hope of escape," Laurence told Hammond on shore, supervising the packing of his sea-
chest: Gerry was not particularly handy, and Laurence was having
to refold every item before it entered the flimsy wooden crate which
should have to serve him for the purpose, "unless you should persuade some other person to inveigle her away from you; I may assure you that given your blessing there are several officers among
our company who would gladly take your place in her affections."

"I give it with all my heart," Hammond said, "and have not the
least hope of its answering. If she meant to be fickle, she might have
remained in her own country; and I dare say she will be perfectly
ready, in the Incan style, to accept any number of suitors, and consider them all her own without letting *me* off: I will count myself
fortunate if I can only persuade her to remain in covert, instead of
romping down the Strand behind me, as I suppose she would be
glad to do. Unless you could contrive to poison her?" he inquired
in a bitter spirit of Gong Su, who had ducked into the tent.

"Did you require me about the provisions?" Laurence asked.

"No, Captain," Gong Su said, "and Mr. Hammond, I cannot
satisfy you; but if I may propose an alternative, you would find
Churki no source of difficulty if she should accompany you to
China."

"Ha; I shall not be posted back to China," Hammond said. "I
will be pushed off into the countryside with vague promises of
some other occasions in future, which will never come—unless
Dom da Câmara decides to try and induce their Lordships to bring
me under charges, which I cannot discount—"

"Pardon me," Gong Su said, gently breaking into this morose
ramble, which trailed away low but showed no sign of immediately
concluding, "but you need not return to England first: the ship may
carry you to China, instead."

"What?" Hammond said, staring.

"And you, of course, Captain," Gong Su said, bowing, "and Lung Tien Xiang; that is what I wish to humbly suggest."

Laurence was rather taken aback himself at what could only be called the effrontery of the suggestion they might virtually commandeer the *Potentate,* particularly when that suggestion came from a source so ordinarily self-effacing: although that Gong Su might desire to return to his own country was no surprise if one considered it; Laurence made it five years since they had left China. "We are very likely to stop a merchantman on its way to Canton, at Madeira if not before," Laurence said, "and I would of course book your passage if you wished—" But Gong Su was shaking his head.

"My own insignificant presence cannot make a difference in these matters," Gong Su said. "But I am of the opinion that my master would, when the fullness of events in this distant part of the world have been laid before him, welcome the chance to consult with you more intimately: and that noble lord, your most honored elder brother and the heir of the dread lord who commands the Celestial Throne, has lately granted me the honor to invite you to visit him, if circumstances should seem to make that desirable: such is his foresight and wisdom."

He concluded this by bringing out a packet of oilcloth, which he unrolled to reveal a narrow and folded letter—the same letter, Laurence realized after a moment, which Lung Shen Li had brought him in Australia, before their departure, and which Laurence had assumed a message from his family: sealed magnificently with red and enclosed in a wrapper labeled all over with Chinese characters. Gong Su placed it across both hands and presented it to Laurence.

"My elder—my what?" Laurence said, baffled, and then said, "Do you mean Prince Mianning? Your *master*? What—" He stopped, and pressed his lips shut against betraying himself into an undignified yammer: having been under the impression, until the present moment, that Gong Su had been his cook, he could only regard with outrage both the shockingly brazen mode and the act itself, the self-acknowledgment of a—

"He is *not* a spy," Hammond hissed at him urgently, having dragged Laurence nearly bodily to the far corner of the tent, "not a spy, at all, Captain; you must not consider him so. He is—" Hammond groped for some excuse. "He has been delegated to your service—"

"Delegated to my service?" Laurence glared at Hammond. "Mr. Hammond, if you will instruct me what else, but a spy, I am to consider a man who has assuredly reported every minute detail of my affairs—he was a guest in my father's house!—and those of the service to a foreign power—"

"To your relations, who surely had some right to an interest," Hammond said, as brazen as Gong Su himself, but hastily altered his course, seeing that Laurence was by no means to be persuaded along these lines, "—to his own government, to whom he surely offers his first allegiance; and in any case," he dashed on, "in any case, you must see the utmost significance—if Prince Mianning invites us to China officially—"

"Prince Mianning has issued no invitation but one hypothetical," Laurence said, "and left the power of making it in the hands of this—"

"—servant of the throne," Hammond said loudly, overriding, "and plainly one of trusted probity and judgment to have been given such license, for, Captain, there can only be one purpose in asking us to make such a journey: they wish to discuss an alliance."

"How you should arrive at a conclusion so wholly unsupported by any past evidence offered by their behavior—" Laurence began.

"I have been laboring these last five years myself, Captain," Hammond said, "and not, I trust, to no purpose: China may not have opened her ports to us, but there has certainly been a softening of—"

"From a softening to alliance?" Laurence said.

"If I may," Gong Su said, apologetically: their voices had risen past even a fiction of private conversation, though Laurence was not much inclined to forgive the reminder that virtually all his conversation, save those conducted under rare circumstances of real privacy, had been exposed to an interest beyond ordinary gossiping curiosity. "I do not presume to speculate as to the motives of my lord, or as to the purpose of his invitation! But I have been impelled to speak as I have by those late events, which one must fear as altering for evil the very balance and the order of the world: and it is with that consideration that I do urge you to hasten without delay to answer the invitation of the crown prince, as is your filial duty."

"Oh! Laurence, it is beyond anything wonderful!" Temeraire said, in delight. "Of course we must go: I should like nothing better than that Maximus and Lily should see China, and all our formation, too. And to think that Gong Su has arranged it all: I should never have imagined it."

"No," Laurence said, stifling the smart of renewed indignation. The first infuriated heat of betrayal past, he had not been able to stand his ground against Hammond's persuasion very long. Gong Su had made his meaning too plain, even if a notion of courtly decorum forbade him outright speaking on behalf of the Emperor's son. Laurence could not despite a certain irritated desire to do so believe him a liar or untrustworthy: indeed it was impossible to fault for loyalty a man who in the service of his throne had left home and family to accept a menial position and keep it across a war, five continents, and so many weary years.

Temeraire peered at him a little anxiously. "I hope," he said tentatively, "that you do not mind we should not go back to England straightaway? But I do understand from Lily that everything there at present is quite at a standstill: and Napoleon will surely have a long time sailing back. And I am sure that this Captain Blaise in charge of the *Potentate* will see the very real importance of our going to China under these circumstances."

Of that, Laurence had less certainty. "Particularly as we have only the crown prince's invitation, and not the Emperor's; and no certainty of success when we have arrived," Laurence added soberly, "but I am persuaded we must make the attempt. If we should indeed find it possible to engage China in alliance, that may be our only hope now of standing for long against Napoleon. But we may have to make the passage overland and far to the north, at the Bering strait. I have no confidence in Blaise's diverting the *Potentate* at our request: he is not Riley."

He stopped and said again, low, "He is not Riley," and swallowed regret once more: the loss not only of a friend, but of that still more priceless treasure, a man on whom he could rely.

"No," Temeraire said, and bent his head to nose gently at Laurence's back in comfort.

ABOUT THE AUTHOR

NAOMI NOVIK was born in New York in 1973, a first-generation American, and raised on Polish fairy tales, Baba Yaga, and Tolkien. Her first novel, *His Majesty's Dragon*, the opening volume of the Temeraire series, was published in 2006 and has been translated into twenty-three languages and optioned by Peter Jackson, the Academy Award–winning director of the Lord of the Rings trilogy.

She has won the John W. Campbell Award for Best New Writer, the Compton Crook Award for Best First Novel, and the Locus Award for Best First Novel. She is one of the founding board members of the Organization for Transformative Works, a nonprofit dedicated to protecting the fair-use rights of fan creators, and is herself a fanfic writer and fan vidder, as well as one of the architects of the open-source Archive of Our Own.

Novik lives in New York City with her husband, Edgar Award–winning mystery novelist Charles Ardai, their shiny new daughter, Evidence, and a recently and ruthlessly winnowed set of ~~four~~ five computers.

You can find out more at her website (http://naomi novik.com/) and follow her as naominovik on Livejournal, Twitter, and Facebook.